LIFE IN THE GOLDEN ERA, EARTH AND BEYOND

LIFE IN THE GOLDEN ERA, EARTH AND BEYOND

Sonja H. Lüsch

Columbus, Ohio

Life in the Golden Era, Earth and Beyond

Published by Gatekeeper Press
2167 Stringtown Rd, Suite 109
Columbus, OH 43123-2989
www.GatekeeperPress.com

Book cover made by Saul Bottcher

Library of Congress Control Number: 2022937273

ISBN (paperback): 9781737491538
eISBN: 9781737491521

Table of Contents

This is a book of fiction and the author is not a medical doctor, therapist or herbalist and makes no guarantees as to the efficacy of the remedies mentioned in the book. All statements of advice listed in the book pertaining to medical advice, mental therapy, herbal remedies and all other advice listed are not a substitute for medical care and are not intended to diagnose, treat, cure or prevent any condition or disease. The reader should consult with a physician or healthcare specialist for personalized medical care.

All suggestions listed in the book pertaining to political systems, banking and business practices, currency and money system, warfare, matters of faith and all other procedures executed in everyday society are all fictional and the author makes no claims any of them will work. Any view or opinions mentioned in the book are not intended to malign any religion, ethnic group, club, organization, company, individual or anyone or anything.

To Tina,

A True and Loyal Friend

This book is a continuation of

Triumph of the Superbug

and the

Rise of the Golden Era

By Sonja H. Lüsch

CHAPTER 1

It was a brilliant summer day with azure blue sky and a mild breeze. Grace looked beautiful in her wedding dress and Berrill smiled as he put the ring on her finger. She was only eighteen years old and still in school. Berrill had spent most weekends with Grace and her family since he arrived from Bantizza five years ago and Rasufilus knew he would be a devoted husband to Grace. His charming personality was hard to resist and the whole family was fond of him. Berrill had patiently waited for Grace to come of age and he had been in love with her since he trained her to ride her mare Ylja. Finally, Grace would be his wife and Berrill felt he lived in the golden era.

The wedding took place by the lake outside the town of Rasunom and it was a small affair with only family members attending. Five miles down the road a horse ranch was ready for the young couple and Rasufilus, Vitzoll and Berrill had built it together. A large barn was part of the ranch and corrals with white fencing gave the ranch an old-world traditional look that was delightful. Grace and her mother Akinom had furnished the home together.

It was an emotional experience for Rasufilus and Akinom to see their youngest child tie the knot and their house would seem so empty now. Akinom was glad Grace would only live a few miles away.

Every time Rasufilus and Vitzoll took off on a mission, Berrill took care of all the chores and hard work around the house and Akinom found his work enormously helpful and Rasufilus was grateful he was around. When Berrill and Grace told them they wanted to get married, they had given their consent right away and Grace' parents knew he would be the best husband Grace could ever get. He was twelve years older than Grace.

Berrill made a good income at the mint and had designed a second coin featuring a mare and her foal. The image captured the mare's love for her foal and the coin was admired by the citizens on Earth2. He was presently working on designing a third coin featuring a gilded image of a rearing stallion. A gilded coin had never been produced before and would require adjustment to the way the coin was made and Berrill hoped it could be achieved. Each design was well paid and Berrill could use the extra money for his ranch.

He worked three days a week at the mint and the rest of the week he would start training horses at the ranch. More people wanted to own a horse and the government had hired him to train the horses and sell them. The herd of horses had increased in size and there were plenty of horses available both on the Bavonilla land and out on the grasslands. Berrill's dream of owning a horse ranch had come true and with Grace at his side, life was a joy.

Rasufilus was planning to retire in a year and Vitzoll would take over the fleet of ships as commander. He had proven himself worthy and Rasufilus had great trust in him and his judgment, courage and fairness. Vitzoll was also very calm and able to think clearly under pressure. He was mature in spite of his young age of twenty-one years and resembled his father both in looks and personality.

In 2194 a new president would be elected on Earth2 and Rasufilus was hoping to run for office. If things went as he planned, he would be fully retired from mercenary work by then.

The population on Earth2 had increased to one hundred and fifty thousand people and Bliss had grown to a large town with suburbs. A few hardy families had moved beyond the suburbs and most of them owned a groundmobile so they could commute to work in Bliss. Immigrants from Etteron and Frejja kept coming and people from Bantizza were eager to move to Earth2 and, so far, five thousand had arrived. Only the affluent from Bantizza could afford the cost involved to immigrate.

Pollox and Lyra were still the only settlers out on the grasslands and their oldest son Janus, now eighteen years old, was a pilot in training in Rasufilus' fleet. Janus was still in school, but on holidays and when school was closed in the summer, Vitzoll had taught Janus how to fly a spaceship. Janus and Vitzoll were best friends and the only career Janus could imagine was being part of Rasufilus' fleet. His parents had no objections and felt he was capable of making his own decisions. Janus had grown up on the grasslands and was fiercely independent, self-sufficient and trusted his instincts. Vitzoll, equally independent, recognized Janus' qualities and was glad he would soon join the fleet.

He planned on making Janus his copilot as soon as he was out of school. Both Vitzoll and Janus had spent time in each other's homes and were familiar with each other's upbringing. All the citizens in Bliss were aware of the lifestyle of Pollox and Lyra and admired their emotional strength. Their three children were equally strong and independent.

***

Atlas and Viola's children were almost grown and Melody was now sixteen years old and Paragonne twelve. Melody was steadfast in her decision to become a doctor and even openminded to live on another planet to her parents' dismay. Paragonne had no such ambitions and wanted to stay on Earth2 and be a farmer. He felt a deep connection with Nature and had always enjoyed gardening with his mother. Xentos, the younger son of Pollox and Lyra, knew Paragonne through school and had invited him to spend a week with his family on the grasslands. After that week, Paragonne knew his future was tied to the land and even though he was only a boy he was in love with Xentos' younger sister Hattie. With her blond ponytail reaching down to her waist, she looked typical Frejjan and was so pretty. Atlas and Viola never interfered with the children's career dreams.

Atlas had undergone a slight aging procedure giving him a dignified look and Viola found him even more handsome. Atlas was not vain and took the whole thing in stride. His focus of attention was his love for Viola and the children. At the hospital, he was the chief surgeon and he also trained the beginner doctors. Viola was involved with her music, but being a mother came first and raising her two children had been an important part of her life. She and Atlas were happy together.

***

Quality of life had increased and Earth2 supplied the citizens with a safe and abundant lifestyle. Crime was rare, jobs were plentiful, the stores were well stocked with consumer goods from both Frejja and Etteron and the food supply was excellent. No one was rich, no one was poor and the government was fair and working for the people. Earth2 was debt free and the citizens paid no taxes. For the time being, the income from the mining was sufficient to pay all the bills the government had.

Earth2 did not export anything, but all imported goods were paid for with the precious metals the planet had an abundance of.

Telly was a keen observer and as the advisor to the president he often introduced ideas no one had thought of before. His solutions to matters of concern were always brilliant. One of his observations was that stagnation due to lack of hardship may occur on Earth2 in the future. Life was so easy, perhaps too easy. No matter how he presented the issue, it would come across as if he wanted hard times to strike his planet to 'toughen up' the people. He decided to keep his thoughts to himself, but he did not forget about them.

A road had been built all the way from Bliss to the grasslands and infrastructure and services were developing. Several manufacturing plants staffed by robots produced consumer goods and less imports were needed. Shipping services had become available and citizens could now send packages for a small fee using cargo drones.

Drugs and alcohol were unavailable on the planet ensuring a low crime rate and no police force was needed. Rasufilus and his men were responsible for law and order on Earth2 and only two incidents had occurred since the planet was occupied. Both of them were homicide and Rasufilus found the murderers after a short investigation. The guilty men had been born on Earth2 so they could not be deported and they were sentenced to ten years of forced labor after which time they would regain their freedom. The men accepted their sentences without dispute and lived in a low security facility.

Earth2 was developing without growing pains and people from various planets had inquired about immigration, but only affluent people could afford to pay the cost of transportation to Earth2. Veehnia, Frejja and Mars still offered free tickets and were popular destinations for adventurers. The most interesting group of people immigrating to Earth2 had come from Ljeviina, a very advanced planet, and two hundred people had paid their own expenses to relocate to Earth2 and start over. They were all nature lovers and much more advanced psychologically than the people on Earth2, well-educated and all of them aided the advancement of their new planet. Their kindness was admirable. All of them were young and unmarried. At first, a small group of them had decided to make Earth2 their new home and by word of mouth more people joined them until they had reached two hundred in number. They knew, of course, Rasufilus lived on Earth2 and the people on

Ljeviina considered him a savior of their planet. Although the Ljeviinans loved their home planet, they wanted to experience the building and shaping of a brand-new planet from 'childhood to adulthood'. All of them would play a part in Earth2's growth into maturity and at the end of their lives they would all say 'yes, it was worth it'. One of them was Lorre, the young pilot who had been Tyler and Jayce' guide on Ljeviina. The Ljeviinans were admired for their kindness, intelligence and highly advanced minds.

Amazingly, a hundred people from Ziggellus had asked if they would be allowed to immigrate and the government had approved their request on Rasufilus' recommendation. Ziggellus was now a peace-loving planet no one needed to fear and the immigrants had arrived using the spaceships gifted to them by the Moon inhabitants. They settled outside Bliss not far from the immigrants from Ljeviina and there was no animosity between them. The past was forgiven and Earth2 was a new beginning for all of them. All the people from Ziggellus had had their tails removed to improve their appearance. The tail had no biological use and was a leftover part of their bodies that evolution had 'forgotten' to eliminate. None of the Ziggellus immigrants had been involved in raiding and all of them were the children of the citizens who had hidden in the countryside during the years when insanity reigned supreme on their planet. These people were peace-loving, respectful and very courteous. They were not as highly evolved as the Frejjans, but would compare well with people on Earth and Mars. The Ziggellus people were fully aware they were not pleasant looking, but they made up for lack of looks by their likable and engaging personalities.

CHAPTER 2

Ten years had passed since Cooper and Rosalie got married and their love for each other was as strong as when they were newlyweds. The children were thriving and Halcyon was nine years old and Celeste six and both had been fitted with an implant. Most of the population now wore the implants, but some of the elderly had refused to wear one.

Reyya and Littiana acted as grandparents and the children spent every other weekend with them in their home. Being grandparents was the highlight of their lives and they relished their time with the children.

In only fifteen years Sorenia had evolved into a prosperous planet with a mostly literate population that had increased from half a million to three quarter million citizens. The beauty of the planet was striking with forests, lakes and rivers, but no ocean. Crops were growing on fertile fields and the food supply was more than adequate. Brand new homes, both in the towns and in the countryside, had replaced the shabby houses that people used to live in. Infrastructure was well organized with roads connecting the three countries and mining and manufacturing were supplying a good income for the people on the planet. The large supply of precious metals available on Sorenia had paid for the goods from Mineata that had been delivered all these years. The old Sorenia had been replaced with a modern, well-functioning planet. Many people owned a computer and understood how to use it and slowly more advanced electronics were introduced into society. Airmobiles and groundmobiles were available to buy and some people owned a vehicle. With the help of the implant people learned faster and could manage even an airmobile. No spaceships existed. A small police force kept law and order, but the crime rate was low and people were mostly honest and showed respect for each other.

Cooper had not introduced communicators yet, but he was planning to do so within the next few years.

The school system was unusually strict and parents did not complain. They understood the value of education and encouraged their children to study hard. Two universities had been established and many of the students graduating from high school were eager to continue their education at the university. Many dreamed of becoming computer programmers and Cooper had just designed a simple Internet system, by no means comparable to anything the advanced planets had, but more of an introduction to what would come later on. The young people understood it, but older people had trouble using it even though they had an implant.

All the citizens were now aware their planet orbited the star Arros and no other planet existed in their solar system. They also understood their solar system was located in the Andromeda Galaxy and the neighboring galaxy was called the Milky Way. Slowly the citizens became more knowledgeable and curiosity drove them to read whatever books they could find. Cooper had made many books available to read on the Internet and as more and more people improved their reading skills, the population was in an upward spiral and evolving fast. Many adults continued attending classes at school even after they had learned how to read and write, but some of the elderly were still illiterate.

A hundred people from Mineata had moved to Sorenia and all of them were well educated. Some of them became teachers at the schools and universities, some were scientists and researchers, a few doctors and several of them were experts in various technology fields. Six of them were spaceship pilots who were capable of flying any modern spaceship and on Cooper's recommendation, they started a school for pilots. One of the pilots was Volrex who had made the trip from Mineata to Sorenia countless times and decided he wanted to be part of Sorenia's development into a modern planet. A flight simulator was imported from Mineata and the brightest high school students were invited to start training to become pilots. The school was enormously popular, but the program was highly demanding and only a small percentage of the students were able to grasp the complexity of the advanced computer systems running a spaceship. The few students who qualified would eventually become the pilots of Sorenia's fleet of starships and fighters.

The people from Mineata faced no discrimination from the Sorenians because of their furry appearance. It was well known that Mineata was a very advanced and prosperous planet and the immigrants were welcomed to their new planet. Volrex had married a girl from Sorenia and was the proud father of a daughter, Jilina. She did not inherit her father's fur.

Halcyon told Cooper he would become a pilot and his parents smiled and said "of course you will". He studied hard and was determined to conquer the universe.

The mindset on the planet was optimistic and people had great trust in Cooper. He had asked the citizens whether they wanted to hold elections and appoint a new president and the response was a resounding *"no"*. As long as the people wanted him to be their president Cooper was willing to stay in office, but he was also flexible and totally ready to step down if the people wanted to replace him.

Rosalie was working part time from home writing books for the school system while also raising her family. Littiana was her best friend and she could always count on her to help out with the children. Cooper allowed Littiana to work flexible hours and take days off as needed. Reyya worked hard as president of Mulerna as well as being Cooper's vice president.

There was no religion on the planet and the ten years of terror Drako and Keid had forced upon the people with their religious war was still fresh in mind. Sorenia had come close to total destruction due to the fanaticism of these two men. Only the immigrants had spiritual beliefs and they preferred to keep their faith private.

Cooper only worked five six-hour days a week to ensure he had time for his children and Rosalie. They always came first and he had great fun with his kids playing games and taking them on trips around the planet with their airmobile. A family favorite was canoeing and camping by the lake and sleeping in an old-fashioned tent. There were no carnivores on Sorenia, only herbivores resembling horses, and they were no threat. Both Cooper and Rosalie enjoyed their family time together.

***

Life on Veehnia had treated Tothellim well and at seventy-three years he was still working full time as was Rheo. His daughter Heidi was married and worked as a veterinarian and his son Logan was a professional pianist with a bright future. His concerts were always sold out and he had already built up a nice nest egg from his many recordings.

Tothellim's life had been all he had dreamed of until a year ago when his beloved wife Anna suddenly died from a blood disorder and he became a widower. The shock of losing her had devastated him and it took a full year until he could accept her death. Anna had been the love of his life and to come home to an empty house had been almost unbearable. Peturuns had long lifespans, often living to one hundred and twenty years, and Tothellim was still physically strong and fully capable of commanding a spaceship. With no dependents, he decided to go back to exploratory space travel. It had been thirty years since Tothellim had flown a spaceship, but as flight instructor he had worked continuously with the flight simulator while teaching his students and he knew all the details of modern space travel. Part of his work had been to send out ships to investigate space and find new planets, but he had not been onboard himself. Now it was his turn and he felt ready to face whatever danger he would encounter out in space.

Tothellim discussed his wish to return to space travel with his supervisor Rear Admiral Fletcher, who was excited to hear Tothellim wanted to explore the universe. Many pilots were unwilling to risk their lives on dangerous exploratory trips and even Tyler and Jayce had not volunteered for many years. They were both married and preferred short distance travel with minimal risk. Tothellim sent a message to Emrak telling him about his plans to explore space once again and had received a reply wishing him well and a safe trip and to report back to him when he returned.

Tothellim spent a month flying the newest starship Veehnia had and within a few weeks he was totally at ease flying through the tunnels and felt as if he had never been absent from flying. He knew he was ready and did not need any more training. Rheo thought he was crazy and tried to discourage him from leaving his comfortable job, but Tothellim had made his decision. He boarded the huge ship as Captain and with a crew of three additional pilots and eight experienced androids he took off. The ship was well equipped with everything the crew could possibly need for two years and a shuttle and two airmobiles were in cargo bay. One of the androids was a medical doctor and one was a chef responsible for all their meals. The other six androids were able to fly the ship as well as repair both the computer systems and engines onboard. They had years of experience in space travel.

***

Emrak and Karol enjoyed a quiet retirement together and were now empty nesters. They had raised five children and Solveiga and Sven were now adults. Solveiga was married and the mother of a baby son and Sven was still in school studying physics. His uncle Leo had offered him a job in his company and Sven had accepted. Uncle Leo had twenty people hired and several new inventions under his belt; the most famous and useful was velcro flooring in spaceships. Leo was determined to invent artificial gravity in spaceships and his father always encouraged him. Emrak knew gravity in spaceships would revolutionize space travel and it was badly needed. Leo had just recently married a young immigrant girl from Earth, Lana, who had decided to try life on another planet. The free ticket Frejja offered had enabled her to follow her dream. Leo was already forty-one years old and had not had time to think of marriage, but when he met Lana, he knew she was the girl for him. Lana's family had respected her wish to leave Earth for good.

Emrak was surprised when he received the message from Tothellim that he would return to space travel, but he understood it may be the only way he could continue living without his wife. Emrak was grateful Karol was still alive and healthy and their forty-two-year marriage had been very happy. In three years Emrak would become one hundred years old, but he did not look it and was still physically active. Brandon and Brianna would often stop by and visit and talk about old times. Their grandchildren were adults and doing well, but Funina and Omunon had passed away. Rigel and Thole still worked together as domestic pilots and were close friends.

Life on Frejja was pleasant but perhaps a little too laid back. The government sent a spaceship to Earth twice a year and always returned with new immigrants filling all the seats on the ship. Some of the new citizens truly added a spark to Frejjan society and with the latest arrival a magician had appeared. His show made people breathless and no one could figure out how he performed his spectacular stunts. Very few immigrants arrived from Mars, but Frejja still offered free tickets to several planets and the population was slowly increasing.

***

Mars was known as the best place for researchers and inventors and funded all sorts of research. The best minds from many planets flocked to Mars and Martia had grown to two hundred thousand citizens. After the housing domes had been reinforced several years ago, the safety of the structures was infallible and the citizens had no fear of the sand storms and marsquakes.

A recent attack by raiders had easily been warded off by a strong counterattack from the Martian fighter ships and Mars was known for having a large fleet of ships equipped with the best weapons available. The raiders were uninformed opportunists and paid with their lives when they failed to back off after the first warning shot from the Martian commander. Within minutes their ships were fireballs with no survivors. As a warning to other invaders in the universe, Mars posted holographic images of the burning ships on the Interstellar Internet with a blunt warning *don't mess with us.*

A very large section had been added to 'the Bubble' and turned into a park with live trees and paths for walking. Birds had been imported and lived in the trees and the popularity of the park was huge. People loved it. The highlight of the park was a small lake in the center where ducks lived a pampered life. Mars was awash with gold from the terrynium exports and building of the park had taken an enormous bite out of the budget, but the government felt it was necessary to create 'Nature within the Bubble' to prevent citizens from leaving. It had taken several years to fill the lake using water ice and the finished park was a true masterpiece, so real it was hard to believe it was man-made. The government knew it would soon recover most of the money spent on the park from the export of the terrynium and Mars was in no danger of running out of the mineral.

Martians who were descendants of people from Earth had undergone a slight mutation with lighter bone structure and muscle tissue. If these people could survive on Earth with its heavy gravity was unknown and so far, no one had tried it. The medical advice to Martians who wanted to leave was to only move to a planet with the same gravity as Mars to avoid problems, but few wanted to leave. It was a known fact no planet offered a higher standard of living than Mars and most Martians were happy to stay. Occasionally, some moved to Frejja which had the same gravity as Mars.

***

Many smaller countries had merged into larger countries on Earth and the Advisory Board had evolved into a *World Government*. North and South America had become one country called *The Americas*; European countries were one country called *Europe; Africa* was one country; Russia and all the '-stan' countries were called *Russia;* most countries in the Middle East had merged into one country called *Arabia;* China and several of the southeast Asian countries, including India and Japan, had merged into *The Far East* and Australia and New Zealand were called *New Australia*. All the mergers were voluntary and approved by the citizens and the World Government was fair and democratic. Each country was free to choose their own ways and the World Government oversaw mostly planetary decisions and defense of planet Earth as well as discourage wars between countries. The World Government never interfered in any country's internal affairs and was by no means authoritarian. So far, the system worked well. People on Earth knew they could be invaded by hostile aliens and felt a world government was needed.

The collapse of 2035 was now just a chapter in the history books and Earth was doing well with good standard of living in all countries. Wealth was more evenly distributed and most countries were self-sufficient. Quality of life was good on Earth and there were no wars going on. Some adventurers still emigrated to Mars, Frejja and Veehnia as long as the cost of travel was free and some spent a year or two on the Moon to save up some money.

The Interstellar Internet had improved and communication between Earth, Mars and Frejja was now possible, but any planet beyond these planets could not be reached.

Many futuristic inventions had been transferred to Earth from both Frejja and Veehnia advancing science and raising quality of life. Robots did all labor work and people worked only four days a week. Some chose not to work and lived on the base income. Most people felt content.

CHAPTER 3

Tothellim's first stop was planet Sorenia and he was eager to visit with Cooper again. Fifteen years had passed since Tyler and Jayce left Cooper on Sorenia and there had been no communication between the two planets. Tothellim was at the controls and skillfully flew the ship through the fifteen-hour tunnel and as soon as the ship was out of the tunnel, he transmitted a message to Cooper he was on his way. Tothellim had trained Cooper to fly a spaceship and liked his gentle and sophisticated nature.

Cooper was excited and surprised to receive Tothellim's message and responded he was delighted to welcome him. The three months' additional travel time went fast and the ship entered orbit around Sorenia. As Tothellim looked down on the surface from the ship he saw a lush, green planet with brilliant blue skies and bright sunshine. He invited the copilots to join him and soon the shuttle landed on the surface close to the government buildings. Modern shuttles were designed to enter any planet's atmosphere without being affected by heat and friction. Cooper, Reyya and Littiana waited for them and Tothellim laughed heartily as he gave Cooper a big hug.

"Gosh, it's good to see you, old friend!"

Cooper laughed and shook hands with all of them and introduced Reyya and Littiana. To shake hands to greet each other was not limited to Earth but the universal way on most planets to welcome people. They went inside and Cooper gave a detailed report about everything that had taken place on the planet, the end of war, the improvements, the new super strict education system, the minerals on the planet that had paid all the bills and the upgrading of the people from illiterates to modern citizens. It was a lot to take in and Tothellim and the pilots listened attentively. They spoke English as both Reyya and Littiana now spoke fluent English. On the ship, Tothellim had shown the pilots the holographic images of Sorenia at the end of the war and as they looked around now, they saw a clean, prosperous planet with crops growing, modern homes and a population that had no resemblance to the primitive people who had greeted Cooper so many years ago. Everyone was neat and clean, fully literate and embraced education and most citizens had an implant to boost cognition. Only some of the elderly were illiterate. What a difference!

"Cooper, your accomplishments are commendable, a true miracle," Tothellim said. "I look forward to a big tour of your society."

Dinner was being prepared by several Sorenian women and Rosalie joined them together with her children. Tothellim could not help but admire her beauty and noticed how well behaved the children were. He understood a donor had been involved and on Veehnia several of the most prominent androids were married, so Tothellim was not surprised to find Cooper married.

The following two weeks were very busy and Tothellim and the pilots toured the whole planet. The androids took turns descending to the surface. Tothellim enjoyed seeing the new school for pilots and the flight simulator imported from Mineata. Volrex, who was chief instructor at the school, was proud to tell them a couple of students were close to mastering the flying of a spaceship and would become the first pilots ever on Sorenia. Tothellim and his pilots were not taken aback by Volrex' furry appearance. They had all seen many unusual looking aliens over the years and they liked Volrex and his friendly, outgoing nature.

Volrex told them Sorenia had ordered two starships from Mineata fully capable of flying through any tunnel and once they were delivered, they would make a trip to Veehnia as well as visiting Ljeviina and Ziggellus. Delivery of the spaceships was expected very soon.

Cooper had made it clear that he had no intention to move from Sorenia even if he would step down as president. His son Halcyon promptly told a smiling Tothellim about his plans to make the universe his future home and to become a captain of a starship.

"You will make it, Halcyon," he told the boy and invited him for a tour of the orbiting spaceship before they took off.

The visit came to an end and the last thing Tothellim did was to invite Cooper and his family as well as Reyya and Littiana to visit the spaceship. Rosalie was as fascinated as her son and the highlight of the visit was to see the Bridge with all its electronics. Halcyon was dizzy with excitement and his little sister was almost as excited. The spaceship was equipped with Leo's velcro flooring, but Rosalie, the children and Reyya and Littiana enjoyed being weightless and tumbled around in the ceiling while laughing out loud. Cooper and the pilots were all laughing as they watched the show.

The visit was over and Tothellim was emotional when he said goodbye to Cooper. He had recorded many images of the planet to show his president how Cooper had transformed a destroyed planet into a thriving society with a totally changed population. He asked himself if he could have done it and had to admit it would have taken him much longer to achieve what Cooper had accomplished.

***

The purpose of Tothellim's trip was to find new planets and he felt there was no need to visit Ljeviina as Tyler and Jayce had already been there years ago. He was hoping to find a new tunnel and if there was one, the vibration would cause the ship to shake as they neared its entry. The ship was traveling towards the center of the Andromeda galaxy and for two months they saw nothing but empty space. Then the ship started shaking, more and more for every hour, and the pilots knew they were in the neighborhood of a tunnel. There it was and they entered not knowing if they would come out alive. The width of the tunnel was more than enough for the ship, but the violence and vibration were more intense than the pilots had experienced when flying through both he fifteen- and eighteen-hour tunnels. It also moved constantly back and forth. Tothellim was at the controls the first three hours and then had to take a break. All the pilots had been trained by Tothellim and Rheo and he had great confidence in their abilities. The ship accelerated in speed the whole time and after an arduous five-hour passage it was hurled out into space at enormous speed. Where were they? The instruments showed they had traveled seven thousand light years straight into the Andromeda galaxy! Every tunnel was different and there were no set rules how far a tunnel would propel a ship or even accelerate its speed. This tunnel was a mega portal.

The monotony of empty space was finally broken after two months when they spotted a single, rather large planet orbiting a small star and within a month they were in orbit around the planet. When daylight ended, the planet was lit up and they knew it was inhabited by a modern civilization. The next morning, Tothellim launched a drone to investigate the planet and to send back holographic images to the ship as well as information about atmospheric conditions. The drone was not damaged by heat and friction from traveling through a planet's atmosphere, the same as modern shuttles. Staying at an elevation of ten thousand feet to avoid the busy air traffic reaching up to five thousand feet, the drone started transmitting images showing white-skinned humans. The city below was teeming with humans both walking and traveling with groundmobiles. But something was wrong! The drone cautioned there was insufficient oxygen in the atmosphere.

Tothellim asked the other three pilots if they were willing to accompany him to the surface and they all agreed. Wearing their spacesuits, they boarded the shuttle and landed a short distance outside the city where they noticed the airmobiles touched down. They were unarmed and within minutes of disembarking, a large vehicle with armed soldiers showed up. The shuttle had been spotted on their screens and the people on the planet knew they were aliens.

"We are from planet Veehnia and come in peace. Please enter your language code." Tothellim held out his two-way translation device and the officer in charge entered the code. The device instantly translated Tothellim's greeting.

"I'm Osaris," the officer in charge responded in a language that was totally unfamiliar to Tothellim. He had heard many languages from the translation device, but this language sounded choppy and unmelodious. "The name of our planet is Ursemic and our star is called Xelin. Let's go inside and we have easy-to-wear oxygen masks for you so you can remove your spacesuits."

Tothellim noticed the gravity was heavier than on Veehnia. They entered a modern government building and were shown into an oxygenated chamber, where they removed their spacesuits. The aliens showed them how to breathe with the help of a lightweight helmet and a small oxygen pack strapped onto their backs. It was easy to talk with the oxygen helmet on and they sat down in a comfortable lounge.

Tothellim explained where they came from and that they were on an exploratory mission to find other planets and exchange information. He also described the five-hour tunnel they had discovered. Using his communicator, Tothellim showed the officers holographic images from Veehnia. The officers listened with great interest and noticed the Veehnians looked like themselves.

"Which planet are you from?" Osaris asked Tothellim.

"Peturun, in the Milky Way galaxy," Tothellim replied. "I moved to Veehnia many years ago. You're humans, but you're able to breathe normally even though there isn't sufficient oxygen in your atmosphere. How did this happen?"

"We're all genetically modified," Osaris explained with a smile. "We're able to survive in spite of the low oxygen. About five hundred years ago our planet started to slowly lose its oxygen atmosphere due to severe atmospheric changes. The oxygen level is now stable and hasn't changed for a long time. In the beginning millions of people died, but over time our scientists were able to genetically modify us and change our lungs so we would survive the new conditions. We may be ahead of you in science and our scientists did a great job changing our bodies so we would remain alive in spite of the lowered oxygen in our atmosphere. If we could survive on your planet Veehnia while breathing normal amounts of oxygen is unknown to us since no one has tried it."

"Remarkable, what a transformation you have been through!"

"Our space travel is limited, but we do trade with another planet that has normal oxygen levels and we always wear space suits. None of our pilots is willing to gamble and remove his suit just to find out if he can breathe normal amounts of oxygen with our changed lungs. It could be fatal to us. We keep oxygen helmets for visitors who need it. Our babies are born genetically modified as our DNA is permanently changed."

Tothellim showed many images from the Milky Way and life on the different planets such as his home planet Peturun, Mars, Earth, Frejja and the officers listened while paying close attention. They knew very little about the Milky Way and no one from their planet had been there. They had done some travel around the Andromeda galaxy and shared valuable information about the planets they had visited and gave the exact locations of them and the tunnels they knew of in the area. All the information was transmitted to the orbiting ship's computers.

Tothellim and his copilots returned to the ship and told Osaris they would come back the next day. There was no way they could eat with the helmets on. Osaris had offered them dinner in an oxygenated chamber, but they politely declined. All of them were fatigued and they just wanted to get back to the ship and share the information with the androids, eat and then collapse in bed.

They spent two weeks touring Ursemic. The people were friendly and their society a little more advanced than Veehnia, no poverty anywhere and only one race and one language. A nice planet, but without any distinct feature setting it apart from so many similar planets.

They departed and decided not to visit the planets Osaris had described to them. Their mission was to find new planets and Osaris had mentioned one planet they could reach with only one tunnel to travel through and the name of the planet was Gellimo orbiting the star Adleni. There were rumors the inhabitants could be hostile and Tothellim was told to orbit the planet first and use the drone for reconnaissance missions before descending to the surface. Osaris did not know of anyone who had visited Gellimo, but had only heard the rumors to avoid the planet.

They used the tunnel Osaris had described and it was a short two-hour tunnel, but it propelled the ship one thousand light years and as they exited, they saw Gellimo and its star. It was a small planet and its blue color reminded Tothellim of Earth. Within a month they were in orbit and launched a drone to transmit images back to the ship. They could not see any air traffic so the drone descended to one thousand feet and started taking pictures. What they saw from the images was amazing. Short humanoids with light brown skin, about five feet tall, stocky build, bow-legged and long arms reaching to their knees. Tothellim sent a message to the drone asking for a close-up of the aliens and they received a blowup showing a face that was fully human, but with two short horns on top of their heads, warty skin and strange light blue eyes with pupils that looked translucent. They had short hair on their heads. Many of them walked around on the surface. They saw no roads and no vehicles of any sort and the dwellings were dome shaped clay buildings of various sizes. The planet appeared lush and beautiful with two large oceans taking up half the space of the planet and small boats were lining the shores. There were no farm fields and no animals.

One of the androids, Rex, offered to descend to the surface and investigate and Tothellim accepted his offer. Rex was a pilot by training, well educated in all the sciences and only a very trained eye could detect he was a machine and not a human. He was thirty years old, blond, six feet tall and with a strong personality. Rex was also a fully trained soldier.

"Let me go alone, Tothellim," he said. "There's no need to risk the life of any of us. If they capture me, so be it. I will use the laser gun if I have to, but hopefully the stun gun is sufficient."

The shuttle landed right outside the little village of about fifty homes and Rex climbed out. Both his stun gun and laser gun were on his belt ready to use and he had his two-way translation device ready.

The planet had a nice oxygen atmosphere, pleasant temperature in the seventies and the same gravity as Veehnia. As Rex climbed out of the shuttle, he was immediately surrounded by a gang of men pointing nasty looking daggers at him. Rex calmly held up the translation device and set it on 'search' and as the men talked among themselves the device flashed. It recognized their language.

"I'm Rex from planet Veehnia and I come in peace. Put your knives down. I'm no danger to you." Rex was towering over the small men.

"Why are you alone?" the leader asked angrily.

"My crew is onboard our spaceship and the ship is in orbit around your planet. We've heard you're hostile to strangers and that's why I came alone. Can we talk?"

The men put their knives back into the sheaths and sat down on the ground. Rex joined them and placed the translation device in front of them.

"Is this planet Gellimo?" he asked.

"It is. I'm Tuvve. We seldom get visitors from outer space. We don't have spaceships and our society is not very advanced, but that's the way we want it. We want to be left alone and we have no use for technology and other modern contraptions. Two years ago, a spaceship landed here and we killed them all and destroyed their ship. They called themselves 'missionaries' and wanted to update us. They didn't respect that we said no, so we had no choice but to kill them. The ship landed here on the surface and we destroyed it with explosives."

Rex noticed Tuvve was eloquent and appeared intelligent. They obviously had no implants, but seemed to get along well without them.

"I noticed you have no farm animals and no crops planted. What do you eat?" Rex asked.

"Only fish and our oceans have lots of it. We also eat root vegetables that grow in our forests, so there's no need to plant crops. Our lives are simple and no one has to work hard. Everything we need is easy to get right here on our planet."

"Do you have schools?"

"No, our kids learn skills from the parents. We have no written language."

"Have schools ever existed here?"

"Yes, long time ago and our ancestors also had spaceships and could read and write. They were warriors and invaded other planets. Then, one day a fleet of ships arrived and killed most of the people on our planet. They had all been invaded by our ancestors and wanted revenge. Some of our people hid and were not found by the invaders and we are the descendants of those people. After that bloodbath, our surviving ancestors decided to never leave this planet and destroyed all written material, all ships and all modern technology to ensure no one from Gellimo could invade another planet again. We adapted to a very simple lifestyle and prefer it this way."

"You can have a modern society without being warriors," Rex said slowly. "We on Veehnia have a very advanced society and have never invaded another planet." He looked into Tuvve's strange eyes and wondered how he could see with his translucent pupils.

"Nothing you say will make us change our society. We prefer our way of life."

"Would you allow the crew from the ship to visit your planet?"

"No!" Tuvve's voice was unyielding.

Rex realized there was no point in staying and thanked them for allowing him to talk to them and said farewell. He had recorded the conversation and taken holographic images of the people with his built-in devices, a fact they had no way of knowing.

Back on the ship Rex transferred the information to the ship's computers and they all watched the images and listened to the conversation.

CHAPTER 4

One year had passed since Tothellim and the crew left Veehnia and Tothellim decided they should try to find one more planet. What they had discovered so far was interesting, but far from extraordinary. Osaris had mentioned there were planets close to Gellimo, but he did not know their location. They left Gellimo and Tothellim steered the ship in the opposite direction of Gellimo and after three months of travel they spotted a planet. As they neared the planet after a few weeks, they were met with a fleet of thirty fighter ships and the pilots transmitted a message in a foreign language. The translation device blared out a message.

"Land the ship on the surface!"

The ship had powerful defense weapons, but their mission was to peacefully explore the universe, not conduct war, and Tothellim knew he could not fight a fleet of thirty ships. He landed the ship and the crew climbed out unarmed. The gravity felt heavy but was manageable. The ship's instruments showed an oxygen atmosphere and it was rather chilly, perhaps in the forties Fahrenheit. Tothellim, the pilots and androids waited quietly outside the ship. None of them feared death.

The fleet of ships landed next to them and the pilots exited their ships. The leader walked up to Tothellim and his crew and promptly immobilized them with a mild charge from his stun gun. They wore spacesuits and helmets. The androids were unaffected, but did not reveal they were not biological beings and only a very keen eye could detect they were machines. The charge was mild, but still very uncomfortable and it was hard to breathe. Their ability to think was not affected. The aliens now removed their helmets and Tothellim and his crew were shocked to see they were all women. They had beautiful, fully human faces, arched eyebrows and elongated ears lying flat against their heads. No hair on the head and their heads were somewhat bumpy and large and the skin on their heads as well as on their necks had black, irregular markings. Tothellim could not see if the markings were tattoos or naturally occurring. What stood out was how good looking they all were in spite of lacking hair.

"Identify yourself!" the leader ordered speaking into a translation device. Her voice was deep, not entirely a masculine voice, but deep base, melodious and almost hypnotic.

"We're from planet Veehnia on a peaceful mission to find new planets. I'm Tothellim." It took all Tothellim's determination to speak and he knew his paralysis was temporary and would soon wear off, but while it lasted the stun gun's effect was painful.

"I notice you're unarmed so I'll give you an antidote." The leader fished out a small gadget from her chest pocket and pushed it against the neck of all the men. Instantly, the stun effect was gone and all the pilots felt big relief.

Tothellim immediately explained their mission, the location of their home planet and emphasized they were not warriors but explorers. All they wanted was to exchange information and to get to know each other.

"I'm Zittana and this is planet Edena. Our star is called Oserik. Let's go inside and talk."

Zittana and her copilot led the way and the other pilots went to a large barrack. It was obvious Zittana was in charge.

They entered a modern building and sat down. Two men appeared with a cart filled with beverages and they were offered several choices of juices and various teas. Tothellim and his pilots all selected tea and when the androids politely declined to drink anything, Zittana understood they were androids. She waved the waiters away with an impatient gesture.

"This planet is run by females and our men function as drones and servants. They have nothing to say and live only to service us females."

"Has it always been that way?" one of the pilots asked.

"Yes, for two hundred years and we women have no intention to change our system. Many generations ago men had equal rights here on Edena, but our women became more and more masculine and eventually just took over everything and made the men into servants. They had become so feminized that they had no will to object and just accepted their new roles as underlings. Marriage does not exist here and any woman in need of a man can just order a man to service her. Our children are raised by the men alone and we use artificial wombs to grow the fetuses."

Tothellim and his copilots as well as the androids were mildly shocked to hear Zittana's statement. Not many planets were run by females and even Arrynia had abandoned their matriarchy many years ago. Tothellim was a 'mature' man, but his copilots were all men in their prime and he noticed Zittana and her copilot checking them out. All pilots from Veehnia had to follow a strict moral code and interaction with aliens was not permitted. The women were stunning and Tothellim understood it would take determination by his pilots to reject the women's seductive overtures.

They talked for a while and Tothellim asked if they could be excused and return to their ship to spend the night and perhaps the following day, they could tour the planet. Zittana agreed and they walked back to the ship and sealed the door. Back inside Tothellim said to his crew -

"I trust you will honor the code you swore to uphold when you became pilots. These women mean business and are used to getting their way."

"Yes, sir," the men replied in chorus.

Tothellim trusted two of his pilots, but the third, Andrew, was known as a skirt-chaser and Tothellim felt he needed to keep an eye on him.

The android doctor onboard, Kody, was in his eighties with a distinguished career behind him and he was also a successful scientist and researcher. Androids often worked beyond their hundredth birthday and Kody was one of the best doctors Veehnia had. He was also adventurous and had asked to be part of the crew, a request Tothellim was delighted to grant.

"Please allow me to run some tests on the men as well as on the women. I have a hunch this planet is dying, but I need proof," he said to Tothellim.

"Of course, please go ahead," Tothellim replied.

Zittana had no objections to being tested and offered herself as a patient. Kody took several blood samples from her. Five men were called in and also gave blood. Kody noticed how weak and feminized they looked and all of them lacked upper body muscles typical of a well-proportioned man. The ship had a modern lab onboard and Kody ran lots of tests. After a few days he asked for a conference with Zittana and her government advisors. Tothellim was also in the room.

"As you know, I've done a detailed study of your hormonal balance and what I found is cause for concern. Your men are basically females with the lowest level of male hormones I have ever seen; they're close to being eunuchs. Within a short time, they will not be able to father children and there will be no reproduction possible. The women are oversupplied with male hormones and are more masculine than the men on this planet." Kody turned to Zittana.

"Did you inject female hormones into your men?" he asked.

"Yes, " she answered. "We wanted to be in charge and gain control of all the power and that meant we had to subdue the men. We also injected ourselves with male hormones to increase our physical strength. Our birthrate has been down for years, but it hasn't stopped so we were not that worried about it."

"You should be, you're facing extinction," Kody said with a stern face. "What you women have done to your men is a human rights atrocity of the worst kind," he continued. "I can reverse the condition, but it will take time and I need your permission to start work."

Zittana and her advisors were silent at first, but then started to talk among themselves in a low voice.

"If we go through with your program, will the men be in charge?" Zittana asked.

"How about sharing power and running your country together as a team," Kody suggested. "Must you women rule? If I can bring your men back to becoming real men again, I have a feeling you would welcome the changes. I will have to decrease the male hormones in the women and increase the levels in the men until both of you reach normal levels for men and women. Do I have your permission to start? I need to involve the doctors in your country to get the job done. If you say no, you as a people will go extinct."

To give up power was a bitter pill for Zittana to swallow. She was a macho woman and was used to being obeyed, but she was intelligent and understood Kody was right.

"Yes, go ahead and start your program," she finally said in a beaten voice.

Kody called in the top doctors of the country, all females, and explained his plan how to give boosters of male hormones to the men, which would cause the men to naturally start producing male hormones again. Male hormone boosters to the women and female hormones to the men must stop immediately. The doctors had orders from Zittana to follow Kody's regimen and did not object.

The population was small and with the involvement of all doctors on the planet, changes in the men were visible within a few weeks. Slowly, they went through an awakening and were more alert and energized and some of them started to exercise to gain muscle. Tothellim decided they should stay on the planet to ensure the program was successful. The crew lived on the ship, which was still on the surface, and Kody's strategy was working well for six weeks.

One of the androids caught Andrew in bed with one of the women, unable to control himself, and he was promptly called to the Bridge.

"You are no longer a member of this crew," Tothellim brusquely informed Andrew. "You have violated the code you swore to uphold as a Star Fleet officer and will remain on this planet. You have disgraced yourself and the Veehnian Star Fleet and don't deserve your Veehnian citizenship. Pack your personal belongings and disembark immediately. *Dismissed!*"

One look at Tothellim's steely face told Andrew negotiations would get him nowhere. His legs were shaking, his heart banging in his chest and the thoughts were racing through his mind. He would never return to Veehnia! He was stuck here on a faraway planet many light years from home. What had he done to himself!

"Please reconsider. You can't leave me here," he pleaded.

"DISMISSED! OUT!" Tothellim's thundering voice cut through the air ending any hope Andrew had Tothellim would mellow.

He packed his suitcase and left the ship. He had lost his dream job and would never have a chance to explore the universe again. Being a member of Tothellim's crew and explore the universe had been the best part of his career. There was only one place he could go and that was back to the woman, who had invited him to her bed, Tilli. To his relief she let him move in.

After two months Kody and Tothellim met with Zittana and her advisors and Zittana made a firm statement.

"We will share power with our men and honor our agreement. The women actually like the rebirth our men are going through and since we stopped taking our male hormones, many of us feel better and more at ease. If you want to leave, please do so, and you should know that we will allow our men to be men from now on, just like you are. We are indebted to you for saving us from ourselves."

Kody and Tothellim laughed good-heartedly and both gave Zittana a hug. A tear rolled down her face, a good sign she was returning to womanhood. All the women had stopped taking male hormones permanently.

They left Edena the following day and Andrew was not visible. The long journey back to Veehnia started and they had fourteen months of travel ahead of them and many tunnels to negotiate until they would land on their home planet. The ship was well equipped with holographic programs, reading material and a huge number of entertainment devices so the year of travel time was bearable. They landed safely on Veehnia a little over two years after they had departed. It had been a trip with many learning experiences and well worth it. All the pilots needed several months off to rebuild their muscles and Tothellim felt he would like to make at least one more trip, perhaps two, before he finally retired.

Tothellim informed Andrew's parents as gently as he could that their son had broken Starfleet rules and had been fired. They understood Tothellim had followed Starfleet regulations, but were still shocked to hear Andrew had been left on Edena and they grieved the loss of their son.

***

Andrew reluctantly came to terms with the idea he was stuck on Edena for the rest of his life. Tilli's apartment was spacious and she had a well-paying job as a math teacher and supported him financially until he could get a job. Tilli was in love with Andrew and admired his masculinity and good looks, but Andrew did not feel the same. He was fond of her, but his heart was not involved and he knew he would not stay with her permanently.

Andrew had stayed mostly in the apartment while Tothellim and the crew were on the planet. He could not face them and felt destroyed inside. He spent his time trying to learn the Edena language using a translation device, but it was hard and he knew he needed a tutor to advance. When the ship finally left, he felt relief. What would his parents and his sister say when they were told he would not come back?

They had seen him off when he left and were so proud of him. Andrew felt anger with himself he had fallen for Tilli, embarrassment and fear of the future.

Tilli had never met a man who stood up to her and would not accept to be ruled and she was astounded when Andrew flatly refused to obey her.

"Listen, Tilli," he said with a stern look on his face. "I'm very grateful you let me live here and I'll pay you back when I have a job, but you have no power over me. *No one owns me,* is it clear?"

"Yes, Andrew, I understand," she said quietly. For the first time in her life, she faced a man not intentionally weakened the way the men were on her planet. After that incident, she never bossed him around.

With Tilli's help a tutor was found, an android that was programmed with the English language downloaded from the Internet. No one on the planet spoke English, but the android learned quickly and was able to speak English with good pronunciation after a few days. The lessons began and Andrew found the Edena language was not too complicated and he learned fast. The alphabet was confusing, but once Andrew had mastered it, he was able to read and write simple text. His plan was to apply for a job as pilot in the Edena Star Fleet. He knew he could never return to Veehnia, but he was a licensed Star Fleet officer and could fly any ship they had. All he needed was to learn the language. With all his might he worked hard and advanced rather quickly.

Three months after the Veehnian ship left, Andrew applied for a job as pilot and was accepted. His command of the Edena language was passable and he was told to continue learning the language. The female officer who tested his flying abilities saw right away he was well qualified and had full control of the ship and the electronics onboard. They flew through one tunnel and Andrew kept the ship perfectly centered in the tunnel. He was an excellent pilot and had been trained by Rheo. All pilots on the planet were female and Andrew would be the first male pilot in the fleet. Edena traded goods with a nearby planet called Birresta and Andrew was hired to fly a cargo ship between Edena and Birresta as full captain. His salary was impressive and he would soon be able to get his own apartment and repay Tilli whatever he owed her. He knew Tilli was in love with him, but he wanted to be free and he had no romantic feelings for her. He regretted deeply his affair with her and had promised himself never to repeat a mistake like that again. The price he had paid for his indiscretion was immense and had aged him several years.

The first flight to Birresta went well and his female copilot was courteous and professional. The trip took only six weeks with the help of two tunnels and their stay on the planet was one week. Andrew got two weeks off between each trip and he liked his schedule. It was easy and the ship was no harder to command than the Veehnian ships. The people on Birresta were humanoids with slightly reptilian features, pleasant and as advanced as the Edena people. Andrew was used to seeing aliens and found the people on Birresta average looking, neither handsome, nor unsightly. They were curious about Andrew and had never seen a human before. Andrew just told them the truth why he was living on Edena and they all smiled and one of them said –

"The power women have over us men is unbelievable."

When Andrew had worked six months, he had saved enough money to move out of Tilli's apartment and found a nice apartment close to his work place. Tilli was devastated and begged him to stay, but Andrew put a pile of money on her table and just thanked her for allowing him to stay with her and they were now even. He gave her a hug, then walked out without looking back. Finally, he was free.

Andrew had now lived on Edena nine months and spoke the language rather well, not fluently, but he was improving all the time. The change he saw in the population was astonishing. The men were slowly becoming men again and the macho women returning to more female behavior. Zittana had kept her promise and the men were given equal rights. The gyms were full of men trying to build muscle and many of them now looked like normal men. Everything had changed and the women helped raise the children, a responsibility they had not faced for generations. It was a normalization of living conditions benefitting both the men and women and Andrew liked what he saw. The men had started to assert themselves and refused to take orders from the women.

In the beginning of his stay on Edena, he had been propositioned several times by women asking him for his services.

"I'm not a whore," he had replied with a cold look on his face totally disarming the women.

As society transformed, women stopped their aggressive behavior and became more respectful of the men. The changeover also involved educating the men. None of them had higher education and they needed to learn various skills to join the work force. Many of them went back to school and pursued higher education. The planet was rather affluent and the government paid all expenses for any man who wanted to study. It would take a generation to undo the damage the Edena society had forced upon the men, but both men and women understood it was a necessity to preserve their race.

Edena was a nice-looking planet with rolling hills, no mountains or oceans, but with enough rainfall to support a beautiful flora of plants and forests throughout the planet. There was no desert anywhere and herds of herbivore animals were often seen on the fields. Rivers and lakes were common sights and a few of the lakes were substantial in size. Andrew decided to buy a boat when he had saved up enough money and the lake close to his apartment was popular with boaters. Edena was a rather small planet, smaller than Mars, and had no moons and was the only planet orbiting its star. It had four seasons and a mild winter with occasional snowfall and the summers were never burning hot.

Meat was hard to find as many people were vegetarians, but fish was popular and grown in large ponds. Andrew loved a hefty steak and was annoyed it was so hard to find beef. Eventually, he found a rancher and bought his meat directly from him. The food supply was not as varied as he was used to on Veehnia.

Zittana had sent a message to Andrew to meet with her in her office when he was back from Birresta and as he quietly observed her, he noticed how much she had changed since she stopped taking male hormones. She appeared more feminine, her voice was not as deep and her aggressive behavior was gone.

"Andrew, I know you're working full time now, but I would like to hire you as a consultant to our government. You have two weeks off between your trips to Birresta and if you would be willing to work here in the office three days on your time off, we would be grateful to have you as part of the government team. You will, of course, be paid." Zittana smiled at Andrew and waited for his reply.

"I am a space pilot and what could I contribute to your government?"

"Information about life on Veehnia and other planets you have visited. As you know, we are redoing our whole society and need input how other planets function as a free society. You could start on a trial basis."

"I start tomorrow and let's try for three days. After that I'll let you know if I want to continue."

"Thank you, Andrew. Your work day is six hours and we'll send a groundmobile to pick you up at ten tomorrow morning."

She shook hands with Andrew and he left.

The three days working with Zittana were hectic and rather demanding. Andrew was asked to give a full report how the Veehnian government worked and how society functioned. He used the translation device so he could express himself more clearly and when the three days were over, he was asked to continue working with them. Andrew agreed. It had been interesting and he was asked to notify them when he returned from Birresta the next time.

His second three days working with Zittana were spent on space travel and mapping the tunnels he knew of in both the Andromeda and Milky Way galaxies. Andrew knew he would need many days to convey all the information and he would need to find some of the information about the tunnels from the Interstellar Internet as his own ship's computer system had no information about the planets and tunnels Andrew knew existed. He decided to continue working with Zittana and he realized his own knowledge of space far surpassed her knowledge and he actually had a wealth of information to pass on to her.

Zittana was both the leader of the planet and a space pilot. There were elections on Edena and she had won the last election. Term limits did not exist and she could be reelected until her retirement, if the voters decided they wanted her as their leader. The challenge she faced was to raise the men to equal status of women and allow men to compete for jobs with women based on merit. Tothellim and Kody had also informed her how governments worked on other planets. Zittana was bright and understood her own planet had gone too far and warped the natural balance between men and women. Andrew's help had been priceless and she valued his work. She was attracted to him, but with the new system in place, she would never proposition him. Those days were over forever.

***

Several months went by and Andrew lived frugally to save money to buy a boat. His government job paid well and with two incomes, he was soon able to buy a used boat and loved spending days out on the lake fishing and swimming. His parents had a boat and he had many fond memories of leisure days on the water on Veehnia. Andrew always went alone and did not miss company. Emotionally, he was far from healed and the time he spent alone on his boat was part of his healing process. Edena was a nice planet and not a bad place to live, but Andrew's heart was firmly anchored on his home planet.

When Zittana heard Andrew had bought a boat, she politely asked if she could join him for a day trip and Andrew said yes. He liked Zittana as a friend and admired her intelligence and they always had lots of things to discuss, but he had no intention to start a romantic relationship with her. The affair with Tilli had taught him a lesson for life. Every decision has consequences and being stuck on Edena was the price he had to pay for his shortsighted weakness to join Tilly in bed.

Andrew found he truly enjoyed Zittana's company onboard his boat and they fished, swam and enjoyed a big lunch together. Zittana brought several homemade salads that were truly delicious. She confided to Andrew she loved cooking and she smiled when she saw Andrew wolfing down his lunch with utmost delight. Zittana's humor and quick wit made Andrew laugh many times. *How good it felt to laugh*, he thought to himself. When they said goodbye, he realized her company had been delightful and he had enjoyed spending the day with her. He saw on Zittana's face she also had enjoyed the day. They shared the fish they had caught and Andrew told her she was welcome again on his boat.

During the rest of the summer Zittana spent many days with Andrew on his boat and he considered her to be his best friend. They had an emotional relationship and he felt he was healing in her presence. She always made lunch for them when they went on the boat and in the office, she often surprised him by bringing lunch for him from home. Andrew enjoyed her various dishes and she was truly a good cook. While they were fishing, they told each other about their lives and childhood. Zittana was in love with Andrew, but did not show it, and Andrew was emotionally not ready for a romantic involvement. He needed more time to heal. Zittana sensed this and was just happy to be with him.

Andrew told Zittana how unnatural their former lifestyle was and no planet he had ever visited had treated men or women the way the women on Edena had treated their men. While Zittana was taking male hormones she was blind to the truth, but now that she had returned to normal levels of hormones for women, she fully understood what

Andrew was telling her. She deeply regretted what they had done and assured Andrew she would do everything she could as a leader to undo the damage done to the men. She asked Andrew to advise her and he promised he would continue to work as her consultant.

Their friendship continued and Zittana showed Andrew much of Edena using her airmobile. The planet was beautiful in a tranquil way, but it lacked high mountains and spectacular scenery. They would stop for lunch at a scenic place and talk. Small towns were scattered throughout the countryside. In the past, children were raised by their fathers and they hardly knew their mothers, but many women now returned to their children and moved in with the men, who had fathered the child. Marriage did not exist on Edena. Andrew knew he would prefer a traditional marriage rather than the strange system they had on Edena and he would propose a change in the law to Zittana. All planets he had visited had some form of marriage in effect and Edena was the only planet without marriage.

Zittana introduced Andrew to her father, who had raised her alone, and she did not know her mother. The mother had never bothered to visit her daughter and perhaps this unnatural behavior had shaped Zittana as she grew up and made her to the macho woman she had been when Andrew first met her. Without the male hormones, she had changed into a rather feminine woman and Andrew liked what he saw. She was beautiful and so easy to be with and her funny remarks caused Andrew to burst into laughter. She had a way of seeing life from a different angle and always with humor. They enjoyed each other's company, but there was no romance between them.

Her father was a pleasant man and had also transformed into more masculine behavior with the help of his hormone shots. He was studying and hoping to become a mechanic. Andrew liked him and they spent a day together. Zittana liked her father and dropped by to see him as often as she could. She had no siblings.

CHAPTER 5

A year passed and Tothellim was ready for space travel once again. He felt a strong yearning to return to the vast vistas only the universe could offer. His soul told him he was needed out there somewhere.

Another trip was approved by the government and the same spaceship was equipped with supplies to last up to three years. The crew from the first trip all volunteered to go along and Andrew was replaced by an experienced pilot; all the pilots had been trained by Tothellim and Rheo and were first rate.

The ship departed at dawn on a snowy winter day with brilliant blue skies. Tothellim's children Heidi and Logan were there to see him off and tried not to show they were worried he would not come back. Neither of them could understand the strong pull the universe had on their father. None of the crew members was married, but their families and the president joined Heidi and Logan to wish the crew success.

Tothellim followed the same route as last time all the way to planet Ursemic and then changed course, so instead of heading to Gellimo, he traveled in the opposite direction. The ship had built up immense speed from the tunnels and they covered long distances very quickly. A dimly lit star appeared far away with a single, small orbiting planet visible and the ship was soon in orbit. The new planet had two large moons, each about a quarter of the planet in size. As they watched the planet from the ship, daylight faded and the planet lit up, but the light was faint. The planet was inhabited. Early next morning, they launched a drone on a reconnaissance mission. No air traffic of any kind was visible so they programmed the drone to descend to five hundred feet and activated its cloaking device. It made very little noise as it was powered with twin electric motors.

The pictures started coming in from the drone and showed images of humans looking the same as Veehnians, but dressed in clothing from antiquity. Women wearing long dresses and men in coveralls were everywhere working in farm fields and performing manual labor. Apparently, they were harvesting a crop. Children were working next to the adults. Large horse-drawn wagons were ready to receive the harvest.

The androids on the ship were searching the computers and found a similar lifestyle on planet Earth long time ago. The drone continued and an impressive large home was visible and they guessed the owner of the farm fields lived there.

"It sure looks like a variation of a feudal society," Kody remarked. "The lord lives in his castle while the people work as his slaves. That type of society disappeared on Earth many centuries ago. I bet the people are corrupted and the lord has instilled fear in the people so they obey his rules.   The big question is what exactly are they afraid of?"

Tothellim decided Kody, Rex and one of the pilots, Eric, should use the shuttle to descend to the surface and investigate. Tothellim was a Peturun and his physical appearance would most likely scare the people to death, so he would remain onboard. The shuttle had cloaking capabilities. A brand new mini-size translation device that could be kept in a pocket would handle the language problems. All they could hope for was that someone would be willing to talk without succumbing to fear. The crew was dressed in casual clothes that would not stand out too much. The ship had a supply of old-fashioned clothing for use in situations like this. All androids had built-in recording devices.

They descended and the temperature was in the seventies, somewhat strange as their sun was dim and did not feel very warm.

"The planet must be heated by its core," Rex noted. "Otherwise, it would be much colder than it is."

The air was fresh and they left the cloaked shuttle a few miles away on a farm field and walked towards the village. The first house they saw was a run-down cabin and an elderly man sat outside with a cat on his lap.

"Who are you?" he said in his language and Kody held the translation device in his hand shielding it from view with his sleeve.

"We're not from here," Kody said in a low voice, but the device spoke loudly and it was hard to tell the sound did not come from Kody but from the device. The man did not notice anything strange.

"You speak with a dialect. Are you from the opposite side of Hydrasol?"

The crew members looked at each other and smiled. The name of the planet was Hydrasol and the ship's computers could probably find all the information about the planet from its library.

"Yes," replied Kody. "Why aren't you working in the fields?"

"I'm injured and they allowed me to take a few days off. I have to go back to the fields tomorrow and I'm not looking forward to it, but if I refuse, I'll be forced to leave this cabin and I have nowhere else to go. The Master owns the cabin. Life is hard and there is not much fun to live, mostly very hard labor," the man sighed.

"Do you get time off?"

"After ten days of work, we get one day off and then we must show up in the House of Worship. I usually fall asleep during the service from exhaustion. Half the day off is spent there and our lives are nothing but hard labor."

"Can't you overthrow the Master?"

The man appeared agitated and frightened and took a second look at the crew members.

"Who exactly are you? Don't you know the rules? Do you want to be beheaded?"

Rex decided to gamble and reveal who they were.

"We come from another planet. Please don't be afraid. We will not harm you. All we want is that you tell us about the living conditions on this planet. Then we will leave you alone."

The man was shocked at first and alarmed, but when Eric gently put his arm around the old man's shoulders and reassured him with his warm smile, he had nothing to fear, the ice was broken and he started to ask questions.

"I didn't know it was possible to fly in the sky like a bird. You mean you really come from another planet?"

The crew members all smiled and nodded.

"Please tell us everything about life here on Hydrasol. Perhaps we can help your people and make your Master change his ways."

The old man had calmed down a little and started talking, eager to get the painful details of his life off his chest.

"We live a hard life, barely worth living," he began. "We start working in the fields when we're ten years old and go to school every other day for only a few hours. We can read and write, but there are no books available, so what good is it to know how to read. They don't teach us anything else and when the crops are harvested, we have to do logging and all labor work to keep up the Master's grounds. When we're kids, we have to listen to hours of preaching by the Minister in the church and it's mostly about how sinful we are and if we don't obey, God will punish us. I don't believe any of it. God is not as cruel as they want us to believe, but most people believe it. I have my own thoughts on most things in life."

"What's your name and how old are you?"

"Teo and I'm fifty-two years old."

Teo was apparently rather intelligent and an independent thinker. He looked twenty years older than his real age from hard work and poor nutrition.

"What do you get to eat?" Kody asked.

"All the crops go straight to the Master after harvest and then we have to go to the Master and ask for our rations. They never give us enough and we're always hungry. If you're known as a troublemaker, they cut your rations as a punishment. We never eat meat, only the Master can have meat. We eat mostly bread, beans and some vegetables. We're forced to marry so the Master has more people as slaves, but I refused to marry and got away with it. Many who marry never share a bed together so no kids will be born. Everyone feels the same. Why have a child who will only become a slave? Very few children are born."

"How long has this system been in place?"

"As long as anyone can remember. If you disobey, they cut your head off. Everyone is afraid of the Master and God's punishment, so we tend to obey and just live out our miserable lives. In a year or two I'll be dead, thank goodness."

"Does the Master have an army?"

"Yes, a big one, so there's no way we could get to him and kill him off."

"From what you're telling us, we understand you live under a full dictatorship," Kody said while stroking his chin. "We need to discuss this among ourselves and we may come back to talk to you again, Teo. You have been most helpful and brave talking to us."

They left and walked back to the shuttle. The only person they met on their way back was a young woman dressed in peasant clothing carrying a load of firewood on her back. She struggled under the heavy load and the men wanted to help her, but Kody signaled 'no'.

Any encounter may reveal they were aliens and set off a panic. They just waved and quickly walked past the woman. She barely looked, too burdened with her heavy load to even look at them. She was around twenty years old and very pretty. The men thought to themselves about the bleak future she faced.

No one was around so Eric started the shuttle and soon they were back on the ship. Tothellim and the rest of the crew were eager to hear the news and Rex transferred all the images from his internal recording device to the ship's computers. After they had finished watching the images, all the men were quiet and thinking deeply.

"We need to make contact with the Master," Tothellim finally said. "Any suggestions?"

"To catch the Master alone and convince him there are better ways won't work," Kody said slowly. "He 'll never give up his power. We don't know how big his army is and what weapons they use. In addition, the Ministers of their churches have to stop corrupting the people and threatening them with God's punishment to keep them in line. This rescue mission won't be easy. We also don't know how many other Masters the planet has, but we can find out if we do a recon with the shuttle."

"Let's do so," Tothellim agreed. "First thing tomorrow, the three of you descend and investigate the whole planet. Keep the shuttle cloaked."

Flying at an elevation of one thousand feet the crew flew around the planet several times and at the end of the day they had the information they needed. The planet was a little smaller than Mars and without oceans, but several large rivers indicated there was no water shortage on the planet. It was very sparsely populated and vast evergreen forests were visible. They noticed some wild animals and herds of herbivores. There were three additional mansions on the planet, so four Masters ruled and kept the people in a vise-grip. All the citizens lived in shabby homes in hamlets spread out around the Master's home.

Back on the ship the crew struggled to come up with an idea that would work. As they discussed several plans, they all agreed the Masters would never willingly submit to a new system. The people themselves had to change the living conditions and the new society had to be more favorable than the present ways.

Slowly a plan emerged and was agreed upon. They would land the shuttle uncloaked and Tothellim and the crew would all descend to the surface. Two of the androids would stay behind and man the ship. With Tothellim present, no one could question they were aliens. Each army's headquarter had been visible from the shuttle and the crew would have to visit each Master's territory separately. There was no way to travel on the planet other than by foot or horse carriage.

The shuttle descended and landed outside the barrack where they assumed the leader of the army resided. They were right. He came storming out holding a short sword ready to fight. When he saw the crew and especially Tothellim he stopped dead in his tracks and gasped.

"Don't be afraid, we're friends," Tothellim said hastily using the language device. "We're visitors from another planet and we need to talk to you. Can we go inside and talk?"

The leader was too shook up to respond and could only manage a nod. As they entered the barrack, they saw the man was trembling. There was a table and chairs in one of the rooms and the whole building was rickety. They all sat down. The translation device was placed on the table.

"I'm Tothellim and we come from a planet far away called Veehnia. We know the name of your planet is Hydrasol. Tell me your name and if you are the leader of your army." Tothellim's deep voice and calm demeanor commanded respect as he spoke into the translation device.

"I'm, I'm Vejjo … and I'm the leader," he finally managed to say.

"Vejjo, how many people belong to your Master?"

"I think it's about two thousand."

"How many soldiers are there in your army?"

"Two hundred."

"If anyone disobeys, how do you deal with the person?"

"We just cut his head off. They have no weapons and can't defend themselves. No one dares to disobey."

"Do the other Masters also have around two thousand people working for them?"

"Yes."

"Are there any other people living on this planet in addition to the people working for the four Masters?"

"Several thousand live deep in the forest, but you never see them. They hide and we leave them alone. They live off the land and hunt for food. There are enough animals to kill and they eat mostly meat."

"The whole planet has about fifteen thousand people tops," Kody said in a low voice to Tothellim. "They may face extinction soon. There's probably a lot of inbreeding going on. The forest people need to intermarry with the Master's people to introduce new genes into the gene pool."

"The land on this planet doesn't belong to the Masters. It belongs to the people, including your soldiers," Tothellim said. "We suggest the land should be divided into parcels of three hundred acres and a parcel of land should be given for free to each family to farm and it doesn't matter if the person is married or not. This will only use up a small area of the land and the rest of the land can be left for future generations. Hopefully, more children will be born. The people in the forest should be notified so they can claim their land. The Masters will be allowed to keep their homes and three hundred acres, but no one needs to work for the Masters unless they are paid a salary. Do you have a money system and is there a government on the planet?"

"We have a money system, but no government," Vejjo said. He had finally managed to calm himself.

A loud voice was heard from outside and the Master marched in with two men at his side holding swords. He was rather young and looked well fed.

"What's going on here?" he yelled. Then he spotted Tothellim and almost fainted.

"WHAT the hell are you?" he managed to utter while hyperventilating. *"SIT DOWN!"*

One look at Tothellim's stern face convinced the Master to shut up and do as he was told. Tothellim explained everything he had told Vejjo and when the Master heard the land would be given out to the people he exploded and turned to Vejjo.

"Will you allow this?"

"Yes, I support the idea and it's fair. From now on you have no army and no one to protect you. You will have to pay the people working for you if you can even find anyone willing to slave away for you. You're on your own now. No one will help you."

The two men who had accompanied the Master left his side and sat down with the army leader clearly showing the Master he was abandoned.

"Are there any people with an education who can form a government?"

"Yes, some of the forest people are educated, more than anyone of us."

"Vejjo, send a few of your men into the forest and ask the leaders to come here so we can talk to them."

Vejjo left the room to notify a team of his soldiers and then returned. Tothellim turned to the Master.

"Whatever money you have stolen from the people you can keep, but no one on this planet owes you anything from now on. The people have been toiling away for hundreds of years as slaves while you and your ancestors lived in splendor and if they dared oppose you, they were beheaded. You will never regain your power over the people and from now on you have no more rights than the people. To defend yourself will be your problem."

The Master was ghostly white in the face, scared witless and cold sweat appeared on his forehead. Would he even make it home alive, he wondered to himself? Who would defend his family?

"Leave this room immediately! You won't be needed by the people ever again," Tothellim declared in an ice-cold voice.

The Master managed to stumble out of the room and onto his horse and disappeared. His chance of survival was slim.

The news spread like wildfire. Teo ran around and told his people the incredible changes that would take place. After two days a group of forest people walked into town and met with Tothellim and the crew. They were self-educated and intelligent and when they heard about the new system they were elated. Tothellim knew they would take charge, form a fair government and build a new society. A feeling of peace came over him and also joy that these abused people finally would have a fair chance at a normal life.

Over the next few weeks, the crew addressed the other Masters and repeated the message. All the forest people returned to the villages and eagerly listened to Tothellim. They stayed another month on the planet to ensure the foundation to a new and fair society was in place and the army leaders were more than happy to assist in the process. They also wanted peace and looked forward to owning land. A new age had begun.

Teo ran into the crew and announced the House of Worship had been empty last time a service was offered. No one would tolerate the Minister's propaganda ever again.

When Tothellim and his men departed for the last time with the shuttle many people saw them off and thanked them. Their faces were full of hope.

Tothellim decided to return to Veehnia and it had been a successful trip. The crew agreed and they started the long journey back home.

CHAPTER 6

Many new inventions had made life on Earth easy and stress free and the population globally had more free time to pursue exploration of their minds. People understood each life had a purpose and consciousness is beyond the physical body and can be expanded. Raised awareness is not tied to religion and people saw it as the new normal, a natural way of being.

Children were taught in school their lives had a meaning and were instructed how their psyche worked. The lessons became more advanced as the children grew older and could absorb more complicated issues. The result was the children matured into self-confident adults with sane minds and a realistic view of themselves. Inflated egos and narcissistic tendencies became rare and as adults, they were comfortable with who they were. Personal freedom and increased functionality rewarded the person following this path.

Physical and verbal abuse of children were a thing of the past and better results were achieved when children had to face the consequences of their actions.

Some children had trouble with mathematics and science and a few people suggested these subjects should be simplified. The students who requested an easier version were offered a simplified explanation of math and science, but the students who grasped the concept of math and science were taught a very advanced curriculum. No stigma was attached to the students who had trouble with the sciences and it was understood students differed in their abilities and neither was superior to the other. The student not adept at science may excel in other subjects.

Karma was taught to be an equalizer, not punishment, a consequence of a decision. We create our own karma by cause and effect and through karma we evolve. It is nothing to fear.

Children understood the importance of making their own decisions and not wait for anyone else to make decisions for them. If the decision is wrong, learn from it and go forward. Wisdom comes from knowing yourself.

People who were advanced in mind exploration were researching matter. Matter is a creation of the mind and not a separate substance and can be changed by the mind. The denser the matter, the harder it is for the human mind to change matter. Dense matter has lower vibration. The study of the mind referring to mind-over-matter was only pursued by the most advanced people on Earth as it was a difficult discipline to engage in. Citizens of planet Ljeviina were involved with mind research and some of them had reached a very high level of competence. Earth was far behind compared to Ljeviina.

Politically, the people on Earth were no longer divided and did not view each other as enemies. Divided people will not prosper and cannot move forward. Cooperation between countries was encouraged and basic humanity emphasized. All countries had democratic governments and People Democracy and variants of it were popular. It was recognized people always knew better than the government what was best for the country. No government was involved in misinformation or restriction of news to the people.

***

Even though spaceships from Mars, Frejja and Veehnia landed on Earth regularly, people on Earth had limited interest in space travel and felt it took too much time to visit other planets. Some adventurous people still emigrated to these planets as long as the transportation was free and usually every ship returned to their home planet filled with people from Earth.

However, *Natural Energy*, not the same as Natural Electricity, had recently been discovered and the cost of space travel had been lowered significantly and interest in exploring space started to grow. Young astronauts living on Earth and flying to the Moon and Mars expressed interest in more distant journeys into space and the governments of The Americas and Europe, with voter approval, decided to share the cost of several new spaceships capable of advanced travel into the universe. Veehnia supplied the design of their ships for free and the Moon had an abundance of terrynium needed in the manufacturing of the ships. A team of four astronauts spent a lot of time practicing flying through the twelve-hour, fifteen-hour and eighteen-hour tunnels in the flight simulator and by the time the first ship was built, the astronauts were well trained and ready.

The first trip was scheduled to be to Frejja and Earth2 and then return to Earth. If all went well, more trips would be offered and also exploratory trips. The four astronauts were all in their early thirties and three males and one female made up the team: Myles, the Captain, and Bonnie were both from The Americas; Hans was from the State of Germany and Claudin from the State of France in Europe. All four were experienced and had been flying about ten years. In addition to the captain and his three copilots, four androids, all pilots, would accompany them. Fifty paying passengers were onboard and were hoping to be allowed to live on Earth2. The passengers were only charged a modest fee as the trip was not risk free.

The travel time from Earth to Frejja was three months and from Frejja to Earth2 nine months and they would have to negotiate the twelve-hour tunnel. The trip would last over two years, but the crew accepted the challenge. None of them was married and they had no dependents. The passengers would have to endure one year on the ship to reach their Earth2 destination, but there were lots of distractions and entertainment onboard and none of them felt the year in space was a problem.

Frejja had been notified a ship was on the way and as soon as they were out of the twelve-hour tunnel, the ship's captain transmitted a message to Frejja they were close by and would land.

The ship was performing flawlessly and the crew and the passengers had adjusted to life in space. After three months they were in orbit around Frejja and asked for permission to land the ship on the surface. It was granted. The reason for not using the shuttle was that the passengers were eager to see the planet and some of them actually expressed interest in staying rather than continuing on to Earth2. People from Earth were well familiar with Frejja as their ships had landed on Earth for years and always returned back to Frejja with every seat taken on the ship. Frejja was popular, especially among single men.

The saucer type ship landed and as the first ship ever to land from Earth it was met with interest. The Frejjan president greeted them and Emrak and Karol were also there. Emrak was one hundred and one years old, but still agile and by no means old looking. He was well known on

Earth and had often been featured on the Interstellar Internet describing life on different planets. Karol was in good shape as well. The crew and passengers disembarked and were offered to stay at a hotel as guests of Frejja. The following two weeks were very busy with sightseeing and interaction with the Frejjan people. Twenty of the passengers fell in love with the planet and decided to stay. When the ship left both the crew and the remaining passengers felt the stay on Frejja had been truly delightful.

Nine months of travel time was now ahead and in six months they would go through the twelve-hour tunnel. The passengers were impatient to land and bored with the ship. The crew handled the tunnel well and the passengers endured the violence and shaking of the ship with bravery.

They landed on Earth2 and were greeted by president Rasufilus and his cabinet members. In addition to Viola, there were only a handful of people from Earth living on Earth2 and they had first settled on Frejja and later moved on to Earth2. The thirty immigrants from Earth were welcomed and allowed to stay. All of them were young and the group consisted of three families with small children and the rest of them were unmarried. The passengers said goodbye to the crew and were taken to a hotel in Bliss where they would be offered housing and jobs. All the immigrants were well educated and would contribute to the society at large.

The crew enjoyed a three-week stay on Earth2 and they all said to each other they would not mind living there. They also visited the grasslands and saw the herds of meat animals as well as the horses. Pollox and Lyra invited them for dinner and they ended up staying several days as their guests. The crew was fascinated to hear how Pollox and Lyra had lived without neighbors for almost twenty years and never felt lonely. The crew had brought along a translation device so they could communicate with the Frejjans. They described life on Earth and showed Pollox and Lyra many holographic images from different areas of Earth, the ethnic variety of its people, the oceans and whales and the wildlife on the African continent. Greenland and its frozen landscape in contrast to the Equator, all of it kept Pollox and Lyra mesmerized. The crew copied the images and gave them to Pollox as a gift.

When they returned to Bliss, a member of the government showed them around the Bliss area, the manufacturing plants and the mines.

They also saw Rasufilus' land Bavonilla and his fleet of fighter ships. It was a lot to absorb, but when the ship departed all of them said they loved the planet. Frejja was a close second.

Now they had a full year of travel to endure until they were back on Earth and even though the ship had Leo's velcro flooring installed, it was still tiresome to deal with the weightlessness. The four pilots and the androids were close friends and got along very well together and they agreed they would accept another trip to space if it was offered. Each trip was a hardship on their bodies and they knew they faced weeks of heavy exercise when they returned to Earth to regenerate their muscles. Bonnie was the only female, but she was one of the guys and all of them were sworn to celibacy as long as they were part of a ship's crew, so flirtation was not an issue and the crew did abide by the code they had sworn to uphold. Bonnie was a pretty girl, but rather masculine and totally dedicated to her job as a pilot.

They took turns flying the ship through the twelve-hour tunnel and each pilot had the controls for three hours. Many practice sessions in the flight simulator had prepared them for this challenge.

The year finally came to an end and they landed on Earth. They had trouble moving around and gratefully accepted the wheelchairs waiting for them. After a short debriefing it was decided they would rest a few days before meeting with the sponsors of their trip.

A week later they all felt better and met with the people in charge of their trip. After all the images had been viewed and discussed, they were offered another trip to any place they wanted including the Andromeda galaxy. The crew agreed immediately and said they would discuss among themselves how far they would like to travel and give their answer in a month. All of them wished someone would invent artificial gravity on spaceships. The lack of gravity took a heavy toll on their bodies.

CHAPTER 7

Rasufilus had been a successful president for five years and had one more year until his term was over. To serve in office had been a dream come true and his advisors Telly and Ássurt had done everything possible to assist him. With the present population of sixty thousand people, the governing of the country had become more complex and planning for the future had to include possible hardships. A troubling rumble had been heard from one of the volcanos located on the far side of the planet, but no eruption had occurred. Former president Ijakull, the geologist, had made several trips to the volcano and found that there was a possibility it could erupt. Steam was coming out of the volcano and a few small quakes had occurred in the area. The government knew they had to stock up on more food for emergency use in case the volcano would erupt.

***

The immigrants from Earth were settling in on their new planet and knew they had made the right choice moving to Earth2. Everyone was friendly and welcomed them. All of them had been offered a starter house, which they could buy later on if they wanted to, and all of them had quality jobs waiting for them as soon as they could speak Frejjan. A tutor spent four hours a day giving them lessons and homework assignments. Everyone was eager to learn quickly and worked hard. One of the immigrants was a young medical doctor and Atlas was asked to train him. Atlas' native language was English as he was created on Earth so the doctor started working right away. A few of them were teachers and as soon as they could speak Frejjan they would start working for the school system. Among the married people, one couple were both chefs and they opened a restaurant that became wildly popular and was well attended. A young filmmaker was planning to make holographic films, both fiction for entertainment and documentaries about the planet. Many people, especially the young, spoke English on Earth2 as it was part of the curriculum and the new immigrants could speak their native language with many of the people on Earth2.

***

Vitzoll and Janus lived next door to each other in the town of Rasunom. Vitzoll was newly married to a girl who was half Arrynian, half Etteron, Attinna. She was the daughter of one of his father's female Arrynian pilots. Attinna's mother was now retired, but she had served as part of Rasufilus' fleet for many years and had been an excellent pilot. Attinna looked mostly like an Etteron and had hair on her head, but she had inherited her mother's petite size and was only five feet tall. Vitzoll and Attinna were hoping to start a family, but Vitzoll was half Morekian and half Etteron and Attinna was half Arrynian and half Etteron, so three different humanoid races were present and there was no guarantee a child could be conceived.   Janus was still single.

Vitzoll was the new Commander in Chief for the mercenary fleet and Janus served as his copilot. Janus' competence and bravery matched Vitzoll's and the two men were more like brothers than just friends. They were very close and had shared the same spaceship since Janus started working for the fleet at age twenty-one. During the three years he had worked as a pilot, Janus had proved himself over and over and his skill and courage were beyond doubt. One of his attributes was his lack of fear as well as being levelheaded.

The Internet call came in to Vitzoll's house and it was from planet Ziela, not far from planet Peturun, orbiting the star Tevarkus and around three months' travel time from Earth2. They had been invaded and with their limited defense capabilities, they had been forced to capitulate to the invaders. Vitzoll was fully familiar with planet Ziela as his father Rasufilus had taught him everything he knew about the different planets. It was a small planet and its citizens were extremely advanced mentally, peace loving and with an aversion to any kind of war. Their mental awareness exceeded the consciousness of the most advanced people on planet Ljeviina, who were considered to be among the most advanced people known. Because of their high vibration, their lifespan was around two hundred and fifty years and the high vibration also protected them from disease. They were seldom sick during their long lives.

The people on Ziela were not affluent, but comfortably 'middle class' and a certain amount of assets in the form of precious metals and gold was present in the government's coffers to pay for society's needs. It was this amount the invaders had demanded at gunpoint. Unknown to the invaders, one of the government officials had managed to send off an emergency message to Vitzoll asking for help. The invaders were still on the planet, but no one knew how long they would stay and if Vitzoll would reach Ziela before they left.

Vitzoll and his pilots were briefed by Rasufilus before they left and he passed on all the information he had about the Ziela people. The mercenary fleet left and, as usual, six fighter ships and twelve pilots were left behind to defend Earth2 from raiders.

Vitzoll and Janus shared one ship and each ship had two pilots and was large enough to live on for extended trips. For a while, Rasufilus had kept three pilots per ship, but the cost became too high and he had been forced to let some of his pilots go to reduce the cost of his operation. He found that two pilots were sufficient as the autopilot did a good job of relieving the pilots from continuous duty in the cockpit.

The eighty-four ships flew in formation towards Ziela and they traveled through three short tunnels, one ship entering the tunnel every ten minutes. Upon arrival on Ziela, they found the invaders had departed taking all the funds the planet owned with them and the planet was bankrupt. Ziela was a beautiful planet, orderly and without crime. All labor work was performed by robots and the people had ample time to develop their psyche. The planet had high oxygen levels at thirty percent oxygen compared to Earth2's twenty-one percent and Vitzoll and his crew noticed it was difficult to breathe. Vitzoll and Janus met with the government officials and found them very pleasant to deal with. They were humanoids with large heads, short brown hair, human facial features, and about five feet tall. Both men and women were dressed in tunics and their serene faces revealed their advanced minds. There was no anxiety in their voices when they disclosed how they had been robbed, only sadness. As pacifists, they did not fight back. The government officials told Vitzoll and Janus the invaders had arrived with sixty ships and were a mix of several races and some late model androids. After they had stolen all the assets the planet had, including lots of expensive electronics, food and other supplies, they had violated many of the women and then abruptly taken off with their ships.

Vitzoll informed the government officials they would most likely find the invaders and what their fee would be and the officials agreed to pay the fee as soon as they had the funds. The planet was engaged in both manufacturing and mining and had a steady income and if the stolen goods could not be returned, they would pay Vitzoll in installments. Vitzoll agreed to the arrangement. He had never been defrauded and had full trust in his clients.

They stayed on the planet to lay the groundwork for their search and all the pilots did their share. Vitzoll had a whole team of well-paid snitches working for him on various planets and orbiting workstations and every single one was notified raiders awash with money may stop by for a shopping spree. After only two days the first call came in notifying Vitzoll a fleet of sixty ships had resupplied at their workstation and paid with gold. They only stayed one day and no one knew where they were headed. Vitzoll told the snitch he would be paid the next time they passed the workstation. All the snitches knew they would always be paid, but it may take a while until Vitzoll was in their area. Vitzoll kept a record of all the informers and how much he owed them and had never missed a payment yet. Several more tips came in, but after four days they had a breakthrough. The sixty ships had landed on a small planet and had erected temporary housing on a remote corner of the planet. They intended to stay for a while. The snitch did not live on the planet, but had overheard them talking about their plans and recorded it for possible sale. To reach the planet would only take a month. Vitzoll informed the government officials they had a lead and a detailed plan and left Ziela.

They entered orbit and engaged their cloaking devices. The planet was occupied and it was unclear if the inhabitants knew the invaders were living on their planet. Vitzoll and Janus descended to the surface fully cloaked and left the fleet in orbit. They saw a group of structures that looked like official government buildings and uncloaked as they neared the surface. They climbed out of their ship unarmed and a team of armed officials surrounded them within minutes. They were humanoids with slightly reptilian features, not as pronounced as the Kodetsian people, but clearly reptilian.

"We're here to help. Let us speak to your officials," Vitzoll said through his translation device. It was set on 'search' and as the guards started speaking it found their language.

"Follow me," the leader replied and they entered one of the buildings. A group of officials were seated around a table and rose when Vitzoll and Janus entered.

"I'm Belvon, the president of this planet. Please state your business."

"I'm Vitzoll, son of Rasufilus, and we are mercenaries."

"I know who your father is and I have great respect for him. Explain why you're here."

Vitzoll and Janus took turns explaining the situation and, as they had guessed, the president had no idea the criminals were living on the planet. The president explained their fleet of fighter ships consisted of only twenty ships and were mostly outdated and the weaponry on the ships antiquated compared to the weapons produced lately. They had never updated their defense as they were short on funds and struggled to make ends meet. Vitzoll assured the president his fleet was capable of defeating the invaders without their help as long as they had permission to conduct armed warfare. The president gratefully gave his consent. Vitzoll instructed the president to stay out of the area until the battle was over and he would return with a full report when the raiders had been defeated.

Vitzoll and Janus returned to the fleet in orbit and engaged the cloaking device. As his crew was listening, Vitzoll addressed them on an encrypted channel and delivered his plan of action. They would strike at daybreak the following morning with the ships cloaked and take out all the enemy ships. Anyone firing on them would have to be eliminated, but if no one retaliated from the ground, they should spare all lives and let the local government deal with the gangsters according to their laws. Vitzoll gave further details to his crew. All of them had years of experience and were ready to do battle.

It started and went well at first. As planned, all the enemy ships were fired on and reduced to heaps of trash and one after the other exploded. Then the firing quickly started from the ground and a weapon of tremendous power was used firing nonstop on Vitzoll's ships, randomly sweeping back and forth in hopes of hitting the cloaked ships. Vitzoll's ships were all made of terrynium, but the power of the weapon firing from the ground was so powerful it might penetrate the terrynium. Vitzoll realized the weapon must be a new design of incredible power.

"*RETREAT,*" Vitzoll shouted.

Too late. Four of his ships had been hit and tumbled to the ground. The rest of the fleet made it safely back into the sky and regrouped at a high elevation waiting for orders.

"Ship two through ship thirty follow me and we have no choice but to eliminate all of them," Vitzoll informed the crew. "I regret the death toll, but we must strike before they get our pilots out of the ships. They may have survived. These people won't capitulate and it's obvious they'll fight to their death, so we have no choice. The rest of the fleet will remain at this elevation until we return."

Vitzoll and the other ships quickly returned to the battle scene fully cloaked. It was chaos on the ground with some of the criminals trying to enter the downed ships while nervously looking up into the sky. Without hesitation Vitzoll gave his orders.

"*FIRE NOW!*" A barrage of firing weapons from Vitzoll's ships hit the temporary housing and they continued firing until no movement was observed from the structure. It was obvious no one was alive in there.

"Land and remain inside your ships, engines on idle," Vitzoll ordered his pilots. He and Janus landed and with their laser guns drawn they exited the ships. A dozen dead enemy bodies lay on the ground. They kicked the door open to the temporary building the criminals lived in and walked in. No one was alive inside. The weapon they had used was at the door and Vitzoll and Janus saw right away it was a new design they had never seen before. Vitzoll quickly ran around inside to make double sure no one was hiding anywhere and was still alive. They were all dead. Rasufilus as well as Vitzoll always tried to avoid bloodshed, but this was one of those times when the adversaries would not surrender and Vitzoll had no way out other than to eliminate them. He felt sad when he saw the dead bodies in spite of knowing they were all criminals. They had been living beings with a soul.

Outside, using his communicator, he ordered his crew to turn off their engines and exit the ships, set their laser weapons on 'fire' and assist in getting the pilots out from the downed ships. The four ships were smoking and badly damaged. The crew carefully opened the doors of the ships and found three pilots alive and five dead. As fast as they could, they brought the three pilots into Vitzoll's ship and they took off to the government buildings in search of medical help. The crew stayed behind and the fleet waiting at high elevation was told to enter orbit and wait for orders. Janus sent a message from the ship to the government officials requesting the location of their best hospital. They received an immediate reply and reassurance the doctors were ready and waiting to assist. To Vitzoll's relief the hospital was modern and the doctors seemed competent and alert.

Vitzoll and Janus were slumped in their chairs, mentally and physically exhausted, and waited for the doctors to come out. After what seemed like an eternity they appeared, shook hands with them and sat down.

"The three of them will all survive," one of the doctors explained. "They took some hard hits when they landed with their ships, but most of the injuries are broken bones and none of them has a head injury, thank goodness. Their helmets did a good job. All the internal organs are undamaged. They have lots of scrapes and bruises, but not life threatening. Our doctors are working on their broken bones right now and gluing them together and we'll clean their wounds and close them up. They must stay at the hospital at least three days until we see they are strong enough for your return trip. Come back tomorrow and then you'll be able to visit with them."

President Belvon showed up before they left the hospital and Vitzoll briefed him about the combat they had been through. He listened attentively and offered his sincere condolences when he heard that four of Vitzoll's ships had been shot down and five pilots were dead. He knew his own fleet could never have defeated the criminals and he shuddered when thinking about what they could have done to his own people when they realized they were defenseless.

"Vitzoll, we're not an affluent planet, but we will still pay for your four downed ships. That's the least we can do. You have saved us from a disaster."

Vitzoll accepted with gratitude the offer and the following day an airmobile showed up at the hideout and delivered payment in gold to cover the cost of the four ships. The team of soldiers delivering the gold asked Vitzoll to meet with their president before they departed.

At the hideout, they easily found all the money and stolen goods belonging to planet Ziela and loaded all of it onto their ships. The five dead pilots were stored in body bags in the cargo bay on the ships and it was a heartbreaking task when they carried them onto the ships, but all of them knew the danger of their jobs and had accepted the risk. There was nothing to salvage from the ships. The electronics were broken and all they could do was to abandon them. The cleanup crew on the planet would have to deal with it. The new weapon the criminals had used was also loaded onto one of the ships together with the ammunition, but the standard weapons they left for the cleanup crew to confiscate. They knew the planet needed supplies.

On the fourth day the pilots were sufficiently recovered to leave the hospital and their broken bones were strong enough so they were able to walk out of the hospital slowly with the help of crutches. The glue used to mend bones together was incredibly strong and had been in use for half a century on most modern planets. Vitzoll, Janus and the pilots stopped by to see president Belvon before they joined the fleet in orbit.

The president was emotional and thanked them several times for their help and would post the heroic effort Vitzoll and his fleet had performed on the Internet.

The fleet landed on planet Ziela and Vitzoll and Janus informed the government about the conflict. The Zielans were sad to hear the invaders had to be killed, but they fully understood the situation. They were against all killing, even their own enemies, and they were unhappy to hear about the tragic death of the pilots. They gratefully accepted all the returned money and electronics stolen from them and promptly paid Vitzoll the full fee in gold from the returned pile of money.

Vitzoll and the fleet stayed a few days on the planet to rest and transmitted a message to planet Peturun inquiring if they had four fighter ships fully equipped in stock. The response came back they did. Vitzoll would fly one of the new ships back to Earth2 with no copilot onboard; two of the injured pilots were well enough to fly a second ship and four of Vitzoll's most experienced pilots volunteered to fly alone; one pilot each for the two remaining new ships and one each to fly their own ships back home. Janus would fly Vitzoll's ship together with the third injured pilot, who was the most injured of the three and not fully recovered. Solo flying was possible with the help of the autopilot, but there was a risk involved.

Vitzoll ordered his fleet to return to Earth2 and he and the pilots, who would fly the new ships home, departed for planet Peturun. All fighter ships in the mercenary fleet were manufactured on Peturun and the quality of their ships was outstanding as was the advanced weaponry and electronics.

They arrived on Peturun and paid for the new ships with the gold they had received from president Belvon and bought food supplies for the trip home. The ships were impressive and met all the requirements Vitzoll had for his ships, such as weaponry, cloaking ability and velcro flooring. The most experienced team on Peturun checked out the new weapon they had taken from the invaders and told Vitzoll they had never seen a weapon of that sort before and did not know who had invented it. The ammunition used for it was also a new design they had never seen. The weapon had no identification markings on it so it was impossible to know where it originated. Most likely, the invaders had stolen it from an advanced planet somewhere.

The return trip back to Earth2 went well with the ships flying in formation and all the pilots communicated several times daily with each other ensuring all was well onboard. They slept for a few hours while the autopilots were running the ships and by the time they landed on Earth2, all of them were severely sleep deprived. Days of rest followed and slowly they were back to normal. It was hard to tell the five widows their husbands were dead, but all the mercenaries and their families knew how dangerous the job was and each mission could be their last. Vitzoll maintained a pension fund for widows and they were allowed to stay in their houses as long as they wanted. Most widows eventually remarried and moved, but a few stayed and were grateful to receive their monthly pension money.

Rasufilus listened carefully to Vitzoll's report and ensured him his decision to eliminate the raiders was the only option and he should not feel he failed. Not every mission goes according to plan and sometimes there will be loss of life. Vitzoll and Janus accepted Rasufilus' reassurance and promised themselves to always save lives on their future missions if it was possible.

Rasufilus and his government members carefully studied the weapon the invaders had used and it was decided to put it into storage in Bliss until it could be determined where it was manufactured. It was of such advanced design that none of the known planets could have invented it and Rasufilus realized that somewhere in the universe a planet existed dedicated to warfare and using weapons of this design. How could the invaders have stolen the weapon? It was a mystery.

CHAPTER 8

Planet Sorenia was the proud owner of two modern spaceships and when they were delivered from planet Mineata five years ago, the whole population celebrated. Volrex had successfully trained six young students to fly the ships and with the help of the flight simulator, they had gained enough experience to qualify as copilots. Two of them could fly through a short tunnel, but Volrex knew they needed more experience to master any tunnel and would only allow them to take the controls in the tunnel for a few minutes while he was ready to take over at the second set of controls. The students were all in their mid-twenties and 'star crazy'.

Volrex and five immigrants from Mineata, all experienced pilots, ran the flight school. When the ships were delivered, Volrex, two copilots and three of the students made a trip to Veehnia. A month later, the second ship took off and the remaining three students were onboard. Their destination was Mineata and Ziggellus.

Both trips were highly successful and the citizens on Veehnia had seen many images from Sorenia recorded by Tyler and Jayce and they knew Cooper had been left behind to restart their society. They were astonished when the ship came to visit them and Volrex transmitted many images from Sorenia the way it looked now. He also showed images of Cooper and his family and the images were available on the Internet for all to view. The Veehnian people were truly impressed to see the improvements Cooper had accomplished and Tyler and Jayce met privately with Volrex to get more details. Volrex knew of Tyler and Jayce and enjoyed meeting them in person.

The ship visiting Mineata and Ziggellus had less distance to travel, but the students found it most interesting to finally see the planet that had supplied so many of the consumer items to Sorenia and it was a good visit. The stay on Ziggellus was also educational and the planet was back to normal. Twenty-five years had passed since Rasufilus ended their raiding and all their manufacturing plants and starships had been rebuilt. Ziggellus was now a fully democratic planet and the citizens wanted nothing to do with their former lifestyle. They were doing well economically and were happy to greet the starship from Sorenia. It was a most enjoyable interaction between the crew and the people on Ziggellus. The pilots noticed all of the Ziggellus people had had their tails removed and one of the pilots asked in a friendly way why. The person replied the tails did not fit their new, nonviolent lifestyle and was associated with their former way of raiding. The tail was a reminder they could do without.

When the ships were back on Sorenia, Cooper asked if Halcyon could start training in the flight simulator and Volrex agreed. Halcyon was now sixteen years old and capable of understanding the computer system on the ship. His father Cooper had worked with him and Cooper knew Halcyon had what it takes to become a pilot. Halcyon was fully dedicated to the training and studied very hard both at school and when attending the courses at the flight school.

Halcyon and Celeste knew by now their father was an android and had recently asked who their biological father was. Cooper replied calmly it was Reyya and he had given the gift of life by helping them out. The children did not react adversely and they now understood why they had spent so much time with Reyya and Littiana, who they loved as much as their maternal grandparents. The children told Reyya and Littiana they would like to continue calling them grandparents. Rosalie's parents also knew Reyya was the father and they often visited with Reyya and Littiana. They had become good friends.

Cooper had just introduced communicators to the people and many saved up to buy one. The people who bought a unit were offered free instructions how to use them and after a while, they grasped the concept and found the units most impressive.

The Internet had also been advanced and was used by most of the citizens. Slowly, more and more people were able to use it and understand how it worked. It took a burden off Cooper as he was able to post government messages directly to the people on the Internet.

Rosalie and Cooper were happy together and soon their children would be on their own. Halcyon would most likely become a pilot and Celeste wanted to work with children as a psychology teacher. She was only thirteen years old, but had a good understanding how the mind worked and would like to help other children and young adults to explore their psyche and find freedom of mind. She needed a university degree to become a psychologist and she worked hard to reach her goal. Rosalie had written most of the books used in the school system. Her books were based on true facts and there was a lot of research behind every book she brought out.

***

Emrak was still agile and healthy at one hundred and four years old, but Karol had started to feel her age. A recent heart transplant had restored some of her energy and she still had several more years left of her life. In one year, Emrak and Karol would celebrate their fiftieth wedding anniversary and it had been a good marriage for both of them. They had several grandchildren and great-grandchildren and enjoyed their visits, but when they were alone at home, they were comfortable with each other and had always been each other's best friend. Their retirement years were pleasant and peaceful. Emrak always looked forward to hearing from Tothellim and his travels. Brandon and Brianna were still alive and, in a year, Brandon would be one hundred years old. They still visited Emrak and Karol and the four of them always had a good time talking about space and new inventions. Rigel was still working as a domestic pilot at sixty-eight years old and he and Sillia were already grandparents. Their beloved pet Rollo was still alive and able to go for short walks, but she preferred to lie in Sillia's lap and be pampered.

***

Back on Earth, a year had passed since Myles and his crew returned to Earth and their spaceship was being equipped for another long journey into space. The same crew would make a second exploratory trip, but this time without passengers. Planet Ljeviina in the Andromeda galaxy would be their first stop and after that the crew was asked to look for a new planet. All the planets that had been visited by spaceships in both the Milky Way and Andromeda galaxies were known to the citizens on various planets thanks to the Interstellar Internet and every new, inhabited planet that was discovered was listed on the Internet. No one from Earth had ever visited the Andromeda galaxy. Brandon and

Brianna had of course been there, but they were citizens of Frejja at that time. The scheduled trip was the talk of planet Earth and the crew was interviewed before departure. The trip was expected to take over three years and had generated lots of excitement on Earth.

The ship had Leo's velcro flooring to make walking upright easier, but one new feature had been added to the ship and it was a gravity chamber invented by Leo and his team. The idea was not new and the invention was by no means high-tech, but it worked rather well and was better than nothing. The chamber was also the exercise room and by spinning at a rather fast rate, it produced a gravity of seventy percent of Earth's gravity by centrifugal force. The crew members were expected to exercise in the chamber at least two hours per day and resistance training and running were part of the program. It was hoped the crew would retain more physical strength by spending time in the gravity chamber and two hours daily was the minimum time needed. The chamber was large enough for three crew members to exercise at the same time.

Tons of foods and supplies were loaded onto the ship and it departed from Earth on a snowy day in December 2200. It was one year since the crew returned from Earth2 and by now all of them were ready for the adventure of their lives. To reach Ljeviina would take one and a half years and they would travel through all three monster tunnels, the twelve-hour, eighteen-hour and the fifteen-hour tunnel and cover a distance of more than two and a half million light years each direction. It was difficult even for the crew to fathom the enormous distance they were about to travel. They were mentally ready for the challenge and in good physical condition.

The first year of travel went by and the ship was moving through space at an incredible speed. They had just passed the eighteen-hour tunnel delivering them into the Andromeda galaxy and they still had the fifteen-hour tunnel to pass through. Life onboard was not boring and the crew was busy running the ship, exercising, learning about the different planets that had been visited by various humanoids and they also were trying to learn a little of the Ljeviinan language. There was a holodeck onboard, a library with holographic movies and educational material, games and lots of other entertainment devices to spend time with. None of the crew felt the trip dragged on and all of them had maintained good physical condition thanks to the gravity chamber.

The last tunnel was behind them and in two months they would be in orbit around Ljeviina. Myles transmitted a message they would soon arrive and received a reply they were welcome. Twenty-eight years had passed since Jayce and Tyler had landed on planet Ljeviina. Two hundred people from Ljeviina had moved to planet Earth2 and Lorre was one of them. He had been Jayce and Tyler's guide on Ljeviina.

The Ljeviinans had long lifespans thanks to their high vibration and they lived on average two hundred years, some even longer than that, and their high vibration also ensured they were free of diseases most of their lives. Their minds were highly evolved and some of them were able to communicate telepathically with each other. Myles and his copilots climbed out of the shuttle and were greeted by Flar and other members of the Ljeviinan Starfleet, who had also greeted Tyler and Jayce years ago. This was the first time a ship from the Milky Way had visited Ljeviina. Flar was now in his mid-sixties, but did not look a day older than forty and the warmth radiating from the Ljeviinans was felt as intensely by the crew as Tyler and Jayce had experienced. A wall of kindness surrounded them and it felt like a divine moment.

"Welcome, all of you, to our planet. I'm Flar and we're delighted to have you visit us. You're the first people from the Milky Way to land here and it's so exciting to meet you." Flar was smiling and shaking hands with them and when he noticed Bonnie, he looked into her eyes and seemed dazzled by her. Bonnie was an attractive woman and self-confident, but she was at the same time humble and unpretentious.

"You're the first female pilot I have ever met," Flar said.

"I'm honored to be here," Bonnie replied and looked into Flar's eyes.

Myles noticed a certain electricity in the air. Bonnie was one of the guys and he never thought of her as a woman, but he did notice she had impressed Flar.

The following month was full of activities and they toured the brand-new capital. The crew knew all about the destruction of the former capital by the Ziggellus raiders and how Rasufilus and his fleet had put an end to their raiding. Ziggellus was now a peaceful planet run by the descendants of the people who had never participated in the raiding and had instead hidden in the countryside. It took years, but the Ljeviinan people had finally forgiven the Ziggellus people and a few years back they had welcomed a spaceship from Ziggellus and treated them as guests. A hundred young people from Ziggellus had moved to Earth2 and President Rasufilus had personally welcomed them.

Flar and Bonnie seemed to enjoy each other's company and Myles knew she was totally loyal and would never break any rules. Flar was their official guide during the whole month. A few days before they were scheduled to depart from Ljeviina, Bonnie knocked on Myles' hotel room door and entered.

"Myles, this is hard for me to say, but Flar has asked me to marry him and I said yes. We're in love and I know it sounds unbelievable, but it just happened. I have no family on Earth, as you know, and I'm willing to resign and stay here on this planet. Flar has offered me a job in his Starfleet, if I want to continue flying, but that decision I will make later on. Can I resign?"

"My intuition told me something was going on, Bonnie," Myles said and gave her a big hug. "Of course, you should follow your heart. Flar is a great man and I understand your affection for him. These people are the kindest and most interesting people I've ever met and I know your life with Flar will be fascinating. Their advanced minds will make your life both exciting and stimulating. You have my support."

"I have always felt you're like a brother to me, Myles, and it would mean a lot to me if you stayed another week and attended our wedding. Would you do it?"

"Absolutely! How are wedding ceremonies performed here?"

"Organized religion doesn't exist on this planet, but the people are spiritual and one of their spiritual leaders will perform the ceremony. The wedding will take place in Flar's home."

Flar had dedicated his life to being a Starfleet captain and had never been married. He was a wealthy man and his home was lovely. Myles knew Bonnie would have a good life and Flar had assured Bonnie he would only take on short distance flights after they were married.

Bonnie was a stunning bride dressed in a traditional Ljeviinan wedding tunic that showed her nice figure and Flar had a matching tunic designed for men. Marriage was important on Ljeviina and the ceremony was rather long. Bonnie had to say her vows through the translation device and she had already started to take lessons in the Ljeviinan language from Flar's housekeeper, a female android called Pendy. Myles had added the English language to her programming and spent several hours making sure she was able to pronounce the English words properly, so Bonnie could work with her. She was a very advanced model and had no trouble acting as a tutor. No one on the planet spoke English.

Myles and the crew stayed through the wedding and the dinner that followed and then it was time to leave the planet. Myles and the two copilots were emotional when they said goodbye to Bonnie and all of them hoped they would meet again. The four of them had worked together for over ten years and Bonnie had been like a sister to the three men. Flar waited discreetly in the background while his new wife said a tearful farewell to the pilots and then gave a bearhug to each of the men. He reassured them he would do his best to make Bonnie happy. Bonnie's personal belongings had been delivered already to Flar's home.

***

Bonnie's life as Flar's wife started and he radiated kindness when he looked at her. She had never been in love before and had not had any serious relationships due to her work. At thirty-three years old, she was thirty years younger than Flar, but he only looked to be in his forties and with a lifespan of two hundred years, he would probably outlive her. Flar was a wonderful husband and Bonnie thrived. She loved her life and Flar. She enjoyed snuggling up to him and she could literally feel his high vibration. Bonnie was an only child and her parents had perished in an accident when she was only fifteen years old. Flar nurtured her and she felt reborn. He was both husband and parent at the same time. Flar adored Bonnie and her youth invigorated him. Bonnie stayed home for the time being and was hoping to become a mother and to her surprise she became pregnant after a few months to Flar's delight.

Pendy worked with Bonnie and she was soon able to understand simple language. The language was not too complicated and reading and writing was also manageable. Bonnie still used the translation device when she talked with Flar to make sure he would understand what she said.

No one discriminated against her and Bonnie soon had a friend in the neighborhood, a woman her own age, named Xiona. She learned a lot from this woman and as the mother of two children, she would advise Bonnie about children's issues for years to come. Xiona was fond of Bonnie and treated her like a sister. There were no immigrants on the planet except Bonnie.

As he had promised, Flar switched to domestic flying and was only gone for two, three days. He always enjoyed coming home to Bonnie and looked forward to the birth of their baby. Flar had never been married and to become a father was very special to him.

Bonnie did not use the artificial womb and went through a natural pregnancy. This was not the norm on the planet and even her doctor tried to convince her to use the womb. Her doctor had never delivered a baby before, but all went well and Bonnie gave birth to a large, healthy boy. He looked like Flar, but he did have hair like his mother. He was truly handsome. They named him Victor after Bonnie's father. Bonnie stayed home while the baby was small and Pendy took care of all the housework. Eventually, she wanted to resume her work as a pilot, but only for short distance trips.

CHAPTER 9

Bonnie was sorely missed onboard, but the crew had to concentrate on their mission now. Three pilots were sufficient to run the ship and the four androids were all pilots. They had trained in the flight simulator and were capable of piloting the ship through all the tunnels.

On the Interstellar Internet, they found the news about Tothellim's visits to planets Ursemic, Gellimo, Edena and Hydrasol and the locations of each planet. They were supposed to look for new planets and Myles entered a new course into the computers away from these planets. Myles and his crew were also aware of Vitzoll's mission to planet Ziela and the futuristic weapon Vitzoll had confiscated. The mission had been posted on the Internet, but the present location of the weapon was not disclosed. All spaceships traveling around the universe were fully updated about the known planets and Vitzoll always posted his missions on the Internet without revealing sensitive data. However, the news about the weapon had been released to warn travelers a hostile planet may exist.

Two months passed and a solar system became visible with a single, medium sized planet orbiting and Myles steered the ship towards the planet. They entered orbit and found the planet was occupied and very lit up after dark indicating a large population. The next morning, they launched a drone with cloaking ability and programmed it to cruise at five thousand feet. There was air traffic below the drone and groundmobiles on the surface. Lots of beings roamed the streets and from the images transmitted by the drone they saw humans with white hair; females with long shoulder length hair and men with short white hair and white beards. They were average height and truly handsome.

"Are they angels?" Claudin asked astonished. The other pilots laughed loudly and Hans said –

"They look just like us, but with that strange white hair."

"They walk slowly and lightly, as if they're floating around," Myles observed. "Let's bring the drone back and launch the shuttle."

The three pilots and two of the androids boarded the shuttle and took off from the ship. The remaining two androids had to stay on the ship and would descend to the surface later on. They landed the shuttle outside the city on a field and climbed out. The planet had an oxygen atmosphere and a little less gravity than Earth and seemed lush with green grass, trees and planted fields. The sun was bright and warm. Soon a groundmobile pulled up and six armed men in uniform jumped out. They did not point their guns at them and with a smiling face the leader entered their language code into the translation device Myles offered him.

"Welcome to our planet Strovea. I'm Tahillo."

Myles introduced himself and his crew and explained they were from the Milky Way galaxy, the huge distance they had traveled to reach them and they had just left planet Ljeviina.

"We know, of course, of the Milky Way, but we haven't heard of your planet Earth. Our ships haven't visited your galaxy, but we have landed on planet Ljeviina several times and we traveled twice to planet Veehnia. Follow me and let's talk inside."

They entered a modern building and sat down in the lobby. An airmobile landed outside and a group of government officials entered, five men and three women. They were all good-looking and both the women and men wore tan leggings with dark blue, close-fitting jackets. All the men had a short white beard and they had green eyes. The leader stretched out his hand and shook hands with all of them and introduced himself.

"We're happy to meet you and my name is Terjo. I'm the leader on this planet. I understand from Tahillo you're from planet Earth. We look forward to hearing how you were able to find us and the route you took to find our planet. There are a billion people on our planet and this is a peaceful planet without wars."

An android pulling a cart with tea and a tray with mini-sized sandwiches served them and then left. The two androids from Myles' crew politely declined and the aliens noticed they were androids.

Myles explained the long travel route from Earth and how one of them had decided to stay on Ljeviina. They all smiled when they heard

Bonnie had married Flar and Tahillo, who was part of the Strovean Starfleet, had met Flar several times.

"Your pilot Bonnie couldn't have married a better man than Flar," he said with a grin. "I know him and respect him very much. He'll be a good husband to Bonnie. She'll be the only foreigner on Ljeviina as far as I know, but the people over there are so kind and no one will discriminate against her."

They continued talking for a few hours and then a soldier took them to a hotel. It was agreed they would meet again the next morning and Terjo asked for exact locations of all the tunnels and the holographic images of the tunnels. All of it could easily be transmitted from the ship's computers as well as images of life on Earth.

The Strovean society was slightly more advanced technologically compared to Earth, but the people's consciousness was perhaps a hundred years ahead of people on Earth and not far behind Ljeviina. Their awareness was high and the people were continuously transcending thanks to their highly advanced psyches. Few people suffered from disease as their vibration supplied enough light to offset most illnesses and the average lifespan was close to two hundred years.

The next morning loads of information were sent from the ship to the government computers together with holographic images of life on Earth. The ethnic diversity on Earth astonished the Stroveans and they found it strange Earth was divided into different countries with different languages, each country with its own government. Most planets in the universe had only one ethnic race and one government unless the planet allowed immigration. The wildlife on Earth was a hit and the Stroveans were both amused and fascinated as they watched all the images from around planet Earth. Elephants, apes, carnivores, herd animals as well as aquatic animals astonished them. Even horseback riding surprised them and watching a rider on a galloping horse took their breath away. They had never seen anything like it. A motorcycle gang with tattoos and earrings made all of them laugh out loud. Myles and his crew were smiling and they knew Earth was very unique and not a typical planet.

Strovea had only one ethnic race and one government and the citizens were similar to the people on Ljeviina in many ways. Their goal in life was to develop their minds and increase their vibration. Myles, Hans and Claudin discussed the matter when they were alone.

"Have they forgotten life is a gift in their pursuit of advancing their minds?" Hans wondered. "Do they ever allow themselves to have fun? It's not a sin to by happy."

"I agree," Claudin said. "I see no problem aiming for both goals. Advance your mind and at the same time have fun and enjoy life. I doubt the Creator minds if people are happy."

"I concur with both of you," Myles said. "Happiness, adventures, challenging life, even taking risks, all those things will make you feel alive and increase your creativity. I did notice they only laughed when they started watching our holographic images from Earth. Before that they were awfully serious."

More images followed of life on Earth and the arts were displayed with a piano player playing classical music, opera singers and ballet dancers. It was so entertaining to the Stroveans that Terjo said in a moment of enthusiasm the images would be shown on the Internet for all the citizens to see. To top it off, Myles displayed a clown and to his surprise the Stroveans laughed heartily. Myles hoped the images had put emphasis on the value of variety in life and not to take life too seriously.

Myles and his crew had succeeded in changing the Strovean people and Terjo finally understood the gift of life includes pursuit of personal happiness and will not interfere with advancing the mind. Terjo announced to Myles he would make this clear to his people. Myles chuckled and patted him on his shoulder.

Myles asked Terjo if he had any information about the weapon Vitzoll had found and to his surprise Terjo nodded.

"There is a planet about ten light years from here called Rotzini, with a violent population who loves war. They're highly advanced technologically and a few years ago, one of their scientists invented a horrific weapon to add to their arsenal. Only two pieces of the weapon were made and one of them was stolen. The planet is ruled by two brothers, Hitzabin and Aboqroll, two sadistic savages incapable of feeling empathy. The women are almost as cruel and they teach their children warfare from an early age."

"Where did you get this information?" Myles asked with surprise.

"Rotzini trades with a planet that supplies them with some of the rare minerals they need to manufacture electronics and weapons. In return, that planet will never be the target of an attack and they're also very well paid for their minerals. One of the pilots of the supply ships delivering the minerals to them is our spy and we pay him very well to report to us anything he hears when he visits Rotzini. His name is Udenni. We live in fear they may invade us. We're pacifists and have no fighter ships or army, only standard cargo ships for space travel. Udenni reported to us a group of the men had left the planet and lived as criminals and they stole one of the monster weapons when they left. They invaded Ziela and robbed them, but we saw on the Internet Rasufilus' son Vitzoll had overpowered them and killed them all. There was no information who has the weapon now, but we assume Vitzoll has it. The problem is Hitzabin and Aboqroll have the remaining weapon and will not hesitate to use it. If they choose to invade us, we have no chance against them."

"How big is Rotzini and how large is the population?"

"Oh, it's a small size planet and the population is around fifty million, give or take a few. The Rotzini people are tall and strongly built humanoids, low foreheads and elongated heads with thick, dark hair. They have small, flat noses and small ears. Hardly a handsome people and I would say they're among the most dangerous people in the universe."

Myles was thinking deeply and finally said –

"Even if Vitzoll or another invading force managed to take the weapon from them, they could just make another weapon since they invented it. What needs to be done is to disarm them completely and try to change their mindset. Actually, to repeat what Rasufilus accomplished on planet Ziggellus years ago."

"We're familiar with the Ziggellus mission. We read about it on the Interstellar Internet."

"Is there a mercenary fleet working here in the Andromeda galaxy with the same high integrity as Vitzoll's fleet?"

"Actually, there is," Terjo replied, "but I think they only have a fleet of thirty ships. That's not enough ships to disarm the people on Rotzini and Vitzoll is too far away to assist in a mission against them."

"I agree," Myles said. "What needs to be done is to change the people's mindset from embracing war to wanting to live in peace with their neighbors. That's not easy to accomplish as they're warriors. I need to talk it over with my crew and if we come up with anything before we leave, I'll let you know."

When Myles and his crew returned to their hotel rooms in the evening, they contacted the two androids onboard the ship, Lenny and

Toby. They quickly informed them of planet Rotzini and the weapon located there and asked them for ideas how to proceed. Lenny was known to be creative and suggested a plan.

"I think I can hack into their computer system and plant a virus that will infect the whole system. While they're occupied removing the virus, we land our ship on Rotzini and the ship will be fully cloaked. Toby and I exit the ship and simply kidnap Hitzabin and Aboqroll. The crux is to find them. If we do find them, we would stun them and just carry them back to our ship. Toby and I can easily carry them. As soon as we're back on the ship, we lock them up and take off. If we're lucky, we'll only be on the surface an hour."

"Good," Myles said and then added "What happens next? How do we change the people from criminals to peace loving citizens?"

"The brothers will never be returned to their planet. They will be dropped off on planet Cerres, where the Cosmic Court is based, and stand trial for all the crimes they have permitted. Most likely, they'll never be free men again. We pass Cerres on our way home to Earth so that part is easy. Once the brothers are gone, it may be possible to convince the citizens on Rotzini to change, if they know for sure the brothers are gone and will never come back. They may want to embrace a new lifestyle, but are too afraid of the brothers to even hint they've had enough. I am, of course, guessing here, but it's worth a try."

Myles and his crew nodded and Myles said –

"We'll discuss the plan with Terjo tomorrow and if he can contact Udenni and find out where the brothers live and their routine, there is a chance we can pull it off. Once we have the brothers locked up on the ship, we would return to Strovea and start negotiating with the leaders. By that time, they have probably neutralized the virus and can communicate with us. Let's start tomorrow. Lenny, thanks for your help. It's a good plan."

Terjo and his advisors supported the plan wholeheartedly and Terjo contacted Udenni right away. Terjo was told the brothers shared a house outside the capital and always returned home in the evening to spend time with their families. Udenni warned him the brothers were always armed and all the family members would have to be stunned so they could kidnap the brothers. Udenni added his own people would be delighted if the plan worked. Everyone dealing with the Rotzini people were disgusted with them and wanted an end to their terror. He added he had sensed the people were worn out and only continued their lifestyle for fear of retaliation by the brothers. Terjo promised to pay Udenni for his help the next time he visited Strovea, but Udenni assured him no payment was necessary if the plan worked.

Lenny and Toby wasted no time and after only a few days they managed to bypass the security system and hack into the main computers on Rotzini. They found the best location to launch the virus and started to write the code. The virus was particularly nasty and Lenny knew it would not be easy to neutralize it and would take time.

Terjo informed Myles the travel time to Rotzini was five weeks and they would have to pass through two tunnels, but both tunnels were rather short and easy to negotiate. The plan of action had been prepared in detail and Myles departed from Strovea promising they would return if all went well.

The trip to Rotzini was easy and the ship was soon orbiting the planet. It was late evening and Lenny successfully launched the virus. Udenni had given them the location of the house the brothers shared and it would only take a short time to descend and land a distance away. Only the ship had cloaking capability, so they could not use the shuttle. It was now time and the ship started descending to the surface with all lights off. The brothers had a large property and they landed two miles behind the house and Lenny and Toby left the ship. Modern space ships were not overly noisy and it was unlikely the sound of the ship had reached the house. They were dressed in dark clothing and the stun guns were ready and set on high. The stun would not kill the victims, but totally paralyze them for several hours. It was completely dark outside.

Lenny looked into the windows and saw the two families having dinner together. No guards were around and they noticed the brothers were armed. They found an unlocked back door and entered the house. No one saw them and they were able to walk past the kitchen without being seen by the chef and his assistant. They quietly opened the door to the dining room and instantly fired the stun guns hitting all family members. They were immobilized and Lenny and Toby raced in and grabbed the brothers. Udenni had sent pictures of the brothers and they recognized them right away. They picked up the brothers and as they ran out of the room, the chef saw them. Toby threw the brother down on the floor and stunned the chef. He collapsed in a heap, but now the chef's assistant tried to block him. Toby recognized the assistant was an android and could not be stunned. He quickly pulled out his laser gun and fired at the android's head and he went down. It was not a fatal shot and he knew the android could be restored, but for now the android was no threat. Toby picked up the brother and ran out. Androids are stronger than humans and the weight of the men on their backs slowed Lenny and Toby down a little, but not by much. They ran as fast as they could to the ship and after fifteen minutes, they were back. The crew saw them and had the door open and pulled them in. The engines were idling and within a minute they were airborne. The brothers were alive, but it was obvious they struggled to breathe and they looked terrified. They were still unable to move. Myles and his crew had six cages onboard for prisoners and the brothers were locked inside a cage each. The cage was twelve feet square and had a cot, an incinerator toilet and a tiny sink for washing, nothing else, and they would have to stay there until they reached Cerres. Myles knew they may not survive inside the cage, but he was not concerned about it and if they died, so be it.

Terjo and his government members waited for them and Myles, his copilots and Lenny and Toby took the shuttle down to the surface. Terjo was overwhelmed with excitement the plan had worked and they contacted Rotzini to no avail. Apparently, they had not conquered the virus yet. The following day, they received a return signal from Rotzini and spoke with the leader. The transmission from Strovea came through as 'unidentified' and Myles explained to the leaders the brothers would never return to their planet and why they had been kidnapped. Would they be willing to destroy their weapon and abandon their criminal lifestyle in exchange for acceptance by the other planets? The leader knew they were hated by everyone and deep inside he felt it was time to return to a peaceful lifestyle. He hesitated and informed Myles he needed to discuss it with his team. The brothers were gone and he felt enormous relief to hear that. He hated them and so did most of the citizens.

When Myles contacted the leader the following day, he had still not made up his mind and told Myles he himself was ready to comply, but some of the leaders were dedicated warriors and refused to surrender. Myles asked if the leaders who refused to capitulate could be incarcerated and the leader said he would discuss it with his team.

The negotiations went on for a week and the leaders had no idea who they were dealing with, only that an unknown force wanted them to abandon their way of living. Myles had made it clear the weapon and its design must be destroyed and never again manufactured.

Another week went by and this time the citizens had been asked if they were ready to abandon invasions of other planets. The reply was 'yes' from most of the citizens. They had had enough. The people in charge who refused to give in had been put in jail and the leader informed Myles the weapon and the design of it had been destroyed and they would comply with all the demands. He asked who Myles was, but was told he was better off not knowing. The leader was aware mercenaries were around and feared they would face an invading fleet of fighter ships. Myles assured him it would not happen if they accepted the peace agreement Terjo had written and never again invaded another planet. Terjo transmitted the agreement and the leader and his government accepted all the terms and returned the signed documents to Strovea.

Myles told Terjo it was time for them to return to Earth and from now on he and his government would have to monitor if the people on Rotzini honored the agreement. Both Myles and Terjo felt it was unlikely the people on Rotzini would return to their criminal ways. The driving force had been the brothers and now that they were off the planet, most likely the leaders they had dealt with would honor the agreement. The leaders had been instructed to post a message on the Interstellar Internet stating they had abandoned their criminal ways and Rotzini was no longer a threat to other planets. The leaders never found out who they had communicated with.

Terjo and his government officials saw Myles and his crew off and expressed immense gratitude for all the help they had offered. He also thanked Myles for showing them that enjoying life would not interfere with advancement of the mind.

The long trip back to Earth started and they dropped the brothers off on planet Cerres. They were still alive. The court officials were fully informed how the people of Rotzini had plundered other planets and promised Myles the brothers would stand trial for all their atrocities. If they were found guilty, they would face a firing squad. The trial would be posted on the Internet so the citizens on Rotzini could see for themselves that criminal behavior is never worth it.

The ship safely passed through all three of the long tunnels and Myles landed the ship on Earth after a year and seven months of travel time. They had been gone three years and four months, but were in remarkably good physical shape thanks to Leo's gravity chamber and Myles and his copilots had spent at least four hours in the chamber every day. Myles sent a message from Earth to Leo praising the chamber and how well it worked. Leo was touched when he read the message and replied to Myles, he would do his best to invent full gravity on spaceships.

Myles and the crew were celebrated and the details of the trip were posted on the Internet, except sensitive data. Myles sent a report to Emrak, who passed it on to Tothellim and Rasufilus. It was also posted on the Interstellar Internet because a new planet, Strovea, had been discovered. Rotzini was only mentioned briefly and the capture of the brothers was not revealed. Myles also sent an encrypted message to Vitzoll and Rasufilus with all the details of the weapon, where it had been made and the removal of the brothers from planet Rotzini. The leaders on Rotzini had destroyed the weapon and Myles suggested to Vitzoll and Rasufilus they do the same. They responded they would neutralize the weapon and sent greetings to Myles thanking him for the report.

Leo's gravity chamber was installed on all new ships being built and significantly improved the health and stamina of all the people using them on the ships.

CHAPTER 10

Bonnie loved being a mother and Victor was already two years old. Another baby, a girl, was developing in the artificial womb and would reach maturity in a few weeks. For her second pregnancy, Bonnie had chosen the womb and Flar had not tried to influence her either way. He felt it was Bonnie's decision.

Bonnie had accompanied Flar on a few of his space trips and were at the controls most of the time. She did not want to become rusty and was determined to maintain her skills. She had no intention to engage in long distance space travel now that she was a mother, but short trips, preferably with Flar, interested her. She had worked hard to become a licensed pilot and it was also the only occupation that appealed to her. Flar was happy to have her as his copilot and noticed how well she handled the ship. He had full confidence in her skills.

When they brought their daughter home, Flar was very emotional and told Bonnie how happy he was. Bonnie smiled and assured him she was honored to be his wife. They were happy together and the age difference was unimportant.

Flar taught her so much about space, his planet, history and advancement of the mind and Bonnie, always eager to learn, soaked it all up. Spirituality was a new concept for Bonnie and Flar taught her how the psyche functions, how to increase her vibration and have control over her emotions. In return, Bonnie told Flar about life on Earth and all the space travel she had done and the aliens she had met. Boredom in the marriage was never an issue as they had endless stories to tell each other and both of them were by nature dedicated to learning new things. Bonnie was teaching Flar how to speak English and she wanted her children to be bilingual. She also enjoyed spending time with Xiona and she told Bonnie lots of things about everyday life on Ljeviina.

***

It was the year 2204 and Andrew had now lived on Edena nine years and had adjusted to his new life. He would never forget Veehnia and he missed his family a lot, but he had made peace with his new life and decided to make the best of it. He and Zittana had been married six years and he truly loved her. Zittana had changed into a loving wife and was the mother of his two children. Marriage contracts had been introduced on Edena to ensure the welfare of the children and Andrew had been the driving force behind the idea. Zittana was no longer president and stayed home with their two boys, Thomas and Roland, four years and two years old respectively. Andrew had insisted on standard Veehnian names for the boys and Zittana had no objection. Zittana's father was a devoted grandpa for the boys and a great help as a babysitter. He had raised Zittana alone and was very good with children. Andrew and grandpa were close and had deep affection and respect for each other.

The current president was a male and Andrew still worked as a consultant to the president, but only two days a week. Andrew's ideas were valued and many of his suggestions were implemented and became law; the marriage contract was one of his proposals.

The normal balance between men and women had been restored and equal rights was the law. The men now looked and behaved like men and the women had lost their masculine ways. All employment was based on merit and it did not matter if a male or female applied for the job. The Edena society was no longer any different from other civilized planets and when Zittana asked Andrew if he still wanted to return to Veehnia, he found to his surprise he hesitated with his answer. He had grown fond of Edena and his life and work were here. Finally, he told Zittana he was perfectly happy to live out his life on Edena. Zittana put her arms around him with a relieved smile.

"I can't be without you, Andrew. I'm so glad you feel that way."

Their lifestyle was free from hardships with Andrew making enough money as a domestic pilot to ensure a comfortable lifestyle and Zittana had recently started to work part time as a flight instructor. She was a skilled pilot and could fly cargo ships as well as fighter ships. They had bought a bigger boat and spent many days on the water and grandpa was often with them. Andrew bought a house when Thomas was born and an android to help Zittana with the housework. The android always came along when they went boating.

Andrew had seen many planets and aliens and had realized the difference between civilized planets was not that big. Basic needs were the same for all humanoids and only customs and habits differed. The Edena society was in many ways similar to Veehnia and Andrew had initiated many changes that had occurred on Edena. Women never propositioned men anymore and treated them with respect. Zittana had told Andrew she finally understood how crazy their society had been and how grateful she was that Tothellim and Kody had opened her eyes to the injustice suffered by the men.

"In retrospect, I can't imagine going back to the old Edena society and we women must have been insane to conduct ourselves in such a barbaric manner as we did," Zittana once told Andrew.

"I would never have asked the former Zittana to be my wife," Andrew replied smiling, "but the new, improved version of Zittana is a dream wife." He held her tight and told her how much he loved her.

Andrew was the only alien on Edena and somewhat of a celebrity. As a consultant to the president, he was successful and many of his ideas had been implemented. He was well paid for his services. Andrew was a practical man, intelligent and a good problem solver. He was also a handsome man. Andrew loved his boys. Both had hair on their heads and they looked mostly like him. There were no barbers on the planet, but their android quickly learned the skill and trimmed Andrew's and the boys' hair. Andrew had never been around children before he married, but now as a father, he treasured his time with his sons. He was dedicated to his family and had abandoned his former ways of womanizing. Zittana was an excellent mother and very maternal. Her love for Andrew was deep and she was grateful he was her husband.

***

Paragonne and Hattie were newly married and their thousand-acre farm was not far from Hattie's parents Pollox and Lyra's home. Paragonne and Hattie had chosen the land themselves and the Earth2 government had gifted the land to them in exchange for an agreement they would farm the land at least ten years. The land could not be sold and must be cultivated. If they decided to leave the land, they would lose ownership.

Paragonne had modern autonomous tractors and six robots helping him plant his crops and it was a proud moment when he harvested his first crops of grain, hay and peas. The Earth2 government bought all his crops. Hattie was as tied to the land as Paragonne and enjoyed being a farm wife. Her parents were frequent visitors and could not be happier their daughter was living so close. Learning how to be a successful large-scale farmer was not easy and Paragonne had a degree in husbandry and Hattie had taken several courses in animal care and cultivation of crops.

Atlas and Viola had a new airmobile capable of much faster speed than their former vehicle and could reach the farm in eight hours. It was still a long distance from Bliss, but once they had entered the destination code into the airmobile's computers, they could rest or watch a movie and just relax. The airmobile was equipped with a mini-sized galley, a tiny restroom and reclining seats for sleeping. Atlas and Viola visited as often as they could and found Paragonne's farm life fascinating. The farm house was quite big and had three large guest rooms and Paragonne had just bought an android to help with the housework.

Melody was now twenty-seven years old and a surgeon. Atlas had trained her and she worked side by side with her father often assisting him in the operating room. Melody was newly married to Lorre, the immigrant pilot from Ljeviina, and even though he was twenty years older than Melody, he looked no older than her. Melody was fascinated by his acute mind and they had met at the hospital when he sought care for a minor injury. As they chatted Melody found she was attracted to him and Lorre apparently felt the same as he asked if he could see her after work. A few months later they were married and Atlas and Viola were very fond of him. Lorre was an interesting man and as all the Ljeviinan people extremely kind.

Rasufilus' presidency was over and he was teaching math and physics at the new university in Bliss. At the age of eighty-one, he was still very active and had no intention to sit home and twiddle his thumbs. Akinom was helping Grace with her three children and loved being a grandma.

Berrill had designed a gilded silver coin featuring a rearing stallion in gold on one side and a herd of horses on the opposite side. The coin was stunning and hugely popular and the extra income from the coin was welcome as running his horse ranch was expensive. He trained horses and they sold rather quickly and Grace helped him with the training. Grace' horse Ylja was twenty years old, but still rock solid and healthy.

She had lived a pampered life as Grace' beloved pet and mount and the bond between them was strong. Grace rode her without a bridle using just a halter and that was sufficient. Ylja understood verbal commands and she and Grace were one. Her breed could easily carry a rider until age thirty.

Vitzoll and Attinna had become parents of a boy and with three humanoid races in their genes, they were relieved they were compatible.

***

Janus had recently married a girl from Earth, Alma. She had been one of the immigrants onboard Myles' ship five years ago and she had booked her ticket using a fake name. By working as a babysitter, she had managed to scrape up the money to pay for the passenger fee to Earth2 and she left Earth with no regrets. At the age of sixteen, she had had a hard life with a dictatorial father who demanded his family live strictly according to the Bible and his own rules. Disobedience would be punished by God, he reminded his family on a daily basis. Her mother could not stand up to her husband and allowed him to rule the household. Alma had not revealed her plan to emigrate to anyone and just walked out of the house pretending to do errands. Nearby, she had hidden her suitcase and no one ever found out what happened to her. Alma wanted it that way. She just wanted to run away and never come back. An airmobile took her straight to the spaceship and she boarded. Her father had tormented her since she was able to understand the spoken word and he was a religious fanatic. No joy was allowed and to enter heaven, one had to suffer here on Earth first. The father never laughed and neither did his suffering wife. Alma had no religious beliefs and just wanted to make her own decisions and be free. On Earth2 she had found freedom and personal peace. No one told her what to believe or what to do. Since she had limited education, she had found a job working in one of the stores in Rasunom and behind the store, she had a little room with a tiny kitchen where she lived. Her living conditions were primitive, but Alma was free and she had no other demands of life, just freedom. Her spare time was used to learning the Frejjan language and she learned fast. Within a year she was able to talk in broken Frejjan and she was working on reading and writing. To read in Frejjan was important as she was planning to educate herself and perhaps enter the Frejjan high school.

One day Janus walked into the store and they talked for a while. He admired her long, dark hair and pretty face. When he noticed Alma's simple living conditions, he felt sorry for her. He asked if he could see her that evening and Alma agreed. They were walking by the lake and she told him her life story. They spoke English as Janus was almost fluent in the language. Janus had had a wonderful childhood and felt great empathy when he listened to her story. He told her there were evening courses at the school and helped her enroll in her first course, an Earth2 history/geology course. She passed the course and took one course after another. It was free and she worked in the store in Rasunom during the day and after a quick dinner she walked to the school in Bliss. She had no free time and did not mind. Learning was important and she enjoyed all the courses she took. Her language skills had improved and she was able to read in Frejjan also.

Between his mercenary work Janus often spent time with her, but they were only friends and Alma preferred it that way. She was afraid of men and marriage in particular. After three years of studying part time, she felt pleased with the additional education she had acquired and applied for a job as lab technician at the hospital in Bliss and got the job. One of the androids trained her and after some time she was able to work independently. She rented a small apartment within walking distance of the hospital. By now, Janus was in love with her and proposed. Alma said 'no' in spite of her strong feelings for him. Janus suspected she was haunted by the memory of her father.

"Alma, I'm not a monster like your father," he said. "You don't have to fear me. If you marry me, we'll be equal partners. I will never force anything on you, no religion, no God and above all I won't rule in the house. Your father is a deranged man. Don't compare me with him."

"I'm afraid of men, all men," Alma said quietly and looked away from him. At that moment, Janus could not reach her. She had walled herself off and could not be approached. Alma was still traumatized and had been both verbally and physically abused by her father. She could still feel the pain when he hit her face with his fist and her emotional scars ached inside her. On one occasion, she had defied him and paid for it with a black eye.

Janus had pieced together the sad story of her childhood from what Alma had told him, but he knew she held more inside and had not revealed all of it. If he could just get her to talk, she may start to heal.

Another year went by and Alma still refused Janus' proposal. She had mellowed a little and responded to his kindness to her. He got her to laugh and slowly Alma allowed herself to feel joy. She had never known happiness and very seldom laughed, but Janus was on a mission to show her life was delightful. By now, Janus had realized Alma had deep emotional scars that may take years to heal, but he trusted he would be able to help her return to normal. Slowly, Alma responded to Janus' affection for her and realized she was 'allowed' to feel happiness. There was no God in the sky ready to punish her if she laughed and when Janus put his arm around her, she let it happen. Before, she had always moved away.

The breaking point came when Janus invited Alma to spend a weekend with his family on the grasslands and his parents greeted her with overwhelming kindness. Their love for each other was evident and Alma saw the difference between Pollox and Lyra's relationship and her parents' sad marriage. Hattie and Paragonne came over to meet her and Alma observed their devotion to each other. Alma felt turmoil inside and her heart opened. Would life permit her to live in a happy marriage and be as content as Janus' parents and his sister? Did she deserve it? Did she have a *right* to be happy?

Janus quietly observed her and guessed her thoughts. She had seen the difference. He took her for a walk along the river.

"Alma, have you reconsidered my proposal? I will be a devoted husband and together we will work on your emotional healing. Say 'yes' and make me the happiest guy on the planet."

"Yes!" Alma's simple answer told Janus what he needed to hear. The first step was taken. Alma put her head against his heart and when he put his arms around her, she looked up at him and smiled.

Janus wasted no time and they were married within two weeks. She moved into Janus' house and Alma was rewarded with a a loving and kind husband who loved her deeply. Her wall was down and she returned his love. For the first time in her life, she was happy and she felt no guilt.

CHAPTER 11

Emrak was in mourning and felt lost. Karol had passed away and shortly thereafter his best friends, Brandon and Brianna, died. Karol had died of a stroke at the age of ninety-eight. Brandon died of old age and was one hundred and three years old and six months after Brandon died, Brianna also passed away. Brandon and Brianna had been inseparable and Brianna lost her will to live when Brandon died.

Emrak was one hundred and eight years old and he had at least ten more years left of his expected lifespan. What would he do with himself? Without Karol, life was empty and meaningless. Their marriage had lasted fifty-three years and his married life had been the best part of his life. He missed Karol enormously. Emrak walked with a cane, but was otherwise still agile and had no cognitive disfunction. For weeks he was wandering around in the house thinking about his future and slowly a plan emerged in his mind. Tothellim had recently sent him a message he was preparing for another exploratory trip to the Andromeda galaxy and Emrak decided he would join him. He had nothing to lose and if he died from the stress, he did not care. He knew the Veehnian ship was on its way back from Earth to Veehnia carrying immigrants and would be passing by Frejja in just a week. The captain of the ship had forwarded the message from Tothellim and Emrak quickly replied to the captain asking him to make a detour to Frejja and pick him up. He would pay any expenses incurred. After an hour, he received a reply from the captain to be ready in one week and they would orbit Frejja and pick him up with the shuttle. There was no charge. Emrak was a friend of the Veehnian government and highly regarded and they had never forgotten the gift from the Frejjan people of the artificial wombs. The captain knew already that his government would never charge Emrak for the trip and there would be no objection to picking him up.

The following week was fast-paced for Emrak. His android would stay in the house and take care of its upkeep and also work for Leo, who lived close by. Emrak had a medical check-up and was told he was in good health and his doctor saw no problem with space travel as long as he kept exercising. The Veehnian ships, and ships from many other planets, had installed Leo's gravity chamber on all their ships to ensure the health of the crew.

Emrak had said goodbye to his children and eagerly boarded the shuttle when it arrived. The captain was a cheerful man and gave Emrak a big hug. He had transmitted many messages between Tothellim and Emrak and felt as if he knew him already. The ship had a spare cabin for unexpected guests and Emrak found it roomy and pleasant. It had its own bathroom and a tiny galley. The seven months of travel time to Veehnia went fast and Emrak used the gravity chamber every day. The ship had three chambers installed. He also spent time with the captain.

When they were within transmission distance of Veehnia, the captain sent a message to Tothellim that Emrak was onboard and to wait for him as he wanted to join him on his next trip. Tothellim replied he was excited to work with Emrak and would delay departure until Emrak arrived.

Tothellim had a beaming smile as he greeted Emrak and the two men were both emotional to finally meet again. Forty-two years had passed since they said goodbye on Frejja and to meet in person again was special. Emrak stayed in Tothellim's house for a few days until departure time. They spoke English with each other. The ship was fully stocked and fueled and after three days they boarded. Three copilots and six androids were onboard and two of the androids were Rex and Kody. The last trip the crew had made was seven years ago when they had visited planet Hydrasol. Tothellim was a young eighty-four-year-old, still full of vitality and a trusted captain for the crew. Emrak would function as copilot and he could choose his duties. Tothellim knew he was able to fly the ship except through the tunnels, which required strong hands and Emrak admitted he had lost some of his hand strength.

Tothellim wanted to explore the area beyond Edena and after fourteen months of travel, they passed the planet at tremendous speed. Emrak knew Tothellim had left Andrew on the planet and if Emrak had been faced with the same situation, he would have dismissed Andrew from the crew, but returned him to Veehnia so he could join his family. This was the only decision Tothellim had made that Emrak did not agree with. The two men were close and had deep respect and affection for each other and engaged in long discussions about life in space. They also told each other about their family lives and children. The ship had two of Leo's gravity chambers onboard and both men used them every day. Tothellim asked Emrak to forward a message to Leo to let him know how useful his gravity chamber was and how much it improved the health of the crew.

Emrak often flew the ship and found he had not forgotten anything and had no trouble with the controls.

They encountered another tunnel and it was a mega portal. It was a six-hour tunnel and propelled them nine thousand light years. Rex checked the computers to ensure the distance they had travelled through the tunnel was accurate and it was. He carefully entered the recording of the interior of the tunnel into the computers and its exact location in space. This information would be posted on the Interstellar Internet for the benefit of all the planets.

They were now in an area of the Andromeda galaxy that no one from the known planets had visited and started looking for a star with an orbiting planet. What they found was extraordinary.

The ship was traveling at enormous speed toward a star visible far away and as they came closer, they noticed a planet the size of Veehnia orbiting two suns and realized they were watching a circumbinary planet. The two suns appeared to orbit each other and the planet orbited the two stars' center of gravity. There were no other orbiting planets and no moons. The ship entered orbit around the planet and waited for sunset to find out if the planet would light up. It did. It was inhabited. Most of the planet had light indicating the inhabitants lived across the whole surface and there were probably no oceans.

The following morning at daybreak a drone with cloaking ability was launched and they noticed air traffic up to five thousand feet, so they programmed the drone to slowly fly over the surface at seven thousand feet. It was a modern planet and the beings were a mix of humanoids and animals. The closeup photos sent by the drone showed humanoids with white skin, fully human faces without fur, but the rest of their bodies had a long, heavy fur coat, including their heads, and erect animal ears similar to a cat. The ears were about three inches tall and located on top of the head slightly to the side and rotated independently of each other. They had no tail. Both men and women wore knee-length short-sleeved tunics with a belt around the waist. None of the crew members had ever seen humanoids resembling these people. The people from Mineata had short fur, but otherwise they looked identical to humans and had human ears. These people were clearly a mix of humans and animals.

As captain of the ship, Tothellim was in charge and suggested they make contact. The shuttle seated eight and the whole crew except three of the androids departed in the shuttle. They found an area with unusually large spaceships parked in rows, but they saw no fighter ships. As they descended, an airmobile almost crashed into them and the people onboard shook their heads as if to say 'watch where you're going'. Not a welcoming sign.

They landed next to the spaceships figuring the people would be close and hear them land and climbed out of the ship. They were not armed. The door opened to the building next to the ships and six people walked out. They were also unarmed. One of them held a translation device.

"Please enter your code," the leader said in his language. He was old and spoke slowly without smiling. Rex quickly complied.

Tothellim explained they were explorers and where they came from in the Andromeda galaxy and the tunnels they had passed through to reach their planet.

"I'm Tzinger and I'm in charge of our space fleet. The name of our planet is Selkoda and as you can see, it's a circumbinary planet. Every twelve days our suns pass each other and we have an eclipse that lasts a couple of hours. During the eclipse it gets cool and dark. Our planet is isolated and we seldom have aliens visiting us." Tzinger had not offered to shake hands with them, nor did he smile or show interest in exchanging information with them. He was distant and reserved.

"May we go inside and talk?" Tothellim suggested not knowing if they would be told to leave.

Tzinger nodded and walked ahead of them inside the building, a modern and architecturally beautiful structure. Emrak suspected these people may be more advanced than both the Frejjans and Veehnians. They sat down in the lobby and the crew noticed elaborate flower arrangements, trees planted in large planters and live, tiny song birds hopping around in the tree branches. The atmosphere was warm and peaceful and did not match the chilly reception by the Selkoda people.

"I take it you prefer not to have visitors," Tothellim said in an opening remark.

"Alien ships have landed on our planet five times and claimed they wanted to trade with us," Tzinger replied. "They were not explorers like you. As we explained what goods we offered them, we realized after a while they were looters, swindlers and totally dishonest. We ordered them to leave our planet immediately and they all did except one large group of people and we had to conduct warfare to get rid of them. The goal of our people is advancing our minds and war is the last resort. Our defense is very advanced, often superior to what the average planet has, and we ended up killing them all. We grieved when we saw all the dead bodies, but since then no ship has landed on Selkoda. The message got out that we will and can defend our planet. That was several years ago and you're the first ship to land here since then."

"I assure you we have only peaceful intentions," Emrak said and looked straight into Tzinger's eyes. "We would be honored if you would exchange information with us and we're willing to share any information you want from our ship's computers. Tothellim and I are from the Milky Way galaxy and the rest of the crew are from the Andromeda galaxy. Both your people and our people would benefit from exchanging information. There are only eleven of us onboard and we're certainly not a threat to your planet. As you can see, we're not even armed." The sincerity in Emrak's voice broke the ice and Tzinger spontaneously offered to shake hands with them all and a smile appeared on his face. It was a warm smile exposing a large soul.

"Welcome to you all," Tzinger said. "We believe you and are happy to have you as our guests. Let me tell you a little about ourselves. We trade goods with only two planets and that's what we use our cargo ships for. Our fighter ships are seldom used and only to defend our sovereignty. We're peace loving and our people engage in advancement of the mind. Our society is technologically advanced, perhaps more so than on your planets, and our education system is quite sophisticated with strong emphasis on psychology and spirituality. We're all vegetarians and our life span is around two hundred years. All labor work is done by robots, but our androids are valued members of our society and many of them work as professionals. Some are even married to our women. Family life is important to us and we consider our children to be gifts. The population is around one billion and our government is honest and we trust them."

"You must have noticed we appear to be a mix of humanoid and animal," Tzinger continued. "This is correct. Our ancestors practiced various forms of genetics and long time ago we had serious cooling of the climate and they spliced in the genes of a long-haired animal to our genes. It took care of the problem and kept our ancestors warm, but nowadays we all would want to remove those genes and return to the way we used to look. None of us want this furry appearance any more. Our climate is stable and the heat from our two suns is sufficient to keep us warm without this troublesome fur. Our scientists have failed to remove the genes and they fear removal of the animal genes may damage our DNA."

"I may be able to help," Kody interjected. "I have worked in genetics for most of my career and have years of experience in changing genes. I'm an android. If you let me study your research, there's a chance I can remove the animal genes. At least let me try."

Tzinger looked at Kody and exclaimed –

"Of course, we'll let you have full access to all our records and if you're successful, our people would be indebted to you."

They returned to the ship as Kody needed to access the computers in his lab on the ship and Tothellim wanted to prepare all the records of their travels to download to the computers on Selkoda. Tzinger had asked for the locations of all the tunnels and planets in both the Milky Way and Andromeda galaxies. Tothellim and Emrak prepared all the material together and it was an enormous file they finally sent down to the planet's computers. They also included holographic images of life on each planet showing culture, education, how people lived and lots of humorous images for entertainment. In return, they received a large file from Selkoda listing every tunnel and planet they knew of with exact location of the planets and tunnels.

The next day Kody started working in the lab on the planet together with the scientists who had tried to remove the animal genes. Kody realized after some time what the problem was and knew he would be able to remove the animal genes without damaging their DNA. It was a delicate operation requiring great skill and Kody was the right person for the job. He needed a volunteer and a young couple offered themselves as test objects. They wanted to start a family and were hoping their children would be spared wearing a fur coat.

Kody studied the genetic material of the young couple and found the animal genes. He carefully removed the genes and infused the changed genes back into their bodies. After four weeks, the couple started to shed some of their fur. Kody did not expect any adverse mutation of the genetic code as a result of the changes he had made, but there was never a guarantee and he was on the look-out for it. The animal ears of the young couple would not be removed by the gene changes, but the children being born to parents with changed DNA would most likely be born with human ears. They were humans originally. The scientists informed Kody that a third of the population had human ears, which was a good sign and with the animal genes removed, Kody did not expect anyone to be born with animal ears in the future.

The couple lost most of their fur including the fur on top of their heads, but slowly human hair started to grow instead. The change was amazing.

Kody took several more samples of their DNA and found only human genes and children born to parents with changed DNA should look fully human. Kody instructed the scientists how to perform the procedure and the citizens were offered to have their genes changed. Everyone was excited and wanted to have the process done, but it would take a long time to take care of the whole population.

In the meantime, the crew was touring the planet and found Selkoda was an advanced, modern society. It was a nice-looking planet, but not spectacular and it lacked oceans and mountains. There were lakes and rivers and the planet had no deserts indicating sufficient rainfall. All the cities were small and the population was spread out over the whole planet. The crew witnessed an eclipse when one of the suns passed in front of the second sun and during the eclipse it was chilly and half dark. Their guide informed them they had an eclipse every twelfth day.

The crew stayed in a large private residence that belonged to the government and the home was elegant and very modern. Privately, the crew all agreed the culinary skills of the Selkoda chefs did not impress them and they all longed for meat and eggs. Only variations of vegetables, beans, peas and grain were served, but they did have milk and different cheeses. The lifespan of the people was two hundred years, so apparently their diet was nutritionally adequate, but the crew found the food unappetizing and boring. Onboard the ship, an android did the cooking and he was a master. The food supply on the ship was superb and they had plenty of freeze-dried meat onboard and loads of frozen eggs. The area of the galley where the chef did the actual cooking was a gravity chamber to enable traditional cooking.

The people on Selkoda were dignified and very calm. The crew could see Tzinger had not exaggerated when he said advancement of the mind was of great importance and they often saw people in deep meditation.

Their visit came to an end and the six weeks they had stayed on Selkoda had been interesting, but the people were not as unique as the crew had first thought. They had seen many planets and interacted with numerous humanoid races and from experience they had found people may look a little different, but basically, they are mostly the same. Tzinger and the scientists had told Kody they were immensely grateful he had solved the gene problem.

Tzinger had forwarded all the information they had on neighboring planets straight to the ship's computers and there was one planet that intrigued both Tothellim and Emrak, a small planet called Cirrkosa ran by only men. Their patriarchal society excluded women from participating in government and business affairs and they were relegated to raising the children and to stay at home. Only basic education was allowed to force the women into submission. Their society was the same as the former systems on Arrynia and Edena, but instead of women being the leaders, the men were in charge. The planet had an oxygen atmosphere, but the carbon dioxide level was ten percent and the humanoid citizens were able to breathe this toxic mix. On Veehnia, the air contained only a fraction of carbon dioxide. Tzinger had informed them the men were not hostile, but totally inflexible and considered women unworthy of everything but motherhood. The women accepted their fate as inevitable and the few women who had fought for women's equality had been drugged to silence them. The people from Selkoda had no interest in contacting them and Selkoda women had full equality.

With three tunnels to shorten the travel distance, the ship reached Cirrkosa after seven weeks of travel. The planet was half the size of Earth and had three small moons. As they entered orbit, they found three fighter ships chasing them and it was apparent they had been spotted by the defense system of Cirrkosa. Tothellim made contact with the ships and transmitted a greeting through the translation device. It was understood by the crew of the ships and they responded Tothellim and his crew were allowed to land with the shuttle.

All of them except three androids manning the ship landed on the surface. Their spacesuits were cumbersome and slowed them down, but the air was toxic. The androids also wore spacesuits as it was unnecessary to reveal they were machines. A group of men waited for them and they were not wearing spacesuits. They were small, barely five feet tall, with humanoid faces and large eyes, no hair and tan skin. All of them were thin and looked almost fragile and they were dressed in brown skintight, shiny pants and jackets. When checking the electronics on his sleeve, Emrak noticed it was only forty degrees Fahrenheit and the sun was low on the horizon. Two of the three moons were visible in the sky. The leader invited them inside with a gesture of his hand and they entered a plain looking building. It was obvious the planet was not affluent.

"Sit, please. I'm Drextuvell and the leader of our planet Cirrkosa. I can see you're not able to breathe our air. We seldom have alien visitors, so tell us why you're here." His voice was high-pitched, almost feminine.

Tothellim explained they were explorers, where they came from and that he and Emrak were from the Milky Way galaxy. He also told them they had just left planet Selkoda and wanted to make contact with one more planet before returning home to Veehnia. The men listened with interest and nodded as Tothellim spoke and they appeared friendly. Emrak asked how they could breathe the air and Drextuvell replied that long time ago the air had been low in carbon dioxide, but then increased very slowly to the present level. The people had been able to adjust to the higher concentration of carbon dioxide and were able to breathe the air without harm.

"We don't trade with any planet," Drextuvell explained. "We don't even have a full-size spaceship. Our fighter ships are for self-defense only. This planet is self-sufficient and we manufacture what we need here on our home planet. We're not a rich planet, but we get by. Selkoda is much more advanced than we are, both as a society and in manufacturing."

Tothellim and Emrak used their communicators and showed a few images from Veehnia, Mars and Frejja, carefully blending in pictures of successful women. One of the images showed Brianna in her captain's uniform in front of her ship and another was of Karol as president on Mars. A female opera singer from Veehnia and various important and successful women on Veehnia. The men looked without saying anything, but it was obvious they were at a loss for words. After a few minutes of silence, Drextuvell commented –

"We can see that in your world women work side by side with the men. Here on our planet, we prefer to have our women stay at home."

"Why? Women are as capable as men," Emrak said.

"That's the tradition on Cirrkosa and we don't intend to change it."

Tothellim quickly changed the subject to avoid causing resentment.

"Please tell us about your society," he asked.

"Our planet is small and we have two hundred million citizens, but our planet can support a much larger population. We manufacture simple robots to do heavy labor work, but we haven't succeeded in inventing androids. The men wear implants, but not the women. We have access to the Interstellar Internet and follow what's happening around the universe, but so much of it is not right for us and we don't agree with most of what we see on the Internet."

"Could you give us some examples?"

"The whole women's issue, for example. They don't have the brains to be involved in society and are inferior in intelligence to men. Perhaps your women are brighter than our women, but here on Cirrkosa women are not capable of working outside the home."

Tothellim and his crew knew how wrong Drextuvell was as all of them had interacted with successful and intelligent women.

"Would you allow me to run some tests on your women?" Kody asked.

"Yes, you can do that," Drextuvell said after hesitating at first. It was apparent he did not like the idea, but felt it would look strange if he refused. He agreed to have ten women meet with Kody the next day for testing and in the meantime, he would show the rest of the crew around the planet. The crew excused themselves and returned to the ship. Drextuvell understood they had to stay on the ship due to their inability to breathe the air.

The following day, Kody found ten small women waiting for him. They were thin, almost apathetic looking, and none of them showed a spark of excitement. Kody felt sad when he looked at them and thought to himself their lives had been stolen from them. They were literate and using the translation device, Kody carefully instructed them how to take the test. Each of them had an electronic tablet and a local teacher had entered the questions and problems to solve into each tablet. The test lasted two hours and at first the women seemed afraid and confused, but as they started to interact with the tablet they woke up from their lethargy and seemed to enjoy the test. After Kody had analyzed the test results, he was pleasantly surprised. Six of the women were of average intelligence and four of them had a high test score indicating a highly advanced mind. None of the women wore an implant and did not have the advantage of a cognitive aid. After the test, Kody talked to the women for a while and asked them if they would like to be educated and hold a job and all said 'yes' with enthusiasm.

When Kody showed the result to Drextuvell, he was surprised and had no comment. He knew he had been wrong about the women, but could not get himself to admit it. Kody reminded him the women wore no implants and still they tested average and above. In his calm and reassuring way, Kody suggested all girls should be educated and participate in life on the planet as equal partners to the men. Kody was never pushy, just stating the facts. Drextuvell responded he would have to consult with his advisors before he made any changes to their way of life.

The crew had had an interesting day and had toured a medical facility, several schools, a few manufacturing plants, their media and they also were invited into a private home to meet a housewife and her daughter. It was clear the planet was far behind advanced planets like Veehnia in discovery of modern electronics and most scientific research. Their homes were plain and small and no one was affluent. If only the women would be allowed to participate in the work force, perhaps their economy would improve. Half the population was excluded and their talent unused. To change these conditions would be difficult as the men looked down on the women as inferior.

"Perhaps we should make them an offer they can't refuse," Rex suggested. They had finished dinner onboard the ship and were discussing what they had seen on the planet. "We could offer them some of our technology in exchange for their guarantee that women will gain equal rights. The people on Selkoda may be willing to come once or twice to inspect the conditions here on Cirrkosa to ensure the leaders have implemented the changes, which will be part of the deal."

"It's a great idea, Rex," Tothellim said and Emrak nodded in agreement.

"Having access to our technology would advance their society a hundred years right away and their economy would certainly improve," Emrak added.

The crew worked out a detailed plan and decided which technology would be suitable to share with the Cirrkosa people. Their knowledge of medical research was far behind and half the package would include improvements to their medical expertise; mining techniques to extract minerals from their own planet; improvements to the skills of their rather primitive robots and improved design of communicators, implants and holographic images. It was a generous package in exchange for giving the women a life worth living. Tothellim and Emrak contacted Tzinger and they were within transmission distance. He listened with great interest to the plan and agreed right away they would participate and check the conditions on Cirrkosa to ensure the changes were implemented.

"We're happy to help in your humanitarian effort and it's a small favor compared to the gift you gave us by resolving our gene problem. You can count on us."

Tothellim ended by saying they would present the plan the same day to the leaders and inform him if the plan was accepted.

Tothellim and Emrak requested a meeting with all the government leaders and presented their plan. No one responded for a while and they were too surprised to know what to say. Here, in front of them, were solutions to most of their problems that would have taken them a hundred years to solve on their own. The price to pay was women's equal rights. There was no way of cheating as the people of Selkoda would visit and ensure all the changes were fully honored and the leaders knew the Selkoda people would never back down and accept anything less than full implementation of the plan. They also knew not to mess with the leaders of Selkoda as they were aware the Selkoda people were fully capable of enforcing what they felt was right. There was only one way to respond and it was a simple 'yes' or 'no'.

Drextuvell stood up and said –

"I agree and my vote is 'yes'. The test Kody performed on our women shows they are our equals. It's time to change and let them be part of our work force and participate in society. They should also be fitted with an implant. Do you agree to the plan?" He looked at the other leaders.

A loud unanimous 'yes' settled the issue and the following three weeks were very busy as the technology was transferred from the ship's computers to the government's computer system.   All the crew was needed to meet with the leaders of different branches of their society to explain how to use the technology. The medical package was highly appreciated by the doctors and would solve many of their medical problems. The leaders were told the Selkoda people would advise them over the Internet if they needed further instructions as they were within transmission distance. When Drextuvell and his advisors realized what they had received, they were almost speechless and also emotional. Drextuvell assured Tothellim and Emrak they would honor their part of the plan and would welcome the visits by the Selkoda people. From that moment on the women had equal rights with men.

The Selkoda leaders were informed in detail what had been transferred to the Cirrkosa people and that they may need to advise them further how to use the new technology. Tzinger responded they would be delighted to assist in the changeover.

A week later the ship departed and Drextuvell and his advisors saw them off. Their wives were present and they had tears in their eyes. The subjugation was over and they were free. Freedom does not have a monetary value, but it is the biggest gift in life.

The long trip back home to Veehnia started and it would take seventeen months to complete, but with the entertainment and the huge electronic library onboard the crew was not bored. The library contained information about space and the various planets as well as everything taught in schools and universities and was heavily used by the crew. Two gravity chambers kept the men in rather good physical shape. Some of their muscle tissue was lost, but it was not severe and the gravity chambers made a big difference.

When the ship landed on Veehnia, the president and several government officials as well as Tothellim's children greeted them and it was with great interest they listened to Tothellim's report. The trip had lasted almost three years, but the distance they had traveled was mind boggling. All the information was posted on the Interstellar Internet and the two new planets, Selkoda and Cirrkosa, were added to the list of newly found planets with inhabitants. The captain of the Veehnian immigration ship usually posted all the information on the Interstellar Internet as soon as he was within transmission distance in the Milky Way and the information reached all the known planets in the Milky Way. The system was efficient, though sometimes it took a while to reach all the planets. The discovery of new, inhabited planets was always met with excitement by citizens everywhere and these reports were treasured reading.

***

Tothellim planned to take one year off and then make another trip beyond Cirrkosa and asked Emrak if he wanted to join him on the next trip and Emrak agreed right away. With a year off until the next journey and another three-year exploratory trip, Emrak would be one hundred and fifteen years by the time they returned safely to Veehnia. Then seven months to travel to Frejja and Emrak knew if he survived all this, it was time to just sit back and reflect on his long and exciting life. Peturuns had a life expectancy of one hundred and twenty years, the same as Frejjans, and Tothellim had many years left to continue space travel. Tothellim invited him to stay with him in his house as a guest until the next trip and Emrak gratefully accepted. The two men were as close as brothers.

Through the captain of the Veehnian ship, Emrak sent a long message to his children and grandchildren telling them about his interesting excursion to the Andromeda galaxy and assured them he would return to Frejja after he completed the next trip. A few months later he received their response and they had read his fascinating report and looked forward to seeing him again in four years.

The year Tothellim and Emrak spent together resting up before their next trip was peaceful, emotionally rewarding for both of them and they bonded even more. Many days were spent fishing on Tothellim's boat and Emrak had never done boating on an ocean and found it very exciting. He had seen oceans, but never had time to experience being on the water on an ocean. When they encountered four-foot waves and were bobbing up and down, Emrak still loved it and was not uneasy. He and Tothellim just laughed together and endured the weather. The boat was rather big and could easily handle the waves. Tothellim's children were frequent visitors and Emrak truly enjoyed meeting them and spending time with them. Emrak loved Veehnia and the easygoing people.

The year the two men spent together was one of the best years in their lives. There was nothing they could not discuss and their outlook on life was the same.

CHAPTER 12

Back on Earth, Alma's parents frantically searched for her to no avail. Alma had no friends so there was no one to ask and she did not attend any school as the father had demanded she should stay at home and concentrate on Bible studies. Her sister Helga had no idea either where Alma was and the two sisters were not close as the age difference was nine years. Her parents finally realized she had run away, but where? They contacted the police and after a few months of investigation without finding a trace of Alma, they asked her parents to come to the police station.

"We're pretty sure your daughter is not on our planet," the police officer told them. "There was a space ship leaving Earth about the same time Alma disappeared. There's a chance she was on that ship. We've checked the passenger records and Alma's name was not on the list, but she may have given a fake name. Did Alma have any reason to want to run away?"

"Yes!" Alma's mother had a stern look on her face and finally all the years of anger she had held inside came out. She felt as if she was suffocating and knew she would be punished later on for speaking out, but at that moment she simply did not care. She had to talk.

"My husband has terrorized her since she was a baby and…." she continued, but was interrupted by her furious husband.

"Hush!" His outburst had no effect on Alma's mother.

"My husband has made our lives a living hell and I fully understand Alma ran away," she said and looked at her husband with disdain. His face was a grimace of rage. "The family has to live according to his rules and follow everything in the Bible or we risk verbal and sometimes physical abuse."

The police officer got the message and felt it was best to interrupt Alma's mother for her own safety.

"We just have to assume Alma took off and is living on another planet and all you can do is to accept it," he declared. One look at Alma's father assured him the mother had told him the truth. "There's nothing more we can do and I'll close this case." The police officer wondered to himself what punishment the mother would suffer when they arrived home. He tried to pay no heed to his nagging thoughts of alarm, but he understood Alma's father was a dangerous man.

Alma's mother knew she would face hell from her husband once they were home and she was right.

"You humiliated me in front of the police officer," he shouted "and you didn't shut up when I told you to stop. I'll teach you a lesson, woman!"

Without thinking of the consequences, he grabbed the fireplace shovel and with full force slammed it on his wife's head. She collapsed on the floor in a pool of blood. The impact of the heavy shovel had cracked her skull and within minutes she was dead. Alma's father woke up from his fit of anger and stared at his wife. He was dumfounded. What had he done! He let out a scream and sank down next to his wife's dead body sobbing. During his rage, he did not know what he was doing.

He managed to get up from the floor and slowly went into the kitchen, grabbed the sharpest knife he could find and without hesitating drove it into his heart.

Alma's sister, Helga, came home a few hours later to a horror scene. She was only eight years old. She howled at the sight and ran to the neighbor's house for help.

"Call the police, my parents are dead on the floor. Don't go there. It's horrible," she managed to say while sobbing and hyperventilating.

The same police officer who had talked to Alma's parents in the morning was now forced to face the grisly scene of them dead on the floor in a pool of blood. He blamed himself thinking he should have done something, but legally he could not have arrested the father as he had not committed any crime. It was one of the worst days of the police officer's life and the crime would haunt him for years to come.

Helga ended up in foster care. The gruesome image of her dead parents was imprinted on her mind and she had to have psychiatric help to overcome the ordeal.

Organized religion and church attendance on Earth had lost popularity in favor of spiritualism and to increase one's consciousness.

Alma's father had adhered to the old ways of believing without a doubt that God was a punishing being up in the sky ready to pounce on anyone disobeying him. He could not perceive God as a loving being and instead feared him. To avoid punishment, he forced himself and his family to live according to his own strict rules and guided by the Bible and removed all joy and happiness from their lives. The consequence of his fanaticism was a suffering family and ending with a murder and suicide as well as inflicting deep mental scars on his daughters.

***

Three years had passed since Myles and his crew returned to Earth from their long trip to Strovea and Rotzini. They were ready for another trip, but much shorter in distance. Most areas of the Milky Way were unexplored and Myles wanted to investigate the Perseus Arm, a rather short distance of around six thousand light years. Compared to their long journey to the Andromeda galaxy it was a short hop, but without a mega portal the distance was still too far. They could gamble on finding a new tunnel and the vibration would alert them to the existence of the tunnel.

Myles suggested to his supervisors he and his crew were willing to try searching for a mega portal to shorten the distance to the Perseus Arm. If they were unable to find a tunnel, they would return to Earth. His supervisors gave Myles the go-ahead for the trip and after a month the ship was ready for departure.

Myles and his regular crew took off not knowing what to expect. After they had passed through the tunnel to Mars, they continued toward the asteroid belt. The ship was vibrating just a little, the following days a slight increase in vibration. Several days passed and then the vibration increased significantly and the crew knew they were nearing a tunnel. A short tunnel would not help them much, only a mega portal would propel the ship thousands of light years. Days later, the vibration was so substantial they all knew a good size tunnel was ahead and they were close to its entry. With Myles at the controls, they were sucked into it and the taxing journey through the tunnel began. This tunnel vibrated as much as the other tunnels, but it was not weaving back and forth making it easier to control the ship. After three hours, Claudin took over to allow Myles to rest his hands. The ship had tripled its speed making it a challenge to control. After seven hours it was over and they flew out of the tunnel. All of them were relieved it was over. Lenny and Toby checked the computers and realized the seven-hour tunnel had propelled them eight thousand light years and they were in the area of the Perseus Arm. They knew they had been unusually lucky to find a mega portal and only two months had passed since their departure from Earth. They celebrated and allowed themselves a beer break while the ship was on autopilot. Lenny and Toby had recorded the ship's passage through the tunnel and were now busy pinpointing their location. A holographic map generated by the computer was visible in front of them and they found their location. They were indeed in the Perseus Arm area.

The ship continued at fantastic speed and a small star became visible. A single planet orbited the star at a distance that probably could support life of some sort, but the planet was closer to the star than Earth was to the sun. It may be very hot on the planet. After two months they were in orbit and when night fell on the planet there were no lights. The crew launched a drone at daybreak and programmed it to fly at an elevation of five hundred feet. The images sent back to the ship gave them the shivers. It was a planet occupied by huge insects and no humanoids or animals were visible. Large reptiles and snakes were on the ground. Flying insects, the size of birds, were clearly visible. The drone sent back closeups of insects crawling on the ground looking like beetles and they were the size of a human hand.

The planet had an oxygen atmosphere and creeks filled with water, but they could not see any mammalian animals. The drone recorded a surface temperature of hundred-and-five degrees Fahrenheit, not as hot as they had expected.

"I volunteer to walk around on the surface," Lenny said. "No insect can hurt me, but we don't know if they're poisonous and they may be very dangerous to humans. Will you come along, Toby?"

Toby nodded and they descended to the surface and climbed out. Lenny closed the door to the shuttle to ensure no unwanted passenger would crawl into the vehicle. Toby was hit on the head almost right away by a flying bee of some sort and it landed on his arm trying to inject its venom. When Toby tried to chase it away it went wild and repeatedly tried to land on him. A quick stun by Lenny's gun finally chased it away, but they realized the planet was deadly for humans and perhaps even androids like themselves could be harmed by the reptiles and snakes. Lenny and Toby continued walking a short distance when they discovered both of them had three huge beetles crawling up their legs and they could not get them off. They were glued onto their legs. Only the stun gun had an effect and they shot them using a mild charge. The beetles fell to the ground. Androids were not harmed by stun guns.

"We must leave. This planet is lethal," Lenny yelled and they ran back to the shuttle. Crawling up the door of the shuttle was a huge, wide diameter snake doing its best to enter the vehicle and was unaffected by a shot from Lenny's stun gun. Lenny increased the stun to maximum and the snake had no reaction. Toby took out his laser gun and fired two shots at the snake's head and it fell down dead. By now, Lenny and Toby realized their own existence was in danger and they quickly checked themselves for insects and jumped inside the shuttle and slammed the door closed as fast as they could. Lenny revved up the engines and took off.

"I'll take a quick tour around the planet just to see if anything else is living on the far side," Lenny said to Toby.

They flew at five hundred feet elevation when Lenny felt something crawling up his leg and to his horror, he saw a medium size snake. Toby grabbed it by its neck and opened the shuttle door just a few inches and tossed it out. They put the shuttle on autopilot to hover and searched the whole shuttle for anything alive. There was nothing, but they found a small air vent they had left open where the snake had entered. Both of them spent another hour checking every corner of the shuttle to ensure they would not bring any insect or snake back to the ship. The engine area was sealed off and nothing could enter.

The rest of the planet was the same and they returned to the ship. The images Lenny and Toby showed the crew made their skin crawl.

The ship left the bug planet and continued in search of another, more hospitable, planet. One of the androids was the chef onboard and as he was preparing dinner for the crew, he looked up and saw a snake floating around in the air and his head was just a few inches from his face. All the androids onboard were equipped with the latest software and had almost as strong feelings as humans. The chef gasped in horror when he saw the snake and realized it came from the shuttle. He grabbed it by the neck and dropped it into the garbage disposal system, where it was sucked down and incinerated. He ran to the Bridge and informed the others to search the shuttle once more.

"It must have hidden in the engine compartment," Toby exclaimed. All of them ran to cargo bay and opened the engine door. There were two more snakes hidden in the engine and they found a tiny opening where they had entered. They quickly killed them and dropped them into the ship's waste disposal system. The crew never forgot *Planet of the Creeps* and talked about it for years.

One month passed and they discovered a short tunnel and when they exited, they saw another star with two planets orbiting. One was very close to the star and most likely too hot to support life, but the second planet was about the right distance from its star to have a favorable climate. As they neared the planet, they noticed it was blue and may have an ocean. The ship entered orbit and at nightfall the planet lit up. It had a population.

The following morning, they launched the drone to get a closer look at the planet. They saw humanoids who were very tall, about seven feet at least, with light brown skin, human looking nose and mouth, eyes twice the size of human eyes, tiny ears flat against the skull and no hair. Their neck was twice the length of a human's and the skull slightly elongated. Each side of the forehead was concave. They had wide cheekbones and the face was narrow by the mouth. The women wore short dresses and the men pants and shirts. The crew noticed they were all slim and muscular, even the women.

"They're good-looking people," Myles noticed. "They look almost like the Ljeviinans. Let's go down. "

The shuttle landed outside the city and they climbed out unarmed as they were explorers, not soldiers. The air was warm and fresh and the gravity a little lighter than on Earth. An airmobile soon landed next to the shuttle and four soldiers jumped out. They did not point their weapons at the crew. Myles held out his two-way translation device and one of the soldiers entered their code. The planet was at least as advanced as Earth from what they saw.

"Welcome to planet Norioon. My name is Litberk. Where are you from?"

Myles explained where they came from and that they were searching for new planets and they had traveled through the seven-hour tunnel to a part of the Milky Way unknown to Earth people.

"We're unfamiliar with the seven-hour tunnel, but we've heard of your area of the Milky Way, the Orion-Cygnus area, from the Interstellar

Internet. We do make trips to other planets ourselves, but not as far as you have traveled. I'm one of the pilots on our ships. Our people embrace peace and want nothing to do with warfare."

Litberk was kind and polite and spoke slowly, almost hesitatingly. It was as if he was listening to instructions. He invited them to follow his airmobile to meet their leaders. It was quite a distance and as they flew at low altitude, they noticed the planet was neither poor nor affluent. It was clean with small cities and rural areas, rather sparsely populated and they also saw what looked like a large ocean. It was a pleasant looking planet with low mountains at the horizon. The government buildings were surprisingly fancy compared to the other buildings. They walked in and Litberk introduced them to the leaders, both men and women. The senior leader shook hands with them.

"My name is Torraforz, welcome. I hear you're from Earth. Please tell us about your trip and your planet."

Myles and the crew showed images of Earth and the other known planets and the lifestyle on these planets. The leaders were interested and asked many questions. None of them spoke with hesitation the way Litberk had done.

"We're not an affluent planet, but the people are comfortable. There are no dissidents here and the people follow our regulations. Norioon is a peaceful planet and we're mostly self-sufficient. We manufacture almost everything we need ourselves and we have limited trade with other planets. I'm happy to say there are no hostile planets in this area, so we don't need fighter ships."

In the evening, Myles excused himself and the crew and told the leaders they would return to the ship for the night, but would appreciate it if they could tour the planet the following day with a guide. Torraforz nodded. He had not invited them to dinner or offered lodging.

They toured the planet the next day and the guide was pleasant, but seemed distant as he talked. There was no spontaneity in his speech, no spark or fire in the man. He showed them the ocean and explained it covered almost half the planet. Several large ships were tied up at the dock as well as smaller boats in an adjacent marina. When they toured the town, some people came over and welcomed them, but not that many.

They returned once again to the ship for the night and reviewed what they had seen.

"The people are friendly," Myles commented, "but I sense something is wrong. Their minds seem to be absent. I can't put my finger on what's wrong, but my gut feeling tells me the people are not themselves. It's as if they're possessed. The leaders are not that way."

"Now that you're mentioning it, I did notice their behavior is robotic without individualism," Claudin said in agreement. "They're all the same and their reactions seem to follow a preset pattern. Normal behavior of humans differs from one person to the next, but the people we saw today agreed on everything without diverging from each other."

Lenny listened carefully, scratched his head, and said slowly –

"Could their minds be hacked? If they all have an implant and a dictator pulls the strings, he can influence everything the person thinks, decision making and feelings. It wouldn't be hard to write a program covering most aspects of life and 'teach' the person what to think and how to react. After a while, the person will forget he has a mind of his own and just follow directions from his implant. If that's the reality of these people, the planet is doomed. Ideas and creativity move society forward. Most likely, the whole education system is part of it also. There may be a reward versus punishment factor involved ensuring the people will obey the orders from the implant. Whoever is doing it is a madman."

"I think you hit the nail on the head, Lenny," Hans said and Myles nodded. "Their brains are hijacked and the dictator can change how people process information. But why? The madman will be rewarded with obedient citizens to the detriment of the planet's prosperity. In the end, the people will be helpless and dependent as they're addicted to instant answers from the implant."

"If we could just pull the plug," Myles said, "but to find the computers controlling the citizens may not be easy. Another way may be to remove people's implants so they can't receive directions, but I doubt they would agree to it. The madman has probably programmed them to think they can't function without it."

"The leaders are not manipulated, we all saw that, so they're part of the scheme," Myles continued. "The whole time we talked to them I had the feeling they wanted us out of there. They pretended to be interested in our journey, but now I believe they were putting on an act. Perhaps they were concerned we would discover their control over the citizens. They know we're explorers and have seen many civilizations and every new planet we find is featured on the Internet. Just imagine, if we posted on the Internet that Norioon manipulates its people like marionettes, not very flattering for a so-called civilized planet."

"The question is *why* the power elite is manipulating the people and, second, is the population *aware* they're manipulated," Toby reflected.

"I suggest we ask the guide tomorrow," Lenny said. "If we do it in an innocent way, he just may start talking."

They all agreed and the next day as they were talking, Lenny asked the guide if the people wore implants to improve cognition. The guide nodded and said enthusiastically –

"Our implants are great and we are guided by them all the time."

"Can I see it?"

The guide pulled it from the back of his neck and it was not surgically implanted and could be removed.

While holding his implant and preventing the guide to listen to the directives from it, Lenny started talking to him while pretending to study the implant.

"Do your leaders also wear an implant?"

"Oh, no, they're so smart. They don't need one."

"Are you guided by your implant or is it only a cognitive boost?"

"The implant tells me what to say and gives me answers to my questions. I love it and it helps me make decisions. Without it, I couldn't function. I don't think it has anything to do with cognition, but I don't know for sure."

"Do you know where the answers come from? I mean, it sounds fantastic and maybe we could learn from it."

"We have a central computer running the whole system and it's located in one of the government buildings, but I don't know where. I hope it never fails, because all of us depend on it. Without my implant, I would have a hard time making a single decision on my own."

Lenny had heard what he needed to know and returned the implant. He thanked the guide for showing it and the guide fastened it behind his neck. He was unaware he had been used for questioning.

On the ship that evening the crew discussed what they had learned. Lenny's guess was obviously correct and the whole population was manipulated and corrupted. Should they care or ignore it? Was it their business to get involved?

"Every trip we make as explorers should aid the people and improve conditions," Myles said. "It means, of course, we butt in to people's affairs. My suggestion is we destroy the computer responsible for the system without anyone knowing it. By the time the leaders have discovered the system is down and not functioning, the people have been without guidance from their implants for days and there is a chance they wake up and start thinking for themselves. That's all we can do for them. We are visitors, not conquerors."

"Why don't we ask to see Litberk's ship and then invite him to tour ours," Hans suggested. "When Litberk is here, we ask him to remove his implant and explain to him they're all manipulated by the leaders. He may know where the computer is located."

The crew accepted the idea and all proceeded according to plan. Litberk and his copilot were eagerly checking out the electronics on the Bridge.

"You have better electronics than we have," Litberk noticed.

After they had seen everything, Lenny politely asked them to remove their implants. At first they refused, but Lenny responded they had a reason for it and they removed them.

"We know your leaders are manipulating all of you, the whole population, through your implants," he said. "You have lost your freedom, your free will, your ability to make independent decisions and we would like your help to destroy the computer running your implants. Would you be willing to help us? Your leaders are what we call a power elite serving only themselves, not the people, and they don't wear implants."

Litberk and his copilot looked bewildered, but then Litberk smiled and admitted –

"My copilot and I know. We never wear the implant on our ship and we both prefer the freedom we feel without it. When we return from our spaceflights, we must wear it or face punishment. You're right, the whole population is corrupted and destroyed. My copilot knows the building where the computer is kept. Scan my implant and you'll find how to enter the computer. Could you plant a virus?"

Lenny nodded and picked up the implant and hooked it up to the ship's computer. Its processor was visible and Lenny recorded it and returned the implant. He had the information he needed and had found an entry into the computer from the implant.

They returned the pilots to the planet and they wished Lenny good luck with his plan. If the leaders would trace the virus to the ship, the crew could take off, but if they found Litberk and his copilot had assisted the crew, they would probably lose their lives. Litberk was scheduled to leave with his space ship the following week and that's when Lenny planned to deliver the virus.

Lenny and Toby created a devastating virus that would destroy all data and if the leaders reloaded the program, it would become infected also. Any computer tied to the system would become infected. Lenny estimated that if they were capable of removing the virus, it would take several months to clean the system, but more likely, they would have to start from scratch and rewrite the whole program. By that time, the people may have discovered freedom and refuse to wear the implants. Litberk had promised to somehow transmit a message that could reach Earth and let the crew know how the people adjusted to life with freedom.

The virus was launched and literally fried the computer. As soon as the crew understood it had done its job, they said goodbye to the leaders and left. No one suspected them and the leaders were looking for a hacker among the population.

Myles and the crew decided to return home and the five month return trip was uneventful and they landed safely on Earth. They had been gone only ten months and thanks to Leo's gravity chamber, all of them were in good physical condition. Myles posted the information about the new mega portal tunnel and the two new planets on the Internet and their locations. He did not reveal anything about the manipulation of the citizens on Norioon as discretion was standard procedure to protect each new planet's reputation.

***

A year later, Myles received a message transmitted by Litberk and forwarded by a trusted captain of another spaceship that had traveled through the new tunnel. As soon as he was through the tunnel, the captain sent off the message. Litberk reported that Myles and his crew had never been suspected of planting the virus and he and his copilot were not under suspicion either since they had been away with their spaceship when the virus hit. The leaders were convinced a genius hacker was guilty and interrogated all known programmers on the planet without finding any lead. Now, one year later, they had failed to repair the computer and there was no one among the programmers capable of rewriting the program to control the people. The original program had been created by an unusually gifted man and he was dead. The power elite had to give up and allow the people to live without their implants. People adjusted to life without computer directions and slowly learned to make their own decisions. They discovered that with freedom, life is a gift.

CHAPTER 13

A peaceful year had passed and the spaceship was waiting for Tothellim, Emrak and the crew. Three copilots and six androids, among them Rex and Kody, were onboard. Emrak could choose his duties.

Tothellim had confided in Emrak he regretted leaving Andrew on Edena and they both agreed they would make a quick stop at Edena on their way back if Andrew wanted to return home.

They passed planet Edena after fourteen months of travel. The time had gone rather fast and the ship was comfortable with velcro flooring and two gravity chambers for exercise. The food onboard was excellent. The crew had maintained good physical condition and felt energetic.

As they passed Edena, Tothellim transmitted an offer to Andrew that the ship could pick him up and give him free passage back to Veehnia and the offer included his family, if he was married. The message was sent to the government offices to be forwarded to Andrew.

Tothellim changed course after passing Edena and they went in a direction they had not explored before. They were hoping to find a mega portal, but so far, the only tunnel they had found was a short one of minor importance, but things were about to change. Vibrations could be felt and the ship started to shake more and more until they were at the entry of a powerful tunnel.

They entered with Tothellim at the controls. Stop! Something was different with this tunnel. It was the smallest size tunnel Tothellim had ever seen and the ship had only ten feet of clearance all around, but the tunnel was straight as an arrow and did not move. There was no way to turn around and Tothellim had to force himself to stay calm and remind himself to trust his flying skills. Eric, his best copilot, was at the second controls ready to assist. All of them were on needles and pins. One short move from the center and the ship would touch the side of the tunnel and crash. The speed and vibration were increasing. If the tunnel had not been totally straight, they would probably have crashed, but Tothellim managed to keep the ship in the center. After an hour, Eric took over and   his flying skills matched Tothellim's. Eric and Tothellim took turns and after four nerve-wracking hours they came out of the tunnel. They had doubled their speed and traveled three thousand light years, according to the computers. The tunnel was not a mega portal, but still impressive and three thousand light years was an enormous distance to cover in only four hours.

Before they entered the tunnel, they received a reply from Andrew declining the offer to return to Veehnia. He and Zittana both agreed their lives were on Edena, their boys were born on the planet and they enjoyed a comfortable lifestyle living in their own house and spending weekends on their boat. Neither of them saw a benefit to live on Veehnia. Andrew included images of his family and gave a brief summary of their lives and asked Tothellim to forward the message and images to his parents. He added a personal message to Tothellim that he felt no animosity toward him and was happily married to Zittana. Men had returned to being men on the planet and with marriage now in effect, children were raised with both parents at home. He added if the Veehnian ship had not visited Edena thirteen years ago and opened the eyes of the leaders, society would have collapsed. Now, after men had gained equal rights, life on Edena was about the same as on Veehnia and he was happy to stay. Andrew ended by saying Zittana had morphed into a very feminine woman and the macho women greeting them on the planet so many years ago were only a memory.

Tothellim and Emrak smiled when they read the message and watched the images and Tothellim felt a heavy burden had left him. All these years, his conscience had bothered him and he knew he had done a disservice to Andrew by denying him to return home. The rest of the crew also watched the images and it was the same crew that had visited Edena years ago.

Tothellim sent off a warm greeting to Andrew how very happy he was to learn about Andrew's life and the success he had enjoyed on Edena. He admitted to Andrew he regretted deeply his decision to leave him on Edena and had been emotionally burdened by it, so knowing it had worked out so well for him was the best news he could ever get. He would be happy to deliver the message in person to his parents.

***

The ship was moving forward at tremendous speed and after two weeks they spotted a large star with four orbiting planets. They picked the planet they estimated had the most favorable conditions for life and entered orbit. The planet was as large as Veehnia and inhabited. Judging from the lights on the planet, the population was very large.

As explorers, the crew knew their safety was never guaranteed when they approached an unknown planet. Even the ship could be blown up. At daybreak, they launched the drone and programmed it to descend to seven thousand feet. The air traffic was heavy and reached up to five thousand feet, but the brand-new drone onboard had cloaking abilities which they engaged. It also had powerful telescopic equipment and was capable of close-up images taken from elevations up to ten thousand feet.

The drone descended and started sending images back to the ship. The images were astonishing. The beings resembled short humanoids, only four feet tall and very thin, but they were capable of flying and gliding. Their arms had folding membranes that acted as wings. They were capable of short distance flight and once up in the air they were gliding. Their wings were attached to the underside of their arms, but did not include their hands, so they had full use of their hands. The lower part of the wings was attached to their thighs. When they opened their arms, they could leap into the air and gain height and their gliding ability was impressive. Just slight flapping of the wings enabled them to glide. They had human faces, short blondish hair, white skin without fur and their hands were human. When the wings were folded, they were barely visible and they walked around like humans on two legs. Their clothing was tight fitting and contoured to allow movement of their wings. Judging from the modern design of their airmobiles, the people were intelligent and advanced.

"They're bat people!" Eric exclaimed. "They have perfect human heads and bodies attached to bat wings."

The rest of the crew agreed and none of them had ever seen beings resembling these people even on the Internet. They were unique. Their tiny size and light body weight were most likely necessary to enable them to lift off the ground.

"Let's visit them and hope they're friendly," Tothellim decided. "Three androids stay behind to man the ship, but Rex and Kody come with us."

Eight of them boarded the shuttle and they took off. They had stun guns on the shuttle, but the weapons were never used when they made initial contact with aliens to make sure they would not be mistaken for warriors.

Tothellim landed the shuttle in a field close to the city and they exited and just waited next to the shuttle. The planet had medium heavy gravity and normal oxygen. It was easy to breathe. Within minutes an airmobile landed and six armed soldiers dressed in jumpsuits hopped out pointing laser guns at them.

"Stop, we're friends!" Tothellim said in a firm voice and showed them the translation device.

The aliens understood they were not enemies and put their guns down and entered their language code into the device.

Tothellim quickly explained their mission was to search for new planets, they came from Veehnia and they offered friendship.

The leader smiled and said in a high-pitched voice –

"Welcome to planet Zollenius. I'm Rikkitar and in charge of our defense. We have spaceships ourselves and I assume you used the tunnel to find us."

The crew nodded and they towered over the tiny men. Rikkitar suggested they follow his airmobile with the shuttle to the government leaders. It was a long distance and they had a chance to tour the planet. It was nice looking, but rather ordinary. Everywhere were houses and buildings and it appeared the planet had a large population. It did not look affluent, but not poverty-stricken either. They noticed most homes had an airmobile parked outside, so they were not behind technologically. Finally, after a two-hour trip, they arrived at the government center and the buildings were drab looking. Rikkitar escorted the crew to the leaders and introduced them and then stayed in the room. Ten people were present, men and women, and they invited the crew to sit down. The chairs were tiny and the crew had a hard time fitting on the chairs, a fact that was noticed. The leader gave a command to a servant and within minutes full size chairs were brought in for the men, which they gratefully accepted.

"I'm Tuscullo, one of the leaders, and our planet is called Zollenius. Welcome. We hear you're explorers. We're tiny people compared to you, but we keep larger pieces of furniture for visitors from other planets. Occasionally, spaceships stop by and the visitors are all your size. That's why we had larger chairs made."

Tothellim explained where they came from and the narrow tunnel they had passed through and Tuscullo was familiar with the tunnel.

"Our planet has only two spaceships and we have financial problems due to severe overpopulation," he remarked. "Families are too large and we have occasional food shortages."

"Do you limit the number of children per family?" Emrak asked.

"No, it's against our religious beliefs," Tuscullo replied. "But something has to change soon. There are too many of us."

"Your ability to fly is unique," Kody said in an opening remark. "We've seen many different aliens, but none had wings. You're humans, just shorter than standard humans, but when in your background did you grow wings?"

"We simply don't know," Tuscullo said. "Only the younger people use their wings and like their flying abilities, but the older generation like me have our wings surgically removed. We never fly and the wings are constantly in the way. It's a simple procedure to have the wings removed and we gain more mobility." Tuscullo got off his chair and stretched out his arms to show he had no wings. The crew was surprised and had not noticed the lack of wings on Tuscullo. Rikkitar also stood up and with a chuckle pulled his arm out of his jumpsuit demonstrating he had no wings either.

"We just use an airmobile when we need to move around," Tuscullo added with a smile. "It's so much easier."

"Our mission when we contact alien people is to offer any help we can," Kody said. "I'm a medical doctor and scientist. If there is any medical problem you have, just ask me, and perhaps I can help."

"Our planet is mostly self-sufficient and apart from overpopulation, we have no serious problems, no wars, no high crime rate and so on. The citizens are healthy. Occasionally, we have food shortages. There is not enough farm land to grow crops and we don't eat meat. Birth control is not permitted by our clergy."

"Would your clergy allow surgical sterilization of the men?" Kody asked. "It's a simple procedure and the recovery is fast."

"Hmm, I actually don't know, it's an interesting idea and would solve our problem," Tuscullo observed. "I need to consult with our church leaders and let you know."

The crew stayed a few hours and they exchanged information. Rikkitar was one of the pilots for their two spaceships and forwarded all the knowledge he had about tunnels and planets in the area to the ship's computers and, in return, Rex sent information back to Rikkitar's computers. The crew returned to the ship to spend the night as they were sure the aliens did not have beds large enough to fit them. They noticed a group of teenagers flying and laughing and enjoyed watching their flying skills. They sure looked like bats.

The next day, Tuscullo told Kody with a big smile on his face the clergy had approved sterilization of the men. He added all the fathers he had talked to approved of the idea and would have the procedure done. Some of the families had ten children and the average was six and especially the women wanted no more than two children. Androids were available to buy as maids, but few families could afford one. The problem with overpopulation would correct itself with the new sterilization project in effect.

The crew realized the people did not need any more help from them and left the planet. Tothellim steered the ship toward a tunnel Rikkitar had recommended. It was a two-hour tunnel and would propel them a thousand light years. Close to the tunnel's exit was a star with an interesting planet. Rikkitar had not visited the planet, but rumors said the citizens were cannibals, violent and had no modern technology. The name of the planet was Sestoona and as far as Rikkitar knew, no spaceship had ever landed on the planet. The crew discussed back and forth whether they should risk landing on the planet and if their translation device would be able to find their language. The device they had was state of the art boasting ability to translate the majority of languages known in the universe. Without communication, there would be no point in landing on the planet. All six androids onboard volunteered to descend to the planet and try to communicate with the aliens. Tothellim and the human pilots would be best off staying on the ship, Rex advised, until the android crew had ascertained exactly how dangerous the aliens were.

"We do have stun guns and most likely these people have only primitive weapons that are harmless to androids," Kody stated. "We have to find out why they're cannibals and if there's a way to make them abandon their barbaric way of life."

Tothellim approved of the idea and after a month of travel they found the tunnel. It was wide, straight and stationary without floating back and forth and they passed through it with ease. Once out of the tunnel they found the star with a single orbiting planet. It must be Sestoona.

The ship was in orbit and they noticed no lights lit up the planet at dusk and apparently electricity had not been discovered. The next morning, they launched their drone and programmed it to fly at a thousand feet. The images transmitted to the ship showed a sparsely populated planet with humans resembling early man on Earth, perhaps similar to Neanderthal. As a scientist and researcher, Kody recognized these people were thousands of years behind most civilizations on the known planets. Sestoona had an oxygen atmosphere, but the drone registered a surface temperature of only thirty degrees Fahrenheit. It was a chilly planet. The houses were simple log cabins in groups of about fifty and smoke came out of the chimneys. Apparently, they heated with wood. The planet had forests all over ensuring ample supply of firewood. A few children played outside dressed in fur clothing. The androids descended to the surface and landed a short distance from a group of cabins.

"Let's not exit the shuttle," Kody suggested. "Then we'll see how they behave toward us and how aggressive they are. We can leave the door open so they can see us, but be ready to close it if they try to attack us."

The androids had both stun guns and laser guns on their belts hoping they would not be necessary. With the shuttle door open, Kody and Rex calmly waited at the door opening and within minutes a gang of men holding loaded bows approached the shuttle. The arrows were on the string and the archers were ready to draw. An arrow would only do superficial damage to an android and was mostly harmless.

Rex calmly walked down the ramp of the shuttle holding the translation device in one hand and a firm grip on the stun gun with the other hand.

"We come in peace," he said, hoping they would talk so the device could search for their language.

The men yelled something and a minute later the device flashed. It was ready to translate and had found the language.

"Put your bows down, we're here in peace," Rex said in a commanding voice. The men looked shocked believing the device was talking and a few of them dropped their bows. The rest of them lowered their weapons and just stared at Rex. Rex was an impressive looking android at six feet tall and a powerful build. With his blond hair, he looked like a Viking from long ago. Rex walked to the closest man, put his hand on the man's shoulder and looked him straight in the eyes.

"I'm Rex. What's your name?"

The man was too shocked to talk and just stared at the translation device convinced it was alive.

"Nenna," another man with more courage replied. "Are you gods?"

"No, just men like yourselves," Rex said with a smile. "We come from very far away and all we want is to talk and make friends with you. Can we go to your cabin and talk?"

Nenna nodded and the men lowered their bows. They were rather short, but muscular and stocky and dressed in fur clothing and fur boots. They wore no hats and their brown hair was straight, but bushy and very thick reaching to their shoulders. They did resemble early man and had short foreheads and protruding eyebrows. They were not handsome. Kody quietly studied them trying to figure out how far back in time this type of human had lived on Earth and perhaps also on Veehnia. They were probably thousands of years behind Veehnia.

The men walked to the largest cabin followed by Rex and the androids and they stepped inside. The cabin had a dirt floor and a crackling fire in the center of the cabin heated the room. Along the outer walls were wooden benches and in the middle of the room was a large, rectangular wooden table and chairs and a primitive kitchen was next to the fireplace. Nenna invited the men to sit down and then added another piece of wood to the fire. A young woman was sitting in the kitchen area looking very afraid. She wore the same type fur clothing as the men and her hair was waist long. She was not pretty compared to modern women, but when comparing her to the way the men looked, she was actually nice looking.

They sat down at the table and the androids all repeated their names. Nenna was apparently the leader.

"You first visitors," he said hesitatingly, not sure how to proceed. "How can you fly like birds?"

"It's similar to a bird and can fly very fast. Where we come from this type of bird is common," Rex started to explain and searching in his mind how to convey information about modern life and technology to someone with no knowledge of anything but life in his little hamlet. He also knew he had to keep his language plain and simple.

"It's cold here. Will it get colder?"

"Winter has started and much snow come. We have little food and are hungry all winter. Animals not here in winter and we must eat people to survive. We hunt them in next village. Animals better to eat, but they not here when snow comes," Nenna explained.

So, it was true. They were cannibals, but it appeared to be of necessity rather than by choice. Apparently, they were not nomads.

"Do people in the next village hunt you?" Kody asked.

"Yes, yes, they do," Nenna said and fear was visible on his face. "They took my child."

"Do you plant vegetables in the summer?"

"No, we pick roots in forest. Roots keep over winter."

"If you capture several of the animals in the summer, you could feed them and keep them for the winter. When the snow comes, you could eat them," Rex suggested. "Then you don't have to hunt people and you will never be hungry."

The idea surprised the men and, apparently, they had never thought of it before, but seemed openminded to this new concept.

"Many animals come here in summer," Nenna admitted, "and easy to trap them. How stop them from running away?"

"You have to build a strong fence with wooden poles and slats. We will show you how to do it."

"How many children do you have?" Kody asked.

"Many, but many die small," Nenna said. Kody realized they could not count numbers. None of the men was that old and he guessed their life expectancy was short, perhaps forty years or less.

"I make sick people feel better," Kody explained. "Can I take a little blood from you? I'm a medicine man."

Nenna nodded and understood 'medicine man' but not the rest of Kody's statement. Kody quickly ran to the shuttle and returned with his medical kit. The instrument used for collecting blood resembled a gun and the needle pierced the vein painlessly. Kody collected the blood from three of the men and asked if they had a medicine man. They said no.

The crew politely declined to eat with the natives and returned to the shuttle for a quick break. A corner of the shuttle functioned as emergency sickbay and had a built-in lab, where Kody started analyzing the blood samples. Soon the first tests showed answers on the computer screen.

"They're malnourished and they all have worms," Kody noticed. "The DNA test shows the three men are related, so there's inbreeding going on. I see a touch of scurvy, which I'm sure will get worse as full winter sets in and they have no greens to eat. The scurvy will promote tooth loss and I'll check the condition of their teeth next. I bet the older people have lost some of their molars." The rest of the testing would take time so Kody and the crew returned to the men.

They had finished their lunch and the leftovers on the wooden platter looked like cooked roots. Kody asked Nenna to open his mouth so he could check his teeth. Several of his molars were missing.

Rex asked to see their tools and behind the cabin Nenna pulled out his axe made of a straight wooden handle with a very sharp stone tied to it with a vine. Rex tested it against a stump and found it was more efficient than he had expected and the stone easily cut into the stump. He asked Nenna if he had more axes and Nenna replied all men had one. Rex told Nenna to get all the men from the hamlet together so they could start building a fence to corral the animals. Each of the men should have his axe with him. Nenna returned with thirty men and Rex walked into the forest followed by the men.

There were plenty of small trees available that could be used to build a simple fence and after the felled trees were limbed, they had a stack of perfect poles on the ground. Rex instructed the men to carry the poles back to the hamlet and showed them how to line up two parallel poles and drive them into the ground with a heavy stone. Nenna ran and returned with a huge flat stone and drove the two poles into the ground. Luckily, the ground was still not frozen and the poles were hammered into the soil rather easily. When the first section of parallel poles was in place, Rex instructed the men how to position the horizontal poles in between the two vertical poles and fasten them with the same vine they used for their stone axes. The design was simple and used materials they had already. The finished fence was five feet tall and the horizontal poles were placed close enough so the animals could not squeeze through. Rex had been told the animals could not jump.

While the men finished the fencing, Rex and the crew took off with the shuttle to find where the animals were and they only had to travel a short distance to spot them. They were stocky and short and looked like a mix of donkey and deer. The herd did not notice the shuttle as they landed a distance away and the crew quietly walked toward them without being seen. A little closer and they fired their stun guns hitting fourteen animals. They fell down unable to move while the rest of the herd took off in a panic. Rex quickly ran to the shuttle and moved it to the animals and opened up the cargo bay of the shuttle. Each animal weighed about three hundred pounds and two androids were able to lift each animal and place it on the floor. There was no room to spare. The shuttle was overloaded, but they flew just above the ground at slow speed and they made it back without incident.

Back at the hamlet, the crew unloaded the animals to the surprise of the men and tied each animal to the fence until the full fence was in place. The natives worked fast and it would only take another day to finish the job.

Rex explained to Nenna the animals would wake up after a while and they would have to stand guard until the fence was done. They also had to supply a water trough and dried grass. Rex suggested the kids could run around the fields and pull as much dry grass as they could find to feed the animals. Nenna understood the instructions and Rex and the crew returned to the ship. It had been an eventful day.

The human crew was eager to hear the news and after Rex and Kody had relayed all the information, they discussed what to do next.

"We humans will come along tomorrow and we leave three androids on the ship," Tothellim said. "It's apparent they won't throw us in the stew pot, so it's safe. They'll freak out when they see me, but they'll get over it after a while."

"Maybe we should ask Nenna to run over to the next hamlet and invite the leaders to take a look at the animal enclosure. If they also copied the idea, there would be no need to slaughter each other. We could collect the animals for them if they build the fence themselves," Emrak suggested.

"Agreed," Tothellim replied. "That will be our goal for tomorrow. We have to ask Nenna if fourteen animals will supply enough meat for the whole winter."

The crew took off at daybreak the next day and landed next to the hamlet. Nenna and a few of the men ran to the shuttle to greet them, but stopped dead in their tracks at the sight of Tothellim. They gasped with their mouths open and Tothellim could not help but laugh.

"I'm not dangerous, calm down, my friends," he said. The men managed to control their fear and understood he was safe.

"Animals awake and fence almost done," Nenna reported. They walked over to the corral and found the animals were calm and did not try to run away. A hollow log was filled with water and a pile of dried grass was next to the water.

"Nenna, listen," Emrak said. "Run over to the next hamlet and ask the leaders to come over here and take a look at your animals and fence. If they build a fence, we 'll get the animals for them and you and they will have enough meat for the winter."

Nenna nodded and told two of his men to follow him. They took off at a jog and disappeared into the forest.

Kody took more blood samples and checked the medical condition of the tribe. None of them had cancer, heart disease or any of the standard diseases of the modern world. They suffered from intestinal worms, scurvy, tooth decay and malnutrition and the tribe had too much inbreeding. Kody spoke to the women and told them to pick any wild berries that were safe to eat and sun dry them for the winter. That would give them some Vitamin C and improve the health of their teeth. Kody also explained to the women some plants had the ability to kill off their worms and one woman stepped forward and said she knew of one plant growing in the forest that could destroy their worms. She had taken it herself and felt stronger when she used it. Kody asked the woman to teach the other women about the plant and make sure to give it to their families. The next problem was the inbreeding and Kody would have to explain to the men to pick their wives from hamlets far away.

The men came back from the neighboring hamlet and when the neighbors had recovered from their fear, they admired the animals and the fence and agreed they would also build a fence. Nenna carefully showed them how to construct the fence and they returned home to start the project. They were told the 'bird people' would get the animals as soon as their fence was finished.

Toward the evening, Nenna's fence was finished and they untied the animals. They were docile by nature and did not seem too frightened living in captivity and as long as they had food, they remained calm.

Emrak asked Nenna if the animals in the corral would supply enough meat for the winter. The tribe could not count, but Nenna understood anyway and replied it was enough.

The crew took off with the shuttle to investigate how many people lived on the planet and found the population was small, but the herds of animals they used for food were huge. If every hamlet had a corral and learned how to trap a small herd of animals for the winter, cannibalism would disappear overnight. Nenna had mentioned he knew how to trap the animals. The planet was not a beauty, mostly small forests mixed with grassland, where the herds lived. There was no desert on the planet.

Back with the tribe, Tothellim asked to see their tools and Nenna proudly showed his tool collection. All the tools were surprisingly efficient and practical and worked well. Kody realized the tribe was more advanced than he had first thought. Their little cabins were sturdy and they had used vines to tie the logs together. After a few years, the vines hardened and became so strong it was impossible to tear the vines.

They sat in the cabin and Kody tried to explain to Nenna they must find their wives from as far away as possible to ensure their children would be healthy. The concept of inbreeding was impossible to explain, but it appeared Nenna somehow knew by instinct that Kody was right. He agreed with Kody and assured him they would follow his advice.

Rex asked if they believed in gods and Nenna nodded. They had several gods they prayed to for guidance.

The crew told the tribe a tiny bit of the modern world, but it overwhelmed them and they could not process the information so they stopped.

"Do you have wars?" Tothellim asked.

"Yes, many and we always afraid we be attacked," Nenna replied. "But if other people have animals to eat for winter, we hope war stop."

The next two days the crew interacted leisurely with the tribe and then the neighbors appeared and announced their fence was ready and they wanted animals. The crew had seen the neighboring tribe from the air and knew the location. The androids took off with the shuttle and returned to the neighbors with another fourteen animals. Nenna was there to help them and gave instructions. Rex told the leader of the neighboring tribe to tell other neighbors they could keep animals for the winter as food and he understood. Hopefully, this was the beginning of the end of cannibalism on the planet.

The crew said goodbye to the people and left the planet. They had done what they could for the people and their mission was over. It was time to return home to Veehnia and the trip would take one and a half years. They passed all the tunnels safely, but the narrow tunnel was as stressful on the return trip as the first time they traveled through it. The recording of it would be entered into the flight simulators on both Frejja and Veehnia for students to navigate.

They landed safely on Veehnia after being gone three years. All of them were in rather good condition thanks to Leo's velcro floor and gravity chambers. It was an emotional reunion for Tothellim to see his children again and a group of government officials were also waiting to welcome them home. As always, Tothellim would submit a full report to the government as soon as he had rested for a few days. To protect the reputation of Sestoona, the report would not mention they had been cannibals and, hopefully, that epoch in the history of their planet was over.

The Veehnian ship to Earth was scheduled to leave in ten days and Emrak was planning to be onboard so he could live out his life on Frejja. Tothellim had offered to retire if Emrak wanted to live out his life with him, but Emrak told him with a smile he wanted to see his children. Emrak stayed with Tothellim until his return trip.

Two days later Tothellim and Emrak visited Andrew's parents and gave them the recordings from their son and the long message. They were totally overwhelmed when they watched the images of Andrew and his family and they told Tothellim they finally had found peace inside. They would have preferred if Andrew had returned with his family, but the only thing that mattered was that he was happy and had a good life.

The ten days went by too quickly and Emrak said an emotional farewell to his best friend Tothellim. They would probably never meet in person again, but the captain of the Veehnian immigration ship would be happy to transmit any greeting they had to each other in the future.

Emrak boarded the Veehnian ship and it was a peaceful return trip to Frejja. He was offered the same guest cabin on the ship and the seven months went by rather quickly. The captain spent many hours with Emrak listening to his description of the many planets the ship had visited.

Emrak's children greeted him on Frejja. He had been gone seven years and was now one hundred and fifteen years old. What a wonderful life he had had and all he wanted to do now was reflect on his life and enjoy his memories.

Emrak's android moved back into his house to take care of him. She had worked for Leo these seven years, but she loved Karol and Emrak and she had grieved when Karol passed away. She wanted to make sure Emrak's last years were comfortable and was glad he had returned.

CHAPTER 14

Six months had passed since Emrak returned to Frejja and Tothellim missed him terribly. He felt as if his soul mate had left. The house was too empty. Emrak's good humor and easy-going personality had been one of the factors that had enabled Tothellim to finally recover emotionally from Anna's death. It had been eighteen years since he returned to space travel and he decided to retire. It was not an easy decision to make, but he felt from within it was time to quit. He invited the whole crew for dinner and even though the androids did not eat food, they were happy to accept the invitation. Tothellim always rented an android maid while he was home and she had prepared a lovely dinner for the guests.

After dinner, Tothellim announced he would retire and spend a year with Emrak on Frejja. Rex let out a whistle.

"You'll be missed more than I can say, Tothellim," he said and the emotion in his voice gave away his sincerity. "You've been the best captain and friend any crew could wish for and we'll never forget you."

The rest of the crew chimed in and Eric would now become the new captain as he was the senior copilot. The crew assured Tothellim they would keep him informed of their space travels.

"Does Emrak know you'll be visiting?" Kody asked.

"No, the Veehnian spaceship to Earth leaves in two weeks and I'll be onboard. The captain told me the guest cabin is available. When we're through the twelve-hour tunnel, he'll send a message to Emrak that I'm on my way. I'm excited to visit Frejja. I only spent a few weeks there many years ago, but I liked the planet a lot. Emrak and I can now sit back and reflect on our lives together and twiddle our thumbs befitting two old men."

The crew laughed and they stayed until early morning. All of them asked Tothellim to let them know when he was back and to send warm regards to Emrak. He was highly respected.

Tothellim arranged with Rheo to look after his house, which he always did when Tothellim was away, and in return he had full use of Tothellim's boat. The arrangement fit both of them.

***

Emrak felt a jolt of happiness when he received the transmission from the captain of the Veehnian ship and responded immediately he was thrilled to have Tothellim as his guest. He was more than welcome.

The captain of the Veehnian ship manned the shuttle himself when Tothellim disembarked. It was his way of showing the two men his respect for them and their many accomplishments. Almost two years had passed since Emrak left Veehnia and at that time Tothellim had not decided he would retire. After the decision was made, he felt liberated and free.

It was a heartwarming reunion when Tothellim climbed out of the shuttle and embraced Emrak. The moment was divine. The captain was happy to see Emrak again and they had enjoyed each other's company on the ship. The captain was fascinated to hear about the planets Emrak and Tothellim had visited and the different aliens. He would have liked to stay a few days on Frejja, but after they talked for an hour, he had to return to his ship.

Emrak's airmobile quickly brought them home and he still lived in the same house he had bought for Karol. Tothellim loved the house and his large room and he knew he would be happy living there. He had used the gravity chamber on the Veehnian ship several hours a day and felt he would be back in shape within a few weeks. Emrak had a full exercise room in the house and they worked out together.

When Emrak received the message that Tothellim was on his way, he bought a lake boat. A large lake was close to his house and he kept his boat in a marina there. Emrak had treasured the fishing trips he and Tothellim had enjoyed on the ocean on Veehnia and he felt it would be nice to do the same on Frejja, albeit on a lake.

Tothellim settled in and loved his life on Frejja. As always, the two men enjoyed each other's company and felt their friendship was special. When Tothellim met Leo, inventor of the velcro flooring for spaceships as well as the gravity chamber, he shook his hand and told him the enormous value his inventions had added to the spaceships, especially the gravity chamber. Leo was touched to hear it and told Tothellim he still hoped to invent artificial gravity for the whole spaceship.

Leo was by now sixty years old and a rich man earning commission from all his inventions. His wife Lana, born on Earth, had given him three boys and the oldest was sixteen years and the youngest nine. Emrak's grandson Sven worked for Leo, his uncle. Leo deliberately kept his company small and he was very choosy who he hired. His employees were part owners of the company and between them many inventions had been created.

The first months of Tothellim's visit almost flew and they toured Frejja using the airmobile, spent long days on the lake fishing and sometimes one of the grandchildren would come along. Emrak also showed Tothellim where he used to work and the flight simulator where he had trained so many pilots to navigate in space and through tunnels. They often ate their dinners in the backyard surrounded by all the flowerbeds Karol had planted and they were still tended to by the android.

Tothellim was sad to hear Brandon and Brianna were dead, but Rigel came over to the house to meet him and he knew his parents had felt great respect for Tothellim. Rigel had been a guest in Emrak's house many times and would stop by and visit him on occasion. He brought Thole along when he came over to Emrak's house. Rigel was now an elderly man, eighty years old, and he and Thole had been retired several years, but remained best friends. The four men spent an interesting day together and Thole told them in person how he had escaped from Morekia and applied for asylum on Frejja. Their wives were still alive.

The rainy season arrived and for three months the rain came down in buckets. Emrak and Tothellim spent a lot of the time watching all the holographic images Emrak had saved, including the pictures Brandon had taken from Earth. Frejja had a few interesting space museums they went to and the three months were over rather fast. Emrak had asked Tothellim several times to stay another year and Emrak also offered him to continue living in his house after he was gone. It was a touching proof of their friendship and Tothellim agreed to stay another year. His life on Frejja was always fun and if he had not had children back home on Veehnia, he would for sure have accepted Emrak's offer to live out his life on Frejja. He loved the planet and had a small group of friends he enjoyed spending time with. No one had ever discriminated against him and he was almost a celebrity. Everyone he dealt with spoke English, so it was easy to communicate. From Emrak's point of view, having his best friend living with him made his last years in life much more enjoyable compared to living alone in his house.

***

Sorenia was a thriving planet and the population had increased to two million. Immigration was open and five thousand people from Mineata and two thousand from Ziggellus had immigrated and become valued members of society. Standard of living was good and modernization continued to advance the planet. Everyone now wore a communicator and an implant to boost cognition; the Internet was updated and not too far behind in sophistication compared to the other planets; Sorenia had a Starfleet of four ships capable of travel through any tunnel, but no fighter ships yet. Cooper was planning to buy a fleet of twelve fighter ships from Mineata, but the cost was prohibitive and he had delayed the purchase until more gold was found.

Cooper and Rosalie had been married thirty years and Cooper had gone through a slight aging to match Rosalie's age. She was now sixty years old, but looked several years younger, and was supervising the writing of all new material for the universities. Grandpa Reyya and grandma Littiana were very involved with the children. Halcyon was a Starfleet captain at twenty-nine years old and Celeste was twenty-six and had fulfilled her dream to become a psychologist.

Volrex' daughter Jilina was already twenty-two years old and worked hard to become a pilot. As a teenager, she had asked her father if she had what it takes to become a Starfleet pilot and he had encouraged her. Halcyon had also supported her to become a pilot. Several times she had joined him when he practiced in the flight simulator and he could see she had the ability to become a good pilot. She understood the advanced computer system and she was also physically strong and able to control the ship through a vibrating tunnel. In two years, she would graduate from flight school and be a junior pilot, the first female pilot on Sorenia.

Celeste taught at one of the universities and her courses were popular among the students. She also saw patients at her office. In addition to teaching everything about a healthy mind, she also had a course in reincarnation that had caught on with the students. Religion was only practiced among the immigrants and the Sorenians had almost aversion toward religion. Over thirty years had passed since the religious war ended, but the people felt no need to pursue religion of any kind. Contrary to most people's atheism, Celeste was guided by strong spiritual beliefs and knew from deep inside there was an afterlife. As part of her course in reincarnation, she included studies of the Akashic Records and was surprised to find a strong interest among the students in her course. Rosalie had studied her course material and had also become a believer and Cooper was openminded. With his keen intellect, he was aware there was more than the material world and his mind was tuned to the universe. He knew spirituality was part of the cosmic forces and had nothing to do with man-made religion. He had always advised Celeste to follow her heart and not be influenced by naysayers.

Reyya and Littiana were in their seventies and had recently retired. Cooper missed them at work and they were not easy to replace. He had asked the citizens again if they wanted to hold presidential elections and vote in another president, but the answer was still 'no'. Cooper knew Volrex would be a good president and he was still young enough to handle the job. He was intelligent and experienced in many fields. Cooper had asked him once if he would be interested to run for president and Volrex had replied he would run if Cooper wanted to retire. For the time being Cooper continued working as president, but he felt it was time for someone else to replace him. As a captain, Halcyon was away most of the time and flew to Mineata and Ziggellus and occasionally to other planets. Celeste worked full time and had her own little house close to the university, so Cooper and Rosalie now had time to pursue new things in life. Cooper had suggested to Rosalie they should visit a few other planets, perhaps Veehnia where he came from, and Rosalie replied she would be thrilled to travel. They both decided it was time to retire in a few years and follow their goal to explore the universe.

Under Cooper's leadership, the planet thrived and was continuously advancing. The economy was good, everyone looking for work could find a job, the mines still produced plenty of valuable ore and the standard of living was comfortable, not affluent, but the citizens had all the basics they needed and the food supply was adequate. Cooper thought to himself he would soon announce his resignation.

***

On Earth2, Janus and Alma were proud parents of a six-year-old daughter and a two-year-old son. Vitzoll and Attinna also had two children and Vitzoll and Janus had agreed to only accept work closer to their planet to avoid being away from their families longer than a year. After a mission, they would often stay home for several months and their pay was sufficient so they could afford to turn down some of the job offers. There was a demand for professional soldiers and Vitzoll and Janus could not handle all the job offers. Another group of mercenaries was needed, but so far there was none. It was a dangerous job, but well paying. Alma and Attinna were close friends and raised their children together. Alma had never had a friend and was truly fond of Attinna.

Vitzoll knew of Tothellim through his father. Rasufilus had received many reports from Tothellim informing him of different planets and Rex had sometimes added to the report. Vitzoll was aware Rex was a trained soldier and a pilot and would be perfect as a leader of a second mercenary group. He decided to give it a try and sent off a message to Rex asking if he would be interested in forming a mercenary group. After a month Rex' reply arrived stating he was owned by the Veehnian government and not free to work on his own. He was part of a crew exploring the universe, but in the future if he would be granted his liberty, he would be interested to work as a mercenary. He would contact Vitzoll if he was free to work on his own.

Viola was still working as a music teacher at sixty-six years old and Atlas had no plans to retire. He had trained Melody as a surgeon and they worked together at the hospital. She and Lorre had a daughter. Paragonne and Hattie worked hard on their farm and their two daughters were copies of Hattie. They also had a son.

The thirty immigrants from Earth had adjusted well and had now lived on Earth2 fifteen years. None of them wanted to return to Earth. One of the men from Earth had married an immigrant girl from Ziggellus and it was the first Ziggellus person to marry outside her race. Ziggellus people were not handsome, but this girl had a heart of gold and her lovely personality made her attractive as a person.

***

On Earth, younger people formed small communities and raised their children together. This was a new lifestyle enabling mothers to pursue a career and someone in the community would always be available to look after the children. It was referred to as 'commune living' and some families found it was right for them while others wanted no part of it preferring an independent lifestyle. Possessions were not shared, only responsibilities for the children and nothing else. It gave parents more free time and when there was a problem, more people were available to address the problem.

Earth was doing well and the World Government was fair and never meddled in the seven countries' internal affairs. No hostile spaceship had ever landed and there were no wars. Women were often leaders and elected by merit, not for political reasons.

Science and technology were moving forward on Earth, but the best minds usually ended up on Mars, known to be a Mecca for scientists. Plenty of money was available to fund research and many new inventions were created on Mars. Mars was nicknamed *Planet of the Brains* and since the huge park had been built, many scientists planning to stay only for a few years ended up as permanent residents. The park supplied the feeling of nature that had been missing before. Mars was unique and there was nothing like it in the universe. The citizens lived a life in luxury, paying no tax and worked short hours. All services were free. The few people who did leave Mars missed outdoor sports such as skiing, boating and being outside, but more people moved to Mars than from Mars.

***

Bonnie's life with Flar was a love affair involving heart and soul. Through Flar's guidance, her consciousness had increased and she was learning to master her mind and feelings. Their twelve-year marriage had been a discovery trip of everyday life as well as the psyche and Bonnie was advancing as a person. She felt an inner peace that had been absent before her marriage to Flar. He made her feel whole.

Their four children were a lively bunch and the oldest, Victor, was boisterous and very funny. Bonnie felt four children were enough and she had told Flar she did not want any more. Flar loved his children and wanted two more, but he respected Bonnie's wishes. Financially, he was affluent and could afford a large family.

Flar was now fluent in English and all the children were taught to speak English. Pendy, their housekeeper, was instructed to speak to them in English on and off and they learned rather fast to master the language.

Bonnie had not lost her flying skills and would accompany Flar as copilot at least once a month and Pendy took care of the children. Her friend Xiona always checked on the children when Bonnie was away. Sometimes the family rented a large boat and spent a week on the ocean. Ljeviina had two oceans and one of them was close to their home. Hiking in the mountains was another favorite and they left early with their airmobile and spent all day in the mountains returning home in the dark. The family was tight-knit and Pendy always came along.

Bonnie found life on Ljeviina more advanced than on Earth, but not that different. Basic life was the same and all basic needs were the same. She and Flar were two different races, but they both agreed their differences were superficial and they knew they were soulmates.

CHAPTER 15

Tothellim knocked on Emrak's bedroom door to wake him up. Emrak was late for breakfast and they were planning to go fishing that day.

"Wake up, old friend," Tothellim said in a loud voice. No response. He opened the door and found Emrak dead. His face was peaceful and he had died in his sleep. He was one hundred nineteen years old. Tothellim had lived on Frejja almost three years and the two men had treasured their time together, always having fun, engaging in deep discussions and sometimes just sitting around and comparing memories. It had been the best years in Tothellim's life since Anna died and he felt as if a knife was stabbing his soul. His bond to Emrak could not be broken.

Tothellim grieved Emrak's death deeply and it was hard to get through the funeral. He felt paralyzed watching Emrak's coffin, the same feeling he had experienced when he buried Anna. Tothellim was ninety-four years old and had many years left and he felt totally lost. When he was alone, he cried from pain and he was overcome with sadness. The Veehnian ship would return from Earth in a month and he would alert the captain to pick him up. Leo had offered him to stay as long as he wanted in Emrak's house, but he declined.

A few weeks after Emrak's death, Tothellim saw Emrak in his dream. He was smiling and assuring Tothellim he was at peace and told him not to grieve. Tothellim was shaken when he woke up not knowing for sure what to make of it. Was it real? Tothellim was not spiritual, but openminded. Was it a message that death is not the end but a transfer to another life beyond the material world? All day he was thinking of the dream and finally decided it was real; it was Emrak telling him not to grieve. So, there was another life after the material life and death was not the end, only a transfer to the afterlife. Emrak had looked so peaceful and without fear when he was dead and Tothellim realized there was no need to fear death. Anna had not been religious and when she died, she had never contacted him in a dream, but he knew Emrak had been a man of strong faith and would have tried to console Tothellim. As he thought about the whole thing, he became convinced there was an afterlife and Emrak had done his best to convey that message to him.

Tothellim said out loud "I understand now, Emrak. Thank you, my friend, for giving me your divine message. I believe you and I understand you want me to stop grieving. I'll never forget you and I miss you more than I can say, but I will live out my life and honor your memory." After he had uttered the words, he felt a wave of comfort and knew it came from Emrak.

Tothellim said goodbye to all his Frejjan friends and Leo took him with his airmobile to the shuttle. A new inner peace had come over him, a divine peace, and it enabled him to function. The captain had a tear in his eye when he greeted Tothellim and he had been very sad to hear of Emrak's death. Leo gave him a hug and asked him to stay in touch through the Internet and any message from him would be shared with Tothellim's friends on Frejja.   Tothellim promised to do so and the shuttle took off.

The return trip to Veehnia went fast and Tothellim and the captain had many talks during the voyage. He was a kind man with a warm heart. Logan and Heidi waited for him when he landed on Veehnia and it was good to see them. He had been gone four years and they were relieved he was finally home again. They took him to his house and stayed overnight. There was so much to catch up with and discuss and Logan and Heidi ended up staying a whole week in Tothellim's house. When they asked him what his plans were for the future, he replied he had no idea.

Rheo came over and he had done a good job maintaining the house. His touch was visible all over the house and Tothellim noticed he had repaired several defects in the house Tothellim had postponed doing. Rheo was very handy and could tackle almost anything. Tothellim was touched when he noticed the improvements and he knew Rheo was a true friend.

"Rheo, my boat is yours to keep. I have no use for it and I know you love boating. If I feel like going on the ocean I can always tag along, but the boat is your property from now on." Tothellim's boat was a beauty and large enough to spend a weekend on.

"Gosh, I don't know how to thank you. I don't deserve such a gift."

"If *anyone* deserves it, it's you, Rheo. You've done a marvelous job looking after my house all these years and I'm truly grateful. You're retired and now you have time to do all the boating and fishing you always wanted to do. Have fun with it."

A month went by and Tothellim felt more at ease. He still was not sure what to do with himself, but he had decided not to return to space. An idea started to form in his mind. As far as he knew, the flight school had no courses in planetary life and customs; perhaps he could write the course material and teach it at the school? It would be a useful course for pilots to take and he would enjoy teaching it. He contacted his former supervisor and presented his proposal and the supervisor showed great interest in the idea and asked Tothellim to go ahead. Over the next months, he was able to assemble the information he had saved about all the known planets in the universe, including planets he had not visited himself, and the course material was finished. It was a fascinating course and he knew it would fill up when it was offered.

Tothellim was right. The course filled up in two days and he was back at work part time. The pilots loved the course and it kept Tothellim busy and his mind occupied. His love of life returned and with it came inner peace.

***

Cooper declared to the citizens he was ready to step down as their president and suggested Volrex would make an excellent president. The constitution required an election must be held and anyone could run for election. The announcement hit the citizens hard and many expressed worry the society would go downhill. Cooper reminded the people he had served thirty-seven years and wanted to pursue other things in life. Volrex entered his name as a candidate on the list together with three other people, two of them women. The constitution was a variation of People Democracy and to use money to promote a candidate was illegal. The candidates were featured on the Internet and were free to explain how they would run the country. All the contenders were qualified and it was a tight race. Term limits had been added to the constitution and no president after Cooper could serve longer than ten years, two five-year terms.

Volrex won the race and was declared the new president and Cooper stepped down. He was ready. He had given many years to build Sorenia's society and he knew Volrex was more than qualified to serve as president. His intelligence and practical outlook on life as well as his substantial experience in all matters of space made him fully competent. Cooper felt liberated and all he wanted now was to sit back and reflect on life before he and Rosalie decided what to do next.

Volrex addressed the citizens after he was sworn in as president and made it clear he would continue to run the country following Cooper's principles. There was no need to change anything as Cooper had built a thriving planet from basically nothing. It was a good speech and the people trusted him. Volrex ended up serving two terms and became very popular among the voters and he deserved it.

Cooper and Rosalie spent a year vacationing on Sorenia. They had no plans, just took one day at the time, and using their airmobile they went from town to town. Neither of them had ever had the time to enjoy Sorenia's beautiful landscape and their vacations had usually been short. Most towns had little inns where they could stay. Towards the end of the year, they decided to join Halcyon on his ship for a trip to another planet.

***

Cooper and Rosalie were onboard Halcyon's ship on their way to Veehnia. The ship would land on Mineata in one month and they would transfer to a Mineatan ship, which would take them to Veehnia. The trip to Mineata was free, but they were paying passengers on the Mineatan ship. Sorenia did not trade with Veehnia, but Mineata did and offered twice a year passenger service to Veehnia on their cargo ships. Cooper and Rosalie would stay on Veehnia six months and then return to Sorenia.

The trip to Mineata went fast and they enjoyed visiting Halcyon on the Bridge. He loved his ship and one day he hoped Jilina would join him as copilot. She would graduate from flight school in a month and by the time he returned to Sorenia, she would be a licensed pilot. He realized, as so many pilots before him, if he wanted a wife, it would be best if she also was a pilot.

Cooper and Rosalie spent a week on Mineata and found it was a modern planet with a friendly population. They boarded the ship to Veehnia and the trip would take four months and they would pass through the fifteen-hour tunnel. The tunnel to Mineata was only an hour long and Rosalie found it unpleasant, but she was not afraid. She did, however, dread the fifteen-hour tunnel and she told Cooper she planned on lying in bed in their cabin while they passed through. Cooper laughed loudly, hugged her, and reassured her it was safe and the pilots were experienced. The ship had two of Leo's gravity chambers onboard and Rosalie worked out a few hours every day.

After two months' travel time they entered the tunnel and Rosalie endured the rollercoaster ride strapped into her bed. For safety reasons, no one was allowed to float around during a tunnel passage and all passengers had to be strapped into their seats. Short trips to the restroom were allowed. Rosalie sighed with relief when they came out of the tunnel like a bolt of lightning and the rest of the journey was only two months.

Tothellim, Tyler and Jayce waited for them when they landed with the shuttle. They had received Cooper's transmission sent from space. Rosalie knew who Tyler and Jayce were and was eager to meet them. Both of them were close to seventy years old and had not participated in long distance space trips for years, but were still flying domestically. With a lifespan of one hundred fifty years, they were not close to retirement for many years.

The three men were truly happy to greet Cooper and Rosalie and all of them continued to Tothellim's house. He insisted they stay in his house for the duration of their visit and Cooper graciously accepted his offer. The house was comfortable and roomy. Tyler and Jayce stayed two days and were fascinated to hear how Cooper had restarted growth on the planet and advanced it into a modern society. They remembered very well how shabby and run down the planet had been and watched with awe the holographic pictures Cooper had brought along of present day Sorenia. Everything was clean and orderly and crops were growing on fertile fields. They asked about the school system, medical care, mining, literacy rate among the people and the trade with Mineata.

"You deserve a medal, Cooper!" Tyler exclaimed and patted Cooper on his shoulder. Jayce agreed and added –

"When we left you on Sorenia, I had my doubts anyone could rescue that planet. It was a royal mess! Look what you turned it into. It's mind boggling."

Cooper just chuckled. He was a modest man and never promoted himself, but when he worked, he always gave his best.

Tyler and Jayce left and Tothellim worked at the school three days a week. The first month Cooper and Rosalie toured the local area and Rosalie saw the ocean for the first time. She loved it and Rheo took them out on the water several times with his boat. Rheo and Tothellim had both trained Cooper to become a pilot and he was also happy to meet Cooper again. Cooper rented an airmobile and he and Rosalie traveled all over Veehnia, often staying overnight in the countryside. They hiked in the mountains; Rosalie slept under the open sky while Cooper was next to her watching the stars; they saw herds of deer-like animals and even a glimpse of a bear. Their stay on Veehnia was delightful and the six months flew. It was time to return to Sorenia and Tothellim, Tyler and Jayce saw them off. It had been emotional for Cooper to see his home planet again and he asked Tothellim to visit Sorenia in the future. Tothellim had enjoyed their stay and to see a woman in the house again. He found Rosalie charming and enjoyed her humor and wit.

The return trip was uneventful and thanks to the gravity chambers Rosalie had not suffered much muscle loss. They had been gone a little over a year and Cooper had to figure out what to do with himself. Rosalie returned to her work as supervisor of the educational material for the university. Cooper was a mechanical engineer as well as a spaceship pilot and he wanted to invent artificial gravity on spaceships to make life easier onboard. He knew Leo's gravity chamber was a temporary solution. While traveling on Halcyon's ship, he had studied them carefully and felt centrifugal force to create gravity was not the answer. He favored a more natural solution mimicking the gravity felt on a planet. To invent natural gravity on a spaceship would be very difficult and was not within reach right now, so he put the project in the back of his mind. All modern spaceships with the gravity chambers installed also had a section of the galley as a gravity chamber to make traditional cooking possible. Without it, cooking was limited to heated freeze-dried foods, but with a galley with gravity a chef could produce almost anything that could be cooked on land.

Airmobiles and groundmobiles were imported from Mineata and very expensive. Only the affluent citizens could afford to buy one and Cooper decided to start a business manufacturing a combined airmobile and groundmobile. To reduce the cost and make it affordable, it would be a practical vehicle without luxury touches. The electronics had to be simplified so anyone could understand how to run the vehicle.

Cooper secured a short-term loan from the government and hired a contractor to build him a manufacturing plant. He also hired a team of engineers and together they set up the production line. The repetitive work was done by robots and humans would handle the rest. After a year, manufacturing started and soon vehicles were offered for sale at a fair price. Reyya came out of retirement and started working at the plant as chief financial officer. Cooper was pleased to have Reyya working with him again and he had full trust in his abilities. Reyya was in his seventies, but full of energy and with an active mind. He often introduced new ideas and saw shortcuts saving the company unnecessary expenses.

The company became a success and with such an affordable price tag, the vehicles sold as soon as they rolled out of the plant. Everyone wanted one and after a few years Cooper had repaid his loan to the government. He enjoyed running the plant and he was able to pay his employees a good salary and in return they gave their best at the plant. After a few years, he offered every employee a stake in the company and Reyya worked out a system that functioned well. All profits were shared with the employees and Cooper and Reyya paid themselves a fair, but not excessive, salary. Business was booming and the plant had to be expanded to meet demand.

Volrex and Cooper designed a detailed traffic system covering both ground and air and every buyer of a vehicle had to carefully study the rules and abide by them. Top speed of the vehicles was deliberately kept moderate to avoid fender benders and abuse. It worked and accidents were rare.

***

Jilina had graduated from flight school and was proud to be Halcyon's copilot. They flew the cargo ship back and forth to Mineata and occasionally to Ziggellus. It was an easy run and they both loved their ship. Jilina was Sorenia's first female pilot and with a father from Mineata, she had a special place in her heart for the planet.

Halcyon and Jilina were close friends and enjoyed working together. They were not romantically involved, but Halcyon was a practical man and knew if he wanted a wife, he should propose to Jilina. She was smart, pretty and fun to be with, but he was not in love with her. He asked himself if love was necessary for a good marriage. He knew few girls would want a husband who was gone for months at the time. Most pilots remained unmarried for that reason. He was sure his mother would look after their children, but he had doubts Jilina would accept a marriage proposal. He decided to wait and see and said nothing to anyone about the matter.

Celeste had recently married a colleague at the university and Cooper and Rosalie were happy for her and liked their son-in-law a lot.

CHAPTER 16

Vitzoll received a transmission from Rex sent from the Veehnian immigration ship stating he was free to pursue any career he wanted. Rex had petitioned the Veehnian government for release of their ownership of him and grant him independence. The government officials felt Rex had been loyal to them and worked for many years and deserved his freedom. When they heard he wanted to form a mercenary fleet and work with Rasufilus' son to learn the business, they were enthusiastic and told Rex he had their full support. All governments knew of Rasufilus and his impeccable work ethic and they also knew an additional mercenary crew was needed to keep law and order among the planets.

The Veehnian government offered Rex an interest free start-up loan to purchase the fighter ships he needed in addition to a long-term lease of a large field where he could park his ships and build houses for his pilots. The lease was moderately priced and very affordable. The field was located a distance away from populated areas and ensured no one could hear the ships land and depart. Rex gratefully accepted the offer and hired a contractor to build twenty houses and the necessary infrastructure for his compound.

Veehnia had a plant that manufactured fighter ships and Rex bought ten ships equipped with the latest weaponry and electronics and strong enough to pass through any of the tunnels. Tothellim helped him select twenty pilots, but half of them politely declined his offer. They knew it was a dangerous job and most of them were married and had children. Rex continued asking around and eventually he had hired twenty male pilots, six of them androids. The human pilots were unmarried and all were young. No female pilot had applied to work with the fleet.

Rex had asked Vitzoll for instructions and information about his mercenary fleet, fees to charge and any tips he was willing to pass on to get Rex started. Vitzoll replied with a large, detailed package and the

Veehnian captain received it on his return trip home and forwarded it to Rex as soon as he was through the tunnel to the Andromeda galaxy. It was a lot for Rex to study and think about. In one month, Rex would take delivery of his ships and the contractor was putting the finishing touches on his houses. He asked the newly hired pilots to come to his apartment and Tothellim and Rheo joined them. Together they went through Vitzoll's information package and worked out all the potential problems, but Rex knew he and his pilots would have to learn on the job and gain experience just by working. Rex was a fully trained soldier, but his pilots were not and had to be trained. They also needed to spend time with the flight simulator and learn how to use the weaponry onboard.

Rex and his crew moved into the houses and the fighter ships had been delivered. The ships were roomy and the two pilots sharing a ship had ample room to exercise and live on the ship without feeling crowded. The ships had velcro flooring but lacked Leo's gravity chamber. Rex planned to add them later on, but they were unaffordable at present. The weaponry installed on each ship was impressive to say the least and the electronics the latest available. Two-way translation devices were built in and loudspeakers and listening devices were part of the electronics. The ships had cloaking ability, an expensive but necessary feature.

The crew went daily to the flight simulators and took turns training while Rex posted an ad on the Interstellar Internet that a new mercenary fleet was available for hire. They needed to start working to pay off the loan to the government.

The first job offer was suspect and when Rex checked out the details, he knew the people trying to hire him were criminals and turned them down. The second offer came soon thereafter and was from a planet invaded by hostile aliens trying to force the government to accept them and their people as immigrants. They claimed their planet was dying and could not support life, but it turned out to be a lie and they were common criminals with plans to take over the planet and exploit the natural resources. The planet was not far from Veehnia and was an excellent opportunity to start working. Direct communication was possible and the alien government agreed to pay the fee to Rex in gold. Their own fleet was small and they needed reinforcement to overpower the invaders. Rex would take orders from their senior captain. He did not mind as they were all rookies, but emphasized he and his men preferred to spare lives when possible.

The mission was valuable and Rex and his men learned a lot. The captain was empathetic and none of the invaders was killed. They were overpowered and incarcerated and the mission ended successfully. Rex' fleet was used mostly as a show of force and they did not fire their weapons. They were paid promptly by the government and returned home.

While they waited for the next mission, Rex trained his pilots in warfare and discoursed on life on every planet he knew of. There were two workstations they used for supplies and he made agreements with one of the workers on each station to become his eyes and ears if he contacted them for a specific job. The snitches understood they would be well paid.

With ten ships in his fleet, Rex could only accept small jobs and he knew he would need at least twenty ships to have an impact on an enemy force. They fulfilled over a dozen small jobs and each time they gained experience and felt more confident.

Rex bought another ten ships and hired twenty more pilots, three of them women. The female pilots were well qualified and had been domestic pilots for several years, but were bored with the job. They were eager to work for Rex and went through the same hard training as the male pilots without complaining. All his pilots were unmarried and six were androids. The contractor built more housing and with twenty ships, Rex was ready to accept more demanding job offers.

His copilot was Elsa, born on Earth. Her parents had been looking for adventures and decided to emigrate from Earth and settle on Veehnia when she was ten years old. Elsa was slim but physically strong, nerves of steel and she had masculine traits. At times, she was tender and feminine, but when she was working, she was all business. Rex enjoyed her company and had full trust in her skills. She was an excellent chess player and often beat Rex at the game. When the ship was on autopilot, they had free time to do whatever they wanted. She was plain looking, but made up for it with an intriguing personality. Her light brown hair was waist long and kept in a ponytail.

A challenging job offer came in and Rex accepted it. A planet not too far from Veehnia, Bedentes, was in the midst of a civil war. The legally elected government had been ousted by an opposing force of citizens and the planet's armed forces had sided with the citizens against the legal government. The government was in hiding and had managed to transmit a message to Rex asking for help to be reinstated. They offered a very high fee as the job was dangerous and the mercenaries would have to bring down the armed forces and the new people running the planet without the help from the former government. The new government outnumbered Rex and his crew and Rex had to invent a strategy where tactics would determine the outcome rather than the size of his fleet. If the mission failed, the fee would be cut in half.

"We can't take sides in this war," Rex reminded his pilots. "We're hired to bring down the illegal government and reinstate the legal government. The citizens voted in that government and if they want a change, they'll have to hold an election and vote in a government of their choice."

Rex transmitted an encrypted message to the government he was planning his strategy and would return shortly when a plan of action had been worked out.

"We'll have to hit them simultaneously from several angles. I suggest we launch a deadly computer virus and immediately afterwards take out their fleet of fighter ships or at least as many as we can manage to blow up. Then we cut off their food supply and starve them out and lastly, we cut off their water. If all of it succeeds, it should bring them to their knees and, hopefully, capitulation. The whole mission is difficult, but with a bit of luck it may succeed." Rex looked at his pilots to see their reaction.

"The timing is crucial," Elsa said. "There can't be any delay in the onslaught. Each attack has to be launched rapidly or the whole thing will fall apart. We can't allow them time to recover."

The plan was accepted and they started to work on the details. Rex hired an android he knew to write the virus program and contacted the legal government to find out the best way to hack into the computer system. He also requested information where the fleet of fighter ships was parked, how the food supplies worked and the capital's access to drinking water. All the information was transmitted back to Rex and he found he had enough details to finalize the mission. He informed the government they were ready to go into action and would depart the following day. They responded they approved of the plan and wished them luck.

The travel time was only six weeks with two shortcut tunnels and they entered orbit with the ships cloaked. The same evening Rex hacked into the computer system and launched the virus. Before daybreak, Rex and Elsa and eleven additional ships took off cloaked and they had no trouble locating the area where most of the fighter ships were parked. Some of the ships were outside and some inside the hangars. They flew at low elevation. It was still dark and they did not see any guards outside. The government had informed them weaponized drones did not exist on the planet, a plus for Rex and his fleet.

"FIRE NOW!" Rex shouted and at full blast every weapon was used. The inferno was huge and the hangars and ships were all on fire and the explosions threw flames high up into the air. There was no response from the ground and Rex was unsure if the guards were alive. As quickly as they had arrived, Rex and his fleet were gone and soon back in orbit.

In the meantime, five ships were at the reservoir serving the capital with drinking water. The government had informed them that if they destroyed the connection to the water pipes, the city would run out of water within a few days. The connection would not be hard to repair and no long-term damage would be inflicted on the system. The planet had plenty of water and whatever spilled out was of no concern.

Under the cover of darkness, the cloaked ships fired and within minutes the water connection to the pipes was destroyed. They saw no one on the ground. The mission was complete and the ships returned to orbit.

The remaining three ships were hovering cloaked above the city and waited for the huge cargo drones to show up. The city was supplied early every morning with fresh foods and the drones were unmanned. It was daylight and without their cloaking ability, the ships would have run the risk of detection. All of a sudden, a fleet of eight drones appeared and the crew fired at close range hitting all of them. They exploded and blasted apart raining tiny pieces onto the planet's surface. A second fleet of drones arrived soon thereafter and they were also fired upon. The ships waited at a high elevation to see if more supply drones would come into view, but no more drones arrived and the ships quickly returned to orbit.

All the ships were now in orbit and Rex addressed the pilots on an encrypted channel.

"We may not have destroyed the entire fleet of fighter ships, so be prepared they may look for us here in orbit using fighter ships from another location. They may also use their cargo ships to come after us.

Remain cloaked and if anyone of you spot an enemy ship, use your built-in alarm system to notify all of us. If a ship appears, break orbit and fly out into space and we reassemble at a safe distance from the planet."

The sound of the alarm made the pilots jump and in the distance two cargo ships were visible firing their guns at random. All the ships flew out into space in an instant and the cargo ships were unaware how close they had been to Rex' fleet. The ships were cloaked, but every ship in Rex' fleet was visible on the instrument panel and each pilot knew exactly where the rest of the fleet was. They hovered in space for half a day and then went back into orbit. The cargo ships had returned to the surface.

"If the virus worked, their computer system is down," Rex announced to his crew using an encrypted channel. "They have no water and the food supply may be low. It appears we destroyed all their fighter ships as they sent their cargo ships after us. We wait another day and then make contact. By then, they may have their computers up and running."

The alarm sounded again and took them by surprise. The cargo ships were back aggressively firing non-stop. Rex' ships were in orbit in formation and the last ship was out of luck and was hit. It exploded in a fireball and the pilots were killed instantly. The rest of the ships made it out into space, but all of them were shocked. The ship that was hit had seen the cargo ships, but too late to escape.

"Let's honor our departed friends. Those who have faith, please say a prayer and the rest of us should wish them a safe journey to wherever they go after life ends," Rex declared when they had reassembled at a safe distance from the planet." He was shaken to the core and the unexpected loss of the two pilots was a rude awakening to the danger of mercenary work.

"We must take out their cargo ships. Before daybreak, we'll have to search for them. It's too risky to try to contact the former government. I'm sure the enemy is listening for transmissions. We split up into four groups and cover the whole planet. Let's spend the night here and try to get some sleep." Rex gave further instructions to his fleet how they should proceed the following day. They all knew it would be dangerous and the only protection they had was their cloaking ability.

Rex woke the pilots up several hours before dawn and the four groups took off hoping to find as many cargo ships as possible. The night vision technology on the ships was excellent and they only needed a small amount of natural light to detect objects on the surface. The whole planet had to be searched. Two of the groups found nothing, not a single cargo ship, and they returned to orbit. The other two groups found the locations where most of the ships were parked. The distance between the two areas was substantial and each group acted independently. One of the fields had eight ships and the other twelve.

Rex and Elsa and the other ships in their group descended quickly to one thousand feet elevation and they knew time was of the essence. Any hesitation and they would be shot down. They saw one guard looking up into the sky and he must have heard their engines. Rex fired a shot and the guard was dead. He always tried to spare lives, but Rex knew the guard would raise the alarm and call for help. He had no choice but to silence him.

"NOW, START FIRING!" Rex called out to Elsa and the other pilots in his group. While the ships were hovering, both pilots on each ship had a set of controls and they fired away until all eight cargo ships were burning and exploding, one after the other. The scene mirrored hell.

Rex revved up the engines and as fast as they had descended, they took off and were out of sight within seconds. A long-distance weapon shot off huge bullets and one of them whistled right past Rex' ship but missed target. A few seconds later, they were out of reach and at full speed they reached orbit and caught up with the rest of the fleet. Rex addressed the crew to follow him out into space and then reassemble.

"Our group fulfilled the mission. We found eight cargo ships and they're all destroyed. Only one life was lost in the process," Rex started. "Group two, please report!"

"Not a single cargo ship in our area."

"Group three, please report."

"Same as group two. Nothing."

"Group four?"

"We found twelve ships and destroyed them all. The ships were kept under guard and I regret to report we had to kill all ten of them. We felt there was no choice. If we had spared them, we couldn't have carried out our orders. Immediately after they were down, we hovered the ships and fired non-stop until all twelve ships were fireballs. We ascended without being shot at and ended our mission."

"Congratulations, to all of you. It's regrettable you had to terminate the guards, but I agree, there was no choice. We have a mission to complete and war is never pleasant. The most likely scenario is we have eliminated their entire fleet of fighters and cargo ships, so the enemy has no way of leaving the planet. They may have a few shuttles, but they can't do space travel with them. They have no water and limited food supply. They may have neutralized the virus we planted, but if they haven't, we still can't communicate with them. We stay right here overnight and I'm sure no one will come after us, but remain cloaked just in case. Eat your dinners and hit the sack."

The following morning, the fleet entered orbit and Rex initiated communication with the planet. They responded immediately.

"We are mercenaries hired by your legally elected government. My name is Rex. Please put your leader on the line so we can talk," Rex stated in a firm non-yielding voice.

"I'm Setterus, the leader of this planet. What the hell do you want?"

"Return ruling of the planet to the legal government. You have not been elected by the people. We will not leave until you step down and reinstate the legal government."

"Go to hell!"

Communication was broken and Rex told his pilots to remain in orbit and just wait them out. With no food and water, they would eventually have to resume communication. Rex realized they may collect water manually from the reservoir, but with thousands of people in the city needing water, the task would soon become overwhelming.

Two days later, they saw a shuttle nearing them in orbit and without second thoughts, Rex fired and the shuttle blew up. They were cloaked so the shuttle was unaware it was nearing them. Rex and the pilots knew the shuttle would fire at them and after that incident, the leaders did not send up any more shuttles.

Rex decided he and Elsa would risk looking for cargo drones again delivering food to the city and they took off the next morning. They flew over the city area at a high elevation to avoid being heard and after an hour they did see a fleet of six drones delivering food supplies to the city. Quickly, they descended and fired eliminating all six drones. The strike was executed so fast that anyone watching from the ground would only see a mass of flames up in the sky and Rex' ship was too fast to detect with the naked eye. They were soon back in orbit.

Rex was unsure if the new government would risk another drone delivery under armed escort with shuttles, but he was willing to make another attack and Elsa agreed. The rest of the pilots offered to assist and Rex chose two ships. Three ships would easily take out six drones and several shuttles and two days later, they made another run. They circled the city at high elevation and were rewarded by detecting the target. Eight cargo drones escorted by four shuttles, most likely well-armed, were on their way to the city. Rex had rehearsed the battle strategy with the crew and the pilots knew exactly what to do.

"Shuttles first, NOW!" Rex shouted and the three ships dive-bombed at full speed while the copilots fired away with devastating accuracy at the shuttles at close range. The shuttle crew had no chance and were not even aware of their approach as the ships were cloaked. All four shuttles went up in flames and within a minute Rex and his pilots returned and took out all the drones. The sky was an inferno of exploding ships and drones and in a blink Rex and his ships were gone. The tremendous speed of Rex' ships combined with the flying skills and bravery of all his pilots made his attacks so lethal to his enemies. Moreover, the computer guided weaponry on the ships were state of the art with tremendous power.

Back in orbit, Rex briefed the other pilots and told them to sit tight and wait. It took another day and the radio silence from the planet was broken.

"We surrender," Setterus yelled into his translation device. "Inform the government to return to the city and we'll step down. The armed forces agree with our decision. The government has nothing to fear. We won't shoot anyone."

"Message received. We'll notify the government," Rex replied.

All the pilots celebrated. It had been a difficult mission and lasted longer than Rex and the pilots had anticipated. The loss of two pilots and a very expensive ship was also a tremendous blow no one had expected.

Rex transmitted a full report to the government and explained they would remain in orbit until they received confirmation from them Setterus and his people were out and the armed forces were under their command. The government responded quickly.

"Well done, congratulations. We'll notify you immediately after Setterus and his people have been arrested. We realize there is a chance we walk into a trap, but we're willing to proceed anyway."

The next day the government sent a message to Rex asking all of them to descend to the surface and spend a few days resting on the planet. All had gone according to plan and it was totally safe for Rex and his pilots to land. Setterus and his people as well as the leaders of the armed forces were safely in jail.

Rex and the pilots landed and parked the ships on a field outside the government complex. A large bus picked them up and took them to a nearby hotel. Rex and Elsa were picked up with a groundmobile and the president and his advisors were waiting for them. The president was a tiny man with a humanoid body, mostly human features and short, reddish-brown hair. The president shook hands with Rex and Elsa and immediately expressed his sincere gratitude that the mission had been executed so well. He also expressed his condolences to Rex over the loss of two pilots.

"We will of course compensate you for your ship in addition to the fee we agreed on. Did the deceased pilots have any dependents?"

Rex replied they were not married.

"If children had been involved, we would have offered financial support for them, but as the pilots weren't married, all we can do is to extend our condolences to their parents. Please give our message to them."

The president explained how the coup had occurred and how he and his cabinet had escaped from the city. There was no mercenary fleet available until one of his advisors had seen Rex' posting on the Interstellar Internet and they decided to hire him. The president stated there is no way they themselves could have overthrown Setterus and they would recommend Rex and his fleet as a first-rate mercenary group.

Rex smiled graciously, gave a small bow and said –

"Thank you, Mr. President, your endorsement of our fleet is truly appreciated and we'll do our best to earn it."

Rex and his pilots rested at the hotel for a few days and their fee and payment for the lost ship was paid in gold. The ships were resupplied free of charge for the trip back to Veehnia. They left the planet and returned home. The mission had been a unique learning experience and the president did post a message on the Internet praising the efficiency of Rex and his crew.

Rex met with the families of the two pilots and conveyed the condolences from the president. They were heartbroken, but knew their sons had chosen the job themselves and knew the dangers involved.

Tothellim and Rheo were very interested to hear about the mission and Rex also sent a report to Vitzoll. He responded he was sad to hear about the loss of his two pilots, but admired how Rex had handled the assignment.

The fee was substantial and Rex was able to pay his first installment to the Veehnian government after he had paid his pilots. He also ordered a new ship and hired two pilots. They were told they replaced two deceased pilots and their job as mercenaries would be highly dangerous, but they agreed to the terms and accepted the job. Rex started their training right away.

CHAPTER 17

Halcyon and Jilina worked well together and enjoyed each other's company. They were good friends. When the ship was on autopilot, Halcyon decided to be forthright with Jilina.

"We've been working together now for a couple of years and I'm truly fond of you. I like being around you and would be honored if you agreed to be my wife. I'm not in love with you, but our friendship may be strong enough to ensure a good marriage. Am I crazy?"

"Certainly not," Jilina said and laughed good-heartedly. "My thoughts exactly. I'm also fond of you and you're my best friend for sure, but I 'm not in love with you. We both know no one wants to marry a pilot who disappears into space for months at the time. I want kids and I know you do, too, so let's go for it and my answer is *yes*. My mom would help us raise the kids; I know that. Let's consider 'falling in love' our work in progress."

Halcyon held her tight. Jilina was a smart and fun person and he had no regrets. She was also very pretty with a nice figure.

"Would you be ready to get married when we return to Sorenia?" he asked.

"Definitely," Jilina said.

Back on Sorenia, Jilina confided in her mother she was not in love, but felt close to Halcyon. Both her parents were hesitant and asked her if she really thought those feelings were sufficient to make the marriage last. At the same time, they knew very few men would commit themselves to a wife who was away most of the time. They told Jilina they did not approve, but the decision was hers to make.

Halcyon also told his parents. Cooper and Rosalie had married for love and reacted the same as Volrex and his wife. Would it last? Cooper and Rosalie were close and still very much in love and Rosalie would never have accepted a marriage proposal from a man she did not love.

They let Halcyon know he had to make the final decision, but they were against it.

"In the future, if you meet another woman you fall in love with, do you just dump Jilina?" Cooper asked.

"I would stay with Jilina," Halcyon replied.

"Feelings are powerful," Cooper continued. "If you stay with her out of loyalty, but fantasize about the other woman, your life will become total misery. If you have kids, that's another complication. My advice is to wait a while and think it over. Don't rush into this. You're only thirty-four years old. There is time."

Halcyon and Jilina went alone to the office where a government administrator officiated the wedding ceremony. They both knew their parents disapproved of their marriage and felt it was best to spare them the experience. Neither of them had second thoughts and felt their friendship was strong enough to support a lasting union. Jilina moved into Halcyon's house and they had two weeks until they had to be back on their ship. Both of them notified their parents they were married using their communicators. Volrex and Cooper were longtime friends and had deep respect for each other. Volrex sent a message to Cooper they should support the marriage and just move on. He and his wife were willing to help raising their children and perhaps Cooper and Rosalie would also help out. Cooper replied he and Rosalie agreed.

***

Halcyon and Jilina were happy, actually as happy as if they had been madly in love. There was nothing they could not discuss and neither of them had psychological problems. They had both had easy childhoods and loving parents and their lack of mental hang-ups had resulted in two stable, confident adults.

Sorenia had only four artificial wombs and Jilina reserved one unit for herself. She could not carry a baby and work at the same time and the second choice was to use a unit at a Mineata hospital. That was Plan B and more complicated, even though they made the trip to Mineata every few months. It worked out as Jilina had hoped. She conceived a few months after they were married and when the embryo was ready to be transferred, the womb was available. It was a girl and they named her Aster.

Both sets of grandparents went every week to check on the baby and Reyya and Littiana were also frequent visitors. Biologically, the baby was Reyya's granddaughter.

It was an exciting day when Halcyon and Jilina brought Aster home. Her grandpa Volrex was Mineatan, but Aster had no fur and looked mostly like her dad. Volrex and his wife and Cooper and Rosalie had worked out a schedule where they would take turns raising the baby while Jilina was working and they all thought it would be fun to care for the baby.

Jilina stayed home three months to take care of her baby and the grandparents were frequent visitors. When she returned to work, she knew the baby would get expert care by the grandparents and she did not feel anxiety when she handed the baby to her mother. She was home and had plenty of time to raise the baby and Volrex was happy to do his part when he came home from work. His first term as president would end in a year and he intended to run for a second term. Rosalie had help from Littiana and she would come over any time Rosalie called her on her communicator. Littiana considered the baby her granddaughter. When Cooper came home from the plant, he was delighted to carry Aster around and relished his role as grandpa. Cooper had wanted more children, but Rosalie felt two was enough. Having Aster in the house was a joy for Cooper. Reyya was also a proud grandfather and enjoyed his time with Aster.

***

Earth citizens were used to spaceships coming and going from Mars, Frejja and Veehnia. Earth was at peace and the citizens of all countries were pleased with their standard of living. No one starved, work was plentiful and most services were free in all countries. Hostilities and wars were a thing of the past. Earthlings were lulled into a sense of security.

It was a sunny spring morning and the sky filled with large spaceships. They were not familiar looking and it was obvious they were not from any of the known planets. About twenty hovered over The Americas and another twenty over Europe and also over The Far East. Strangely enough, they appeared to be passenger ships, not fighters, and the design was a mix of a standard saucer type and the elongated type the Peturuns used. The World Government immediately contacted the Venusians for consultations.

One of the ships landed outside the White House in one of the large parks that had replaced the former housing areas. It was a gigantic ship, larger than any ship people on Earth had ever seen. The rest of the ships hovered at about ten thousand feet elevation. An exit door opened on the side of the ship and a long staircase gently floated out. Four humanoid men climbed out dressed in tan uniforms and were apparently able to breathe oxygen. The president, his advisors and four generals arrived in a large groundmobile to find out the reason why the aliens had landed on Earth. They drove out to the aliens and exited the groundmobile. The president held a two-way translation device.

"Welcome to Earth," he managed to say even though he felt panicky inside. "I'm President Thorson, the leader of the country called The Americas. Why are you here and where do you come from?"

The humanoids were handsome and their faces were mostly human. They had large eyes, larger than humans', their noses and mouths looked the same as humans', the ears were slightly elongated and their heads a little bigger than humans'. They had no hair and their skin was light tan. Their facial features were delicate and refined and they exuded dignity and self-respect. Two of the men had dark blue eyes and the other two hazel-colored eyes.

"Thank you, President Thorson," the leader said. "I'm Zerventos, captain of our fleet of ships, and we come from planet Nuvirenn in the Milky Way galaxy. We speak English. Have no fear, we're here in peace."

President Thorson invited the men to the White House and when all of them were seated, Zerventos gave an explanation.

"Our ancestors were humans from planet Earth and a long time ago, our people landed here on Earth and returned to our planet with our ships full of humans. These humans lived before your recorded history and you may refer to them as 'ancient civilizations'. They were more advanced than you are now. We're half humans and we'll show you images how our people look like. There are not many of them left as almost all of us are half human. We're hoping to return to our planet with as many humans as our ships can seat. The last hundred years our women haven't been able to have many children and our population has decreased to less than half. We invite men and women to settle on our planet and in return we offer them a life in luxury, increased brain capacity and a lifespan of about three hundred years. We've found a way to regenerate a person's cells and prolong life threefold and the person will not suffer from diseases or lowered stamina. I'm one hundred and sixty years and considered young."

"I'm truly amazed, Captain Zerventos," President Thorson exclaimed. "I don't mean to be disrespectful, but you need humans for reproduction, if I understand you correctly. With your advanced society, can't you improve your birth rate without bringing humans to your planet?"

"No, there is a problem with our genes. We must have new blood and the people coming to our planet would, hopefully, marry our young men and women and reproduce. The women all use the artificial womb, so each pregnancy is easy and all labor and housework are done by androids. Our society is more advanced than yours and I'm sure your people will find our technology interesting. Anyone who wants to can attend classes and become trained in whatever field they want. It's free. Your people would have all the comforts of life and they can choose to work or not to work. Our doctors will adjust their genes and with minimal medical interference, they can renew the cells in your people and prolong their lives. We will show holographic images of life on our planet so your citizens can choose for themselves whether to settle on our planet. We will, of course, not force anyone. Our food supply is excellent and sports and recreational activities are plentiful. There are four seasons on Nuvirenn and the winters have enough snow to allow skiing, which we know is popular here on Earth. Boating is also common and our people often go fishing on the ocean. There are wild herbivore animals on our planet, but no carnivores, so it's totally safe to go anywhere on the planet."

Zerventos was offered to display images of his home planet and to set up a recruiting office in one of the government buildings. His fleet of ships were in orbit until enough people had signed up to emigrate to Nuvirenn. Each ship could seat five hundred people and the travel time to Nuvirenn was seven months with three long tunnels to pass through.

The Venusians had issued a statement announcing the people from Nuvirenn were fully trustworthy and sincere. People flocked to the recruiting office and watched all the images of the planet. It was the same size as Earth with one ocean, a large mountain chain and enough rain to make the planet green and attractive looking. The current population was only half a billion. The native people were typical alien, about five feet tall, thin and with large eyes, wide cheekbones and no hair. They were not bad looking, but the mixed people were better looking and many were very handsome. After only a week, one thousand people had signed up. They were lured by the promise of a long life and an easy lifestyle free of diseases. Life on Earth was considered very good, but there were always people who were eager to try something new. Food was similar to what people ate on Earth and housing was more elegant than most people could afford on Earth. Nuvirenn was an affluent planet and traded their valuable natural resources with other planets.

Captain Zerventos was pleased when he realized the people on Earth were very enthusiastic to settle on his planet and within a month ten thousand people had signed up. Most were young and unmarried, but there were around fifty families with children who had also signed up. They were welcomed as well and the children would, hopefully, one day marry a native.

The twenty ships under Captain Zerventos' command departed and carried ten thousand people from Earth to a new life on a planet no one had heard about just a few weeks ago. Direct communication was not possible and future messages would have to be transmitted from spaceships in transit and close to Earth.

The ships visiting Europe and The Far East had also departed with every seat taken and all together thirty thousand Earth citizens had left to face a new future. The captains of each fleet had told the president of the three countries they would return one more time, perhaps twice, and extend invitations to people on Earth to emigrate. The global population on Earth was four billion people and had not increased for years. Earth was by no means overpopulated, but if people wanted to leave, they had free will to do so and no government wanted to meddle in the citizens' decisions.

CHAPTER 18

Alma's sister Helga was onboard Captain Zerventos' ship and she was a scarred twenty-eight-year-old girl. Her soul was still aching from the memory of her parents lying dead on the floor and the abuse she had endured by her father growing up. She had spent lots of time trying to find Alma, her older sister, to no avail as Alma had used a fake name and there was no way to find her. Helga knew she was probably living on Frejja or Earth2, but it was not for sure and she did not want to go to a planet and find out her sister was not there, so she had given up trying to find her. The offer to go to Nuvirenn free of charge gave her a chance to leave Earth and the memories behind and start a new life.

The psychiatric help she had received after her parents' death had helped some, but she still felt haunted, lonely and tormented. She had lived in a foster home until she was eighteen years old and her foster parents had been kind, but Helga's heart was frozen and she had been unable to open her heart and receive their kindness. She left as soon as she found a job and a tiny apartment. She had no friends and had never had a boyfriend and she often had the feeling she was wasting away with no purpose in life. Sometimes she was tempted to end her life, but lacked the courage.

The spaceship did not feel crowded and the five hundred passengers learned to hold themselves down with the help of all the handrails. Helga had never been on a spaceship and found it fascinating. She had her own private cabin and bathroom. It was very small, but she was grateful she did not have to share with anyone. The food was good and the crew serving the passengers were all androids. Helga often had conversations with one of them and learned a lot about her new planet. She knew it was expected of her to marry a man from Nuvirenn and she was openminded about it and hoped she would find someone she would be able to love. Instinctively, she knew it was the only way she would heal.

The three tunnels were long and each tunnel took almost a whole day to pass through. All the passengers had been thoroughly prepared by the androids and no one was afraid. They knew it would shake and vibrate a lot. Some chose to strap themselves down to their beds and some preferred to stay in their seats and endure the shaking. Helga was lying in her bed each time they went through a tunnel and the straps lessened the vibration.

At long last the seven months were over and the twenty ships landed on an enormous field on Nuvirenn. They had flown in formation the whole distance to their home planet and Helga had watched them in awe through the windows. As each ship exited the three tunnels, it had circled until all the ships were through and then the ships continued in formation as a group. As they descended, she noticed the planet was lovely looking and she felt she would be happy here.

She climbed down to the surface and the gravity was a little less than on Earth. She felt wobbly on her legs even though she had participated in all the exercise classes led by the androids to preserve muscle mass. The air was fresh and easy to breathe. It was a sunny spring day and the trees had just opened their leaves. All the passengers were taken by large buses to a hotel and they would stay there until each of them had been assigned a private house and employment, if they wanted to work. The people were kind, welcoming and rather good looking. Their eyes had such an intelligent look and the people were dignified. Some of them had hair. Helga was an attractive girl and some of the native people complimented her on her long, dark blond hair that reached to her waist.

It was soon Helga's turn to go through the paper process and when she was asked if she wanted to work, she said yes. Their native language was English so communication was easy. She had no formal degree and had worked in a building producing vegetables using the hydroponics system. Together with five robots, she had overseen production of the crops and she felt safe working there. She could not handle interacting with too many people, it scared her, and the robots were just enough for her to deal with. They were non-threatening and kind and watching the plants grow from seed to mature plants was emotionally rewarding.

"There's a job opening in the countryside that may be right for you. It's on a privately owned farm growing grain crops and the owner is looking for an assistant to run the computers. The whole farm is automated and run from the farmer's office. He also produces milk, but the milking process is carried out by worker robots. The farmer needs someone looking over the process to ensure cleanliness is maintained at all times and also to check on the health of the cow udders on a daily basis. You will be trained by the farmer himself. It's a healthy lifestyle and I've seen images of the farm. It is located in a scenic area of our planet and very tranquil."

Helga's heart jumped with excitement and she immediately accepted the job. She did not ask about salary or lodging, it was not important, the idea of working with animals and living in the country was a dream come true.

"The pay is generous and you'll live in the farm house with the farmer. He isn't married and I hope that fact won't bother you. He is a gentleman and the housework is done by two androids that do all the work in the house and also maintain a large vegetable garden."

The following day, Helga was taken by airmobile to the farm and it was located in a remote area of the planet. The scenery was lovely with planted farm fields stretching as far as the eye could see. A corral with ten cows grazing was also visible and the farmer's home was spacious and inviting. A distance from the home was a lake that looked rather big. No other home was visible and when Helga looked around, she saw rolling hills with stands of deciduous trees here and there, like little oases to heal a broken soul like hers. She sighed with happiness; it was home.

The door burst open and the farmer ran out with a welcoming smile. He was a young, nice-looking man with short brown hair, a mix, and his kind eyes looked at her with approval.

"Welcome, Helga, what a pleasure to meet you. I'm Settie," he greeted her. He shook her hand with enthusiasm and grabbed her suitcase as the airmobile left.

The inside of the house was large and nicely furnished, very comfortable. The two android maids came out from the kitchen and shook hands with her and welcomed her to the house.

"We're Monna and Nita," one of them said. Helga observed they were more advanced than the models she had seen on Earth and it was almost impossible to distinguish whether they were humans or androids. They smiled at her and looked pleased to see her. Helga felt emotional inside. A feeling of immense gratitude came over her and she felt a touch of peace, a feeling she had only experienced when she worked with the plants in the hydroponics building.

"Please have dinner ready for Helga and me in an hour," Settie told the maids and they nodded and went back to the kitchen. "I'll show you your room, Helga. Please follow me."

On the second floor, Settie opened the door to a large bedroom that was comfortably furnished. It had a private bathroom.

"Just come down when you're ready. I'll be in the living room."

Helga unpacked her suitcase and changed into a skirt and blouse. She brushed her long, thick hair and pinned it back with two barrettes. Her legs were still weak from the space travel and she knew more exercise was needed to regain her strength.

Settie waited for her and they sat down and talked. He told her he had inherited the farm from his parents and they lived in the city now, at least for a while. They wanted a new experience and had decided to hand over the farm to their only son. His mother had not been able to have any more children after he was born and they were relieved Settie wanted to continue running the farm. He was fifty-two years old, but did not look a day older than Helga and he had never been married.

Helga told him briefly why she had left Earth and he was shocked to hear how her parents had died, Alma's disappearance and Helga's decision to also leave Earth behind and start a new life somewhere far away. He immediately understood Helga had emotional scars and was fragile. A protective feeling came over him and that hour they spent before dinner was the first step of their bonding. Settie looked mostly human with a touch of the native alien look, but Helga found him quite attractive. He was quick-witted, compassionate and funny.

The dinner was very tasty and Helga had a healthy appetite. Settie smiled when he noticed how she appreciated her food.

The following month Settie trained Helga and he was pleased to see how fast she picked up all the details of the job she was supposed to do. Helga was intelligent and found her duties easy but fun. She oversaw the milk production and bonded with the cows, always giving them a hug after milking and the cows looked at her with affection. They knew Helga loved them. The milk was picked up daily by a cargo drone. Her computer work was a little more time-consuming to learn, but she mastered it after a few weeks giving Settie more time to look over his farm machinery with his robots assisting him. He was pleased with her work and hoped she would never leave.

They often walked to the lake and swam in the clear water. There were no people around and the lake was partly owned by Settie. A corner of it was on his property. The closest neighbor was one hour away using an airmobile, so the farm was definitely in an isolated area.

"Would you be interested in learning how to ride a horse?" Settie asked.

"I would love to, of course," Helga replied.

"I've always wanted to have a horse for riding and there are still horses on this planet. In the past, they were common, but most people prefer their airmobiles and there aren't many horses left. My closest neighbor has two horses we can buy and we'll learn how to ride together."

Settie finalized the purchase with the neighbor using his communicator and the following day a large cargo drone delivered the tranquillized horses hanging in two sturdy slings. The neighbor was accompanying the drone in his airmobile. Helga had to giggle when she saw the sight. The drone lowered the horses gently and the neighbor jumped out and gave each horse an antidote to the tranquillizer. Within minutes they jumped up and looked around. The neighbor took hold of the lead ropes and turned to Helga.

"I'm Vomerus and it's a pleasure to see a woman here. There are so few people in this area. My wife and I and our daughter would love to have you visit our farm."

"Thank you, of course I want to," Helga responded. She observed Vomerus was not a mix but a full native. Settie told her later that his wife was also a native and they had wanted to have more children, but it had not worked out that way. Fertility was a medical problem on the planet.

Helga found Vomerus pleasant to talk to and he stayed for dinner. His farm was about the same size as Settie's and they grew only grain crops. When they said goodbye, Helga assured him she would visit.

The summer was coming to an end and Helga had already spent five months at the farm. She felt emotionally nurtured by her new lifestyle and her memories of Earth slowly lost importance. She was healing faster than Alma had done. She and Settie had learned how to ride their horses together and the robots did a good job taking care of them. They had visited Vomerus and his family twice and Helga enjoyed meeting his daughter Trenna. She had promised her parents to take over the farm when they retired, but with no husband it would be a lonely life and she confided in Helga she would love to have a husband from Earth. Helga told her the ships were scheduled to make two more trips to Earth and each time they returned with thirty thousand passengers. If her father advertised for a male farm helper, perhaps he would turn out to be a suitable husband for her. Trenna was pleasant looking, but Helga was unsure if a man from Earth would find her attractive enough to share his life with. Those thoughts she kept to herself.

Settie proposed to Helga and she said yes right away. He was so kind, so intelligent and caring about her and she was in love with him. Settie had been in love with Helga from day one and using their airmobile, they traveled to the closest city and applied for a marriage contract. Religion did not exist on the planet, but spiritualism was strong among the citizens. Settie had a strong faith and Helga was openminded. She knew her father's religious beliefs were insanity, but her heart was not closed to spirituality. Their trip to the city took three hours with the airmobile, so it was quite a distance away.

Their marriage contract had no expiration date and she felt peace and happiness when Settie put the ring on her finger. She knew she had the best husband she could ever find and the scars in her soul were fading away.

Their married life was all Helga had dreamed about and she never tired of Settie's company. They both wore implants to boost cognition, but Settie was much more advanced than Helga as his people were ahead in awareness and consciousness compared to people from Earth. His people had used spaceships when Earth was a Stone Age planet. Settie taught Helga so much, both practical and spiritual matters, and their bond and devotion to each other were strong. His parents came to visit from the city and Helga liked them right away. They were truly pleased to see Settie married and embraced Helga with smiling faces.

Helga was fertile and the first baby was on the way to Settie's surprise. He was so used to hear about fertility problems among his people that he was slightly shocked when Helga whispered in his ear she was expecting. At the end of her third month, they traveled to the city and the baby was transferred to the artificial womb.

Monna and Nita helped Helga furnish a nursery. All supplies the farm needed, including groceries, were delivered by a cargo drone from the city. There were no stores in the area.

The firstborn son was finally home and they named him Peter after Helga's paternal grandfather, who had been a kind and loving man and the opposite of his insane son, Helga's father. Helga did not nurse Peter as the baby formula was of outstanding quality. Settie was a proud father and enjoyed feeding the baby his milk. Helga relished being a mother and with two androids doing all the work, she could take as much time as she wanted to just be with the baby and hold him.

***

Vomerus had followed Helga's advice and a man from Earth now worked on their farm. He was a young, pleasant looking man from China, Jianyu, and just like Helga, he fell in love with the area. Trenna found him attractive and to her surprise, he seemed to feel the same for her. It was happy news when Settie and Helga were told Trenna and Jianyu were married. Vomerus and his wife were relieved to see Trenna with a solid husband by her side and they had secretly worried how she would run the farm all alone. Now they could turn over the farm any time they wanted to the young couple and pursue other things in life. Jianyu appeared to truly love Trenna and Helga noticed his affection for her. She felt happy for Trenna.

Settie had told Helga she needed to visit the hospital in the city to have her cells renewed and her genes adjusted. The doctors would also improve her brain capacity. The process would take two days and Settie had been through the procedure twice and told her it was easy.

Settie went with her and the medical procedure was performed without problems. Afterwards, Helga found she could think so much faster and marveled at the result. The doctors had found a way to remove old cells and regenerate the whole system. This knowledge was unique to Nuvirenn and they had discovered it. Settie was not sure how many planets were aware of the technique and how well it worked to prolong life. It had been invented a long time ago and was appreciated by all the citizens. The doctors had told her she would be fertile until the age of one hundred and fifty years.

CHAPTER 19

The last five years since Rex had executed the mission to reinstate the elected government on planet Bedentes, the mercenary fleet had been swamped with work. They could not accept all assignments and Rex was adamant his crew had to have at least a month rest time between each mission. Until recently, none of his pilots were married and Rex knew not many women would want to devote their lives to a husband who was seldom home. He had three female pilots hired and two of them had married the human copilot they usually teamed up with. The androids were not married. Rex himself was in love with Elsa and found her personality energizing, almost hypnotizing. She was a quick-thinking pilot with fast reflexes and her command over the ship was superb. Rex was unsure if she would be willing to share her life with an android and had delayed proposing. What he did not know was that Elsa adored him and had decided to take action. She was somewhat masculine, but her yearning to become a wife and mother was rock solid and Rex was the man of her choice. To become a mother would involve a donor, but she put that issue on the back burner for the time being.

Rex and Elsa were between assignments and Rex was keeping Elsa company while she ate her dinner. She enjoyed cooking and Rex smiled as she was eating her dinner with gusto. She had no hang-ups and never pretended to be what she was not. Elsa was one of a kind and a connoisseur of life.

"I'm glad you're willing to keep me company, Rex," Elsa started. "I enjoy your company."

"Enough to keep me around forever?" Rex asked in a teasing voice.

"Till death do us part, my dear," Elsa said and laughed.

"Would you consider marrying an android?"

Elsa got up from the table and put her arms around Rex' neck.

"The sooner the better, yes, I'm all yours."

Rex laughed and lifted her up. His feelings were as intense as a biological man's and he hugged her and kissed her.

The following week they were married and Elsa's parents and sister, Hanna, were the only guests. All of them liked Rex and were not taken aback by the fact he was an android. Marriages between humans and androids were not common, but they did occur and were fully accepted.

Elsa moved in with Rex and they skipped a honeymoon trip. Elsa faced everything in life with enthusiasm and her wedding night was no exception. She found Rex so human she forgot most of the time he was an android. He kept her company during dinner and would lie down a few hours every night until Elsa was asleep, always holding her hand. He did not need to sleep, of course, and spent the rest of the night doing research, checking over job offers and learning new skills. He always woke her up with a breakfast tray and was learning how to cook. This was a new skill he had never before even thought about, but breakfast in bed made Elsa feel like a queen and Rex enjoyed seeing her happy face. Elsa was a good cook, but when Rex offered to make dinner, she always accepted with gratitude. Eventually, he learned the basics of cooking and did not mind it. They were very much in love.

***

A new job offer came in and it was time to return to work. One of the workstations had been robbed and the theft had been very profitable for the criminals. It appeared they had been tipped off as they made their hit just before the workstation had scheduled to deposit their gold in one of the banks on the surface. The station orbited a large inhabited planet and only the two owners knew when there was excess money onboard. Obviously, they would not rob themselves, so one of the employees must be the informer. Rex knew from experience it could be almost impossible to find a gang of criminals and many criminal gangs were dashing between planets and workstations playing cat and mouse with legal authorities. The fee was very generous and Rex accepted the job telling the two owners he could not guarantee he and his crew would find the gang.

Rex and Elsa departed alone on a reconnaissance mission and left the other pilots on Veehnia. It was only two months' travel time to the workstation thanks to three short tunnels and the trip was easy.

They arrived and docked with the rotating station and entered it. The gravity was light, but enough so they could walk with relative ease. It was a humongous metal world of walkways, restaurants, hotel, gambling casino, holodeck, auditorium and various workshops for repairs. Many races of humanoids walked around and Elsa observed them with her standard curiosity. Rex was more experienced and had seen more aliens than Elsa and did not scrutinize them the way Elsa did. He could not help but laugh when he peeked at her. They found the owners' office and entered. The two men were inside and they had seen Rex' ship arrive. They were Morekians.

"Rex, I presume," one of them said in broken English and Rex nodded. He introduced Elsa and they sat down.

"We're the owners and I'm Zakkarim and my partner's name is Ijondelli. The value of the gold stolen from us is worth millions in Cosmic Currency and we have no lead whatsoever. Someone onboard may have figured out when we have gold on the station and tipped off the criminals for a fee. It could also be someone on the planet, probably working at the bank we use, who knew when we were planning to deposit. I doubt any crew member on our workstation is involved as we do background checks on all our employees before we hire them. I personally believe the tip to the gangsters came from someone working at the bank. Ijondelli here is not so sure the crew is innocent and wants you to question the crew also."

"There is a famous case involving a hit on a workstation orbiting planet Earth's Moon, where the informer was the workstation's cook. We have to assume anyone can be guilty," Rex said slowly and philosophically.

"I heard of that case," Zakkarim said and nodded. "It's well known."

"Elsa and I will stay a few days here and start the investigation. Then we take it from there. We'll brief you before we leave, but there's a chance we won't be able to find them."

"Please try," Zakkarim said.

Rex and Elsa checked into the hotel and Elsa called room service and ordered her dinner. Rex went to the bar hoping to find a bartender he could make a deal with. Bartenders were known to overhear many secret conversations. Two worked the bar and Rex pushed a gold coin over to the bartender when he was asked what he wanted to drink. There was no one sitting close to him.

"I want information about the theft of the gold. Do you have anything?"

The bartender, a mix of several races, quickly put the coin in his pocket and whispered "Cabin forty-three, tonight at midnight".

Rex nodded and quickly left. He did not want to be seen talking to the bartender. Elsa had finished her dinner and Rex told her he had made an initial contact. At midnight, he went alone to the bartender's cabin and he was expected.

"I'm Bo-Bonn. I haven't heard any rumor the informant is a crew member," he said in a whispering voice. "Personally, I suspect the bank. I'm planning to spend a few days on the surface next week and I know someone working at the bank. I'll check with him if he knows anything."

"I'm part of the investigation team and a mercenary. Call me Rex. If you give me a tip that leads to the capture of the gang, I'll pay you ten gold coins. Do you have an account in the Cosmic Bank?"

Bo-Bonn nodded and gave Rex his account number. He had heard of Rex' mercenary business and trusted him. Rex handed his card to Bo-Bonn with his encrypted Internet address to his communicator.

Rex and Elsa left the workstation and continued to another workstation that was a combination fuel station and supply station. Modern ships were fueled by Natural Energy, but the old ships still used traditional fuel. This workstation supplied ships with everything they needed for extended space travel and there was nothing they could not supply. They even had shuttles and airmobiles in stock. They also orbited an inhabited planet. Rex bought some supplies even though they did not need anything, but it was a way to make contact. The clerk that took their order was an elderly man with an alert look.

"Want to make some money?" Rex asked him in a low voice. "I'm ready to do business with someone who is discreet and can keep a secret."

"You found him," the man said and smiled. "I take it you look for an informant. I'll be your ears if you pay me well."

Rex explained who he was and that he was investigating the hit on the workstation. The clerk had heard of the crime through the Internet and Rex asked him to be on the lookout for big spenders and listen in on conversations with clues where the gang lived. The clerk understood perfectly and Rex made a deal with him.

All sales of fighter ships had to be recorded and approved by the *Cosmic Alliance* for security reasons. Cargo and passenger ships were exempt, but strict rules applied to fighter ships. There was a black-market selling fighters at inflated prices and Rex had a contact at one of those places. They sold fighter ships to buyers who could present legal papers, but on the side, they secretly made deals with criminals and sold ships at twice the price to them. Rex and Elsa made a quick stop on the planet, Zorrelus, and found Rex' informant. He agreed to notify Rex if a big spender appeared. His fee was high, but he justified it by stating if he was caught, he would be killed. Rex agreed to the deal. He knew the informant risked his neck.

Rex and Elsa returned home and now all they could do was to check the Interstellar Internet for unusual news or events hinting someone was spending large amounts of money.

A week went by and Bo-Bonn sent a message he had not seen or heard anything yet. The clerk at the supply station reported no unusual large spending had occurred.

Another week went by. Then a message came in on Rex' communicator from the informant on Zorrelus. He had overheard a secret deal between his employer and five men arriving in a single fighter ship. They had bought four ships very quickly and the five men had piloted a ship each. The fighters had been fully equipped with the latest weaponry and technology. The informant thought he had heard them mention they stayed on a planet called *Terreress* or something like that. Rex responded he would be paid right away if his tip led to the capture of the gang.

The Cosmic Alliance had a database listing every planet known and Rex contacted them immediately for information on any planet that sounded like 'Terreress'. Only one showed up with the name *Ferreress*. The Alliance gave Rex the location of the planet. It was inhabited and located close to planet Peturun in the Milky Way. It was only two months' travel time from Veehnia, but they had to pass through the eighteen-hour tunnel, a monster of a tunnel not easy to deal with that would take them from the Andromeda galaxy to the Milky Way, a distance of two and a half million light years. Each of Rex' ships had only two pilots and they would have to take turns piloting the ship eighteen long hours through the tunnel. He called his pilots to a meeting and explained the conditions to them. All his pilots were experienced and they assured him they accepted the challenge and if they had the controls one hour on, then one hour off, they could handle the job. All of them were competent enough to fly the ship through the tunnel, including the female pilots. Rex thanked them and it was agreed they would ready the ships with supplies and take off in two days. Rex sent an encrypted message to Zakkarim and Ijondelli he had a lead and would travel to the Milky Way.

After a month, they reached the tunnel and every ten minutes one of the ships entered. Rex had instructed the pilots to continue to the planet and not wait for the rest of the fleet in order to take advantage of the acceleration in speed the tunnel supplied. The pilots should reassemble a short distance from Ferreress and the fleet would enter orbit together.

Elsa and Rex had no trouble with the tunnel and alternated being at the controls. Elsa was a little fatigued when they blasted out of the tunnel, but they had one month of easy travel to the planet and she took advantage of it by resting and sleeping more than she usually did. All the pilots made it safely through the tunnel.

They spent the night in orbit and the following morning at daybreak the ships descended fully cloaked to ten thousand feet. Rex had worked out a plan and each ship covered a section of the planet. With a little luck, one of them would find the parked fleet of fighter ships belonging to the criminals. The air traffic was light and no airmobile was visible above three thousand feet. Rex' ships were not within sound level of the airmobiles and anyone on the surface would not be able to hear them either. The engines of modern ships were rather quiet compared to the old ships. They flew all day over the planet's surface and returned to orbit in the evening. Rex and Elsa had not seen anything on their survey of Ferreress.

"Please report," Rex asked his crew.

"We found them," the male and female pilots of Ship Eleven yelled with excitement in their voices. They were a married couple working well together as a team. "The ships are hidden in a camouflaged hangar, but when we descended to five thousand feet, the electromagnetic system detected a huge amount of metal inside the hangar. We couldn't see the ships, obviously, but the amount of metal was too much to just be a few shuttles or airmobiles. We estimate the fleet is around fifteen ships. There are guards outside the building and the area is in an isolated, uninhabited desert area of the planet. There's a chance no one knows they are there. Perhaps the government owns the hangar and it's not used for the time being and the gangsters just moved in."

"Congratulations, great work," Rex said in a relieved voice. At least they had a start now. "Our goal is to preserve the ships so the four ships they just bought can be returned and exchanged for money. That money belongs to Zakkarim and Ijondelli. If we catch the gang and turn them over to the government officials of Ferreress, they can confiscate the remaining ships. We have to assume there are at least thirty pilots. Lastly, we have to find the rest of the gold. The gold they stole could have bought at least ten fighter ships, so there's a pile of gold we must find and return to Zakkarim and Ijondelli. If anyone has any suggestion how we can overpower them without being detected, tell me now."

No one had any plan and they decided to sleep on it.

"I have a plan, but it may not work," Rex told his pilots the next morning using his communicator. "This mission is complicated, because we want to save all the ships and this raid is not without danger. First, all of our ships will be used in the mission and we land on the ground far enough away so they can't detect us or hear us. We leave two pilots to guard the ships and the rest of us strap on our portable electrical engines and fly as close to the hangar as we can. The sound from the portable engines isn't very loud and we can get relatively close without being detected. We remove the engines and leave them without a guard. I think it's safe to do so. No one lives over there. We hike in and stun the guards at maximum power. They'll be out for three hours and that's all the time we need. We storm the hangar and stun the gang. Since there are no barracks or houses, they probably live in the hangar or perhaps on the ships. If we hit them while they're all in a group and not on the ships, we may be able to quickly stun them and take them out. The weakness of the plan is we have no idea where they are inside the hangar and they may be well armed and shoot us all. We'll carry our laser guns as backup. The rest of the plan is just practical details and I'll reveal those later."

The pilots were analyzing the plan in their heads and knew they would be vulnerable as they entered the hangar. The replies came in and Rex listened carefully.

"I'm in. The plan is good if it works. I'm willing to risk it," the first pilot replied.

All of them agreed and the plan was accepted. Rex went over the details and they decided to leave that same afternoon. Flying time was about two hours and they would reach the hangar in the evening. They departed and flew at high altitude fully cloaked and descended quickly.

No one saw them land and there was no air traffic overhead. The pilots selected to guard the ships stayed onboard to be able to use their ship's weapons if needed. The rest of them strapped on their portable engines. The storage compartment on the engines was just big enough to hold chains and the equipment needed to subdue the gang. They took off and flew ten feet above ground. The sound from the engines was very low and they traveled at high speed as close to the hangar as they dared with Rex and Elsa in the lead. Rex gave a signal with his hand they should touch down. They quickly removed the equipment from the engine storage compartments and jammed it into their backpacks. It was dusk and daylight was fading. The crew spread out and their dark clothing made them almost invisible. The hangar was in sight and only three guards walked around outside. They looked bored and were by no means on alert. There were no trees or bushes for cover and Rex, Elsa and two additional pilots dragged themselves close to the ground slowly inching their way towards the guards. The rest of the pilots were lying flat on the ground and waited in silence until the guards were immobilized by the stun guns.

NOW! Rex gave a hand signal to the others to fire the stun guns and all four jumped up and discharged the guns. It was almost instant and the guards went down without uttering a sound. They were paralyzed and would remain in that state for three hours. The guards were quickly dragged off a distance and chained up. It was fully dark outside.

Without making a sound, Rex and the pilots surrounded the hangar looking for exit doors and windows. There were no windows and the only doors they found were in front of the building. It was time. With the stun guns on maximum power and the laser guns ready to grab, Rex gave the signal to storm the building. They kicked the door open and swooped in shocking the gangsters inside. Rex had the element of surprise on his side. The gangsters were unarmed and totally relaxed not expecting anything could happen to them.

Rex and his pilots opened fire and within seconds the whole gang was immobilized and sank down gasping for air. Inside the hangar were twelve fighter ships and four of them did not match the rest of the fleet and were obviously the brand-new ships. Twenty-two men were in a pile on the floor and with the three guards, the gangsters numbered twenty-five. As fast as they could, Rex and his crew chained them up and placed them against the wall. The guards were dragged inside and joined them. They were all alive, but totally paralyzed and struggled to breathe. The stun gun set at maximum force delivered a powerful punch, but was seldom fatal. Cots for sleeping were in the back of the hangar and they had rigged up a corner of the back as kitchen and dining area. The gangsters were of several races and Rex recognized Morekians, several from Humbrus and various mixed races. There were no androids among them. The heist had taken place in the Andromeda galaxy and the gangsters had probably figured no one would look for them in the Milky Way galaxy. They were lulled into a false sense of security now wrecked by Rex and his crew.

Rex left two of his pilots to guard the criminals and they ran back to their portable engines and strapped them on. It was hard to see in the dark, but the androids had night vision and led the way. They picked up the two extra engines and held them against their chest while traveling. Everything was quiet at the ships and the pilots were briefed. Both of them cheered when they heard the good news. The pilots boarded their ships and flew them to the hangar. Everything was now in one place. Rex suggested the pilots stay on their ships overnight, eat and then go to sleep until daybreak. He would give them the details the following morning how they would proceed. The androids took over guarding the prisoners so the two pilots could catch some sleep on their ship. During the night, one of the androids started to chitchat with a prisoner, who seemed to be less violent, and asked him how they got the tip the gold was on the workstation.

"Bo-Bonn told us," he replied.

The following morning all the gangsters were back to normal and the stun effect had worn off. They were swearing, spitting at the androids and complaining they had to relieve themselves. Their complaints were unanswered and they had to let nature take over and wet themselves. No mercy was shown. The chains tied their hands and feet together and they were unable to raise themselves off the floor. The pilots found the gold in canvas bags in a corner of the hangar and packed the bags in several of their own ships.

Rex and Elsa were astounded when the android pilot told them Bo-Bonn had been the informant and he was well paid by the gangsters.

"He sure fooled me," Rex said and sighed. "What an actor."

Rex and Elsa took off alone and flew across half the planet to the government buildings. They had seen them on one of their trips. Outside the buildings was a large parking area for airmobiles and Rex landed the ship skillfully on a corner of the lot by allowing the ship to hover, then gently descend to the ground. Five armed guards came running, but realized quickly Rex and Elsa were no threat when they noticed they were unarmed. Using his portable translation device, Rex told them he had urgent news and needed to speak to their leader. The guards led the way to the president's office. He was a pleasant man of large proportions with a hefty girth, a humanoid.

"Welcome to planet Ferreress, I'm President Dedeen. It's a pleasure to have aliens visit us. How can I help you?"

Rex explained the whole story about the robbery of the workstation and how he and his men had finally traced the gangsters to his planet. As expected, the president had no idea the gang was living on his planet and explained the hangar was only used occasionally to park out of service ships. No one lived in that area.

"We'll prosecute the criminals to the full extent of the law and the trial will be held on our planet since they're living here. Our judges will, of course, decide the sentence, but I'm pretty sure they will face death by lethal injection. That's how the law works on this planet. Yes, I fully agree the four ships must be returned to the seller on planet Zorrelus and the money, or the gold, returned. One of our cargo ships is big enough to carry the weight of the four fighter ships to be returned as well as your twenty ships. It will be a full load, but that ship can do the job by stacking the ships three high. Our pilots will transport all of you to planet Zorrelus. There we unload the ships and our cargo ship will return home. Our pilots have been through the Andromeda tunnel several times and have the skill to fly through it. This way, you'll return to Zorrelus a little faster and the eight ships you offer us from the criminals are more than enough to pay for our transport of your ships to Zorrelus. Our fleet of fighters could use a few more ships and these eight ships would be a welcome addition."

Rex and Elsa were excited to hear the president's suggestion and agreed right away. It was decided the police force would immediately get ready to pick up the criminals and the cargo ship would land by the hangar the following morning at daybreak to load all the ships. Using his communicator, Rex sent a message to his crew the gang would be picked up in a short time by the government police force. The eight ships would be collected within a few days by pilots working for the Ferreress fleet.

The president contacted the police chief and gave orders to get the gang. He was talkative and very nice and listened with great interest when Rex explained his line of work. He had read about Rex and his mercenary work on the Internet. They had a pleasant conversation and after a few hours Rex and Elsa said goodbye and left.

When they arrived at the hangar, the criminals had been picked up already and were gone. Rex' crew were grinning when they reported the circus they had witnessed when the gang members were picked up by a cargo drone and mercilessly dropped inside animal cages that were then dropped inside a small cargo ship. They were screaming, swearing and spitting to no avail. Two pilots and five guards made sure all went well and no escape was possible.

The next day the huge cargo ship arrived and it was the largest ship the crew had ever seen, a monster of a ship. It was accompanied by an airmobile seating six mechanics who would be in charge of loading the fighter ships. Four pilots manned the cargo ship and two commercial size drones were unloaded from the cargo ship. The drones worked as a team and picked up each ship gently and placed them in padded slots three high inside the cargo ship. The mechanics secured each ship with chains to make sure they would be secure when they traveled through the tunnel. They were experts and Rex and his crew watched them with admiration.

Everything was packed and ready and only the eight ships were left in the hangar. Rex and his crew boarded the cargo ship and it took off with the power expected of a true beast and the engines were roaring. The travel time from Ferreress to planet Zorrelus was two and a half months and Rex and his crew had nothing to do but exercise, rest and watch holographic movies. Since it was a cargo ship, there were few entertainment devices onboard. The pilots were skilled and took the ship through the tunnel with ease. Accommodations onboard were rustic and two men shared a cabin with bunk beds. The food was all freeze-dried, but rather good and plentiful and to their delight, lots of fruits and berries were also available.

They landed on Zorrelus on a large field adjacent to the dealer selling the fighter ships. Within minutes a groundmobile from the dealer was racing over to the ship to investigate what was going on.

Rex and Elsa climbed out of the ship and swiftly walked over to them. Rex asked them with a stern voice to accompany him to the president's office and refused to explain why. The president was surprised to see them and asked them all to sit down and explain their business. Elsa excused herself for a minute and then returned. Rex quickly described the situation and when he was finished, the people from the dealer rushed out of the room trying to escape only to be stopped by a team of armed police officers outside the door. Elsa had suspected they would try to slip away and had notified the police. They were handcuffed and arrested and would stand trial.

The Ferreress pilots and Rex' crew had no trouble untying the ships and the drones unloaded them. The pilots would stay a week on the planet to rest up and then return to their home planet.

The president conducted a short investigation and realized the dealer was selling ships illegally and closed down their business. He had not been aware of their illegal activities and thanked Rex for exposing them. The ships were exchanged for the full amount of gold the gang had paid for them.

The following day, all the gold belonging to Zakkarim and Ijondelli was loaded onto Rex and Elsa's ship and they took off to the workstation. The crew could now return home to Veehnia and wait for Rex and Elsa to join them. They said goodbye to the pilots from Ferreress wishing them a safe trip home.

Rex sent an encrypted message to Zakkarim they were on the way and be ready to deposit the gold on the planet without delay. He received a reply they were relieved to hear from him and would comply.

After docking with the workstation, Zakkarim and Ijondelli greeted Rex and Elsa with big smiles and together they carried the concealed bags into the office. No one noticed them and the shuttle to the surface was expected within the hour. Zakkarim checked the gold and assured Rex the full amount was there and nothing was missing. He immediately separated Rex' payment from the pile of gold and handed the canvas bag over to Rex with a handshake. The payment was very generous. The shuttle from the bank arrived and the armed team quickly took the bags and returned to the planet. Rex and Elsa explained how the mission had played out and Zakkarim and Ijondelli were fascinated to hear their story. When Rex revealed Bo-Bonn was the informant they were shocked. He had been a trusted employee for years and they could hardly believe their ears when Rex told them how Bo-Bonn had promised to work for Rex when, in fact, he was the informant himself. Zakkarim would deal with him after Rex and Elsa left and have him arrested.

They departed the next day and returned safely to Veehnia. Zakkarim posted the mission on the Internet praising Rex for his competence. After all the pilots were paid and the expenses deducted for the trip, a sizable amount of gold was left and Rex bought twenty of Leo's gravity chambers for his twenty ships. He knew his pilots would be so much stronger at the end of each trip by having access to gravity every day in space. A small amount of gold was left and Rex paid down his loan to the Veehnian government. They were surprised at how fast they were reimbursed and congratulated Rex on his accomplishments and when Rex told them the details of his latest mission, they were amazed.

Rex also paid the informant on planet Zorrelus by depositing the fee into his account. For safety reasons, Rex had not approached him on the planet and no one knew he was an informant. Without his help, Rex knew it would have been almost impossible to find the gangsters. He deserved his payment. Rex received a thank-you and the informant told him the government had confiscated the dealer's business and he was now working for the government. He assured Rex he would always be willing to help out in the future if he needed him. Rex paid great attention to all his spies knowing full well they were a necessary part of his organization.

Tothellim and Rheo were always waiting to be briefed after each mission and their input and experience were highly valued by Rex.

***

Elsa told Rex she would use the time until their next assignment to try to conceive and her sister Hanna had assured Elsa, she would be happy to help raise her baby. Rex was excited to hear her suggestion and Elsa was artificially inseminated shortly thereafter. It took two tries until she was pregnant and Rex did not accept any work until the embryo was safely transferred to the artificial womb. They had been told the father was Veehnian, not a mix, and the baby was a boy. They named him Adrian.

Rex accepted only short job assignments until the baby was due and it was a special moment when they brought him home. Hanna was along as she would be substitute mother to Adrian. She had only one child herself and was looking forward to having the baby in her care. The baby was handsome and did not look like Elsa, so apparently, he resembled his father. Rex had never been around children and felt awkward at first, but soon learned how to hold him and became a proud and devoted father. Elsa was a loving mother in spite of her occasional macho behavior when she worked. Deep down she was actually quite feminine. Both Rex and Elsa were grateful they had been rewarded with a healthy baby.

CHAPTER 20

Bonnie and Flar were the parents of seven children and Flar was still working full time at eighty-five years old, but with a life expectancy of two hundred years, he was considered middle-aged and in good physical shape. Their oldest son Victor was already twenty-one years old and studied art. His oil paintings, both landscapes and portraits, were of such high quality that his exhibits were well attended and most of his paintings sold quickly. His soul came through in his landscape paintings and they were considered 'intense' and sparkled with color. Bonnie had told Flar when the fourth child was born, she did not want any more children, but Flar wanted a few more and Bonnie changed her mind and ended up as the mother of seven. It had not been a hardship for Bonnie as all the babies except Victor were transferred to the artificial womb and she had two android maids doing all the housework. Flar was well off and had supplied a comfortable life for Bonnie and the children. Bonnie was now fifty-five years old and in good health. The family and the two maids spent many weekends and holidays on their large houseboat and the ocean was mostly very calm. English was the preferred language at home, but the children were bilingual. Flar had been an excellent teacher to Bonnie and their emotional bond was as strong as their spiritual bond. Her consciousness had increased and with it her peace of mind. She knew her life expectancy was only half of Flar's and Flar had started to investigate the latest technology to prolong life for humans. He had seen a brief statement on the Internet how planet Nuvirenn had gained knowledge to manipulate cells and prolong life to three hundred years and he planned to find out how they did it. The thought of outliving Bonnie was painful. He had hired one of the best medical scientists on Ljeviina hoping he could somehow retrieve the information from Nuvirenn. The scientist was willing to travel to Nuvirenn and kept his eyes open for any spaceship heading in that direction.

Bonnie had lived over twenty years on Ljeviina and found the difference between Earth and her new planet was not that big. Basic needs were all the same as well as emotional needs. The Ljeviina people were ahead of Earth in consciousness and awareness, but technologically Earth was not far behind. Even the reptilian people had the same basic needs as all the other humanoid races and only their looks were radically different. The majority of alien races were kind and did not want to hurt any other population. Bonnie knew, of course, wars existed on some planets and space had a fair number of criminal gangs roaming the universe, but she had also met many alien societies where peace was treasured and respect for others honored.

A month later, the scientist Flar had hired informed him he had found a ship traveling to a planet close to Nuvirenn and from that planet he would hire a small ship to take him to Nuvirenn. Would Flar agree to the arrangement? The proposition was expensive, but Flar said yes and the scientist took off. He would stay on Nuvirenn until he had studied the method and understood how to apply it.

A year later he returned full of eagerness to share his new knowledge. He had met with the brightest minds on Nuvirenn and they generously shared their medical discoveries knowing their pioneering work would spread across the universe. They had not tried to profit from their knowledge and transmitted the entire method to the scientist's portable computer, an enormous file with graphics and holographic lectures.

"This is our gift to humanity. Share it with the other planets. We have only one demand and that is you can't charge for it. It must be free for all to use."

Flar's hired scientist felt emotional and his eyes filled with tears. Their discovery would impact people on all the planets and change humanity everywhere. He assured the team he would put the knowledge on the Interstellar Internet and that way no one could charge for the discovery or try to sell it. It would be disclosed that the method had been discovered on planet Nuvirenn and they had generously shared it with all people. With a handshake and a loving smile, the leader of the medical team on Nuvirenn said goodbye to the scientist.

Flar was ecstatic to hear the news. He went with the scientist to the most advanced medical facility on Ljeviina and a copy of the method was downloaded for the doctors and scientists to examine. The scientist also posted the whole discovery on local Internets as well as the Interstellar

Internet and the posting went wild. The information hopscotched from planet to planet and even reached Earth after a while. Nuvirenn became famous almost overnight and received endless outpourings of love and gratitude from every planet that heard of the procedure. The citizens on Nuvirenn read all the postings and were grateful their doctors had shared the science for free with all the other planets.

People on Earth had among the shortest lifespans of the known planets and the new method would impact Earth tremendously. The Earth doctors went to work without delay to learn how to use the system and the information was clearly detailed to ensure it was easy to follow. It would take time to train the doctors at every hospital and also to treat every citizen and new hospitals would have to be built to accommodate all the people.

On Ljeviina, the doctors started full speed to learn the method and after a few months they had mastered the technique and the first patients were Bonnie and her family. Flar had paid the whole cost of the scientist's expenses and the doctors felt it was fair to treat Flar, Bonnie and their children first. The first treatment was complex, but the patient only needed a follow-up treatment every twenty years. Both Bonnie and Flar felt reborn after they had been through the treatment, almost buoyant, and their brain capacity was increased. With their cells renewed, they were told they would live mostly free of diseases. Flar looked at Bonnie with love knowing he would not lose her prematurely and end up a widower.

Ljeviina quickly started building new hospitals using their 3D printers and encouraged medical students to specialize in the new system. Most planets did the same.

***

Every country on Earth was building new hospitals and training doctors how to treat patients with the Nuvirenn procedure. It was estimated it would take a decade or two to treat every citizen on Earth and people received their place on the waiting list according to a lottery system. The waiting list in each country was posted on the Internet right from the beginning. No one was given priority and, as an example, the president of The Americas was listed toward the end of the waiting list. It was a totally fair system and was accepted by the citizens.

All the known planets built hospitals and trained their doctors to treat the citizens with the Nuvirenn process. On planets with small populations the waiting list was only a few years on average. The leaders on overpopulated planets suggested some citizens may consider emigrating to an underpopulated planet at government's expense. The longer lifespan would tax the resources of their planet otherwise. Many planets were looking for more citizens and the Nuvirenn procedure caused a large migration of peoples between planets. No overpopulated planet had ever considered 'culling' the population as it was considered a most barbaric method unfit for a civilized society.

***

On Earth2, Atlas was in charge of the Nuvirenn procedure and with a population of three hundred thousand, only a few additional hospitals needed to be built. Atlas trained Melody and a few additional doctors and after a couple of months they started accepting patients. Everyone who went through the process was amazed at how much better they felt afterwards. The lottery system on Earth2 was by family, so each family was counted as one unit and treated together. This avoided competition within the family unit as those who had been treated evolved with higher brain capacity compared to before the treatment. Earth2 had a team of doctors with excellent credentials who had chosen to relocate to Earth2 based on the beauty of the planet and a stress-free lifestyle. Atlas estimated the whole population would be treated within five years. He found the process fascinating and dedicated himself fully to oversee the treatment plan. Melody and Lorre were in the middle of the waiting list and Viola had landed among the first on the list. Viola was seventy-eight years old and dying to get her treatment. She had started to feel her age, but was in no way mentally ready for a senior lifestyle and after her treatment she felt jubilant and young again. She also looked younger and the aging process was reversed and she barely aged for years. Atlas looked at her and complimented her how great she looked and how bright her mind was. As an android, Atlas could easily exist three hundred years and with occasional upgrades and exchange of parts, he would last as long as Viola. They were tightly bonded and enjoyed life and each other's company. Older people may live a little less than three hundred years as their bodies had already started the aging process. No one knew for sure the life expectancy of elderly people who had received their first treatment late in life.

The planets with small populations treated their citizens rather quickly and planets with large populations needed close to two decades to finish the job. No one complained. Every citizen knew they would have better health after the procedure was done and it was worth waiting for.

***

Among the citizens on most planets, about five percent declined to be treated claiming religious reasons, not knowing what to do with the extra time and having limited enjoyment from life. Their wishes were respectfully honored and they were told if they changed their mind, the treatment would be available. The cost of the treatment was minimal ensuring everyone could afford it.

Everywhere, people were asking themselves what to do with the extra two hundred years they had been awarded and, after a while, most people decided to let destiny decide their future. Many people took a few years off from working and engaged in soul searching and exploring former lives in addition to efforts to remove unbecoming feelings such as envy, bitterness and hate. On Earth, to pay for living expenses during these non-working years, people applied for the free base income. When working, most people opted out of the base income treating it as an emergency solution for hard times and when people retired, they applied for it. The system had never been abused and had functioned successfully one hundred and sixty-three years since it was launched in 2062.

Girls receiving their first treatment at age twenty were expected to be able to bear children until at least one hundred and fifty years old. Exact details were not available, as each race was slightly different and what was the norm on Nuvirenn may not match conditions on another planet. Governments did not expect a dramatic increase in population as some couples may not have any more children compared to their lifestyle before the treatment. Moreover, most planets were underpopulated and welcomed more citizens. The planets with overpopulation paid for emigration of people who agreed to start a new life on another planet and the increased lifespan on all planets had no detrimental effect anywhere in the long run. The opposite was actually true. Elderly people with acquired experience and wisdom contributed vastly to society and were sought after as consultants and leaders.

CHAPTER 21

The ships from Nuvirenn returned to Earth three more times and each seat was filled every time. One hundred and twenty thousand people from Earth ended up immigrating to Nuvirenn and no one returned to Earth. The immigrants to Nuvirenn loved the planet and married natives thereby introducing the 'new blood' Zerventos had described when he visited Earth in 2220 for the first time. It was a successful rescue of a dying people and the birth rate was steadily increasing. Both native men and women, who were unable to have children with a Nuvirenn person, easily produced offspring with an Earth person, so Zerventos was correct when he said they must have new blood to save the population. All people from Earth had almost celebrity status and the easy lifestyle and nice living conditions were very appreciated by the new immigrants. Everybody agreed they lived a pampered life.

Helga and Settie had three children keeping Monna and Nita very busy. Helga loved her children and she could enjoy being a mother without having to do the grunt work. Settie would not allow Helga to do any physical hard work and he pampered her to no end. Monna and Nita had never taken care of children, but they learned fast and became very fond of them. Helga made it clear to the children the maids should be treated with respect and they were. Monna and Nita played with them as well as being substitute mothers and they always came along when the family went away on trips or visited Trenna and Jianyu.

Trenna and Jianyu had two children and the two families had become close friends. There were no neighbors around so they were glad to visit with each other as often as they could. Vomerus was training his son-in-law to run the farm and Jianyu was eager to learn. His heart was involved and he loved the land and Vomerus was pleasantly surprised to see how dedicated Jianyu was. Moreover, he was a heck of a nice guy to be around and his love for Trenna was apparent. Vomerus and his wife were planning to move to the city as soon as Jianyu was able to run the farm alone. He had several robots as helpers and an android doing more sophisticated work as well as running his computers when needed. An android maid did all the housework.

No schools were available in the whole area and the two families had decided to home-school their children together. The distance between the two farms was a full hour with airmobile so they would have to work out a schedule to make the commuting easy. Settie suggested they build a little school halfway between their two farms and the children would only have to commute half an hour to the school. Settie's airmobile was autonomous, but while the children were small one of the maids would accompany the children to school. Trenna and Jianyu agreed to the arrangement and Settle had a school house built. A contractor from the city erected the building using 3D printers and it was an adorable little house. Peter, Helga's oldest son, was three years old and at four years of age he would start school. The government had promised to supply an android as a teacher who would live in the school building. Trenna's oldest, a girl, was two years old.

Helga had healed emotionally and her memories had no longer an impact on her. Settie and her family were of paramount importance and living on a farm and having a horse of her own and cows to hug gave her a feeling of bliss. Nuvirenn was a lovely planet and the leaders cared about all citizens.

***

Elsa had become a mother for the second time and a girl had been born. It was only a year between the children and Rex and Elsa wanted it that way. Rex had adjusted to being a father and enjoyed all aspects of it. He loved his children as much as a biological man. Elsa was scheduled to have her Nuvirenn procedure the following year and looked forward to it. Rex and Elsa had decided not to take on overly risky assignments while the children were small and with Elsa's extended life span, they felt there was plenty of time later on to accept more challenging assignments. Rex' life span was easily as long as Elsa's.

The shorter assignments did not bring in as much income as the dangerous job offers, but they still lived comfortably on the money they had. The rest of the pilots agreed the children came first and not to 'rock the boat' for the next ten years or so. The other two female pilots in Rex' fleet also had children. Both of them had hired an android to care for the children while they were away on assignment.

***

Tothellim was now one hundred and five years old and was, at first, unwilling to accept the Nuvirenn procedure. He was alone, his children were living their own lives and what would he do with an additional two hundred years, he asked himself. Physically, he was still strong and worked three days a week giving lessons at the flight school. His appointment was coming up soon and he had been placed at the beginning of the waiting list. Something from within nudged him to agree to the procedure and he said to himself 'why not' and had it done. What a difference. He felt fifty years had been erased from his age and his mental abilities had increased considerably. He felt on top of the world. As he was adjusting to his new 'youth' he decided to return to space travel and contacted Eric, who was now captain of his former spaceship. Thirteen years had passed since Tothellim retired from space travel and he found Eric and his crew on Veehnia resting between trips. He invited them to his house and after dinner, he told them how well he felt after his Nuvirenn treatment.

"Can I join you again?" he asked. To his surprise they applauded and whistled.

"Join me as captain. Let's share the job," Eric graciously offered Tothellim.

"My dear friend, *you* will remain as captain and I'll be honored serving as your copilot," Tothellim replied humbly. "I'm ready to start working on your next trip into space. When will you leave?"

"In one week, Tothellim. We love to have you join us. None of us have had the Nuvirenn procedure done, but we also look forward to our own treatment."

A busy week followed and Rheo assured Tothellim he would look after his house. Old times had returned.

Erik, Tothellim, 2 additional copilots, Rhett and Matthias, and six androids boarded the ship. Kody, the doctor and scientist, was still part of the crew and even though he was now one hundred fifteen years old, he was in full swing with no plans to slow down. The huge ship was equipped with all supplies they would need for three years and two of Leo's gravity chambers were installed. Tothellim worked out in the gravity chamber to build as much muscle as he could and he was full of energy.

After two months' time they reached the fifteen-hour tunnel propelling them a distance of thirty thousand light years. The ship continued straight ahead and towards the center of the Andromeda galaxy. There were several stars with orbiting planets in the area and they hoped to locate a new planet they had not visited before. Rhett was watching the instrument panel and looked concerned.

"Captain, we are being followed. They're gaining on us."

The ship had a windowed dome and a staircase led up to the observation area of the ship. All of them quickly climbed upstairs and peered towards the back of the ship. It was hard to see in the darkness, but far back they saw the faint lights of what appeared to be fourteen fighter ships following them. Tothellim had been a space pilot since he was twenty-five years old and had never seen another ship while traveling through space and he remembered Emrak had only seen another ship once during his many years of flying. The odds were low these ships following them were friendly and Tothellim's gut instinct told him trouble was ahead. Their ship was moving at maximum speed, but the fighters were faster and would soon catch up with them. The ship was constructed of an almost impenetrable alloy, easily as strong as terrynium, and would most likely be unharmed if fired on except the dome. The weapons onboard were the best Veehnia had and could blow up a fighter ship, even if it was made of terrynium.

"I believe they'll try to hijack us," Tothellim said and his voice was uneasy. "The value of this ship and all its equipment is worth a fortune and the ship can easily be sold on the black market for a vast sum of gold. We can't outrun them and we may have to open fire to defend ourselves. Most likely, they will ask us to land on some desolate planet and kill us off. If they can't fly this complicated ship, they'll keep one or two of us alive to pilot the ship and then gun the pilots down."

"I agree with your assumption," Eric said. He was immensely grateful to have Tothellim onboard and trusted his experience and wisdom. "I will open fire if the ship is compromised in any way. We're on a peaceful mission as explorers, but we can't risk the ship for a bunch of space criminals."

They quickly readied the weapons onboard and the whole crew was on the Bridge. Two of the androids were at the controls for the weapons and they had been trained how to fire them. The weapons were computer guided and would not miss. After a short time, the fighters caught up with them and announced their presence over the communication system. There were fourteen ships and they were all of late design.

"Follow us and land when we arrive at the planet. If you refuse, we open fire." The voice was hoarse, typical of the way reptilians sounded, and the person spoke in broken English.

Eric and Tothellim looked at each other and Tothellim nodded. Without hesitation, Eric ordered the androids to fire on all the ships. They were most likely made of terrynium, but the enormous power of the weaponry on a Starfleet ship was more than even fourteen fighter ships could compete with.

"FIRE ON ALL THE SHIPS!" Eric's usually so calm demeanor was replaced by a warrior mentality and he knew all the ships had to be blown up. Parts of their own ship were vulnerable and the dome may not survive a direct hit from the fighters' weapons. If the dome was hit, they would all die. The androids fired, over and over, and only one of the fighter ships managed to fire off a shot at the Veehnian ship and it just bounced off the fuselage without damaging the ship.

All the criminals' ships were hit and the scene in front of them was a hellish view of burning ships with explosions lighting up the area. All the ships succumbed and debris were all over the area. The Veehnian ship was moving forward at maximum speed and had not slowed down during the attack. Within minutes they were out of the area leaving the inferno behind them. The crew breathed a sigh of relief. It had been a close call and they were sad about the loss of life. Every mission was geared to saving lives, helping aliens and remove injustices, not killing. They all knew they had no choice but to kill the criminals, but the crew still felt the whole incident had been tragic.

The crew concentrated on finding a new planet and after a month they saw a star with three planets orbiting. Two of the planets were too close to their star to support life, but the third planet looked promising and they entered orbit. It had a large moon, about a third of the size of the planet. A dust cloud circulated around the planet making it impossible to see the surface. At night, the planet did not light up. To their surprise, the moon was brightly lit and apparently had a population. The next day, they launched a drone to investigate the planet's surface and programmed the drone to fly at low elevation and take closeup images. The land looked dry and dead and no water sources were visible. They saw no signs of life and nothing was growing. Abandoned buildings were everywhere and it was obvious the population had relocated to the moon and left the planet. They entered orbit around the moon and found it heavily populated so they launched a drone to investigate the surface. A fully modern society was visible from the images the drone sent to the ship and humanoid reptilians occupied the moon. They appeared to breathe air and apparently the moon had an atmosphere. Rivers were visible and fields with crops had been planted. Domestic animals were grazing on the fields.

"They have moved from the planet to the moon. Wonder why?" Tothellim said to the crew. "It must have something to do with the dust cloud."

"Let's descend to the surface tomorrow," Eric suggested. "If we take the shuttle, all of us will fit in the shuttle and two of the androids stay on the ship. The androids who stay will come with us to the surface the following day."

The shuttle landed gently on the moon's surface and the oxygen measured twenty-two percent, well within the ideal zone for humanoids. Gravity was light, perhaps half of Veehnia's, but the crew had no trouble walking. Eric had landed the shuttle close to what they were guessing were the government buildings and they exited the vehicle. It did not take long until a military vehicle pulled up and a group of soldiers jumped out. They were reptilians, very similar looking to the people living on planet Kodetsia. The soldiers noticed the crew was unarmed and did not draw their weapons.

"We're from planet Veehnia and are space explorers," Eric said using the translation device. "My name is Eric and this is my crew. Can we speak to your leaders?"

The lead soldier nodded and waved at them to follow him. They entered the government building, which appeared to be brand-new and was rather elegant looking. He opened the door to the leader's office and they entered. The leader was elderly and moved with difficulty, but smiled at them and wished them welcome to his planet.

"I'm Chikkito, president of our planet Cerrestus and its moon. We seldom have alien visitors and I truly welcome you. Is there a specific reason you chose to visit us?"

Eric introduced himself and his crew and explained they were space explorers with a mission to offer assistance to any aliens who asked for help.

"As you probably saw, our planet has become uninhabitable," Chikkito explained. "An asteroid hit the planet a few years ago and a dust cloud engulfed the entire planet and obscured the sunlight. Nothing grows and we had no choice but to evacuate and move to the moon. Many people were killed when the asteroid hit. The weather is ideal here and there's plenty of water. Our population is small and there's no overcrowding, so the relocation has been a total success. We have only a single spaceship which we used to move the people to the moon, but we did have fourteen fighter ships that were stolen by a gang of criminals. While the evacuation was taking place, they saw the opportunity to steal all the ships and took off before we were even aware the ships had been stolen. The people were trusted citizens and none of us would have suspected they would steal our ships and just vanish from the planet. I have no idea where they are, why they did it and what their intentions were. I'm sorry to say one of them was my own son. His mother was heartbroken when she found out."

Eric looked at Tothellim and when he nodded, Eric started talking.

"I regret to tell you the fourteen ships you refer to tried to hijack us and force us to follow them to a planet. We knew, of course, they would have killed us once we landed on the planet. To save our ship and our lives, we opened fire and all the ships were destroyed. We're so sorry to have to bring this sad news."

Chikkito was quiet, contemplating, and then replied with a reassuring voice.

"Eric, and all of you, you did what you had to do to save your lives and your ship. Don't feel bad. My son deserved his destiny and it was better he died than to pursue a career in crime. Sooner or later, he would have been caught anyway. Now my wife and I can find closure and stop speculating what he's up to. In truth, Eric, you did us a favor." Chikkito put his hand on Eric's shoulder and patted him in a fatherly way. Eric felt moved, but also relieved.

"Eventually, the dust cloud will fall to the surface and the sun will return. Will you move back to your planet then?" Tothellim asked.

"We'll let our citizens decide that for themselves," Chikkito replied. "Our ship seats two hundred people and it takes only a day to travel to the planet. If they want to return to the planet, they are free to do so. My wife and I will stay on the moon and most of the citizens prefer the moon to the planet."

The crew stayed on the moon a week and found it scenic and peaceful. The people were unhurried and seemed to live with the rhythm of the land. It was not an advanced society, but quality of life was good and the people were of sound mind and pleased with life.

The crew left Cerrestus and continued their journey in pursuit of planets in need of help. For two months, all they saw was empty space and then a tunnel appeared. It was a three-hour tunnel moving the ship two thousand light years in distance and doubled the speed of the ship. They were now in an area that was unfamiliar to the crew and the androids knew from the charts onboard a star with a single planet should soon be visible. They had to travel another month and there it was. It was a small star and the planet was also small, about the size of Mars, without a moon.

They entered orbit and at night the planet was brightly lit, so it was inhabited. The following morning, they launched a reconnaissance drone as usual and waited with excitement for the first images from the drone. The first pictures showed a city in turmoil. Many buildings were burned down and armed gangs were roaming the streets. Humanoid people were firing on gangs of people with different looks and dead bodies were lying on the streets here and there. No normal activity could be seen.

The drone continued to the countryside and a very different world appeared with nice looking neighborhoods occupied by people of one race only. As the drone continued across the countryside, images of towns were transmitted showing where the other race lived. The neighborhoods were less affluent and not well maintained. It was clearly a difference in standard of living between the two races. It was obvious the two races lived segregated and did not want to mix. In the cities, they were at full war with each other. The drone flew across the whole planet and segregation was the norm everywhere. Eric recalled the drone and it was soon back onboard.

"It seems we have a planet here with a full-scale race war, similar to what planet Earth had in the twentieth and twenty-first centuries," Kody said slowly, pondering over the images he had just observed. "They solved the problem through segregation, but in the cities, it looks like they're fighting to gain territory. Each gang has its own fiefdom and defends it with full warfare. My gosh, this is not an easy problem to solve. They apparently hate each other."

"What's your thoughts, Tothellim?" Eric asked. "Should we move on or stay and try to help? Would they even listen to us?"

"Tough question to answer," Tothellim said, contemplating pros and cons. "Our mission is to try to make a difference. If we fail, we can at least say we tried. I suggest we make contact with both sides and offer to mediate. I saw no spaceships and no air traffic so it may be a less advanced society. Perhaps we can offer them some of our technology in exchange for a peace agreement. Yes, I know it's bribery, but if it works, there's no harm in using whatever technique that works. If you remember, when we visited planet Cirrkosa in 2206, it was a patriarchy and we bribed them with our technology to give the women equal rights. It worked. Perhaps it will work here, too. But our first move should be to mediate."

Eric and the crew smiled and nodded and Kody interjected he remembered he tested the women and they were just as smart as the men, which came as a surprise to the men. Tothellim's suggestion was accepted and they agreed they would make contact the following day with the people living in the nicer area.

The next morning, the crew boarded the shuttle and descended to the surface. The biggest building looked official and they hovered the shuttle while looking around and then lowered the vehicle to the ground. They climbed out and no one came out at first. Two young boys cautiously walked over to them and stared. They were humanoids with short, dark hair, tall and skinny. Their heads were average size and elongated with shiny, green eyes and they were rather nice looking.

"We're looking for your leaders. Can you show us where they are?" Eric said using the translation device. The boys jumped when they heard sound from the device and quickly talked to each other. The device flashed and it had found the language. Eric's question was translated to the boys.

"Who are you?" one of them managed to ask.

"We're from another planet far from here. We need to talk to your leader. Please show us where to go."

Kody locked the shuttle and they all followed the boys inside the large building. It was a nice structure, but old-fashioned without any modern touches. A door opened and a very tall, skinny, elderly woman looked out to see what was going on. Her dress was full length and her grey hair was in a bun on top of her head. She jumped when she saw Tothellim.

"Don't be afraid. We're visitors from a planet called Veehnia. We come in peace." Tothellim's voice was calm and reassuring and the woman was able to regain her composure.

"I'm President Dori-Venn and this is planet Leto-1. Please come inside my office." The president moved slowly and she was leaning on a cane.

Her assistant, a young male, got up from his desk and looked at them in amazement. The president asked them to sit down and explain why they were on the planet. Tothellim and Eric took turns explaining who they were and their mission.

"Madam President, please explain to us why there's war in your cities and why the two races on your planet are segregated," Kody asked.

"It's a nightmare," Dori-Venn sighed and put her hand against her forehead in frustration. "We're two different races and my race is ahead of the other race in evolvement. This has caused envy and hate from their side and no matter how much we help them, they will not accept us and agree that we can all live together in peace. We don't hate them, but they can't get past their envy of us. The cities became unlivable and everyone moved out to the countryside, but we had no choice but to live segregated. We didn't suggest segregation; they insisted on it. Criminal gangs from both races are now running amok in the cities and killing each other in sport. We want nothing more than to integrate them into our society and make peace with them. We accept them as they are, but they won't listen to anything we say."

"Who is their leader and where can we find the leader?" Eric asked.

"The leader's name is Vrenbeesol and he lives an hour away by car. He is not an appointed government official, but he acts as the spokesman for his race."

"You mentioned you travel by car," Kody remarked. "Do people on this planet not use groundmobiles and airmobiles?"

"I'm not familiar with those words. What is it?"

"Vehicles that can travel both on the ground and in the air. They are computer driven and autonomous." Tothellim noticed the president had no idea what he was talking about. Most planets they had visited had modern electronics and spaceships. It was unusual to find a planet like Leto-1 with living conditions from the early twentieth century. It was obvious computers had not been discovered yet.

"Allow me, Madam, to show you," Kody said and activated his communicator. Using voice command, he pulled up images and they were displayed holographically showing airmobiles and groundmobiles. The president and her assistant watched in disbelief with their mouths open.

"How can that thing fly like a bird?" the assistant whispered, too amazed to find his voice.

"We'll explain it to your scientists," Kody said with a smile.

They stayed several hours and when they left, the crew had a clear picture in their minds how far the people had evolved. They had offered to mediate and Dori-Venn had accepted the offer. The following day, they would try to find Vrenbeesol.

Flying at low altitude, they picked the largest building hoping it was Vrenbeesol's office building. They were lucky, it was. The building was shabby and needed lots of maintenance. Trash was lying around on the roads and the people had a dull look on their faces. The neighborhood did not look inviting and creativity was apparently stifled.

The door flew open and an angry Vrenbeesol stood in the doorway. When he saw the shuttle and the crew climbing out, he was gasping for breath. *What was that?*

"Vrenbeesol, I presume?" Eric said with a smile. "We would like to talk to you. Can we come in?"

"Yea," was all he managed to say, too startled to be able to think straight. He was as tall as Dori-Venn's race, but his facial features were different and it was obvious the two races were not closely related.

They were shown into a room that appeared to be a cafeteria and sat down. Vrenbeesol used what looked like an old-fashioned telephone to call his assistants into the room. Eric explained their mission and where they came from, but Vrenbeesol and his men were not able to understand everything they were told, so Eric showed them images from his communicator. That clarified some of the information, but the concept of space travel and life on other planets was way beyond their understanding.

"Why do you hate the other race?" Eric asked. "They want to live in peace with you. Can't you accept that?"

"They look down on us," Vrenbeesol started, "and...   "

"*NO*, you're dead wrong. Again, *no!*" Eric's voice was commanding and he would not allow Vrenbeesol to ramble on. "We just spoke to President Dori-Venn and she assured us you and your people are most welcome to live in their neighborhoods and participate on equal terms in all aspects of life. Your hate is based on total lies and misunderstanding. Dori-Venn is a good woman and the reason why you can't see that is because you *don't want* to acknowledge it. You enjoy wallowing in self-pity. Wake up, accept her offer and end this useless war and self-imposed segregation. You would benefit greatly, if you did."

Vrenbeesol and his men were quiet and two of his men nodded and looked at their leader. They accepted the terms. Vrenbeesol looked undecided.

"How many of you belong to your race?" Kody asked.

"The whole population is sixty million and we are twenty million," Vrenbeesol replied.

"If you accept Dori-Venn's offer and agree to end this war once and for all, we will meet with your scientists and share some of our technology with you and all of you will be better off. Our technology will move your society forward one hundred years and improve your technical abilities as well as your understanding of medical cures. We only have one demand – stop the war, accept each other as equals and live together in peace. President Dori-Venn's army will end the wars in the cities."

Vrenbeesol was clearly impressed by Kody's offer and Kody helped him save face by adding –

"You can always say you went along with your advisors' wishes."

"I accept!" Vrenbeesol jumped up and Kody shook hands with him and congratulated him on his decision. The whole crew shook hands with Vrenbeesol and his men.

The following month was busy and there were daily meetings with the brightest minds on the planet. The six androids from the crew worked around the clock as they had no need to sleep and Kody transferred a huge amount of medical information to the doctors. Some of the medical technology was not understood by the doctors at the present time, but Kody knew they would eventually grasp the knowledge and be able to use it to cure patients. Computers did not exist on the planet and the information had to be printed on paper.

The human crew was also transferring simple technology that could be used by the scientists. Design of a beginner computer system, groundmobiles and airmobiles were transferred to storage devices and could be used in the future, when the scientists were more advanced and able to understand the information. Half of the transferred knowledge was usable right away by the scientists, but half of it was too advanced and the people would have to save it for later use when they were more sophisticated. The crew made sure Vrenbeesol and his people were present at all the meetings. Vrenbeesol had several consultations with the president and they reached a peace agreement. The army put a quick end to the mess in the cities and it would be a big effort to restore the buildings to their former appearance. It would take decades.

Eric took Vrenbeesol and his men for a spin in the shuttle and they were breathless with excitement. Overnight, they had become technology buffs and Eric knew that feeling was necessary to ensure their minds were occupied with creativity and not war.

After an exhausting month, the crew had finished their work and when they left, Vrenbeesol and the president stood side by side and wished them a safe journey in space. Dori-Venn leaned for support on Vrenbeesol's arm and their faces were peaceful. They knew the spaceship was in orbit from the holographic images they had seen, but if they could actually understand how the ship orbited and what made it work was unclear. Anyway, all the information was safely saved on storage devices and the scientists would eventually piece it all together. It would take many years, but with the technology they did comprehend, their planet had advanced a hundred years.

***

The ship was back in space and continued through unchartered areas traveling towards the center of the galaxy. For three months, it was just open space, then the vibration started and they knew a portal with a sizeable tunnel was ahead. As they neared the tunnel, the ship shook with such force no one could stand up on the Bridge and they had to strap themselves down. The crew felt as if the tunnel swallowed the ship and they were sucked inside with enormous power. To their relief, the tunnel was very wide and they had no trouble staying in the middle of it. The copilots watched the instrument panel carefully and reported loud they had tripled their speed. Most tunnels would double the speed of a ship, but to triple the speed was unusual and they understood it was a mega portal. For nine long hours the crew took turns at the controls and when they finally catapulted out of the tunnel, their speed was breathtakingly fast. Perhaps the fastest any of the crew had ever traveled. The androids reported they had advanced a distance of fifteen thousand light years and carefully entered all the data into the computer system. Images of each tunnel were always entered into the computers and then used in flight simulators to train new pilots.

A large star was visible with two planets orbiting. The first planet was too close to its star to be habitable and the second planet was orbiting too far from the star to have comfortable conditions for living. They entered orbit around the second planet and to their surprise the planet was brightly lit after dark. It had a population. Early the next morning, they launched the drone and waited impatiently for the images to be sent to the ship. A world of snow and ice appeared on the images and short, stocky humanoids dressed in heavy furs were walking around on the ground. No air traffic and no vehicles were visible on the surface, but they did notice various designs of sleds pulled by short animals resembling goats. The surface temperature registered twenty degrees below freezing.

"They have apparently discovered natural electricity, but still live a totally primitive lifestyle," Matthias, the copilot, remarked. "Wonder who helped them."

"Probably missionaries," Kody said. "There is arctic clothing onboard and let's descend and find out."

Dressed in survival gear, they landed the shuttle outside a little town and exited. When they opened the shuttle door, a blast of ice-cold wind hit them hard and they felt as if their bare faces would freeze in an instant. The androids were also dressed in winter clothes, mostly to fit in with the crew, as they could withstand the harshest conditions without damage.

"Brrr! This wind will for sure wake you up!" Tothellim grumbled. "Good God, it's the worst I've ever felt. We'll become ice cubes if we stay out in this weather."

They locked the shuttle and walked bent over to avoid the fury of the wind and within ten minutes they reached the little town. When they passed the first house, the door opened and a tiny, middle-aged humanoid woman took pity on them and waved them in. The crew gratefully nodded and entered the modest house. Inside was neat and clean and very warm, about eighty degrees Fahrenheit, and it felt wonderful. To their surprise, the woman had a translation device in her hand. She was barely five feet tall, stocky without being fat, her long, dark hair braided and her skin was yellowish tan. Her features were mostly human, but her wide cheekbones and large dark eyes reminded the crew of pictures they had seen of Eskimos on planet Earth.

"Welcome to planet Tsettimon. My name is Ecksel," the woman said in a pleasant-sounding language.

"We come from planet Veehnia, a long distance from here and we're space exploders," Eric explained.

They removed their jackets and sat down around the woman's kitchen table.

Ecksel told them that a generation ago, missionaries had visited the planet and dealt out simple electronics, translation devices and other useful gadgets that had made their lives easier. But the biggest gift from the missionaries had been teaching them how natural electricity worked. They had supplied all the black boxes they had on their ship and stayed on the planet until they had built a large supply of black boxes, so every house and building had natural electricity. When Ecksel saw the shuttle, she understood they were from another planet.

"Do you have a summer on this planet?" Eric asked.

"Yes, but very short and the snow doesn't always melt completely in the summer. We can grow a few fast-growing crops and hay for our animals, but it's always a fight against the weather and it's very difficult to live here. We eat mostly fish. The ocean is frozen now, but in the summer, everyone must buy fish from the fishermen so it lasts the whole winter. We store the fish outside. Most of the people on our planet would like to leave, but we have no spaceships and we don't know if any planet would want us."

Kody reflected on what she said. "There are plenty of underpopulated planets in the universe and if they knew you are willing to emigrate, they would allow you to settle on their planet. The problem is they don't know you're here. This planet is unfit for life. You will never prosper living under such harsh conditions. If we can find a planet not too far from here, would you be willing to move?"

"*Yes!* It would be a dream come true."

"How many citizens live on Tsettimon?"

"There are only about five million of us left now. People die young on this planet from the hardships we must endure. There is no joy in our lives and many married couples choose not to have children because they have no future. Suicides are common. My husband is dead. He froze to death five years ago and I have only one daughter. She is alive, but struggling with depression and has lost her will to live. I think everyone wants to leave."

"Is the climate stable or is it getting more severe?"

"More severe. Every year the winters are colder and soon no crops will grow. We just barely survive now and if it gets any colder, we'll all die."

"Who is your leader and what's his or her name?" Eric asked.

"It's a woman and her name is Isrella. She lives in the next town over from here."

"Ecksel, this is what we'll do," Eric said. "We'll return to our ship, which is orbiting your planet right now, and do a thorough search through our computers and try to find a planet that will evacuate you. From what you tell us, I strongly believe your planet has entered into an ice age and the climate will only get worse. Ice ages come and go on many planets, it's cyclical. You will not survive on Tsettimon."

Ecksel smiled and said "I hope you're successful."

The crew said goodbye to Ecksel and fought their way back to the shuttle. The wind had intensified and they were frozen to the bone when they entered the shuttle. Rhett piloted the shuttle and turned up the heat full blast. Back on the ship they discussed what to do and all of them agreed it was just a matter of time until the planet would freeze over and enter into an ice age and it was anyone's guess how long it would last. They knew it could last several thousand years and the people on Tsettimon had no chance. They were doomed.

All of them searched for nearby planets using the ship's computer system and Kody finally found a planet not too far away with an advanced society and a pleasant climate. People from the planet had posted messages many times on the Interstellar Internet and the planet was large, about the size of Veehnia, but with a rather small population compared to the size of the planet. Kody prepared a message explaining the situation and sent it to the planet using the code listed on the Internet.

To their surprise, they received a lengthy reply the next day from the leader of the planet they would send five of their cargo ships right away, each ship could take five hundred people. The travel time was two months with the help of four short tunnels. Using only five cargo ships would require two thousand trips, but two neighboring planets had offered to assist as it was a humanitarian crisis. Pooling their resources, they were hoping to evacuate all the people on Tsettimon within a couple of years. They would contact a few other planets asking for additional assistance to speed up the process. The first ships would leave in two days as soon as supplies had been loaded onto the ships. The citizens on Tsettimon would have to use some kind of lottery system to decide in what order the people would leave. The first group of two thousand five hundred people should be ready to be picked up in two months. The planet extended a welcome to all the people on Tsettimon and they would receive help to start a new life.

Kody replied immediately they had received the message and would inform the people. The next day, they took the shuttle and landed in the town where Isrella lived. It was even colder than the day before and they found Isrella's house after they had knocked on a few doors asking for directions. She opened and realized right away they were from outer space and invited them in. She was in her thirties with a bright mind.

They sat down in her cabin and explained to her they had met Ecksel and had arranged to have all the citizens evacuated from the planet. Kody told her they were sure the planet had entered into an ice age and would soon freeze over. Isrella nodded and agreed. She knew it was true.

"You'll have to arrange a lottery system to decide which citizens should leave first. It will probably take a couple of years to move all of you out of here. Our ship will take one hundred of you and we'll drop you off on your new planet on our way back to our home planet."

"I and many of us knew we were entering into an ice age and our gratitude to you for helping us is beyond words," Isrella said with tears in her eyes. "We will never forget your assistance. I'll just move the families out in alphabetical order. Our people are unselfish and I know there will be no fighting over who should move first. I'll be the last to go as I'm the president. If I don't make it, so be it. My people must come first."

"We leave in two days at dawn and please have one hundred people ready to come with us. It will take too long to use the shuttle to bring so many people to the ship, so we intend to land the ship here on the surface so they can board the ship here. Remind your people to limit their luggage. Only what they need for the trip."

They said goodbye and returned to the ship. The androids checked the food supply and told Eric there was sufficient food onboard to feed a hundred people for two months and also for the crew for the return trip to Veehnia. The ship was not equipped with extra cabins and the passengers would have to sleep in their seats, but they reclined and were comfortable.

At daybreak, the ship descended to the surface. The wind was blowing and it was snowing lightly. A hundred people were waiting and they were all shivering in the freezing temperature. It was twenty-five degrees below freezing with a biting wind making it almost unbearable. The androids opened up the cargo bay and all the people were loaded onto the ship in record time so they could close up the ship. They were shown to their seats and strapped in and Eric was at the controls when they took off. The only person on the ground was Isrella waving farewell to the ship as it took off, a lone figure braving the elements. None of the passengers had ever been off the ground, but they showed remarkable courage and the androids sat with them and explained what was happening. They were willing to endure anything just to get off their frigid planet. The temperature on the ship was comfortably warm and the passengers stopped shivering after a while. While the ship increased the speed, they were not allowed to leave their seats. They were model passengers and none of them ever complained. These were truly hardy people. The androids prepared them for the passage through the tunnels and explained it was totally safe, but would shake tremendously. Still, all of them remained calm.

Tothellim had become a lover of classical music from Earth by listening to hours and hours of Logan's playing and had all his music downloaded onto the ship's entertainment system. He would often play Chopin's nocturnes for the passengers and they would stop and just listen, almost spellbound. Logan played with intense sensitivity that came through in his playing and the passengers absorbed the music with their souls.

They arrived at the new planet and landed on a sunny and warm surface. What a difference. The passengers laughed, cheered and some even cried with gratitude. Eleven small children were among the passengers and the parents' eyes radiated hope for the future. The government of their new planet had built 3D printed houses and most of them were ready for occupancy.

The leaders of the planet welcomed the crew and the passengers. The native people were tall, handsome humanoids and carried themselves with dignity and it was obvious the people were highly advanced and had deep respect for all life. The crew felt admiration and almost a sense of awe when interacting with them and their sophistication was noticeable. They met with the leaders and explained the dire conditions on Tsettimon and the leaders responded several planets had agreed to assist in the evacuation and they hoped to have all of them off the planet within a year and a half.

The crew thanked the leaders and left the next day. The trip home to Veehnia would take eleven months and they looked forward to coming home. The long return trip went well and Leo's gravity chambers were very appreciated and in use for hours every day. They prevented loss of muscle tone and bone loss and kept the crew almost as strong as when they were not up in space.

When they landed on Veehnia, they were met by their families, a group of government people and the president. They had been gone two years and they had so much to tell. Every return trip by a crew sent out on an exploratory mission was an event met with excitement and the highlights of the expedition were always posted on the Internet. The citizens had been alerted the ship was on its way home and people looked forward with eagerness to read about their adventures.

The crew would take three months off and then depart again. In the meantime, Eric, Rhett and Matthias were scheduled to have their Nuvirenn procedure done and all of them looked forward to it.

CHAPTER 22

On Earth2, Telly felt great after his Nuvirenn procedure and so did his wife Ellala. Both of them were one hundred and eight years old and felt fifty years younger. They had lived on their beloved planet Earth2 for sixty-three years and considered it the best planet in the universe. Before the Nuvirenn procedure, they were both retired and found it boring to be home, but after they were 'updated' they both went back to work. Telly got his old job back as advisor to the president and Ellala loved her work as a nurse.

For years, Telly had been bothered by a nagging thought there was trouble on the first planet. His second trip to the first planet had occurred forty-five years ago and he discussed his suspicions all may not be well on the first planet with his best friend Ássurt. He listened carefully and suggested they should take a trip over there and check it out. Ássurt had never retired and was full of energy after his Nuvirenn procedure and looked forward to an adventurous trip to the first planet. He was one hundred and five years old, a widower. His wife had died before the Nuvirenn procedure was available. He was close to a Ziggelus woman, Trebbie, only forty years old and with a heart of pure gold. The Ziggelus people were not attractive, but Ássurt was in love with her personality and soul and overlooked her lack of beauty. Not even his wife had showered him with such kindness and love as Trebbie did. He had recently asked her to marry him and she had accepted his proposal. She had never been married. Ássurt's wife had not been able to have children, but he was hoping Trebbie would give him a child, a dream of his.

The Tellyship was still going strong and the government agreed to fund a trip to the first planet. Telly, Ássurt, Atlas, Rasufilus and Ijakull, the geologist, would be the crew and the four pilots, who had in the past always manned the Tellyship, would again be at the controls. They were by now elderly men, but had been returned to younger age by their 'updating'.

When Ássurt last visited the first planet, he had recorded the speech of the natives and in his spare time, he had managed to write a program translating their language into Frejjan. Ássurt was a brilliant man with an incredible intellect and he was known as Earth2's 'scholar'. The translation device was now loaded with the natives' language and communication would finally be possible. In the past, conversation had been very slow and limited. Atlas, Rasufilus and Ijakull were eager to come along. Rasufilus and Ijakull were both one hundred and three years old, but felt 'peppy' and vibrant after their Nuvirenn procedure.

Telly visited with Vitzoll and Janus before they left and confided in them he had bad feelings something was wrong on planet one and perhaps the natives were in danger. Vitzoll assured him he would check his communication system often and if they needed military intervention, his fleet would leave within a day. The ships were always stocked with the basics and could be readied in less than a day.

Before departure, Ássurt married Trebbie and they spent a week honeymooning. He was deeply in love with her and in his eyes, she was lovely. All he saw was her angelic personality.

The Tellyship took off and it was only two months' travel time to reach the first planet. The whole trip Telly felt anxious inside. He just knew something was not right.

They entered orbit in the morning and sent out a reconnaissance drone to make sure it was safe to descend with the shuttle. The images transmitted back to the ship confirmed Telly's worst fears. The planet was invaded! A large mining operation was visible. Humanoid people were supervising and next to the mine were barracks for living and two large cargo ships. The drone took closeups of the ore and Ijakull recognized right away it was unrefined gold. The planet was being stripped of anything of value and no one stopped the thieves.

The crew agreed they had no choice but to contact Vitzoll and Janus and Rasufilus used an encrypted channel and explained the situation to Vitzoll. Vitzoll asked them to stay in orbit until he and his fleet reached the planet. His ships traveled twice as fast as the Tellyship and they would leave the same day and reach them in one month. Rasufilus agreed and ended the transmission. Unfortunately, the Tellyship had no cloaking ability and if one of the cargo ships left the planet, they could be discovered and shot down. From the images the drone had sent back, they had noticed the cargo ships were of late design and most likely equipped with powerful weaponry.

"We may be able to land on the surface and hide the ship," Telly suggested. "It may be safer than staying in orbit. The jungle is full of huge, green leaves and if we all chip in, we can have the ship covered in a day. The natives will help, I'm sure. It's safer than being shot down in orbit. We can notify Vitzoll where we are."

"I agree," Rasufilus said. "We're sitting ducks in orbit. We can descend in early evening when it's almost dark with all the lights turned off. Based on my experience, I can tell you we're dealing with a large outfit of organized crime and these people are highly dangerous. We have no chance alone and when Vitzoll arrives, I will join him in his spaceship and assist him."

They launched the drone again and the area where Sidji used to live was about fifty miles from the mining area. They retrieved the drone and agreed they would descend to the surface that same evening.

All the lights were off and the ship was dark. The pilots were experienced and put the ship down gently a mile from Sidji's hamlet. They were sure no one had seen them as it was almost totally dark outside. They stayed on the ship and slept for a few hours and at first light, they climbed out. It was not yet hot outside and Telly and Ássurt jogged over to the hamlet. Telly banged on the door to the first hut and a man opened the door. Telly had the translation device in his hand and quickly asked where Sidji was. The man recognized him even though it had been forty-five years since Telly had visited. He smiled and shook hands with them and replied Sidji and Vuula had been dead 'long, long'. Ássurt was relieved his translation of their language apparently worked.

"This is a translation device so we can talk. What's happening on the planet?"

The man told them his name was Kvetros and his face showed terror as he started to explain.

"People from sky come and kill our people. They have big birds come and go to sky. They take stone and put on birds. They say they kill us we come to them."

Ássurt listened carefully to the way the man handled his own language and noticed the language did not have any real grammar, time was an unknown concept and sentences were not structured; a series of single words were used instead of sentences.

"Our bird is here, on ground," Telly explained, hoping the man would get it. "We fight the men. Many birds will arrive and kill the men."

Kvetros nodded his head and looked hopeful hearing help was on the way. How much he understood was not clear, but he did understand Telly and his men were on their side and would help them.

Telly took a stick and started to draw in the sand showing many 'birds' were on the way and would help. Now Kvetros got it. He understood reinforcement was on the way. Telly tried to explain it would take a month for the ships to arrive and he said "take many days". The device said the words in the native language, but Kvetros could not understand the meaning, so Telly lay down pretending to sleep, got up, then down again. Now Kvetros understood. He nodded wildly with his head and made it known he understood it would take a while. He had no concept of time, only that some things happened 'now' and some things 'not now'. Telly was inventive and knew how to get past the language barrier. He asked Kvetros to assemble his men and come with them to cover the ship. After a few tries he understood and came back with all the men in the hamlet. Some remembered Telly and Ássurt and smiled at them.

The group walked back to the ship and the men were in awe when they saw the huge ship. Telly put leaves on the ship and, strangely enough, they did figure out they must hide the ship. It took several hours, but when the men were done the ship was totally hidden under a canopy of jungle leaves. Afterwards, the men and the crew sat down on the ground together and talked. The sun was out and the heat was intense even in the shade. Slowly and with much effort, the crew got the message across there would be war when the birds arrived and they did not want the natives to help. They also conveyed the foreign men were dangerous. The natives understood. They explained the foreigners had been on the planet 'long, long' and taken 'much stone' from the planet, so apparently the mining had been going on for years. Telly remarked to the crew they must have stolen tons of gold from the planet worth a fortune.

"Men come here?" Atlas asked.

"Come take woman," one of them said and looked down with a sad face. So, the women had been raped. Rasufilus felt fury inside. He could hardly wait to catch the criminals.

"Men hurt children?" he asked.

"Girl, yes."

Telly was usually so calm, but when he heard even the girls had been raped, he was fuming. He made the natives understand the foreigners would be punished and removed from the planet.

The crew lived on the ship and sent a transmission to Vitzoll to land his ship on the surface. Vitzoll's fleet had cloaking capabilities and were invisible to the miners. Most likely, the miners had no idea they were under surveillance.

The crew interacted with the natives while they were waiting for Vitzoll to arrive. Atlas took care of medical problems. The Tellyship had a nicely equipped sickbay and Atlas examined all the natives. They were mostly healthy and he found no serious diseases. Their teeth were in poor condition from chewing on a mildly narcotic root. Ássurt continued studying their language and made some corrections to the program he had written for the translation device. Rasufilus was working on strategy how to take out all the miners. Telly and Ijakull were busy recording the history of the natives, a tedious affair due to the language problem. A group of native men did their best to describe their past and important events that had occurred.

Vitzoll and his fleet arrived after one month, just as he had said, and the fleet stayed in orbit cloaked. Only Vitzoll and Janus landed their cloaked ship at dusk next to the Tellyship. They knew the exact location of the ship from their instruments, but Vitzoll told them the ship was so well hidden it was totally invisible from the air. All of them sat down together in the dining area on the Tellyship.

"I have some tactics worked out, but we need more information to ensure the plan will work," Rasufilus started his explanation. "I would like to capture one of the worker robots. If we can get close to one of them and get to his kill-switch, we can get all the information we need from his memory package. Option two is to stun one of the guards and hope we can get him to talk. That may not work. There is no guarantee he will talk. We need to know how often the cargo ships leave and if there are additional ships in their fleet or if the two ships we see on the surface are the only ships they have. The worker robots can easily be reprogrammed and used in the mines on Earth2. The gangsters should stand trial, either on the planet they came from or at the Cosmic Court on planet Cerres. Some of the gold Vitzoll can take as payment for his services and the rest of it belongs to the natives. The problem is, they have no use for it. To offer them modern housing and various gadgets would overwhelm them. They have to be allowed to evolve at their own rate. The mine should be abandoned and the natives will rediscover it in the future when they are more evolved."

"It's a good idea to catch one of the robots, Rasufilus," Telly said. "How the heck did the gangsters find out about the first planet? Our citizens have never revealed its existence to anyone."

"Gangs like this roam all over the universe and they must have happened on the planet by accident," Vitzoll replied. "I suggest we don't fire on the two cargo ships, if possible. They will become the property of our planet. One of the ships should be used for transport of the gangsters to wherever they will stand trial and the second ship can be flown to Earth2.

The men agreed with Vitzoll.

"The people at the other end receiving the gold must also be charged," Janus remarked. "They all know the location of this planet and that it's loaded with gold. Other criminals may return in a few years when this mission is forgotten and then start mining again."

"There's no choice but to check on the natives on an annual basis," Rasufilus said. "None of us can live here in this boiling heat, so the next best remedy is to check on the natives as often as we can."

"If we leave a black box supplying electricity, we can give the natives a simple communication device," Ássurt interjected. "If they're invaded again in the future, they can reach us and report it. The miners must have the equipment we need and I'll teach the natives how to send a simple signal to us. All they have to do is to send an SOS to us."

"Good idea, let's do so," Telly replied.

"Vitzoll has a spy drone with cloaking ability and let's launch it right now and see how they have placed their guards," Rasufilus continued. "The drone only needs a little light to function and the mining area may be lit up. When we have all the information from the robot's memory, we can continue working out a plan how to shut them down."

The plan was accepted and they launched the drone. It was almost silent when it took off and at a few hundred feet elevation, no one on the ground would be able to hear it. The drone reached the camp within fifteen minutes and the images arrived. The area was illuminated and the robots were still working. Two armed humanoid men were outside the entry to the mine, probably acting as guards. Vitzoll directed the drone to the barracks and they noticed two humanoid chefs preparing food. No guard was outside the barracks. It was obvious they did not expect anyone to interfere with their business.

"They'll take a dinner break soon and that's when we have our chance to catch one of the robots," Rasufilus exclaimed. "Vitzoll, Janus and I will leave right away and transport ourselves with the portable engines to the camp. We'll bring an extra engine for the robot. We have to hurry."

There were six portable engines stowed away on Vitzoll's ship and the three men strapped an engine onto their backs and armed themselves with stun guns and laser guns. Rasufilus carried a fourth engine as well as the electronic device to remotely shut down the robot's kill-switch. It could also be done manually, if they could get close enough to the robot. They took off in a hurry. It would take thirty minutes to reach the camp.

They stopped a short distance from the camp and left the engines on the ground and then jogged to the mining area. As they expected, the guards had left to have their dinner and Rasufilus, Vitzoll and Janus slowly approached the entrance. Janus stayed outside to be on the lookout for the guards and Rasufilus and Vitzoll walked into the narrow entrance of the mine. They heard the sound of mining drills and all of a sudden one of the robots came walking out of the tunnel and Rasufilus instantly used his device to shut down his kill-switch. The robot stopped dead in his tracks and was immobilized. Rasufilus grabbed him and tossed him onto Vitzoll's back and they ran out of the tunnel as fast as they could. The robot was heavier than a man and Vitzoll struggled carrying his weight, but he managed to do it and they were soon out of the tunnel. Janus was relieved to see them and they ran toward the engines. They all knew the camp may be under surveillance while the guards had dinner, but they had to take that chance. Rasufilus strapped an engine onto the back of the robot and all four took off with Rasufilus holding the robot in a firm grip. All of them breathed a sigh of relief when they were safely back at the ship. Rasufilus removed the memory package from the slot in the robot's back and entered it into the Tellyship's computer. The robot would remain immobilized as long as his kill-switch was set on 'off'.

Atlas, being an android, stayed with the robot and scanned him. As he expected, he had a backup memory chip and Atlas downloaded the information onto his own memory package and went over to the men. The information on the robot's memory package did not give the whole story, but the additional information from Atlas' memory supplied all the information they needed. The robot was strictly a worker robot without much individuality, but he had been able to make a few observations and these tidbits of information were on the backup memory chip.

The memory revealed the gangsters worked out of a planet called Tiira-3, a planet located in the Pleiades group of stars, about four months' travel time from the first planet. The mining had started five years ago and the gold deposit in the mine was enormous and would probably last for several more decades. The company on Tiira-3 had already made a fortune from the gold they had extracted and probably sold on the black market. All the names of the people involved were listed, including the number of ships they had. They only had the two cargo ships and no shuttle or fighter ships. The number of people working at the mine was listed as eight and twenty-two robots were doing the work in the mine. Four pilots stayed in the barracks while waiting for the ships to fill with ore. The robot had apparently been a good observer and whatever he noticed was added to his memory chips.

"There are only eight of them and that will make the mission easier to finish," Rasufilus observed. "The robots are never armed and can't strike back at us. There are two guards, two chefs and four humanoids inside the mine. The four pilots will be armed and dangerous. My plan is to remove the only transportation they have, namely the cargo ships. It requires that two of Vitzoll's ships will descend and land here. We leave their ships here and the four pilots will use the portable engines to get to the cargo ships while the gangsters sleep. Remember, they have no idea we're here and won't be on guard. We have to hope they haven't noticed one of the robots is missing. Once the cargo ships are removed, we have them. They have no way to escape. Vitzoll's fleet can descend and they have no choice but to surrender. There are only twelve of them altogether and whatever weapon they fire at our ships will not make serious damage. It's still time to pull it off tonight. Vitzoll, please contact your fleet and ask for two ships to descend and the pilots must know how to fly a cargo ship."

Vitzoll knew which pilots could fly the large ships and quickly got in touch with them. They had formerly worked as pilots on large ships and had the skill to fly just about anything that could lift off the ground.

Within half an hour the four pilots joined the team. Rasufilus quickly briefed them and they took off with the portable engines. It would be dawn in three hours, but by that time the cargo ships would be off the ground. The pilots landed close to the mining camp and without removing the engines from their backs, they crawled up to the cargo ships. The entry doors were open and they dragged themselves inside to avoid being spotted on the surveillance system, in case there was such a system. Once inside, they quickly locked the entry door and fired up the engines. The pilots noticed the ships were state of the art and very modern with the latest weaponry installed and powerful engines to haul heavy cargo. The roar of the two ships' engines echoed throughout the camp and at the moment the ships lifted off the ground, the shooting started to no avail. Several bullets hit the ships and just bounced off without doing any damage. Within a minute they were airborne and out of sight. The mining team was shocked, speechless and totally caught off guard. Both cargo ships would wait in orbit. The pilots noticed the ships had plenty of food stocked onboard.

Rasufilus and his men saw the ships in the sky and knew the pilots had been successful. Vitzoll called his fleet asking them to descend and stay in the air above the camp until he, Janus and Rasufilus joined them in Vitzoll's ship. When they arrived at the camp, all the ships were hovering in the air and almost covered the sky, a frightful scene to say the least. Vitzoll descended to five hundred feet and using his loudspeaker, he spoke in their language through the translation device.

"Come out of the mine unarmed and stay on your knees, hands behind your neck. Bring all the robots out and activate their kill-switch."

The criminals followed the orders and did not shoot. One of the fighter ships hovered above the barracks and commanded the chefs and the four pilots to join the men at the mine. They obeyed. They knew it was over and there was nowhere to escape to.

The rest of the mission was finished without loss of life and four of the fighter ships landed. The pilots gave a mild stun shot to each of the criminals so they could be put into chains without resistance. The robots were all immobilized with their kill-switch set on 'off'. Vitzoll checked each of them to see for himself they had been turned off. They were.

Once the twelve gangsters were securely restrained by chains and the stun wore off, Rasufilus and Telly interrogated them.

"What planet are you from?" Telly asked in a demanding voice.

"Tiira-3," one of them replied. The men showed no resistance and appeared apathetic.

"Are all of you from Tiira-3?"

"Yes."

"How many people are involved in this operation?" Rasufilus asked.

"Only twenty or so. The company we work for wants to keep a low profile. The government doesn't know the company is mining here."

"How many ships do you have?"

"Only the two you stole from us."

"How many of the natives did you kill?"

"Five, in the beginning. They tried to stop us from staying and we had to kill them."

"How much gold did you extract so far?"

"Several tons. We were well paid, but the owners of the company took most of the profits. The gold was sold unrefined on the black market and we heard the owners have accounts in the Cosmic Bank, but we think the money they could deposit wasn't much. They just recently paid off the last installment for the two ships and the robots. The ships were incredibly expensive and these five years, most of the money was used to pay for the ships. Only now, when the ships are paid for, would the company start making money they could keep. We were promised to get some of the profits when the ships were paid off."

Dawn had arrived and Telly and the men had heard what they needed to hear to finish the mission. Vitzoll contacted the cargo ships in orbit and asked them to land at the camp. The robots were loaded inside a locked compartment on one of the ships to be reprogrammed and used in the mines on Earth2. The two fighter ships Vitzoll's pilots had flown were carefully rolled inside the cargo bay and chained down and the pilots were told to return to Earth2. They left and landed safely back home. The pilots got the feel of the ship during the return flight and reported to Vitzoll later on they were truly excellent ships with tremendous power and speed.

The prisoners, still in chains, were safely held in a secure storage area on the second ship and even though the room was rather large, they would have to endure real hardships during the trip back to Tiira-3. There were no comforts on the ship for the prisoners. The sewage system on the ship worked by suction and the waste was incinerated. An extension of the sewage pipe was added and inserted into the room holding the prisoners. They would have to use the pipe for their bathroom needs hoping for a good aim. There was a small opening in the door so food could be distributed and the men would have to sleep on the floor.

Rasufilus informed the two pilots he would contact the government on Tiira-3 and notify them the ship was on its way and also give them all the information about the illegal mining operation. The ship took off and it would take them four months to reach Tiira-3. After unloading the criminals on the planet, the pilots would fly the ship to Earth 2.

Telly and the men removed all the electronics from the barracks as well as the mining equipment, which could be used on Earth2. Ássurt programmed one of the communication devices with an SOS signal capable of reaching Earth2. All the natives were told to watch as Ássurt went through the few simple steps to send the signal. They understood it would send an alarm to Earth2, but Ássurt had to repeat the steps over and over until they had it memorized. They were told never to play with the system and only use it if the miners came back.

Vitzoll took the gold he needed to pay for his fee and the rest of it was just abandoned and left in the tunnels. Sometime in the future when the natives were more sophisticated, the mine could be restarted by the natives. Vitzoll and his fleet returned to Earth2.

Telly and his men loaded the mining drills and electronics onto the Tellyship, said farewell to the natives and left. The natives were visibly sad to see them leave. The return trip went well and they landed on Earth2. The government had already been informed by Vitzoll about the mission and the cargo ship was admired by the citizens. It would be put to good use and there were several pilots among the citizens with the skill to fly the two ships. The robots were stripped of all their programming and after they were reprogrammed, they worked faithfully in the mines on Earth2.

The second cargo ship would arrive in a few months.

Ássurt was greeted by Trebbie whispering into his ear a baby was on the way. It was a boy, doing well in the artificial womb, and would be born in four months. A tearful Ássurt held his wife a long time hardly able to believe he would become a father at the age of one hundred and five years old.

***

The ship with the prisoners arrived at Tiira-3 and they were expected. A group of police officers took the prisoners away and they would face trial together with all the people involved. Most of them would be put to death by lethal injection as was the law on the planet. Illegal mining on a sovereign planet was considered a serious offense and usually punished by death. Government officials assured Vitzoll's pilots they would not reveal the location of the first planet as the natives were defenseless and needed protection. They also agreed the two cargo ships belonged to Earth2 as they had been in charge of the mission and rescued the natives.

CHAPTER 23

Life on Earth was good and most of the people had gone through the Nuvirenn procedure. Rejuvenation of the people had swept across Earth and Nuvirenn continuously received transmission messages from grateful people. Direct communication between Earth and Nuvirenn was not possible, but twice a year a single Nuvirenn ship landed on Earth and always returned with the ship fully loaded with immigrants to their planet. When the ship landed on Earth, people were able to upload their greetings to relatives living on Nuvirenn as well as express their gratitude to the doctors who had so generously shared their discovery. The ship transmitted all the messages once it was back on Nuvirenn. People from Earth now living on Nuvirenn sent messages back to their families on Earth praising the lifestyle on their new planet and many married natives. The natives were able to have children with people from Earth, but seldom with a spouse from their own planet and that was the reason why the ships kept coming from Nuvirenn. Moreover, the planet was seriously underpopulated.

Every time the ship visited Earth, a few scholars and advanced spiritual people from Nuvirenn would discourse over the Internet sharing their advanced minds. They traveled along on the ship with the sole purpose of informing the people on Earth and increase their awareness and mental abilities. These lectures were immensely popular and did result in an upgrade of Earth's population. People saw what was possible and realized the power of the mind. Nuvirenn became a true sister planet to Earth and was loved and admired by people in all countries on Earth. By learning about the power of the mind from the people of Nuvirenn, many people on Earth declared they felt liberated, calmer and they experienced a general sense of bliss. With a life expectancy of three hundred years, people had the time to experiment with mental exploration.

Materialism lost its grip over people and was replaced by mental abilities, getting to know oneself and accepting oneself. Self-hate, for example, was a hindrance to a person's advancement and finding the reason for it was an important exercise. People adhering to the Nuvirenn beliefs became refined and sophisticated and had the inner strength to transcend trivial problems. Parents taught their children and healthy minds were born.

***

On Nuvirenn, Helga and Settie had four children and Trenna and Jianyu had three. Both Helga and Trenna had had children every year since they married, but they did, of course, use the artificial womb. Peter and his brother Tommy and Trenna's daughter Liling were now attending the little schoolhouse and an android teacher, Miss Nellie, resided in the school building. Peter was four years old and Tommy and Liling three. Helga had three boys and a girl and Trenna three girls.

Miss Nellie was wonderful with the children and Nita, the maid, went along every day in the airmobile. Peter could read already and his implant was replaced annually to boost his cognition. The children thought school was the best thing in their lives and were eager to learn.

Helga felt four children were enough, but Settie wanted one more and she gave in. She was very fertile and was soon pregnant again. When the baby was transferred to the womb, they found out it was a girl.

Helga's life was easy and she never had to work hard physically. She and Settie rode their horses every day and the maids did all the cooking and cleaning. She helped Settie with his computer work and enjoyed overseeing the milking process. Tending the garden was one of Helga's hobbies and she liked watching the seedlings grow into full size plants.

It was winter and a light snow cover made skiing possible. Helga and Settie enjoyed cross-country skiing and would often take off for an hour or two, just to be out in the fresh air. The winters were mild and never severe. The next day they would travel to the city to bring their baby girl home and they were so excited to pick her up. Helga had told Settie no more children and he had agreed with her. Settie was an enthusiastic dad and spent a lot of time with his children. They had a happy marriage.

***

Rex and Elsa had accepted a dangerous job, but it was only a month's travel time to the workstation that had hired them and the crew had agreed they should take the job. All of them were running low on cash and the bid had been very generous as the job involved a high risk.

Elsa's sister Hanna was looking after the children in her home and Elsa was determined not to take unnecessary chances. Since she became a mother, Elsa was not so macho anymore.

The huge workstation had been hijacked by a criminal gang and their nine fighter ships were docked all around the station. The station sold fuel to ships as well as supplies and was fully stocked when the hijacking occurred. To try to shoot any of the fighter ships down was too dangerous as a miss would jeopardize the workstation itself. All the fuel tanks had been filled and a powerful hit on the area where the tanks were located could blow up the station. It was in orbit around a toxic, uninhabited planet and the workstation was on its own without sufficient defense. To orbit an uninhabited planet was free and perhaps not such a good idea. The fee to orbit an inhabited planet was high, but much more secure as the planet supplied security for the workstation. The station had been in orbit for many years and never been attacked and the owners had been lulled into a false sense of security. The two owners and the crew of thirty men and twenty robots were locked up on the station. Before they were locked up, one of the owners had managed to quickly contact Rex and offer him the job in exchange for a substantial amount of gold and Rex accepted. He knew it was a highly dangerous mission, but he felt sorry for the crew and told himself he would outfox the criminals. The hijackers had not noticed the owner sent off the transmission and were unaware that Rex and his fleet were on their way.

Rex told Elsa he suspected the gangsters would throw the owners and the crew out through the cargo bay, keep the robots and strip them of their memory. That way they had nothing to report. Their next step would probably be to move the station to a new location and take it over as their property. Most likely, they would sell it on the black market. Workstations popped up here and there all the time and they often moved to better locations, so the fact that this station 'disappeared' would not raise suspicion. A fully stocked workstation of this huge size was worth a fortune and not hard to sell, so Rex was not surprised the criminals had taken the chance to hijack it and succeeded. The probability the workstation had moved out of the area already was small as the criminals had to arrange where to take it and find a buyer.

They were close enough now to see the planet and the workstation and Rex ordered his fleet to stop and hover. Using the encrypted channel, he informed them he was launching his cloaked spy drone and if they opened their transmission channel, they would receive the images from the drone. Soon the pictures were visible and they saw humanoids through the windows. Rex guessed there were at least twenty of them. No engines were running on the workstation, so there was time to invent a military plan. Rex had no strategy yet, but his mind was working hard to create a safe, but efficient attack. Rex brought back the drone. It had confirmed the station was hijacked.

Workstations were too big to ever land on a planet. They were built in orbit by robots and the hijackers were probably trying to find a planet to orbit and sell the station from that location. It would not be easy as they risked detection by the planet they orbited illegally, if the planet was inhabited. If they could find an uninhabited planet, it would be safer for the hijackers. Distance was of importance as a workstation was too large to pass through a tunnel and their travel speed was slow due to their size. Rex checked his navigation charts and saw one possible planet, three weeks' travel time from the present location and marked as 'uninhabited'. That was the best choice the hijackers had and Rex told his crew he guessed that would probably be the new location for the station.

"They have nine ships, we have twenty," Rex addressed his fleet. "My plan is not perfect, but this is what I suggest. Please give me your input when I'm done. We can't do battle here with the fighter ships docked and it's too risky to start shooting so close to the station's fuel tanks. In a few days, they'll most likely move the station. The pilots will fly the fighter ships and perhaps two or three of them will pilot the station. Once they break orbit, the ships may fly in formation to protect the station. Our ships will be fully cloaked and we can get close enough to blow up the nine ships. This is one of the few times we can't spare the lives of the criminals. If we do, we risk being fired on ourselves. After the fighter ships are blown up, we make contact with the pilots on the station and order them to return to the planet. If they threaten to kill the owners and the crew, we respond we will retaliate by launching a full attack on the station. I can see where the tanks are and we'll aim on the cargo bay where the station cannot be damaged enough to be in danger. 'A full attack' is obviously a bluff, but they don't know that. We should do our utmost not to damage the station. If we're lucky, they will return to orbit and before the station starts its centrifugal spin, ten of our ships must quickly dock with the station and the other ten, cloaked, will act as a threat. They don't know how many ships we have that are cloaked. No station has any powerful weaponry and, besides, they can't see our cloaked ships. Once we have docked our ships, we storm the station and, hopefully, stun them with maximum charge. It will be very risky and we'll have to wear our protective gear to avoid being shot. There is a chance they'll surrender and don't try to fight us. They have no ships to escape with and no way out. Even if there's a shuttle on the station, it's useless for space travel."

The crew agreed to the plan and told Rex they would only fire on the station on his command. None of them had a better plan so Rex' plan was accepted.

Now, all they could do was to wait for signs the hijackers were ready to leave. All the ships were cloaked and hovered in space. On day two, they noticed activity and all nine fighter ships detached from the station and broke orbit. They noticed the engines were igniting on the station and it stopped spinning and left orbit. Within minutes the station was on its way and the nine ships were following behind the station at a safe distance. They traveled at slow speed, but it was probably top speed for the station. Rex told his crew to wait and only go forward on his command. The pilots ordered to dock with the station had their protective gear on.

"*FORWARD! NOW!*" Rex yelled. The whole fleet of twenty ships revved up the engines and moved forward at full blast.

"*FIRE ON ALL SHIPS, NOW!* "Rex commanded in a loud voice.

All hell broke loose and Rex' ships fired at maximum power on the nine fighter ships hitting them simultaneously. It was obvious they had not heard them or been aware anyone was following behind them as they blew up without firing back. The ships exploded and fire engulfed them. Debris rained from the broken-up ships and after a short time there was nothing left of them.

"Move around the fire zone and catch up with the station," Rex ordered. All the ships flew around the area and were next to the station and Rex initiated communication with the station.

"*TURN AROUND THE WORKSTATION AND RETURN TO THE PLANET!* "Rex demanded in English.

The pilots looked out the window and saw nothing. They knew Rex' ships were cloaked and could only guess how many ships were after them. The pilots were reptilian.

"Don't shoot. We'll return," they yelled in broken English.

"Surrender!" Rex demanded.

"We surrender. Don't shoot," they pleaded. They were terrified and the shock of seeing all the fighter ships explode had horrified them. The workstation made a wide turn and started the short trip back to the planet. Within an hour they were back in orbit and Rex and nine additional ships instantly docked with the station. They stormed out of their ships and ran to the Bridge finding three terrified reptilian pilots with their arms up.

"Where are the others?" Rex barked.

"It's only us, there is no one else." Rex saw the man was telling the truth. He was shaking with fear.

Rex and Elsa fired their stun guns set at medium stun to immobilize them.

"Search the station to ensure no one is hiding anywhere. Chain the prisoners. Elsa and I will look for the owners and the crew."

Rex and Elsa ran around the station looking for the owners. The station was enormous and they ran up and down endless corridors calling out the names of the owners.

"Over here, Rex," they finally heard a weak voice trying to make himself heard.

Rex kicked the door open and all of them were on the floor tied up, including the robots. Rex and Elsa helped the owners to get up and they were swaying and almost fainted once they stood up. Both of them were elderly and looked frail. The robots helped the crew to get up and all of them walked out of the room. They had heard the attack and guessed Rex and his fleet had taken out the criminals. There was no window in the room.

"Let's go to the conference room," the owner suggested to Rex and Elsa. He turned to his crew and said "Fix yourselves something to eat.

Take anything you want in the kitchen. Robots, please walk around the station and make sure everything is in order."

"I'll be right back," Rex said. "Let me check on my men first."

Rex ran back to the Bridge and found the hijackers in chains immobilized from the stun. He contacted his fleet outside the workstation and told them to just hover. All was safe on the station. Two of his pilots guarded the gangsters and the rest searched the station to ensure no other member of the gang was hiding somewhere on the ship. He ran back to the conference room and sat down with the owners and Elsa.

"The nine ships took us by surprise," the owner explained. "They docked with the station in the middle of the night and the crew and us two were asleep in our cabins. The robots were also in their cabins. We couldn't defend ourselves and they stunned us and threw us inside that room where you found us. They fed us once a day a little bit, just to stay alive, and unchained us one by one so we could go to the restroom. We've been locked up a whole month in that room. It was horrible."

Rex and Elsa nodded showing sympathy. Rex explained exactly how they had carried out the mission and the owners were pleased to hear all of them were dead except the three on the Bridge.

Rex suggested he and his fleet should escort the workstation to an inhabited planet, where they could apply for permission to orbit and just pay the fee to the planet. They would get security as well and it was worth paying the money.

The owners nodded and agreed.

"We're too old to endure another attack like this. We gladly pay for a permit to orbit," one of the owners said. "There is a planet we know will take us and the distance is about five weeks from here traveling at the fastest speed this station is capable of."

They talked for a while and Rex' pilots reported the ship was empty and no one was hiding anywhere. The three reptilian pilots were dragged into the same room as the owners and his men had been kept. Rex and his men spent the night onboard their own ships and the following morning the owners paid Rex his fee in gold. It was a huge amount and when Rex and Elsa shook hands with the owners, they assured them they deserved the fee.

"You saved our lives," one of the owners said with tears in his eyes. "We all figured they would throw us out of the station during transit.

The gold is a small payment compared to what you did for us, saving thirty-two lives and the station."

The owners contacted the planet they wanted to orbit and the agreement was arranged over the Internet. There was no problem and the workstation would be met with the planet's fighter ships to ensure there were no complications entering orbit. The planet's security team would also arrest the prisoners and they would stand trial on the planet. Hijacking was usually punished with a death sentence.

Before departure, Rex and Elsa went to the prisoners and asked them why they had decided to hijack the workstation.

"We got fuel here once and saw they had no defense. We were totally broke and desperate to get some money and just took a chance we could pull it off. No one told us anything. The hijacking was our own idea."

"What planet are you from?"

"Kodetsia."

Rex and Elsa left and the three pilots were sitting on the floor in chains and from the look on their faces, they knew they faced a death sentence.

Rex and his fleet escorted the workstation to its new location and then returned to Veehnia. After all the pilots had received their part of the gold, Rex paid a large installment to the government. His loan was shrinking fast and he looked forward to being debt free. After the loan was paid off, all the pilots would get a pay raise. Rex also saved some money to replace a ship in case they would lose one in battle.

The owners of the workstation posted a report on the Interstellar Internet describing how Rex and his fleet had saved their station from hijackers. They also announced their new location and made it known they were under full protection of the new planet's fighter ships. Each Internet report brought more work to Rex and his fleet.

Hanna brought the children over and Rex and Elsa were grateful to be alive and hugged their children. They had been gone three months. It was good to be back.

CHAPTER 24

On planet Sorenia, the Nuvirenn process had arrived recently and the doctors were eagerly learning how to treat all citizens with the procedure. The population had increased to almost three million and immigrants were welcome. The planet was the size of Mars and underpopulated. Several thousand people from both Mineata and Ziggellus had immigrated and enjoyed life on Sorenia. The Mineatans had informed the president of Sorenia about the Nuvirenn method and forwarded all the details to the doctors on Sorenia. Most of the people on Mineata had gone through the process and raved about how good they felt. Sorenia, Mineata and Ziggellus were trading partners and supported each other. Ziggellus had rebuilt all their factories that were destroyed fifty-three years earlier when Rasufilus and his fleet removed the former government of plunderers. Ziggellus was an exemplary planet now valuing sophistication, peace and very high moral standards. They were known for their kind demeanor and, as immigrants, they were welcome everywhere. Some of them lived on Earth2, Mineata and also Sorenia. Their faces lacked beauty, but they had plenty of it on the inside.

Rosalie had gone through her Nuvirenn process and felt young again. She was seventy-four years old and felt like forty. Cooper had gone through a slight aging process and looked dignified with his new looks. He had traveled to Mineata to have the procedure done as Sorenia had no such facility. Their marriage of forty-four years had been happy and joyful and Rosalie and Cooper were still very much in love. They had never argued or raised their voice to each other. Their two granddaughters, Aster and Miina, were lively little girls and they had helped raise them together with Volrex and his wife.

Halcyon and Jilina had proven their parents wrong by enjoying a strong marriage. Their lives together had evolved from a strong friendship into a mature love and neither of them felt it had been a mistake. Their parents had been against the marriage and never thought it would last, but they were dead wrong. Perhaps the success of their union was based on their willingness to openly admit to each other they were not in love. Neither of them had faked their feelings. The first time Halcyon told Jilina he loved her, she responded right away she felt the same for him. Their marriage was strengthened by their commitment to truth.

Reyya and Littiana had their Nuvirenn appointments scheduled and were eager to experience the results. They were in their eighties and had started to feel their age. Mentally, they were not ready for a senior lifestyle.

***

Cooper was proud of his manufacturing plant and the combined groundmobile-airmobile vehicles were sold as soon as they rolled off the assembly line. People loved them. They were a simpler version of the vehicles available on the more advanced planets, but just right for the people on Sorenia. Technology was still in its infancy on the planet and it would take a few generations to catch up with the more modern planets.

Cooper inspected the assembly line and leaned over below a half-finished vehicle hanging above him. He was working in his mind on a shortcut and his attention was focused on the new design. The vehicle came down, just as it should, but Cooper was not fast enough to jump aside and within a second his arm was caught under the vehicle and ripped off. The robots raced to stop the assembly line and several employees ran over to help. Cooper was loved by his staff and they all knew he was the brains behind the plant. Cooper felt no pain as he was a machine, but the power of his feelings was not different from a biological person's. He felt totally bewildered and asked himself how he could have been so careless and clumsy. Reyya came running and he was shocked when he saw Cooper's arm had been detached. The robots had already pried up the vehicle and one of them held the arm in his hands in a protective way. Sorenia had a workshop for robots, but Cooper's body was as sophisticated as a human body and they could not handle such as delicate repair. Reyya contacted Volrex and he assured Reyya he would ready one of the spaceships immediately and deliver Cooper to the best android workshop on Mineata. He assured Reyya they were very skilled and would be able to restore his arm with full functionality. It would be a difficult repair, but they knew how to do it. Volrex guessed it would take several days to perform the repair.

Volrex had finished two terms as president and was now working again with the space program. He oversaw the education of future pilots and programmed the flight simulator to display all the different tunnels the students had to master in order to travel in space. Sorenia had four spaceships, two for cargo and two for passengers. Volrex prepared one of the passenger ships and it was ready to fly after a few hours with Halcyon and Jilina as pilots. Rosalie and Cooper arrived and Cooper was bandaged where his arm had been to prevent any kind of dust or debris to enter the area. Obviously, a bacterial infection was not an issue, but Cooper's body was a complex design and to repair it was on a par with human surgery. His arm was safely packed in a large box.

The month-long trip to Mineata dragged on, perhaps because Cooper and Rosalie were anxious and worried. Cooper felt embarrassed and Rosalie tried to comfort him. This was the first time Cooper had been dependent on others and it made him feel awkward. When the ship was on autopilot, Halcyon and Jilina spent all their time with Cooper and Rosalie. They were the only passengers onboard. Halcyon was worried about his father and had always been very close to him.

Jilina landed the ship on Mineata and a groundmobile took them straight to the repair shop, which looked like a hospital for people. Two androids and three Mineatan engineers would perform the repair and they told Roalie it may take several days. They would have to deactivate Cooper during the procedure as he had to be immobilized.

It was a tense waiting time for Rosalie, Halcyon and Jilina, but after three days the repair team had reattached the arm. They woke Cooper up and asked him to go through a series of tests to ensure the arm functioned exactly the way it should by 'brain' command and Cooper passed the test. It had been a very difficult procedure as they had to enter his mechanical brain to ensure the connection to his arm functioned flawlessly.

A humble Cooper walked out to the waiting room to his family and Rosalie hugged him half crying.

"You look great, Dad," Halcyon said and he and Jilina also hugged him. All of them were emotional and Rex and Rosalie thanked the team for their work. They refused payment as Cooper had placed so many orders for goods from Mineata that their whole economy had flourished as a result. Cooper was well known on Mineata and all the citizens had heard how he rescued planet Sorenia from total destruction. The team explained to Cooper and his family the details of the repair and ensured Cooper his arm should function as well as it had done before the accident. Cooper and his family thanked the team again and left.

The return trip to Sorenia was peaceful and the anxiety they all had felt going to Mineata was gone. Cooper himself had experienced many emotions he had never felt before and he emerged with added compassion for other people's suffering. He had always felt sympathy for people in distress, but going through his own ordeal had changed him into a very sensitive and humble man with strong empathy for people suffering physical and emotional pain.

Cooper returned to work and was met with applauding and whistling employees. They were so relieved he was safe and able to run the plant as usual. Cooper never again allowed himself to be careless in the plant and Reyya wrote a new set of safety rules all employees had to abide by.

***

The new president who succeeded Volrex was a Ziggellus man with a great mind named Mitse-Tun. He was a physician and had lived on Sorenia the last ten years and decided to run for office. His efficiency and practical solutions were appreciated by the people and his presidency was effective. Sorenia was an evolving planet with a promising future and a population dedicated to learning, a good recipe for success. The small population was a problem and the native population would soon become a minority on their own planet if millions immigrated. Would such diversity help or hamper the planet? No one knew for sure. On the Internet, Sorenia had posted a news message immigrants were welcome and so far, the only people who had responded were citizens from Mineata and Ziggellus.

Planet Ljeviina was twice the size of Earth and with a population of three billion people it was by no means a crowded planet. The citizens were highly advanced, several hundred years ahead of the people on Sorenia, and the planet was known in the universe as a greatly evolved planet. President Mitse-Tun received a transmission from Ljeviina stating one million people had signed up to move to Sorenia and be part of modernizing the growing planet. They would supply some of their own transportation and would Sorenia offer their two passenger ships to assist in moving the people? The president was mildly shocked when he read the message, but he knew the Ljeviinans were adventurous by nature and many had a 'missionary fixation'. One million new citizens coming from such an advanced planet would be a boon to Sorenia and his advisors agreed. He replied immediately all of them were welcome and Sorenia's two passenger ships would help with the transport. There was no fee for the passengers.

And so, it started. Ships from Ljeviina began to arrive carrying five hundred people each and Sorenia's two ships traveled back and forth as well. The journey took only three months and was easy. Halcyon and Jilina were assigned as pilots on one of the ships and they found it hectic. Between trips, they only had three weeks off to spend with their daughters and then it was time to take off again. There was a lack of Sorenian pilots, but some of the new immigrants were licensed pilots and they had agreed to help out as soon as they arrived and had settled in. It would take years to move a million people, but it would be a steady influx of new citizens and the people on Sorenia were in favor of the new arrivals. A building boom started to supply housing for the new citizens and the economy thrived.

CHAPTER 25

On Earth2, the communication system was buzzing over and over and the signal came from the first planet. Ássurt was called to the government's office and using the translation device, he calmly transmitted "we are on our way to you". He knew they had no way of responding, but Ássurt was sure they had been able to hear his message.

"Not again!" he exclaimed to the people in the office."

"Maybe there is some other disaster, not an invasion," one of the people said.

Since no one knew for sure what the problem was, Rasufilus and Vitzoll took off in Vitzoll's ship and landed after a month's travel time. Kvetros and a group of men waited for them with an anxious look on their faces. They had heard the message from Ássurt and understood they would soon arrive.

"We all dying," Kvetros said to the translation device. "Many, many dead. It started from miners."

Rasufilus and Vitzoll understood right away what had happened. The last batch of miners had carried a disease they themselves were immune to, but the natives had no immunity and had become infected with a virus or bacteria that was killing them. The mining had been going on for five years and those miners had apparently not transmitted any diseases to the natives, but one or more of the miners who had joined them the last year of mining must have spread the disease. They had raped the women and most likely infected them.

"Show me sick person," Rasufilus asked.

Kvetros walked them into one of the huts where all the family members were lying on the floor on mats. Rasufilus put his hand on the forehead on one of them and the man was burning up with fever. They were coughing and all of them had labored breathing.

"I think it's space flu," Rasufilus said. "Let me contact Atlas. It's fatal if not treated with antibiotics."

Rasufilus contacted Atlas from the ship and described the symptoms.

"From your description of symptoms, it's almost for sure space flu," Atlas explained. "It's caused by a bacterium and a fungus that have entered into a mutually beneficial symbiotic relationship. The lungs slowly fill with fluid and the patient dies. Incubation time is long, several months. No one on Earth2 has it, as far as I know, so the miners brought it and they used the women and infected them. They will all die if we don't treat them. Melody and I and another doctor will leave tonight on your ships and we'll arrive in four weeks. We'll bring all the medicines we need for the whole population. There's a highly effective vaccine available, which we'll bring for the people who are not sick. We have all the drugs in stock at the hospital."

"You and Vitzoll can return to Earth2," Atlas continued. "There's nothing you can do to help them and if you explain to Kvetros we're on our way, he won't be upset when you leave. When you're back, go to the hospital and get immunized right away."

Vitzoll and Rasufilus had a long talk to Kvetros and Rasufilus patiently taught Kvetros and his son how to transmit a message through the communication system. Neither of them was sick, perhaps they were immune, and after hours of training they understood how to speak into the translation device and send a simple message to Earth2. Rasufilus did not stop until he was sure both Kvetros and his son had memorized the process. If one of them would forget, the other one may remember the method. Both of them understood help was on the way and waved farewell to Rasufilus and Vitzoll. Before they left, Vitzoll took a small amount of gold from the mine to cover the cost of running his ships back and forth to planet one and to pay the hospital on Earth2 for the cost of all the medicines Atlas would bring.

On their return trip home, they saw two of Vitzoll's ships and Vitzoll flashed his lights as a greeting. The ships returned the greeting and were out of sight within seconds.

Atlas, Melody and the third doctor worked hard to treat the sick people and immunized all the others who still had not been affected by the flu. The population was small and Atlas realized only twelve thousand people were alive on the whole planet. By using one of the ships, they covered the whole planet in three weeks and the first patients they had treated in Kvetros' hamlet were already well and able to slowly return to their normal lives. They had acquired natural immunity and did not need to be immunized.

The work was finally done and Kvetros and his people said a tearful farewell to the doctors. Many of the women cried. Their gratitude was obvious and no words were needed. Kvetros and his son assured Atlas they would remember how to send a message if they were in trouble.

When they were back on Earth2, Atlas recommended all the citizens should go to their doctors and be vaccinated.

***

Inventors and scientists continued to move to planet Mars and it was known as the tech and science hub of the universe. Life was good for the Martians and with the new park, even 'nature' was available. All the citizens had gone through their first treatment with the Nuvirenn procedure and could hardly believe they would live an extra two hundred years. Additional housing was added all the time to make room for new arrivals and the government had hinted one million people was the maximum size population. Mars had grown to three hundred thousand people and it would take several generations to reach a million inhabitants. The government felt more than a million people may lower the standard of living and immigration should be closed when they reached that number.

Some of the inventors on Mars had a touch of megalomania and competition between the 'brains' had started to show up. This was a new phenomenon among the younger scientists and not approved of by the old-timers. They preferred cooperation, sharing ideas and shunning personal pride. *Our achievements are to further humanity, not ourselves,* they used to remind the 'youngsters'. They spoke to deaf ears.

A small group of young scientists were working on a new brain implant for the people and the implant would boost cognition twice as much as the present implants. Many hours of work were behind the invention and the group took pride in their design. The implant was a totally new creation and readily interacted with the physical brain in a different way compared to the implants used by people up to this time. The older scientists asked if they could test it and make sure it was safe to use, but the group refused and swore by their design. They wanted fame and the glory of being the creators of such an advanced implant and denied the older scientists access to their work. This had never happened before as all work had been 'open' and anyone working within the group was allowed to inspect the design.

When the implant was ready to use, the group of young scientists had their doctors attach a sample behind the ear on all of them and turned them on. They left the doctor's office and returned to work expecting a brainstorming session among themselves. Within an hour, a horrendous headache started and their brains went into chaos. The young scientists could not think straight, forgot who they were and some of them had to throw up. After an hour, two suffered a stroke and at this point, it was too late. All of them had suffered irreversible brain damage and only two survived, the rest died. The survivors were never the same and needed help around the clock to manage their lives. Their memories did not function and they had no idea who they were and what they had been. A sad ending of brilliant minds caused by their egos.

The tragedy was a bitter pill to swallow and served as a lesson to the other younger scientists that safety must come before personal recognition. No invention was released in the future without thorough testing ensuring every new design was safe.

***

Mars had a fair amount of space tourists as it was a unique place and no other known planet had citizens living inside domes as they did on Mars. The only exception was Earth's Moon, but with a population of only four thousand citizens and only tourists from Earth allowed, it was not a tourist destination. Income from tourism was not the bread and butter for the Martian economy, terrynium was. Tourists had spread the word about Mars praising it as a fun place to visit and several hundred visitors spent their vacation on Mars every year. Nothing was missing and lots of entertainment was available except gambling, which was illegal. The Martian Symphony Orchestra gave regular performances and the Martia City Ballet was also popular. Food was an interesting mix of the best from many planets and the variety was quite large. Several museums had been built and a library featuring printed books, a rarity, was open to the public. Many of the printed books were two hundred years old and people borrowing the books were required to handle them with gloved hands to preserve them as long as possible. People enjoyed the feeling of holding a book and reading it as the standard method of reading was always through an electronic device.

***

The concert hall in Martia was full and the performer had the attention of the audience, when a man and a woman walked onto the stage and removed their jackets. They had explosives strapped to their bodies and they held a device in one of their hands to detonate the bombs with a simple switch and in the other hand they had a laser gun.

"Stay in your seats, no one can leave the concert hall," the man yelled in broken English. "Call the president and ask him to come over here at once."

Too terrified to move, no one tried to escape from the concert hall. The criminals were of mixed races and it was impossible to tell where they came from. The president came running with his advisors and entered the hall. He was unarmed. *Suicide bombers were a thing of the past and had not been an issue for two hundred years. Where did the gangsters even get the idea from?* the president thought to himself. He was a calm man by nature and was able to keep a cool head even under pressure.

"We demand you load fifty gold bars onto one of your fighter ships and dock the ship with the closest cargo bay so we can enter the ship from the building. No one will get hurt if you comply with our demands." The alien man spoke with a high-pitched, nervous voice.

"We will comply. Let me notify our space fleet commander and give me an hour to have the gold loaded." The calm, reassuring voice of the president put the audience at ease and they knew he was resourceful and may have a trick up his sleeve.

The president ran off and returned after an hour.

"The fighter ship is docked with a cargo bay five minutes from here. I will escort you to the ship and you can see for yourselves we have loaded the gold onto he ship. Just follow me."

The president alone escorted the two gangsters to the ship and the gold was in full view. The area had been cleared and no one was around. The president stopped and waved the aliens toward the ship and waited until they had entered the ship and locked the door. The engines started and they took off.

The president ran to the concert hall informing the people the aliens were gone and he would release news the following day with more details. The audience was enormously relieved and the performer asked them if he could finish the concert. Everyone cheered and shouted 'yes'.

The Internet revealed just how clever their president was and the news made the Martians both laugh and admire their leader. Inside the pressurized air system, the commander of the Martian fleet had hidden a vial releasing a sedative and very slowly the aliens would be sedated and fall asleep. The commander estimated it would take about an hour. Following at a safe distance and out of sight were two Martian fighter ships, the commander piloting one of them with his copilot at his side. They noticed when the aliens fell asleep as their ship wobbled for a while. The commander caught up with the aliens and saw through the window both of them slumped over fast asleep. While his copilot flew the ship, the commander took over control of the aliens' ship and using remote control, he flew the ship using instruments in his own ship. He turned the ship around and all three ships returned to Mars and landed a short distance outside Martia. To fly a ship by remote control was a new feature and only the new ships had this ability. It had been added to fighter ships in order to save a ship when the pilot was incapacitated or dead and only by entering a specific code could another pilot take over the ship.

The president and the police force of Martia waited for them and with a smile the president gave the order to arrest the aliens. The aliens woke up hours later in jail totally baffled how they got there and no explanation was ever given. During interrogation, the aliens reluctantly disclosed they had accidentally come across the idea to use explosives from a website showing warfare from long time ago. They moved from planet to planet and had no citizenship anywhere. They were sentenced to twenty years in jail and transferred to a remote prison where escape was impossible.

***

Strange sounds were occasionally heard by Martian instruments from the Asteroid Belt, located between Mars and planet Jupiter. No one was concerned as no life could possibly survive on an asteroid, but the astronomers were intrigued. The sounds had been picked up for a month and who or what transmitted them? Finally, the astronomers asked the space fleet if they could investigate where the sounds came from. It would take about a month to travel to the Belt as a shortcut tunnel had recently been discovered. Three fighter ships flew in formation and as they exited the tunnel, the sounds from one of the large asteroids were unmistakably humanoid sounds. The pilots had spotted a large asteroid and zeroed in on it as the possible target. They estimated the asteroid to be one hundred and fifty miles long and a hundred miles wide and it was an empty, hostile place, just a giant rock. Could anything possibly live there?

The spaceships hovered above the rock and the captain transmitted a message in English.

"I'm Captain Foster. We're from planet Mars. Respond, if you're living on the asteroid."

Immediately a reply could be heard.

"We're living in a bunker below the surface. There are twenty of us here and an android. It's a prison colony. We're dying." The voice was mechanical and generated by a translation device.

"Do you have spacesuits?" the Martian captain asked.

"Yes, but we only need them when we leave our enclosure. We live in a bunker that's radiation proof. Water and air are recycled. The gravity on the surface is so low we have to be tethered to stay on the surface and not disappear into space. If you look on the surface, you'll see we've hammered in spikes we can tie ourselves to when we go outside. Without a spacesuit you freeze to death instantly. It's usually two hundred degrees below freezing."

"Who dumped you on this rock?"

"Our jailers from another solar system. They knew of the Asteroid Belt and left us here as a punishment a month ago. We have enough food and water for several years and several black boxes generate heat, but we're still dying. Please rescue us. Prison is better than this hell."

"We'll send for a cargo plane and pick you up. It will take a month for them to get here. We'll return to Mars, but first we'll transmit a message to send a cargo ship. Be patient. Captain out."

Looking at the rock, the captain felt no one, regardless of crime, should have to endure life on an asteroid rock. It was worse than hell. He sent a detailed report back home and was told a ship would be leaving the next day and pick up the prisoners. On Mars, they would be questioned and then a decision would be made what to do with them.

The three ships returned to Mars and the pilots waited for the cargo ship to return with the prisoners. They were interested to hear their story.

The cargo ship hovered a few feet above the asteroid surface and with the door to the cargo bay open, a team of robots were ready to pull the prisoners inside the ship. The robots were tethered to the ship as a safety measure. One by one the prisoners appeared wearing a spacesuit. They were holding a long hook in their hand and grasping a spike on the surface for every small jump they took. Walking was not possible, but small jumps propelled them forward. Slowly, they reached the safety of the ship and were pulled inside. The robots placed them on a bench along the wall and fastened a safety harness around them. It took several hours until all of them were inside and the door could close. The android came out last and he also wore a spacesuit to protect his electronics from the extreme cold. He was an antiquated android, at least a hundred years old. Once the prisoners were inside, the ship departed right away.

All the prisoners were a mix of different races and they were told to put on jumpsuits and were locked up in a large room on the ship. They were treated with respect, but not coddled.

Back on Mars, they were taken to the small prison in Martia, which was used as a temporary holding place for prisoners while interrogation was taking place. The memory chips from the android were removed to verify whether the prisoners spoke the truth. They all did. The horror of living on a 'rock' had been so frightening that none of them had any fighting spirit left and they had totally collapsed emotionally. Each prisoner was questioned separately and they conveyed the same confession and it matched the information from the android's memory chips. They had lived on a planet unknown to the Martians and after a series of armed robberies, they were caught and deported to the asteroid. Law and order were paramount on the planet and mercy did not exist. Most prisoners faced death or deportation, usually to an asteroid where they would slowly die.

The prisoners had not committed murder and all of them were full of remorse. Since all of them had confessed and assured the Martians they were no threat to anyone, a judge ruled no trial was necessary. He sentenced them to ten years of unpaid labor and they would all live on the outskirts of Martia without being locked up. Food and lodging were free. If any of them would step out of line, all of them would be transferred to the prison on Mars and be locked up for ten years. After serving the ten-year sentence, they would be allowed to stay on Mars and be free. They were warned several times the smallest offense would revoke the sentence and they would face jail time. The judge had sensed the prisoners were no threat to society and he was right. They and the android were model prisoners and for ten long years they worked hard without complaining and eventually earned their freedom. All of them felt loyalty and gratitude to the Martians and they lived out their lives on Mars. Most of them married and had families.

CHAPTER 26

Andrew had lived on Edena thirty-three years and at sixty years old, he was still handsome and in good physical shape. His marriage to Zittana had been happy and they had been married thirty years. Their sons were now adults and on their own. Zittana was Andrew's copilot and they enjoyed working together. Edena still traded with planet Birresta and a few other planets not too far from Edena. One of those planets had alerted Andrew to the Nuvirenn procedure and transmitted all the details to their ship. When they returned to Edena, Andrew and Zittana turned the information over to the president, who immediately called in the leading doctors for a briefing. None of them had heard about the procedure.

The doctors studied the information carefully and found additional information on the Interstellar Internet and requested the government authorize building three additional hospitals to accommodate the increase in patient load. It was granted and it would only take a few months to erect the buildings with the help of 3D printers.

Within one year the doctors were ready and prepared and the first patients were Andrew and Zittana, as they had delivered the information. They went through the same feeling of 'new youth' as all the patients before them had experienced and were astonished how good they felt. Edena was a small planet, the size of Mars, with a small population and it would not take more than a couple of years to treat the whole population.

Andrew was still the only alien on the planet, but immigration was open. The lack of vigorous advertising inviting new people to settle on the planet was the reason why no one moved to Edena. Andrew decided to change that fact and, as a consultant to the president, he carried a lot of clout. More citizens would benefit the planet and for years couples had been nudged to have more children. The planet was rather beautiful with rolling hills, enough rainfall and mild winters. There was no ocean and no tall mountains, but life was pleasant with a good standard of living and jobs were plentiful.

Andrew posted information on the Internet stating immigrants were welcome and soon citizens living on an overcrowded planet six months' travel time from Edena sent inquiries asking for more details. After they had studied Andrew's information packet, thousands applied to immigrate. The president was delighted and asked Andrew and Zittana to start moving the people. Transportation was free and Edena had three passenger ships with three hundred seats each.

The planet was called Versulan and Andrew suspected there may be a tunnel somewhere on the route shortening the travel time. He contacted the planets Edena traded with and one of them sent information there were two short tunnels between Edena and Versulan reducing the trip from six months to two months. Wow, what a shortcut.

Andrew and Zittana gently landed the ship on Versulan's surface. It was an ordinary planet, not spectacular, but pleasant looking and clean. They were met by a group of officials. Andrew had seen lots of aliens, but none looking similar to these people. They were feathered humans, very good looking with delicate faces, large hazel-colored eyes and fully human bodies. Tan-colored feathers grew from their heads, about five inches long, and their arms and bodies were covered with very short, silky, tan feathers looking like down. What made them so handsome was their delicate, perfectly proportioned facial features. Their faces and necks had no feathers.

The group greeting them were four males and three females and they smiled warmly at Andrew and Zittana.

"Welcome, we're so happy to see you," one of the males said through the translation device. "Our people are ready to leave as soon as you are. Let's go inside and talk. My name is Trokenus."

Andrew explained he was the only alien on Edena and the planet needed more citizens. He introduced Zittana as his wife and they talked for a few hours. Trokenus explained all the people were unmarried and young, but well educated and fully willing to integrate with the Edena people. Their planet was overpopulated and natural resources were taxed.

They departed the following day and the journey went fast.

"I wonder if they go through a molting," Zittana said to Andrew as they worked on the Bridge.

Andrew laughed and replied "I would not be surprised if they do. Probably a little at a time. We humans lose hair when we use a hairbrush and animals shed their fur, so most likely they do molt."

Versulan had no passenger ships and could not assist in moving the people, but Edena used their three ships and moved nine hundred people per year. Eventually, ten thousand people from Versulan had settled on Edena and there were no problems or racial issues. Many of them married Edenans and most of their children were born without feathers, so the Edenan genes were apparently dominant.

The immigration continued over the years, but at a slower rate and the new citizens were valued members of society.

Andrew and Zittana had three weeks off between every trip and they treasured their time off. Their android kept the house clean and made sure everything was in order and she was a terrific cook. Zittana loved cooking, but now that she was working full time with Andrew it was a relief their android took care of everything in the house.

Between trips, they spent several days on their boat with their adult sons, Grandpa and the android. Their oldest son was married and their younger son ended up marrying a girl from Versulan. She was cute as a pin and so pleasant.

***

Earth was going through a climate change and it was freezing cold outside in the northern hemisphere. It seemed every winter was more severe and lasted longer than people were accustomed to. The Gulf Stream was not as warm as it had been and it had an impact on the European harbors causing them to freeze solid for a month or so every winter. Growing seasons were shortened and farmers switched to faster growing crops. There was no shortage of food yet, but the long winters were hard on the people with lots of snow to deal with. The scientists knew weather patterns repeat and are cyclical and eventually milder winters would return.

The winter of 2229 was hard in the northern hemisphere and the snow started to fall in late October and by January, the snowpack was ten feet and spring was months away. In northwest Montana, Linnéa's old cabin had been torn down and replaced by a sturdy log cabin three times larger than the original cabin. Bjorn and Linnéa's great, great,

great grandson Tom and his wife Gail lived in the cabin and they were in their late seventies. They had built the cabin themselves as a vacation house and had moved into it when they retired ten years ago. Both had had the Nuvirenn procedure done and felt well physically, but they had a son, Greg, living with them who was not doing well. Greg was forty-eight years old and unmarried and the last years he had been suicidal. He felt he had been shortchanged in life and his wish to have a loving wife and family had not materialized. Recurring thoughts popped up in his head to end it all with a bullet to his head. Going through the Nuvirenn procedure had not helped him emotionally. Greg was not bad looking or unpleasant and the true reason he had not attracted a wife was living in an isolated area and low self-esteem rather than lacking in personality. He worked from home for the government as a professional hacker keeping the Internet free of crime. When Gail found him sitting with a gun in his hand, she knew it was time for him to leave and she strongly suggested he should move to Frejja. Their ship was still arriving twice a year and Gail had seen on the Internet the next ship was scheduled to land in San Francisco in April.

Greg was uninterested at first and almost apathetic. He was in a rut of negative thoughts and had convinced himself he was unwanted and not worthy of life. Gail and Tom had always been loving parents and never put him down, so his low self-esteem came from his own mind. He had had only two romantic relationships in his life and both women had left him when he failed to propose out of fear they would reject him. Part of his problem was taking himself too seriously and also inability to conquer his fears. Fear is an illusion, a fantasy of the mind, but Greg was stuck in a rut of self-loathing, which was uncalled for. His parents saw it, but Greg did not. With no religious or spiritual beliefs to guide him, he was on his own.

Gail found a psychic medium on the Internet, a young man with an inspirational voice, and Greg agreed to a session with him over the Internet. The medium announced with a happy voice he saw Greg living on Frejja surrounded with wife and family. That statement was exactly what Greg needed to hear to get him out of the rut. When the session was over, Greg told his parents he was willing to book a seat on the ship to Frejja and give it a try. Tom and Gail would miss him, of course, but his survival and happiness were more important. Besides Greg, they had two more children.

The winter dragged on and the aged worker robot Tom had picked up for a song at an estate sale was busy removing snow all winter long. When spring arrived, the snowmelt caused local flooding and the robot had to dig interceptor drains around the cabin leading the water away from the building.

Greg and his parents took off in their airmobile and landed in San Francisco. The immense size of the Frejjan ship was overwhelming and after saying goodbye to his parents, Greg boarded with a feeling of excitement he had never experienced before. He sensed he had made the right decision to move. This was his first trip on a spaceship and on weak legs he followed an android to his cabin. He had a single with a tiny bathroom and it would be his home for the next three months. Greg knew all the details of space travel from the Internet, but he had never even been a tourist on a ship. With Velcro flooring and six of Leo's gravity chambers onboard, Greg was not concerned about lack of gravity on the ship.

The trip went fast and Greg endured the two tunnels without fear. He knew the ship would shake and accelerate in speed and he found he had achieved the beginning of inner peace. This new feeling of peace had started when he boarded the ship and he felt he had dumped emotional baggage when he entered the ship. Daily language lessons with homework kept him busy and he was lucky to have an ear for languages and advanced at a fast clip. He engaged in conversation with the androids to practice his pronunciation and they easily understood him.

***

Greg had just finished his first week working as a hacker for the Frejjan Internet and felt happy. This was a new feeling. How good it felt to be happy and to laugh. He lived in a tiny starter house not far from his office and walked to work. The following weekend he had been invited to a party at Fenul's house, now eighty-two years old. Fenul and Rhea were the children of Maija and Arvin. Cellie and Gordon's son Jonas, also eighty-two, would be there as well and Adora and Drujin's daughter Ingrid would also attend the party. By now, Cellie was one hundred and thirty-three years old, but looking fifty years younger after going through her Nuvirenn procedure. All of them were descendants of the Nordin family and Greg was excited to meet them. His parents had stayed in touch with the relatives on Frejja and had told Greg about them, so he knew a little bit about all of them. Gail had notified them Greg was moving to Frejja and they looked forward to meeting him.

Greg was the highlight of the party and meeting his relatives on his new planet was a joyous experience. He felt at home. These people came from the same family as he did. At the party was a girl who made his heart jump. She was a typical Frejjan with long, blond hair and in her thirties. It turned out she was the granddaughter of Maija's younger sister and her name was Naomi. Gail had hinted to the relatives Greg was shy and a little awkward among strangers and Naomi was informed. She was unmarried and liked Greg at first sight. All the Nordins spoke English, some well, some not so well. Naomi spoke broken English, but well enough to start a conversation with Greg.

"I'm Naomi. I am not a Nordin, but my grandmother's sister Maija is married to a Nordin. I'm glad to meet you," she introduced herself.

"I, I, I'm happy to meet you, too," Greg blurted out, stuttering from the excitement of talking to her. "You have an Earth name, how come?"

"Maija and Arvin made a trip to Earth about fifty years ago and they often show us the holographic images. My parents saw the pictures when they were expecting me and decided to give me an Earth name. I like my name."

"So do I. May I see you sometime?"

"I'm off from work tomorrow and I could take you on a sightseeing trip in my groundmobile. I pack lunch for us. Will you come?"

"I'd love to." Greg's heart was beating fast and he was astounded such a beautiful girl had any interest in him. What he did not know is that Naomi liked him at first sight and had no hang-ups about courting him. She was thirty-four years old and even though thousands of men from Earth had settled on Frejja, she had not met any of them. Her maternal instinct was awakened when she noticed Greg's shyness and she wanted to embrace him and protect him.

Their day together opened the pathway to love and they started seeing each other on a daily basis. She lived close to Greg's house sharing a small house with a female roommate. The two of them ran a business selling antique coins for collectors and were doing well enough to support themselves.

Naomi knew Greg was too shy to propose and took charge. They had known each other four months and that was long enough for Naomi to know Greg was the man she wanted to share her life with.

"You mean a lot to me, Greg," she said and held his hand.

"I feel the same for you, Naomi," he replied in an emotional voice. He felt almost faint.

Naomi threw her arms around him and Greg finally found the courage to ask her the magic question.

"Will you be my wife?"

"You know I want to. Yes, *yes*." Her enthusiastic answer caused Greg to change and at that moment he felt self-worth and gratitude that this beautiful girl wanted him as her husband. For a long time he just held her close while the thoughts tumbled around in his head. The psychic had been right. He sent a thought of thanks to his mother for arranging the session.

With Naomi making the arrangements, they got married the following week and Naomi moved into Greg's house. Their marriage would last over two hundred and fifty years with the help of the Nuvirenn process and produce several children. The Nordin relatives on Frejja were happily surprised when they heard the news and they thought they were a good match.

Naomi continued working and since she had her own business, she could take days off as she needed. Greg sent a message to his parents he was married and they celebrated when they received the happy news. A big burden came off them and they were relieved and grateful Greg had a wife who loved him.

CHAPTER 27

Tothellim was in love with an immigrant woman from Earth, Amelia, and felt like a youngster despite being one hundred and ten years old. Amelia was a licensed Starfleet captain and only needed a few lessons in the flight simulator to qualify for her Veehnian license. She could fly any spaceship and fighter ship, but needed a few lessons to fly through the tunnels and that is where she met Tothellim. Between space trips, he still gave lessons at the flight school. He was fifty years her senior and Amelia did not look a day older than forty. She had also gone through the Nuvirenn process and felt reborn. As a dedicated career woman, she had forgone marriage and children, something she now deeply regretted. Her maternal instinct longed for motherhood and after going through the Nuvirenn process, the doctors told her she could have children until at least the age of one hundred and fifty years old. She and Tothellim connected and a spark ignited. They both felt it. Tothellim had been a widower for thirty-seven years and had put Anna's death behind him. He would never forget her. Even though Tothellim was old, he was still a handsome man and full of vitality. Amelia fell in love with him and they got married. It was mature love, but no less intense. Tothellim's children welcomed her into the family and they were about the same age as their stepmother. Heidi and Amelia liked each other right away.

Amelia passed her test and received a Veehnian license as a Starfleet captain, but she was now a married woman and pregnant, so she and Tothellim decided to postpone all space travel until the babies were born. Amelia was carrying twins and they were transferred to the artificial wombs. It was two boys and they named them Aten and Seleus, both names space inspired. Tothellim and Amelia were overjoyed when they found out they would soon become parents and Heidi offered right away to take care of them if they were away on a space trip. Heidi's children were adults and she herself had no intention to have any more children. She looked forward to having little ones in the house again and her husband agreed. She ran her own veterinary clinic and could choose to work or not to work. To take time off and care for her half siblings was a welcome change in her schedule and a new, fun project.

Tothellim adjusted to being a married man once again and Amelia felt loved and cared for in the marriage. She had had a few relationships, but her career had always ended long-term commitments. Now, as she had reached the age of sixty, she knew beyond a doubt no career can replace motherhood and the Nuvirenn procedure had given her a second chance. Having children was unimportant for some women and until now, Amelia had not given it much thought. She was grateful she had conceived so easily and her soul longed to join with the boys' souls. She stayed home and enjoyed making a nursery in Tothellim's house while Tothellim went to work as a flight instructor. Amelia wanted to return to work exploring space, but there was no rush to do so.

They picked up the boys and Heidi came along, all of them eager to welcome the new members of the family. The boys were identical twins and looked mostly human with hair on their heads and no growths on their cheeks, but both had ridged eyebrows like their father. They were handsome and the eyebrows did not diminish their good looks. Amelia was emotional as she held one of the babies and Tothellim the other and she felt it was the greatest gift life had awarded her.

Heidi stayed with Amelia for a month to help out with the twins and Tothellim bought an android, the latest model available, an efficient female programmed to handle everything in a household in addition to child care. Her name was Nilla and she was competence personified with a lovely personality to boot. The gentleness with which she handled the babies reassured Amelia and Heidi she was fully trustworthy.

Amelia stayed home a full year and then she and Tothellim notified Eric they were ready to join his crew. The twins and Nilla moved in with Heidi and her husband while Tothellim and Amelia were away. Eric was the captain in charge and Tothellim, Amelia and Rhett were the copilots. Matthias had been assigned to another crew. Kody and four additional androids were also part of the crew. No passengers were allowed as every exploratory journey carried a definite risk. The plan was to travel two months to the fifteen-hour tunnel, pass through the tunnel and exit close to planet Ziggellus. Then continue towards the center of the Andromeda Galaxy and start exploring. It was a long distance to travel, but measured in time the journey was short. This was Amelia's first trip into the Andromeda galaxy and she was excited to explore. She knew the babies were well cared for and did not worry over their welfare. The saucer type spaceship was huge and, as usual, equipped with foods and material goods to last for years. Since every trip was dedicated to help and aid aliens, onboard the ship were vehicles and electronics to give away as gifts and the cargo area of the ship was always full when the ship took off. Velcro flooring and several of Leo's exercise chambers were part of the equipment making life onboard quite pleasant.

They exited the tunnel and continued straight to the center of the galaxy. Amelia was at the controls most of the time to gain experience with a Veehnian ship and her skills impressed the rest of the crew. She was an ace and they liked her a lot. After a month, a small star became visible with four planets orbiting and they entered orbit around the planet most likely to have a temperate climate. As far as they knew, this star and its planets were unknown and not entered on the Interstellar Internet.

The planet was smaller than Mars and half of it was one continuous ocean. The rest was land and when nighttime arrived, all of the landmass lit up indicating the whole planet was inhabited. From space, they saw there was no sparsely populated countryside, but the land area was evenly illuminated.

At daybreak, they launched a cloaked drone and waited for the images to be sent back. There was air traffic at an elevation of five thousand feet indicating an advanced society. The drone flew over the beach area of the ocean and humans were swimming under the water in an undulating pattern without ever coming up for air. Their shape was long and slender, but they were humanoids. The drone was directed to fly over the ocean several miles from the shore and more humanoids were seen just below the surface.

"They must have gills," Kody observed. "None of them lifts their head above water to breathe."

The drone was steered back to land showing modern cities evenly built all over the land area and in between were farm fields with crops growing. The buildings were not tall and the cities looked more like big towns than large cities. Most planets the crew had visited had tall buildings to fit more people, but on this planet, there were mostly five-story buildings.

"They may have a problem with quakes. There must be a reason why the buildings are so small," Amelia remarked.

Humanoids walked around on the surface and the closeup images showed people of average height, large heads with light to dark brown hair. The men had short hair and the women had long hair reaching to their waist and either braided or tied into ponytails. Their skin was white and they had fully human faces. The only difference in looks between these people and the crew was the size of their heads. They were dressed in loose fitting tunics reaching to their knees and the drone had registered a surface temperature of ninety-six degrees, so that may explain why they wore tunics. It was just too hot for tight fitting clothes. The men wore mostly white tunics while the women had colored ones. They moved slowly and looked sophisticated, almost serene.

"Let's go down to the surface. It looks safe," Eric decided. He was the captain and made the decisions, but he always welcomed input from his crew and had deep respect for their opinions. The whole crew, including the androids, was functioning as a family and they all liked each other.

They brought the drone back and all of them except two androids entered the shuttle in cargo bay. No spacesuits were needed as the surface had a normal oxygen atmosphere. The crew was unarmed and dressed in uniforms. Rhett landed the shuttle a short distance outside the town and within minutes a groundmobile showed up. Five men climbed out and they had seen the shuttle land. Stun guns were in their holsters, but the men smiled and looked welcoming.

"Welcome to our planet," one of them said through a translation device strapped to his wrist. It was a tiny device indicating their electronics were advanced, perhaps more so than the Veehnian instruments.

"I'm Eric and we're from planet Veehnia. Our mission is to explore and help aliens. This is my crew."

The aliens were handsome and they shook hands with Eric and the crew. They escorted them to a modern looking government building and invited them to sit down in the lobby. Everything was ultra-modern, clean and inviting and comfortably cooled. A sculpture was mounted on a pedestal featuring a humanoid and the crew recognized the statue was a copy of the water humanoids. It had a human body, gills on the side of the head, webbed hands and feet, no hair, but looked otherwise mostly like any typical humanoid. Three government officials, two men and a woman, joined them in the lobby and introduced themselves.

"My name is Leekee and I'm one of the leaders on this planet. It's called Tulem2, since it's the second planet in orbit. The other three planets are uninhabitable. Please describe where your planet is located." Leekee spoke slowly and his sophistication and dignity were unmistakable. There was no question these people were highly advanced with very developed minds.

Eric introduced himself and the crew and then displayed a holographic map of the galaxy using his communicator. He showed the fifteen-hour tunnel and the location of Veehnia.

"We know of the tunnel you used, but haven't been through it ourselves. Our trading planets are in the opposite direction. Tulem2 has an advanced society, but we have terrible problems with violent quakes. Our water citizens are capable of life on the surface, but prefer the ocean. About a third of them have joined us and our doctors converted their gills to lungs capable of breathing air and improved their vocal cords so they now have the ability to speak. Their genes have to be changed also so the babies are born with full size lungs and normal vocal cords. This planet has a small population and we would like all of them to live on the surface and participate in society. Those who did join us are happy they did go through the transformation and are respected members of our society. They are not as advanced as the land citizens, but learn fast and will soon catch up. The water people who decide to join us usually swim to an area known as a 'rescue center' and wait for us to pick them up. They can communicate with each other underwater and exchange information and they're aware they can join us land citizens. Their lives in the ocean are primitive and they never advance mentally. It's a dead end."

"How many are water citizens?" Kody asked.

"Half a million."

"Do they live on fish?"

"Yes, they eat raw fish and seaweeds."

"How often do you have quakes?" Tothellim asked.

"At least once a year, but most of them are mild. A severe quake only happens once every five years or so. Our buildings are strong enough to withstand all but the most powerful quakes."

"Have you tried to communicate with your water citizens using converted citizens?" Kody asked. "Do they have enough information about life on land and is there an incentive to make them change their minds?"

"We use converted citizens as missionaries and they visit with them using small boats. They can't go back into the water as their gills are removed, but they are able to communicate with them. The water people have a primitive language and understand some of our speech. No one is forced to convert, but those who willingly give up their water life are helped to establish a new life on land. They have to learn everything from scratch and the first years are not easy for them. To answer your question more precisely, our missionaries cannot illustrate the benefits of life on land and hence the water people have no incentive to leave the ocean."

"Why not just leave them alone? If they prefer their water life, allow them to remain water citizens," Amelia said.

"Ideally, each lifetime should be an opportunity to advance mind and soul," Leekee explained with a smile. "A lifetime where nothing is learned is a wasted lifetime. Life in the ocean has nothing to teach the water citizens and they live mostly like large fish. Beyond survival in the water, they learn nothing and they never transcend."

One of the androids, Roy, was exceptionally good with electronics. He had been quiet, but now made a suggestion.

"I can show life on land using an old-fashioned video camera that's just as effective as a holographic image. This camera is waterproof and was used by divers a long time ago. I can put together a film showing how life functions on land and join the missionaries and display the images to the water citizens. Do I have your permission to do it?"

"Of course, it's a great idea!" Leekee looked excited. "We would like all of the water citizens to join us here on land. Let me call in one of them and introduce you. He converted five years ago and can now master speech and his intellectual abilities grow all the time. His name is Soovy and he works here in the office."

Leekee gave a voice command to his communicator and soon a young, thin man walked in. He had little resemblance to the land citizens, but he looked alert and eager to please. His physical appearance was not much different from the water citizens. He bowed lightly and sat down.

"Soovy, I have a special film camera to show your people how life on land functions," Roy explained. "They may not really understand how big the difference is between their way of life and how you live here on land. Would you want to help me put this film together?"

Soovy smiled and responded "I would be happy to assist you. I believe my people don't join us because they don't understand how life is on land. The missionaries do a good job, but they haven't managed to fully explain the quality of life on land, which is so much better than life in the water. Life in the ocean can be dangerous and there are several species of large fish that use our water people for food. On land, we have enough to eat and are safe. I'm newly married to a converted water girl and we have a baby, who was born with full size lungs and a human voice box. In the water, having babies is very risky and many babies are eaten right away. When can we start?"

Soovy's voice was hoarse and his vocal cords were partially made by the doctors. To convert a water person into a land person was a difficult undertaking and involved two major surgeries lasting a day each. The success rate was high and most of the patients survived, but occasionally the doctors lost a patient when the new lungs failed to inflate. The water people were born with small, underdeveloped lungs that the doctors enlarged. The method was complicated, but their lungs grew to adequate size with the help of their own stem cells.

"Let's start tomorrow morning, if you can take the time off," Roy said.

Leekee nodded, put his hand on Soovy's shoulder and exclaimed –

"Take all the time you need, Soovy, this is a great experiment. We support you."

Roy and Soovy started and after a week they had produced a captivating film depicting many interesting aspects of life from raising children, education, adult life, variety of foods, entertainment, medical care and so on. It was presented with humor and was fun to watch. Roy transferred the film to the antique diver's camera that had once been used to film the ocean life on Veehnia. Soovy narrated the film using the water people's primitive language.

About a mile from the beach, they stopped their boat and Roy slipped into the water with the camera. All late model androids were 'waterproof' and he wore a light flotation jacket to keep himself steady in the water. Soovy stayed in the boat and kept it still. It did not take more than five minutes until Roy had a small audience of water people and he started playing the film. It was a hit. More and more people arrived and Roy kept repeating the film. They were hooked on it and stared in disbelief at the many images they saw, the safety of life, babies in strollers, foods, houses and so on. Many started swimming to the closest rescue center where land citizens were waiting for them. They could process fifty water people every week and, in the film, Soovy explained all of them were welcome, but they had to be patient and wait for their turn. The water people were kept in large pools until the doctors were ready to perform the surgeries.

Kody was considered the best android doctor Veehnia had. He was invited to assist with the surgeries and he added valuable tips when he watched the doctors construct the vocal cords and enlarge the lungs of the patients. After watching a few surgeries, he was totally familiar with the procedure and took over his own patients and worked side by side with the Tulem2 doctors. They watched him, admiring his skills, and were grateful for his assistance. Kody was also an expert in gene manipulation and proposed several suggestions to ensure all water features would be removed from babies born to the converted water people.

Leekee asked Eric if they could stay for a month as Kody was needed at the hospital and Eric agreed. Their mission was to aid and help aliens and Eric felt the support his crew offered was exactly what they were supposed to do. Kody worked night and day as he did not need to sleep and performed an enormous number of surgeries. He became an expert.

The androids onboard were rotated so all of them had a chance to spend time on the surface and the crew stayed in a comfortable home next to the hospital. Roy and Soovy were out every day showing the film. Roy had learned their language from the translation device and communicated with them answering their questions and telling them the doctors on land would help all of them, but since they were so many, they had to wait for their turn. They understood Roy's explanation and told him they would all move to the land. Some of them explained as clearly as they could that until they saw the film, they had no idea what life on the surface was and now that they had seen it, they could hardly wait for their turn. With half a million water citizens, it would take several years to convert them all. This fact was difficult for Roy to convey, as they had no idea what time and numbers were, but he did manage to explain that a 'group' of people could be picked up at a time and they did comprehend that message. They were not unintelligent, only lacking understanding of life on land. Roy found Soovy easy to work with and he learned quickly new concepts Roy introduced to him.

Eric spent many hours with Leekee and they exchanged information and the rest of the crew stayed by the large pools communicating with the water people. They were so grateful to have their questions answered and the crew had translation devices making conversation possible.

They ended up staying six weeks and then said goodbye. Roy left the camera with Soovy and he would continue the work with a few other converted water people. The doctors were sad to see Kody leave and would miss him, but they understood the crew was on a mission and had stayed longer than intended. It had been a productive time and Eric and his crew felt they had made a difference on planet Tulem2.

***

The ship took off and Eric had been told by Leekee about planet Cyros, located only two months' travel time from Tulem2. It was eight thousand light years away, but a six-hour tunnel, a mega portal, shortened the travel time to only two months. Cyros had a small population of humanoid people with highly advanced minds, but upholding certain beliefs that threatened to undermine their own survival. Under no circumstances would they harm any living person or animal. The planet was overrun by carnivorous animals resembling small wolves and they hunted in large packs. The Cyros people called them 'witzos' and they ruled the planet. Herds of grazing animals were slowly going extinct from the constant attacks by the witzos. Lately, the witzos had started to prey on the humanoid population and found them easy to kill. To survive, the people were restricted to their towns and were afraid to venture into the countryside. Leekee had pleaded with Eric to try to resolve the problem. The Cyros people were highly admired for their accomplishments and gentle personalities and the planets that traded with them wanted to help, but the Cyros citizens would not allow killing of the witzos. It was against their spiritual beliefs. The crew agreed they had no choice but to eliminate all the witzos, but they had not found the right solution yet.

The first two hours, Amelia flew the ship through the tunnel and then Eric took over the controls to give her a break. When they came out of the tunnel, they saw planet Cyros in the far distance orbiting a medium size star and it was the only orbiting planet. Once they were in orbit, Kody and Roy suggested a plan.

"I suggest we do not make contact with the people," Kody started. "In this case, they're better off not knowing what happened. I have, on the ship, a biological weapon in the form of a virus we can inject into the animals by shooting them with a gun that injects the virus. The virus will invade and paralyze their lungs and they suffocate. It's not contagious in any way and a scavenger eating the carcass won't be harmed. We have it onboard for situations just like this one."

"We have three shuttles onboard the ship," Roy continued. "If two of us stay with the ship, the remaining seven crew members can use the three shuttles and wipe out most of the witzos. If we don't find all of them, it's OK, because the virus will decimate the population and the few witzos that survive won't pose any danger to the people. I think we can finish the job in a week."

The rest of the crew members agreed and they launched a cloaked drone to find where the witzos were on the planet. From the images, they found them living on the fields in the open and not hiding, probably because they had no enemies. Roy and Kody were busy preparing the guns with the virus. Each gun could hold a hundred shots. Eric and Tothellim checked out the stored shuttles and found them all ready to fly. Everything was set to go.

The following morning, the three shuttles took off and they were cloaked. No one lived in the countryside and the crew did not expect to find any people wandering around or even flying in an airmobile. The shuttles spread out and soon hovered over a large group of animals. The noise from the engines was minimal and the witzos looked up into the sky, but when they did not see anything, they ignored the sound and stayed where they were. With the shuttles hovering on autopilot, the crew started shooting rapidly and soon the whole pack had been shot. They moved on and found another large pack and by the end of the day, hundreds had been hit with the virus. Kody had informed them it would take about a week for the witzos to start dying and none of them would try to hunt during their last week. Their lungs would be starved for oxygen and even to move around would become difficult after a day. They covered the whole planet and after one week, they noticed dead animals lying around everywhere. The three shuttles continued looking for survivors, but after ten days they could not find a single animal that had not been affected by the virus. The project had been a success.

They stayed another two days in orbit and sent out the drone for a reconnaissance tour. Everywhere were dead animals and none walked around.

"If even a hundred of them hid somewhere and were alive, I'd be surprised," Kody remarked. "If any remain, which I doubt, they're of no consequence and would hunt the herbivores, not the people. Our work here is done."

They had not seen a single person the whole time and they left the planet. They had intended to visit one more planet that Leekee had asked them to visit, but Nature had a surprise for them. Amelia was four months pregnant. This was not supposed to happen, but all the time off on Tulem2 had put Tothellim and Amelia in a romantic mood and now they had to face the consequences. Abortion was out of the question and the crew discussed what to do. They were like a big family and their lives were closely connected. All of them shared their thoughts and feelings with each other and their lives were intertwined.

"Our mission is to explore," Kody said slowly. "A pregnancy onboard a spaceship has never happened, as far as I know, and to observe the development of a baby carried the natural way by the mother in zero gravity would add important biological knowledge to the scientific community. It is a way to explore. I will monitor Amelia closely. If we decide to head home, Amelia will be close to giving birth by the time we land on Veehnia, but if we continue to the next planet, the baby will be born on the ship."

"I think we should just continue our mission as planned," Amelia said.

Tothellim nodded in agreement.

"There's no blame here," Eric interjected. "We're all adults, things happen, and personally I feel we should celebrate this new life. As the captain, I would prefer if Amelia and Tothellim make the decision whether we should return to Veehnia or continue our mission."

"Continue our mission," Amelia said immediately.

"I agree," Tothellim said.

"I respect your decision and let's continue then to planet Armitis," Eric said. "Leekee explained to me that no one has ever visited the planet, but they've made several attempts to establish contact with the people and never received a reply. There's a chance it's an uninhabited planet and, if so, it would be a gift to humanity. It would be another Earth2 discovery and any new habitable planet would help humanoids of all kinds. I promised Leekee we would take a look and report back to him."

Eric entered the location of Armitis into the computers and it was a three months' trip with a single short tunnel to pass through. Kody had examined Amelia and told her the baby was doing well and everything looked normal. It was a girl. She spent more time than normal exercising in the gravity chamber to ensure her physical strength would remain at peak. By the time they reached Armitis, Amelia was seven months along and with a sizeable belly. She had no trouble working as normal and had not missed a single day of her scheduled work shift. In the cargo bay, she had found maternity clothes.

They entered orbit around Armitis. It was a single, medium size planet orbiting a rather large star. From space, it appeared to be lovely with flowing water and sunshine. They launched the drone and waited with excitement for the pictures to be transmitted back to the ship. They were lovely. The drone registered a surface temperature of eighty-one degrees Fahrenheit and an oxygen atmosphere of twenty-two percent, perfect conditions. The planet had many lakes, no ocean, and several large rivers meandering through the landscape of rolling hills. Deciduous trees hinted the planet had four seasons. Low mountains could be seen at the horizon. No humanoids were visible, but herds of animals were grazing on the planet.

"We have a winner here," Eric exclaimed excitedly. "Another Earth2 planet. We have to check it out."

They all jumped into the shuttle and left two androids on the ship. Eric suggested they should fly over a large area and no humanoids were visible, only small herds of grazing animals here and there. Birds were plentiful, but they could not see any additional animal species. The planet was peaceful and tranquil.

"There are so many overcrowded planets with people looking for a new place to settle," Eric said. "I'll notify Leekee and let him and his advisors decide who they should share this information with. The planet should be turned over to people, not mining companies exploiting the natural resources."

They spent several days touring the planet and it was indeed an uninhabited gem. The androids took turns descending to the surface and enjoyed the planet as much as the rest of the crew. They also went for walks on the planet and swam in one of the rivers. Someday it would be home to some very fortunate people.

They departed after enjoying the planet for a week and started the long trip home to Veehnia. Once they had passed through the tunnel, they were within transmission distance of Tulem2. Roy sent a message to Leekee with explanations about the new planet as well as telling them all the witzos on Cyros were dead. They received a response within an hour with lots of thanks and assured the crew they would only share the information about the new planet with people who truly needed a new home planet to move to. The ship was now traveling at full speed and they estimated it would take eight months to reach Veehnia.

Amelia was in labor and Kody had diagnosed a breech presentation. The baby's feet were pointing down to the birth canal rather than the head and very gently and slowly Kody managed to turn the baby. It was a lengthy process, but necessary to ensure a safe birth. After that, it was a normal delivery and the baby was born without medical problems. Amelia felt no pain and her little girl was strong and healthy. She looked like her twin brothers with hair on her head and only slightly ridged eyebrows. She was really cute. It was a magic moment and the crew celebrated. All the men onboard felt like fathers and even the androids joined in the celebration. Amelia named her Tulema as she had been conceived on Tulem2. The ship had infant formula onboard, but Amelia decided to nurse the baby the old-fashioned way. One of the gravity chambers was turned into nursery and Kody felt it would be better for the baby to spend the rest of the trip with at least some gravity instead of being in zero gravity. It worked out well and the baby was thriving and developed normally the six months she lived on the ship. All the men and even the androids enjoyed carrying little Tulema around while Amelia worked and they showered her with love. Kody kept meticulous notes for the doctors on Veehnia. Amelia recovered quickly from the delivery and was back to her normal weight after a few months. She looked radiant and enjoyed motherhood. To her surprise, there were baby clothes and diapers on the ship and the cargo area had a little bit of everything people needed to live.

They landed safely on Veehnia and what a trip it had been. The mission to aid and help other planets had been fulfilled; a new habitable planet had been discovered; and a new life had been born. Truly, a successful trip that had lasted one and a half years.

Heidi, Logan, family members of the crew and several government officials greeted them and wished them welcome home. Little Tulema was a celebrity and featured on the Internet as the first space baby. Eric and the crew would meet with the government officials and leave a full report of the trip within a few days.

Thanks to the gravity chamber, Tulema had normal bone structure for babies her age and adjusted quickly to Veehnia's gravity. She had never been sick and her immune system appeared to be strong as she did not catch even a cold during her first winter on Veehnia. Amelia stayed home one year to take care of her three children with the help of Nilla, but she and Tothellim agreed they both wanted to continue their space trips. Heidi loved her half siblings and assured Amelia and Tothellim she was willing to be their substitute mother.

CHAPTER 28

On Earth, Tina had passed away and her son James had reached the age of one hundred and thirty-one years old, but after going through the Nuvirenn procedure, he felt young and strong. He and his adopted son Sidney, now one hundred and ten years old, were partners and had a thriving fishing business going. Their wives, Beth and Maria, often came along and their new boat was a sturdy ninety-foot vessel. Four worker robots were permanently onboard as the boat was too large to manage by James and Sidney alone. The robots were rather advanced, not quite up to android standards, but they had basic feelings and communicated well. They felt affection for James and Sidney and were totally loyal to them and truly enjoyed their life on the water.

James never trusted official weather reports and had the most sophisticated electronics onboard so he could monitor the weather himself. He had lost his father due to faulty weather predictions and he had never forgotten Drew.

The ocean had become home to thousands of people living on huge, man-made floating islands. The dwellings were totally waterproof and anchored into the island and capable of withstanding enormous waves. The islands were unsinkable and the people living on these islands did not get seasick. Most of the time the ocean was calm and placid and life on the islands was very peaceful. Small storms had little effect and the islands would just roll a little and even major storms were not life threatening. People looking for peace and quiet loved the islands and bought a home on one of them when they retired. Each island functioned almost like an independent country with its own rules and regulations. Cargo drones delivered their supplies from the mainland and drinking water was desalinated ocean water. Artists and writers found the peace they needed to create their work and favored living on an island. All around the islands were docks, where the homeowners could keep a boat and these boats were also unsinkable. Between the homes were ample space to go for walks and little shops were concentrated in the center of the island. Bicycles were the most popular way to travel and some were motorized. Crime did not exist on any of these islands and no one locked their doors. The islands could move at a slow speed with the help of large engines and the people preferred to be at least a hundred miles from shore.

James and Sidney delivered fish to one of the islands, Neptune, once a week and the island was usually floating a hundred miles from the San Francisco shore. The return trip back to the harbor took about three hours, but if the weather report was threatening, James and Sidney tied up to the island and stayed until the waters were calm again. The memory of the storm when Drew and their boat went down was forever etched in James' mind.

A well-known psychiatrist, Takara, lived on Neptune and she was one hundred and ten years old, but very much alive and kicking. She had had a prosperous career and was now semi-retired and enjoyed time off from her land life. Her home on Neptune was her sanctuary and she spent several months every year on Neptune. She was a widow and had lost her husband before the Nuvirenn procedure was introduced to Earth and her three children sometimes joined her on the island. Takara had never forgotten her sister Mio and the promise she had made to her to be the best psychiatrist she could ever be and she had kept her promise. Some of her most difficult cases had turned out well with full recovery of the patients and Takara knew she was guided by Mio's divine expertise. They worked as a team. She had a small practice on Neptune and worked two days a week. In San Francisco, her practice was very busy, but Takara was driven by her promise to Mio to make a difference and never turned down a new patient. When she felt worn out, she took an airmobile taxi to Neptune to wind down for a few months.

Her next-door neighbor on the island was a physician, Tojjo-Lin, a permanent resident on Neptune. He was from Nuvirenn, half native and half human, with true compassion for his patients. Ten years ago, he had been part of the group of scholars who had traveled along to Earth from Nuvirenn to hold lectures on Earth and teach people about the power of the mind. He liked Earth and decided to stay. Tojjo-Lin was the only Nuvirenn immigrant to Earth and was respected and well-liked by the people he met. The reason why he lived on Neptune was the residents had advertised for a doctor and when he saw the island, he fell in love with it and took the job.

Takara and Tojjo-Lin often discussed their patients and advised each other. They enjoyed each other's company, often having a glass of wine together in the evening. Takara also made dinner for them quite often. When James delivered his fish, Takara always bought several days' worth of fish and made tasty dinners for herself and Tojjo-Lin. His practice on Neptune was busy and he was always grateful when Takara cooked for him. He was a widower and his wife had passed away on Nuvirenn many years ago. They had no children. He adored Takara and one day after dinner he proposed to her. Takara felt mature love for him, different than the infatuation people would feel at a young age, and said 'yes' immediately. She kissed him on the cheek and told him how special he was in her life and how happy she would be to marry him. He was one hundred and fifty years old, but with the energy and health of a much younger man. Tojjo-Lin understood Takara was not ready to give up her practice on land and they agreed she should work two months on land and then return to Neptune for two months, so every two months he would see her. It was a doable schedule for both of them and it turned out well in the future.

They tied the knot the following week and sold Tojjo-Lin's home and lived in Takara's home. In addition to their mature love, they were joined in divine love. Both of them shared devotion to spirituality and felt their souls were connected. Tojjo-Lin fully understood Takara's closeness to Mio and never questioned its existence.

***

Takara and Tojjo-Lin prepared for the first real storm on the island. The leaders of Neptune assured the residents it was safe to stay and their homes were designed to weather the storm. James and Sidney had just delivered fish and decided to hunker down and wait until the storm had blown over. The boat was chained to the island and very secure.

Fifteen-foot waves rolled over Neptune with no harm done. Inside the watertight homes, it was nice and dry and everything outside was secured and could not be washed away. The island was a marvel of engineering and came through the storm with flying colors. Tojjo-Lin and Takara watched with fascination as the waves washed over their home and inside, they were safe and cozy. James' boat rolled around and the waves pounded the boat, but no harm was done. The door to the interior of the boat was tightly closed and not even a drop entered the living area of the boat. The storm was over the following day and the ocean was calm. James listened to the weather report and it was safe to return to the harbor.

Halfway back, one of the robots yelled *'man overboard'* and James and Sydney ran outside and saw six men fighting for their lives and held up by their orange lifejackets. The memory of Drew's death flashed in front of James' eyes and he revved up the engines and steered toward the men. Within minutes, they reached them and tossed out flotation devices and the men seemed to use their last strength to hold on to them. Slowly, they pulled all six of them inside the boat. The men were frozen stiff, shivering and almost blue in the face. The robots stripped all their clothing off and gave them dry underwear to put on and thick wool blankets to wrap themselves in. Sidney heated Beth's pea soup and as soon as the men had recovered a little from the shock of almost drowning, they gratefully drank several mugs of the hot soup to warm their bellies. All of them were only in their twenties with limited sea experience and they told James and the crew they had been fishing and the storm surprised them. Their boat was too small to survive the waves and had gone down in the beginning of the storm. None of them had drowned, but their boat was at the bottom of the ocean. They were enormously grateful James had saved their lives and said they were ready to give up when they saw James' boat.

By the time the boat was back in harbor, the men had warmed up and felt much better and their families were waiting for them at the dock. Sidney had contacted them from the boat. James had a supply of extra clothing onboard and the men had gratefully accepted dry clothes. None of the men wanted to go to the hospital and all they longed for was a warm bed. They gave James and Sidney a hug and James knew how they felt. He had clear memories of his own nightmarish night in the water, when he was swallowing sea water and gasping for air. He was thankful he had been able to save them.

***

Airships, both blimps and zeppelins, were popular with some people on Earth and they were not too expensive. Some families, who owned one, spent weekends on their airship and floated around up in the sky. The ships were the size of a large bus and the interior had a few tiny cabins, a galley, a head and a family room. Large windows made visibility possible and they traveled at an elevation above standard airmobile traffic. They were quiet, peaceful and safe and catered to people preferring a sedentary lifestyle as well as to people needing silence and solitude in order to create. Writers would often live on them and found the peace up in the sky increased their creativity.

Another way to live was to buy a waterproof home anchored to the bottom of the ocean, usually at shallow depths so the sun could reach the home. They were used mostly as vacation homes and were popular with people who enjoyed scuba diving.

So far, there had been no fatalities involving the airships and the underwater homes and adventurous people continued to look for different lifestyles. With a life expectancy of three hundred years to look forward to, many people searched for variety in their lives and truly immersed themselves in one adventure after another.

Cave living attracted a small following of explorers attracted to wandering around in underground tunnels, some of which stretched for miles. They would often portage small inflatable boats and follow subterraneous rivers snaking their way long distances.

Very popular, but unaffordable by most, were orbiting homes around Earth. These homes had simulated gravity by spinning and were safe, comfortable and offered a spectacular view of planet Earth. Supplies were delivered by small spaceships docking with the orbiting homes and the cost of these deliveries was so expensive most people simply could not afford this lifestyle.

Some people on a budget bought a mule to carry the supplies and spent a year or two wandering the wilderness areas. It was safe to do so as crime on Earth was very low.

Then there were the beach bums living on the beaches, surfing, fishing and 'finding' themselves through meditation and soul searching. Most of them returned to work after a few years of this lifestyle while some picked up a different lifestyle to immerse in.

The new, long lifespan on Earth inspired people to try a variety of ways to live and the basic income made it possible. Very few indulged in these alternative lifestyles for more than a couple of years and most returned to work feeling rejuvenated and actually produced more after their adventures compared to before.

The most dauntless people emigrated to Mars, Frejja, Veehnia, Nuvirenn or Earth2.

***

Takara was pregnant and experienced a mild shock when she found out. She was one hundred and ten years old and Tojjo-Lin one hundred and fifty years. Neither of them looked older than about fifty thanks to the Nuvirenn procedure. When Takara had recovered from the surprise of her life, she told Tojjo-Lin and he was beyond happy. His whole life he had longed to become a father to no avail and he begged her not to abort the child. That was never an option for Takara, but she needed reassurance from Tojjo-Lin, as a medical doctor, she was not too old to go through with the pregnancy. He chuckled and with a warm smile he told her she would be fertile and fully capable to have children for another forty years! Takara hugged him and told him she looked forward to the baby's birth. The baby was transferred to the artificial womb at a San Francisco hospital and it was a girl. They named her Marigold.

When they brought her home, they took an airmobile taxi to Neptune and Takara closed her practice in San Francisco for six months. She only worked two days a week on Neptune and felt it was no need to stop working as it was easy to hire an android for those two days while she was working. She found a reliable android experienced with babies and hired her. It worked out fine and the android was very capable. Takara's adult children came to visit and admired their new sister. Tojjo-Lin was a proud father and felt the birth of his daughter was a dream come true. Secretly, he hoped for at least one more child.

CHAPTER 29

Rex and Elsa were on their way to a rogue planet and the fleet followed in formation. It would take them five months to reach the planet and three tunnels had to be negotiated, two short and one major tunnel, a four-hour mega portal that would propel them seven thousand light years and triple the speed of the ship. The tunnel was known as a dangerous passage as it was narrow and winding in a perilous way. Utmost caution had to be exercised to pass it, but Rex trusted Elsa's skill and he also knew she had nerves of steel. Their children were now half grown, ten and eleven years old, and in good hands. Their Aunt Hanna was their second mother and they adored her.

They had been hired by a mining company, Rogue Mining, as mediators in an effort to resolve a dispute with another mining company. The goal was to resolve the conflict without starting a war, but Rex' whole fleet was necessary both as a show of strength and as a backup force in case the mediation would fail. The name of the planet was Rogue-436, a free-floating, large planet not orbiting a star. No one knew for sure why these rogue planets were traveling through the universe all by themselves, but it was believed they may have been ejected from orbit around a star by gravity from a close fly-by cosmic body. This was speculation and nothing had so far been proven. They were probably affected by the gravity from the galaxy itself and possibly 'steered' by gravitational forces. As they were not warmed by a star, these rogue planets were too cold to support life. No one owned them and any mining company could extract minerals from them.

Rogue Mining was extracting both gold and platinum on one side of the planet and they had entered orbit with their workstation as the second mining company to work on the planet. The first company, Cosmic Quarry, had their work station in orbit as well and claimed they had full rights to the planet as they had discovered it first. They were mining gold, lots of it, from the planet. Both workstations were enormous in size and the refining of the ore was done on the stations. The humanoid crews lived on the workstations and robots did all the work on the planet. Cosmic Quarry had tried to expel Rogue Mining to no avail and was now threatening to shoot down Rogue Mining's workstation. It was a sensitive situation, but actually rather petty since Rogue-436 was large enough for several companies to operate mines at the same time. The two mining companies came from the same planet and competed with each other at home as well.

Rex and his fleet entered orbit behind Rogue Mining's workstation and he contacted the leader requesting a meeting the following day. Both companies agreed to a meeting.

Rex docked his ship with the station and a shuttle from Cosmic Quarry soon arrived. They sat down and the atmosphere in the room was hostile, almost antagonistic. The people were humanoids, very tall and thin with dark spiked hair and dressed in leather. Their angry faces told Rex and Elsa diplomacy may not work.

"Your problem is you compete with each other and are hell-bent to win the game," Rex started with a firm, unyielding voice. "This is not an issue of supply, but an issue of *winning*. The planet has enough precious metals for half a dozen companies to extract ore at the same time and from my sources I know the supply will last for several generations. Both companies can work around the clock a whole lifetime and still not deplete the supply. I did a careful investigation before we left and your own metallurgists and geologists confirmed to me the supply is immense. To threaten to shoot each other down is counterproductive and both companies would benefit from cooperation instead. I look at your situation from an outsider's point of view and see both of you *play a game* you feel you must win."

The room was silent and it was clear Rex' point-blank remarks had hit target. The two men looked angry, perhaps a little embarrassed, but both of them knew Rex was right.

"I want to cooperate and let's help each other," the Rogue Mining leader said after a few minutes.

"I'll give my answer tomorrow," the Cosmic Quarry leader replied. He looked irritated.

"I hope you can reach an agreement," Rex said. "If you refuse, I have no choice but to contact the Cosmic Court on planet Cerres and we all know they would stop all mining until the Court decides what to do.

It will take several years perhaps until they reach a decision about this planet. In the meantime, neither of you will earn any money. The easy way out with no loss of income is to cooperate and respect each other's right to work on the planet."

The leader of Rogue Mining stretched out his hand and Rex watched intently to see if the Cosmic Quarry leader would return the handshake. He hesitated at first, but then shook hands and said –

"Rex is right. If the Cosmic Court gets involved, we may sit here and wait forever. Let's make peace and stop this fight."

To prove to Rex they were serious, the two leaders agreed to split Rex' fee and end the matter. This was the first time Rex and Elsa had acted as mediators and they were thankful it had worked out without doing battle. Part of the reason why it ended so fast was that Rex had realized the true cause of the fight was *winning,* an ego game, not lack of supplies.

They departed the following day and in transit, Rex and Elsa briefed the pilots of their fleet about the details. The return trip went well and they landed on Veehnia in a snowstorm. The fee covered their expenses, but it was not their most profitable mission.

***

The Ljeviinans kept arriving and their numbers on planet Sorenia had increased to eighty thousand. Among the immigrants were many licensed pilots and they volunteered to help out flying the spaceships from Ljeviina to Sorenia. It would take several years to move the one million people who had signed up for the move, but the impact they had on Sorenia's ascension was remarkable. The planet was propelled forward perhaps a hundred years as the new immigrants started working and infiltrated all the sciences and universities. They worked as teachers, doctors, scientists, lecturers and their kind personalities and patient teaching gave Sorenia a second jumpstart. Most of them were middle aged and experienced in their field of work and many married Sorenian women. President Mitse-Tun's comment the Ljeviinans had a missionary fixation was perhaps true, but the 'fixation' was a big bonus to the planet.

Halcyon and Jilina had done the Ljeviina route for nine years and felt they needed a break. They asked for time off and the supervisor allowed them three months off with full pay. Halcyon asked if they could get their old route to Mineata back and it was also approved. The Mineata route was easy and they had more time to spend with their daughters. Aster was already seventeen years old and would soon start her studies at the university and Miina was fifteen. Halcyon and Jilina had spent all their time off with the girls, but still felt it had not been enough time. Jilina was only forty-five years old and wanted another child and they decided to let Nature make the decision. All space pilots sacrificed family life for their occupation. At the end of their time off, Jilina was pregnant and she stayed home until it was time to transfer the baby to the womb at the hospital.

Their parents came along when they picked up the baby boy from the hospital and they had enjoyed helping to raise their granddaughters. Jilina and Halcyon were allowed maternity leave and looked forward to three months off with the new baby.

***

Vitzoll and Janus were on their way to a small planet in the Milky Way called Tejra and their mission was a first of its kind that the mercenary fleet had been hired to resolve. The whole fleet of eighty-five ships followed behind them and five ships remained on Earth2 as usual to protect their home planet. Vitzoll's father Rasufilus was onboard to act as advisor and at the age of one hundred fourteen years, he felt strong and young again due to the Nuvirenn process. He and his wife Akinom had been among the last of the citizens on Earth2 to have the procedure done and now that it was over, they both enjoyed their newfound youth. Vitzoll was commander in chief and made all decisions, but to have his father along and be able to tap into his expertise based on years of work was reassuring. The ship was large enough for three people to live onboard without feeling crowded.

One of the ships was piloted by Vitzoll's thirty-year old son Erronne. He would take over the mercenary business when Vitzoll retired.

Tejra orbited a star not far from planet Bantizza, only three months' travel time from Earth2. The leaders had managed to contact Vitzoll right before they were overthrown in an android coup and most of the humanoid citizens were held in large camps with no escape possible. The androids had not yet decided what to do with the 'useless' humanoids and they had secured their kill-switches so they could not be remotely deactivated. They were unstoppable, more intelligent than the people and very advanced. All of them had the latest software installed, the same feelings as humanoids and ability to design their own replacements. They did not need people. In the hasty transmission, the leaders had begged Vitzoll to either kill the androids or shut them down and remove their entire package of software. The androids hated people and wanted the planet for themselves. The fee was huge as the leaders felt they had nothing to lose and suspected all of them would most likely be killed anyway.

The number of androids was about two hundred thousand and while they were traveling to Tejra, the crew members discussed various military strategies using an encrypted channel. Traveling on one of the ships was a software mastermind, who would launch a virus and try to infect the androids. It was a long shot as the androids were experts at removing malware. They had threatened to kill all people if any military action was taken against them, so Vitzoll and his crew were planning to take them out without being seen. To shoot them down was not the best way either as some of them would probably survive and just execute all the people. Some of the people were under house arrest and some in camps. Anyone venturing outside was killed. The androids had seized all weapons and killed thousands of people already. The coup had been totally unexpected and that is why it had succeeded and with no weapons to aid them, the citizens had no way of defeating the androids.

Two of Vitzoll's pilots were androids, Jeff and Scott, and they flew together on one ship. They suggested they would mingle with the androids pretending to be from Tejra. They had already downloaded their language and practiced the pronunciation on a daily basis and the machine language used between androids they knew already. If they were caught they would be deactivated, but the pilots assured Vitzoll and Rasufilus they were willing to risk it. They were hoping to overpower one of the androids, remove the software and scan it using their ship's computers. Vitzoll agreed to the plan. Once they had the information from the android's software package, they would make the final plans. The computer expert onboard was hoping to find an entryway to launch his virus by viewing the software package.

One of the pilots from the fleet would have to put a spacesuit on and strap an engine on his back so he could travel to Jeff and Scott's ship while they executed their mission. In theory, a ship in orbit could be unmanned for a short time, but it was risky and Vitzoll had no intention to jeopardize a ship.

The ships arrived at Tejra and entered orbit and engaged the cloaking system. Each ship had a small shuttle with two seats in the cargo bay of the ship. Unfortunately, the shuttle had no cloaking ability, so the androids would descend to the surface in the dark. One benefit was the shuttle engines were very quiet. The pilot from the closest ship was ready in cargo bay of his ship and his copilot gave him thumbs up and closed off cargo bay. The pilot started his engine and as an extra measure of security he was tethered to his ship in case his engine would quit. Jeff and Scott had their cargo bay open and within fifteen minutes the pilot was safely inside their ship. Once the exterior door was closed, the cargo bay was pressurized and he could remove his spacesuit and enter the ship.

As darkness fell over the planet, lights were turned on and it was easy to see the cities. Jeff and Scott took off and landed the shuttle on a field about a mile from the closest house. Each of them wore a backpack with tools, handcuffs, chains and security items and in holsters they had a stun gun and a laser gun concealed under their jackets. They locked the shuttle and started jogging towards the town. No one saw them and they were soon at the outskirts of town. Some androids walked around on the streets. A police station was visible with androids inside and Jeff and Scott decided to make it their target. They needed an android with as much information stored as possible, so they took a chance those androids had the information they needed. Jeff and Scott were dressed in casual clothes so they would not stand out and entered the station.

"We're looking for an android called Leon. Where can we find him?" Jeff asked the clerk speaking in the Tejran language.

"No one here has that name," the clerk replied, not suspecting foul play. "Maybe I can help?"

"Yes, I want to show you a map. Let me take off my backpack and get the map out," Jeff said and smiled at the clerk. He wanted him to stand up and be away from his desk, where he just may have an alarm button hidden. By now, the clerk was curious and stood next to Jeff as he pretended to look for his map. In the meantime, Scott quickly went behind him and saw his kill-switch. In a flash, Scott turned it off and the clerk was fully deactivated and immobile. They removed all his software and put it inside Jeff's backpack and looked for a hiding place for the android. They found a storage closet in the same room and stuffed him in a corner carefully covering him with some of the equipment in the closet. He was not visible if anyone opened the door to the closet.

Jeff and Scott walked outside. Only one person saw them and waved, believing they were from Tejra. They waved back and walked out of town and as soon as they were out of sight, they ran at full speed back to the shuttle. They stayed in the shadows and no one saw them. The shuttle started up and the whole mission had taken only an hour and a half. They felt lucky and grateful and soon they were back with the fleet. Once the shuttle was in cargo bay and they entered the ship, they thanked the stand-in pilot and waited until he was safely back on his own ship.

Jeff connected the software package to his ship's computers and scanned the information and it was now available to all the pilots to download on their own ships. It contained a wealth of information, how the coup had been planned and executed, names of important androids and government people, future plans for the planet under android leadership and plans how to murder all the people on the planet. The government leaders had suspected they would all be killed and they were right. That was in fact the plan.

The computer expert did not waste any time and carefully looked for an entryway for his virus. Time was of the essence. If the clerk in the storage closet was discovered, the androids would know they were under attack and probably check for ships in orbit. If they did, full war would break out. The other androids at the police station may not have noticed the android clerk was missing from his desk. Vitzoll had eighty-five ships with state-of-the-art weapons onboard, but he did not know how many fighter ships the planet had and the strength of their weapons. Vitzoll's ships were made of terrynium and could withstand tremendous force, but not knowing the enemy's defense system was uncomfortable. None of the pilots was afraid and they had all faced danger without succumbing to fear. Vitzoll had full trust in his pilots and their warrior skills. The government leaders had had just a few minutes to transmit their emergency message, offer the fee and hope Vitzoll would accept the mission. They did receive Vitzoll's affirmative reply and by that time the androids were already inside the government building and the leaders quickly deleted the message. There had been no time to ask any questions and Vitzoll had no information to rely on. The software from the android did not offer any information about the planet's defense.

Within an hour the computer expert had found the only entry for his virus and launched it hoping to target all the androids on the planet. It was a powerful and nasty virus, but there was no guarantee it would shut down the androids.

The next day, Vitzoll launched a spy drone with cloaking ability and waited for the transmission to return to the ship. It was informative. The drone flew at an elevation of a thousand feet and the androids walking around on the streets appeared drunk, swaying back and forth and many of them were sitting down. The virus was working, but the expert could not predict how long the effect would last. It all depended on the skill of the androids to remove malware. Rasufilus suggested they should descend to the surface right away and destroy the androids using the weapons onboard.

"We can't remove the software from two hundred thousand androids," he told the pilots over the communication system. "It would take forever. Since we don't know how fast they can reboot themselves, time is of the essence. The leaders would most likely prefer to see the androids dead rather than inactivated considering the terror these androids have afflicted on them. Any suggestions?"

Vitzoll and Janus agreed wholeheartedly to military action and all the pilots approved of the idea. The plan was accepted. The whole fleet of eighty-five ships descended to a low elevation and under the protection of cloaking, they spread out over the whole planet and destroyed any android they saw. All the buildings with androids hiding inside were demolished and all the guards by the camps were quickly eliminated. The pilots were successful as the virus was still working and they could see the androids had not been able to reboot and rid themselves of the virus. They were helpless and of no danger. The pilots worked all day and only returned to orbit when it turned dark. Rasufilus suggested they should not risk their ships by landing overnight on the surface and it was safer to return to orbit and continue the mission the following day. Any android they could see was extinct and if any was still alive, there were not enough of them to pose a major threat anymore.

The following day at daybreak they continued. A few androids were seen here and there and were quickly destroyed. Those androids were still affected by the virus and unable to defend themselves. By the afternoon, not a single android could be found anywhere on the planet and Rasufilus declared all the ships should land outside the largest camp and hope to find the leaders.

As they ran inside the camp, the scene in front of them was shocking. Dead people were lying on the floor and in dirty beds; the air smelled of death; sanitation was a row of buckets that were overflowing and moaning could be heard from some of the dying people. Those still alive were too weak to notice the pilots running around checking on the people.

"Mr. President, where are you?" Rasufilus called out. "We're the mercenaries you hired."

"Here, here." A weak, labored voice barely above a whisper alerted Vitzoll and he found the president half dead.

"They stopped feeding us two weeks ago and only gave us water every two days. That's how they were planning to kill us, by starving us to death," the president whispered. "Thank God, you're here. Please tell me you killed them all."

Rasufilus took the president's weak hand and assured him all were destroyed. The pilots ran into the camp's kitchen and returned with pitchers of water and offered water to all the people who were still alive. They were seriously dehydrated and gratefully took the water. The president drank two glasses of water and then he was able to sit up and explain to the pilots what had happened. His voice was weak, but he was determined to describe what had happened.

"It started three months ago with a gang of corrupted androids. They were power crazy and wanted to rule and I don't know how they got that way. Their software had all the safety rules in the code. They reprogrammed the other androids and corrupted them also. We people were in their way so they disarmed the whole population. This planet doesn't have armed forces, most of us are pacifists, so after the coup they just forced the people who owned guns to hand them over or get killed."

The president had to rest a few minutes before he continued. Vitzoll offered him more water and he drank some.

"They decided the easiest way to kill us was to starve us and half the population is probably dead," he continued. "If you hadn't saved us, we would all have been victims of genocide. I had just time enough to send you our plea for help when they stormed into the government building, but I did see you agreed to come here before I deleted the message.

That's what kept us alive. We knew it would take you three months to reach us and that you were the best there is. Thank you to all of you."

The president had tears in his eyes and needed to calm himself.

"We'll stay as long as it takes to make sure the people are safely back in their homes and can function on their own," Vitzoll assured the president.

Some of the pilots were in the kitchen making food for the people in the camp hoping it would revive them. There was a large supply of freeze-dried foods in the storage room in the kitchen that the androids had decided not to use and instead starve the people to death.

The crew fed and nurtured the people and after a few days, many of them were strong enough to return home. Slowly, their society started to function again and people could return to work. Everyone was told to only work according to their ability and anyone who was feeling weak could return home. Rasufilus accompanied the president to his home and he and his wife were strong enough to cook for themselves and gather strength. There was no lack of food and the stores opened again offering an adequate supply of food. Since all the androids were destroyed, the people had to learn to run their own households. Before the coup, most families had owned an android maid. No one complained. They were just grateful to have survived.

Vitzoll, Janus and Rasufilus spent the last day on the planet with the president. One month had passed and he and his wife looked much better. They were still weak, but not in danger anymore. The president had paid the crew the fee he had promised and assured Vitzoll they were not overpaid.

"The fee is a token compared to the value of a life. Without you, there wouldn't be a single person alive on this planet. Please take the fee. We can afford it." The president shook hands with them and the last thing he said was there would never be any androids on their planet again as long as he was president. Worker robots, yes, but no androids.

The men understood his condemnation after what he had been through, but they knew almost all androids were loyal and would never turn against people. Under the circumstances, they felt it was more diplomatic to just listen and be quiet. They had stayed in a hotel in town and the pilots had made daily tours of the planet with the ships to ensure no android was alive. No one was found. The pilots had helped anywhere they were needed on the planet and even helped cook for the ones too weak to fend for themselves. It had been a busy month for them and their help was truly appreciated by the people. In the countryside, more people had survived by hiding from the androids and they also came to the cities offering their help to get the country back on its feet. When the crew left, the president assured them they were now strong enough to go back to work and continue life. The crew never found out why the first group of androids had become corrupted, but they suspected an insane person with software knowledge may have started the mission. The president posted a report on the Interstellar Internet how their androids had taken over the planet and cautioned other planets to exercise caution. He also posted how Vitzoll and his fleet had eliminated the androids.

The trip back to Earth2 went well and it had been an emotional mission. Every job offer they accepted was different and this was the first time the enemy was not living people but machines.

CHAPTER 30

The tranquility on Earth2 was in jeopardy. Pollox and Lyra were still living on the grasslands and were now in their late eighties. The only neighbor was their daughter Hattie and her husband Paragonne and they lived just a few miles away. Pollox and Lyra had lived their pioneer life all alone on the grasslands until Hattie and Paragonne started farming the land and raised their family. No one else lived on the grasslands and Pollox and Lyra liked it that way. So did Hattie and Paragonne. The four of them shared their love of nature and felt the herds of meat animals and the wild horses were the only neighbors they needed. Hattie and Paragonne were now in their fifties and their children were already adults. It had been a busy life running the thousand-acre farm even with the help of six worker robots. The government had bought all their crops. Their twenty-five-year-old son, Tikkim, lived with them and was going to take over the farm when Paragonne retired. He was not married and he knew many girls would find life out on the grasslands too isolated, but he was by nature a cheerful person and accepted life as it was. Perhaps one day a girl would share his life on the farm and he had not lost hope by any means.

The last few weeks tremors had shaken the ground and Pollox contacted Ijakull, the former president. Ijakull was the best geologist on Earth2 and very familiar with the planet and its history. Before he had undergone the Nuvirenn procedure, he had felt old and accepted his life was soon over, but after the process he felt well in spite of being one hundred and twenty years old. He worked full time again and decided to investigate the opposite side of the planet. The three volcanoes had always worried him and the skeletons they had found from the former population was a warning the planet had not always been peaceful. Ijakull was rather certain the former population died from the impact of a meteorite a thousand years ago, but there was a chance the volcanoes were the true reason. He just did not know for sure.

Two geologists accompanied him and they reached the volcanoes on the opposite side of the planet. They flew the airmobile above the volcanoes and all three looked dormant and non-threatening. No steam or smoke could be seen and they decided to set up camp close to the largest volcano and continue their inspection the next day. It was summer and warm and they just put their sleeping bags on the ground and slept under the starry sky. A violent shaking woke them up in the middle of the night, so powerful they almost panicked. It lasted several minutes and then died down. Then two more tremors could be felt and then it was quiet again. The three men knew it was a sign something serious was going on and they decided to rise at first daylight.

After a quick breakfast, they flew again over the volcano and saw smoke coming out. The other two volcanoes were a distance away and one of them also emitted smoke while the third volcano was dormant looking. The airmobile was hovering over the large volcano and the men peered into the crater trying to see through the smoke. Suddenly, without warning, an explosive eruption occurred and gases and hot magma blasted out of the crater with incredible force. Ijakull was at the controls and could not get away fast enough. The airmobile was hit and thrown up into the air with the escaping gases and lava and within minutes it was incinerated and the three men died instantly. What was left of the airmobile was hit by a molten volcanic rock. There was nothing left of the airmobile.

For three days the large volcano was spewing its material out and then slowed down. After a week, the eruption was over. The other two volcanoes did not erupt, but the damage from the large volcano was substantial. The eruption was serious, but by no means the maximum the volcano was capable of.

Pollox and Lyra had felt the shaking of the ground and contacted the government in Bliss. They were told the three geologists were on the site and Pollox jumped into his airmobile and at full speed he traveled to the volcano. From a safe distance, he saw the eruption taking place and stopped his vehicle and just hovered in place. He recorded the eruption so he could transmit it to the government. It was too dangerous to get closer and his gut feeling told him the men had not survived. He sensed it from within. Later on, when it was safe to get closer to the volcano, robots searched the area and when they could not find even a trace of the geologists, they realized they had perished.

Earth2 was in mourning. Ijakull was a former president and loved by the people and his death while serving the country was tragic. All the people lived around Bliss on the opposite side of the planet and only Pollox, Lyra, Hattie and her family lived on the grasslands. It was quite a distance from the volcano to the grasslands and Pollox was unsure if they would be affected by the ash. All they could do was wait and see where the ash would come down once it started to fall from the sky. Right now, the ash was at a high elevation.

The larger particles from the eruption started to fall down to the ground within days of the eruption and fell close to the volcano, but volcanic eruption clouds high up in the atmosphere traveled toward the grasslands and slowly dropped ash over Paragonne and Hattie's fields. The crops were a month away from harvest and beautiful looking and these thousand acres of planted fields were the breadbasket for Bliss.

Paragonne and Hattie watched their crops of grain, potatoes and vegetables being smothered by the falling ash and small, sharp ash particles adhered to the plants. Not all of the grasslands were affected and the ash never reached Bliss. It was hard to breathe and they wore masks. The drinking water from the river had to be filtered. Paragonne realized the crops were lost and all he could do at harvest time was to plow the crops under and hope the following year would be normal. He and Hattie were resilient and they were sad to lose all their crops, but they knew Nature is often unpredictable and they accepted their loss without allowing themselves to fall apart emotionally. They took the disaster in stride. For over thirty years they had been rewarded with beautiful crops and the loss of one year's harvest was not so bad when viewing the total number of harvests. The government reimbursed them for the cost of seed and it was enough to live on until the next harvest.

Pollox and Lyra waited to check on the animal herds until the ash had fallen and the air was mostly free of ash. For days the skies had been dark as the ash reduced the sunlight. Pollox was concerned the ash would affect the engines of his airmobile and he was not willing to risk the only vehicle they had. When they finally started their tour, they found a third of the animals had died and were lying dead on the ground. Large groups of meat animals and horses had sensed the danger and moved away from the affected area and found grass fields free of ash. Somehow, the animals had relied on their instinct and it saved their lives. Pollox decided to leave the dead animals where they were and they would soon decompose naturally.

Outside Bliss were fields planted with vegetables and hay, but far from sufficient to last a year. The government decided to use the two cargo ships taken from the first planet and one of the ships would travel to Etteron and load up on grains and legumes. They were told by the Etteron government they had had a good harvest and would be able to supply Earth2 for a year. The other ship would travel to Bantizza, which was closer. They were willing to sell their surplus crops and between the two planets, Earth2 had sufficient supplies to last a year. The Earth2 government was grateful they had two heavy duty cargo ships at their disposal.

The citizens in Bliss watched the Internet images of the eruption transmitted by Pollox and were relieved the ash clouds did not reach their area. It was a reminder more eruptions may occur in the future, but for now, the volcanos were quiet and peace restored.

***

Melody talked to Viola using her communicator.

"Mom, this sounds crazy, but I think Dad is sick. Yes, I know an android can't be sick, he's not biological, but Dad hasn't been himself for a week. Have you noticed it?" Melody's concern came through in her voice. She loved her father deeply.

"Now that you're mentioning it, yes, he has acted strange the last few days, as if he couldn't think straight. I noticed it yesterday when we talked and he couldn't remember what we were talking about." Viola felt angst welling up inside her and the thought of losing Atlas made her almost numb. "Could you take him home now?"

"Yes, I'll get him right away."

Melody and Atlas walked home from the hospital and Atlas was swaying lightly. He was leaning on Melody and it was obvious something was wrong. They sat down and Atlas started talking.

"Something is going on with me. I ran a virus check on myself yesterday and it was negative, but I think I've been infected with malware of some sort and the virus check missed it. I've never felt like this. I can't think and analyze normally."

"Do you have an enemy, another android perhaps, who could have done this to you?" Viola asked in a trembling voice.

"There is a human doctor from Earth, Joshua, at the hospital and I think he wants my job. If I'm out of the way, he'll be the chief surgeon instead of me. I doubt he's savvy enough to spring a virus of this magnitude on me, but perhaps he hired someone to do it. All I know is I'm fighting something."

"There's a computer expert from Ljeviina, Noron, working in Bliss," Melody said suddenly. "He's a friend of Lorre's and I've met him several times. Let me contact him." Lorre was not home. He was one of the pilots on the cargo ship traveling to Bantizza to buy food. He would not be back for several months. Melody found Noron at home and he assured her he would be right over.

Noron had brought along a sophisticated scanner from Ljeviina and he hooked it up to Atlas' software package and started running a full scan. It took only five minutes and the scanner had located the virus. Noron promptly removed it and then ran a full scan to ensure nothing else was hidden inside Atlas' software. Nothing was found.

"This was a very advanced and serious virus," Noron said. "There is only one person I know of who could have done this. He works in our office and he is an expert in malware. He must have been well paid to pull a stunt like this."

Noron contacted the expert using his communicator and he admitted he had done it. Right after he launched the virus, he had felt terrible and was planning to undo it. He asked Atlas to try to forgive him and the holographic image showed he was sincere. Atlas told him he had already forgiven him and would not press charges. The expert admitted Joshua had hired him.

Atlas and his family thanked Noron several times for his help and he left. Atlas hugged Viola and Melody and assured them he was perfectly well now and back to normal. The following day he asked Joshua to step into his office and asked him if he had hired the expert to launch the virus on him. Joshua was silent for a minute and then confessed.

"Please don't fire me," he begged Atlas with an anxious look on his face.

"Joshua, you're a top-of-the-line doctor and we need experts like you. Let's put this incident behind us and never talk about it again. There's no need for you and me to compete. We're both needed here at the hospital and all I ask is that we cooperate. It doesn't matter *who* is chief surgeon. You're as needed here as I am. I admire your skills and I consider you to be my friend."

Atlas held out his hand and Joshua gratefully shook hands with him. This was a lesson in kindness he would never forget and Atlas and Joshua worked together for many years with deep respect for each other.

CHAPTER 31

Life was hard on planet Ruovo. It was poverty-stricken without natural resources. The food supply was less than adequate, the people were pawns of the government and the leaders owned most of the meager amount of wealth available on the planet. Parents struggled to put food on the table and took their frustrations out on the children and many felt their own children were a drag on their quality of life. Children were told from early childhood they were 'bad' and 'no good' and, worst of all, 'you should never had been born'. Many parents did not mean what they said and only vented their anger. There were also parents who never verbally abused their children, but they were in the minority. By the time the children were half grown, many died by suicide driven by the belief they were unwanted burdens. Many parents felt only relief when they died, no guilt and no sorrow. Their feelings were dead. The children who refrained from suicide were mentally unstable. Most people lived in fear of everything and looked to the government to keep them safe, not understanding the government was the cause, not the savior. The population was shrinking fast, but few bothered to notice.

Ruovo was totally isolated and the conditions were not known to the more advanced planets. Many affluent planets helped the less fortunate planets and often established a business model to generate income.

A stroke of luck changed the future of Ruovo. A missionary spaceship from a nearby planet had decided to check out Ruovo since no one knew anything about the planet, only that it was inhabited. They came from an advanced planet and it did not take long until they realized the sad conditions. When they happened to see five children jumping from the rooftop of a building while holding hands, they were horrified and the sight of the little bodies lying dead on the ground was heart-wrenching.

The missionaries rushed inside the government building confronting the leaders without success. They were totally indifferent and shrugged their shoulders.

"That's how it is here. It happens every day," one of them said in an uncaring voice.

"Can we sit down somewhere and discuss the conditions on Ruovo? Maybe we can help."

The missionaries were not fooled by the leaders and after a few hours they had a good understanding how the planet worked, who owned the money generated and the fate of the citizens. The planet was in serious violation of human rights and the population brainwashed. There was only one university and one of the professors was willing to talk while the missionaries recorded what he said. He told them of all the injustices he had witnessed and the never-ending deterioration of quality of life, the people's hard-earned money ending up in the leaders' pockets, lack of food even though the planet was fertile and could support a much larger population. It was a lot to take in by the missionaries and they returned to their orbiting ship to analyze what they had heard. They relied on the testimony of the professor, but would never reveal his name.

"The planet is attractive," one of them remarked as he looked out the window of the spaceship. "We know Ruovo has no natural resources, but they have enough open spaces, lakes and beautiful scenery to attract tourists."

The following day, the missionaries presented a business plan to the leaders and suggested they start building hotels in the countryside for tourists. When the leaders heard it may generate income, their interest was piqued. The missionaries emphasized a new constitution was needed and were met with silence. They realized they were dealing with hard core tyrants unwilling to give up their power over the people. The whole government must be removed and replaced by leaders elected by the people.

There were no armed forces on the planet, but a strong police force feared by the people. The missionaries requested a meeting with the leaders of the police and asked them to stage a coup and overthrow the whole government. They explained it would benefit all the citizens and if they continued on the current path, the planet would cease to exist within a generation. The leaders of the police force had sensed for years the planet was doomed and living conditions had deteriorated from bad to worse with no hope for the people. They themselves had added to the people's burden by terrorizing them, but many of the officers were waking up and wanted change. When they listened to the missionaries' proposal to make Ruovo a tourist planet they agreed to a coup.

A turbulent period followed and the whole government was overthrown and incarcerated. The people were invited to run for office and scholars from the university wrote a new constitution that benefitted the people, not the government. Everything from the old system was declared invalid and the new system was fair and matched what most civilized planets would call a just and democratic government. The missionaries continued suggesting ways to increase the food supply and how to raise the standard of living.

Hotel building started and after a year the government was ready to offer the planet as a resort for tourists. It was a slow start and few arrived the first year, but eventually the word got out and more people found Ruovo a pleasant place to visit. The missionaries had stayed the whole time to guide the new government and one of their missions had been to teach parents parental skills. They were taught to respect their children as individuals with free will, how to nurture them and instill in them they were loved and wanted. The suicide rate dropped to zero and the children looked to the future with excitement. The older children were slowly healing and went from being unstable to children with healthy minds. In the end, parents understood the disservice they had done to their children and adopted the new ways suggested by the missionaries.

Psychology lessons became part of the curriculum and were considered one of the most important subjects. The lessons shaped the children's minds and made them mentally stronger, removed fear, enabled them to make decisions and gave them self-worth.

After staying a year and a half, the missionaries left and the new democratic government was functioning well with an expanding and fair economy and a raised standard of living. It had been the most challenging rescue operation the missionaries had undertaken and, at times, they had been unsure if they would succeed. When they left, they looked around and saw children happily playing and knew in their hearts they had succeeded. They would return annually to continue guiding the new government.

***

A year had passed since the volcano erupted on Earth2 and it was spring and planting time. Paragonne and his son Tikkim had inspected the fields and found no damage from the volcano eruption. In the fall, they had plowed under last year's harvest together with the ash and the plants had decomposed nicely. The soil looked good and they went ahead and planted all the fields with the help of their worker robots. When the plants emerged as usual, Paragonne was relieved the ash had not prevented germination.

The imported grains and foods from Etteron and Bantizza had sustained the people on Earth2 over the winter, but the government favored self-sufficiency and hoped for a plentiful harvest from Paragonne's fields. They had offered Paragonne more land, but he politely declined. He took pride in producing excellent quality crops and for over thirty years he had sold his harvest to the government. Paragonne felt a thousand acres was the maximum he could manage and still maintain top quality. The government knew that as the population increased, more farmers were needed. Several fields had been planted outside Bliss, but in the future larger tracts of land would have to be cultivated.

Last fall, Tikkim had put an ad on the Frejjan Internet stating 'Earth2 farmer looking for wife' and to his great surprise he got an answer. He had done it just for fun and then forgot about it. A girl responded through the Interstellar Internet and said she was planning to visit and see if they would be a good match. Her name was Kazinna and she was nineteen years old. She had booked space on the next ship leaving Frejja in a few days and would arrive in nine months on Earth2. Was she welcome? Tikkim sent a reply right away she was more than welcome and when he watched the image she had transmitted of herself his heart jumped. She looked like his mother Hattie with a blond ponytail to her waist and she was so pretty he could hardly take his eyes off her. The ship was due to arrive in a few days and his mother had the guest room ready. Tikkim had left with his airmobile already and stayed at the little hotel in Bliss anxiously waiting for the shuttle to deliver the passengers. Frejjans still immigrated to Earth2 and usually at least fifty passengers would be onboard every time the ship arrived from Frejja.

There she was! Tikkim recognized her right away as she climbed out of the shuttle. Most Frejjans were tall, but Kazinna was tiny. Tikkim ran up to her and gave her a hug. He knew it was inappropriate, but she did not mind at all and just smiled at him.

"Here I am, Tikkim," she said and looked up at him with her blue eyes.

"I'm so happy to meet you, Kazinna. I have my airmobile over there and as soon as we get your luggage, we take off to the farm."

A robot came over to them with her bags and they left Bliss. The airmobile was autonomous and Tikkim and Kazinna could talk and get to know each other during the eight-hour trip. She told him she had always wanted to live on a farm and when she saw his ad, she knew she should reply. Her chances to find a husband farmer on Frejja were next to none and her parents and sister had supported her when she told them she would reply to Tikkim's ad. When Tikkim explained there were no neighbors except for his grandparents a few miles away, she replied she did not mind and he, his parents and grandparents were enough people for her. Kazinna had just finished school and did not want to continue studying. She was practically inclined and loved being outside and when she heard Tikkim had several horses, she was excited. She would love to learn how to ride.

Tikkim told her about their farm life, last year's volcano eruption and how he and his father Paragonne ran the farm. She was a good listener and enjoyed hearing Tikkim talk.

Paragonne and Hattie liked Kazinna from the minute they shook hands with her and she liked them. The following two months Kazinna took part in all facets of farm life and bonded with all three of them. Tikkim taught her how to ride a horse and she and Tikkim went horseback riding several times a week and it was a treat for Kazinna. She knew already this was the life she wanted and when Tikkim proposed after only two months, she said 'yes' with an emotional voice. Tikkim was a nice-looking guy, three quarters Frejjan and a quarter Etteron. He was tall and muscular from working on the farm, but his heart was tender and full of love, a fact that came through when he talked to his horse. The horse clearly showed his affection for Tikkim and Kazinna knew animals do not fake love and the human owner must earn the animal's devotion. She let her heart guide her and put analytical thoughts aside when she accepted Tikkim's proposal.

The marriage took place the following week with a government official in Bliss officiating the wedding remotely over the Internet. Their marriage license could be picked up the next time they visited Bliss. Paragonne, Hattie, Pollox and Lyra attended and it was an emotional time for all of them. Viola, Atlas, Melody and her husband Lorre had promised to visit in a few weeks. Paragonne and Hattie's older daughters lived in Bliss and also looked forward to meeting Kazinna as did Xentos, Janus and Alma.

Tikkim and Kazinna's union lasted over two hundred and fifty years and it was a happy marriage. They were well-suited for each other and shared the same interests. Paragonne and Hattie felt they had a new daughter in the house and the extended family lived in harmony under the same roof. Tikkim was a spiritual man and talked to his divine guides on a daily basis. Everyday issues were discussed and he would receive guidance from them through his thoughts. Feeling their presence gave him inner peace and strength and Kazinna shared his divine beliefs.

***

Rex and Elsa loved dogs, especially a breed looking similar to the German Shepherd breed found on planet Earth, and this breed was popular on Veehnia. Rex had contacted the scientists on Veehnia and asked them if they could invent an implant for dogs similar to the implant worn by people. They responded with enthusiasm they would get to it right away. The implant was pricey, but Rex would only be charged if the dog responded to it and it actually worked, so Rex ordered one.

Rex and Elsa bought a male puppy and named him Yambo and began training him as a space dog. Their children were already teenagers and were disappointed Yambo would travel with their parents, but they were still happy to have a dog in the house between trips. Once Yambo was house trained, Rex and Elsa took him on daily trips with their spaceship and he adjusted to being weightless rather quickly, 'swimming' with his legs in the air. Rex made booties for him to enable him to walk on the velcro floor and he adjusted to that as well. He loved the gravity chamber and stayed there while Elsa exercised and his 'litterbox' was kept in there so he could make his bathroom trips with the help of gravity. His intelligence was remarkable and Rex and Elsa looked forward to fitting him with his implant and find out how he would react to it.

When the implant was ready, Rex and Elsa took Yambo to the lab and a veterinarian attached it behind Yambo's ear. The first days they noticed Yambo looked bewildered and they realized he was in 'discovery mood' and from there on his understanding took a big leap forward. It seemed as if he understood everything around him and his command of words was impressive. He responded to at least a hundred words with perfect understanding of the word as well as an array of whistles. Rex was an expert whistler and could change his whistles almost like a bird and each whistle had a specific meaning, from 'danger' to 'everything is normal now' and Yambo understood every whistle. The whole family was in awe of Yambo as well as thoroughly entertained. Rex and Elsa now started training him for serious space work and to face explosions and to be dressed in his very own spacesuit, which Rex had ordered custom-made for him. He was trained not to eliminate in the suit and he never had an accident. The inventors of the implant and the dog spacesuit came over to check how Yambo had adjusted to his new world and were truly impressed by what they saw. Rex and Elsa had only one rule – no Internet coverage of Yambo to eliminate the risk he would be stolen.

Yambo was one and a half years old and still growing when he went on his first mission with Rex and Elsa. He resembled a large wolf and weighed more than Elsa. Yambo understood the difference between family life and his life as a working dog on the spaceship and he obeyed Rex instantly. He obeyed Elsa as well, but Rex had done most of the training and he considered Rex to be the alpha male.

The new assignment was a dangerous job involving sex trafficking of very young girls. As the father of a fourteen-year-old girl, Rex could hardly wait to nab the gang who raked in a fortune when selling these innocent girls. Some of the girls were only ten years old. Rex and his fleet had been hired by the police force of a planet located rather close to Veehnia and with three shortcut tunnels, the travel time was only two months. The criminal organization had avoided being caught and the police force had not been able to find where the girls were hidden before they were shipped to other planets for sale. So far, sixty very young girls had disappeared from the planet and the parents were traumatized and overwhelmed with grief. There were no armed forces on the planet.

The advanced planets did not have sex trafficking, but there were still primitive planets with low moral standards willing to buy young girls as sex toys and destroying the poor girls' lives.

When they arrived at the planet, the fleet stayed in orbit and Rex and Elsa descended to the surface with Yambo. They knew the location of the headquarters of the police force and landed a mile away on a field. Two officers met them and jumped when they saw Yambo. Rex put his hand up reassuring them Yambo was fully trained. He was not on a leash.

As they walked inside the building, Yambo heeled and looked to Rex for instructions. He created quite a stir when entering the room and Rex calmly explained Yambo was part of the team and they had nothing to worry about. He only took orders from them.

The officers told them the details of the case. The planet had a low crime rate, but a year ago a gang of alien criminals had arrived and stayed somewhere on the planet. No one had been able to figure out where they were hiding and young girls were kidnapped and just disappeared never to be seen again. Time was of the essence as parents were frantic with worry to lose their girls and the police on the planet needed help to put a stop to the kidnappings. The fee would be paid by the government. No one had ever seen a ship leave and the police said they thought the ships left during the night. Apparently, they had sufficient supplies as no theft of foods or other supplies had ever occurred.

Rex had a rough idea what was going on and told the officers he needed to discuss the case with his crew and would let them know later on what the plan was.

In orbit, the fleet listened in on an encrypted channel and Rex gave them the details.

"I suspect they're all hiding in an abandoned mine, in the mine shafts, probably in the countryside far from the cities. If their ships are not too large, they can slowly enter the tunnels and hide the ships. That's a place no one would think of looking and when they leave the planet, they may be cloaked. That takes care of their hiding place. To kidnap the girls, how do they do that? A cloaked cargo drone could transport the girl and if she is drugged, she would be unconscious during transit to the mine. The criminals must operate where there are children and look like the local population. They may be former citizens of the planet and that's why they don't stand out and can just pick the girls as needed.

I suggest we start at daybreak and cover the whole planet looking for mines with the ships cloaked. I will not inform the police force ahead of time what we plan to do as there may be a mole within the force."

The fleet flew at slow speed just high enough to avoid being heard from the ground and the ships covered the whole planet. There it was! Rex and Elsa heard the encrypted message from one of the ships announcing they had found the mine. The surrounding mountains were impressive and cast a shadow over the opening to the mine. A narrow road led to the mine and from the condition of the road, it was clear the mine had been out of production for years.

Rex got the coordinates to the mine and ordered the rest of the fleet to return to orbit while he and Elsa would check out the mine and the surroundings. They hovered the ship at a high elevation and used their high-powered telescope for closeups. The entrance to the mine was wide enough to accommodate a medium-sized ship and a cargo drone could easily pull it inside. In front of the mine was enough room for five ships and they could block the entrance and prevent the criminals from leaving. No guards were outside, but suddenly one man came out of the mine to relieve himself. That was the proof Rex and Elsa needed. They had found the hiding place. They returned to orbit and opened the communication channel to the fleet.

"We've found the right mine and we saw a man come outside, so it's almost for sure that's the hiding place," Rex started explaining. "Tomorrow at daybreak, all ships will fly cloaked to the mine at twenty thousand feet elevation. Ships number two through five will descend with my ship to the surface and our five ships will block the entrance to the mine so they can't escape. I doubt there are more than six of their ships inside the mine and perhaps twenty men inside. We stay inside our ships, engines running and fully cloaked, ready to fire on my command only. The rest of the ships will hover at two thousand feet and act as backup force. If the men come out and fire weapons at us, we have no choice but to shoot them down. If they hide inside the mine, I'll send Yambo in. My ship will be at the edge so they can't see him exit the ship. Yambo will enter the mine and be instructed to 'track' and 'hide' with a camera attached to his collar. He will find where the men hide and he knows how to hide and return to us. A spy drone can also be used, but drones make noise and I prefer to send in Yambo. Once we know how many are inside, I'll give you your orders. We should avoid firing into the tunnel to prevent it from collapsing."

Everything went according to plan and once the five ships were outside the mine, no one came out. For sure, the men must have heard the engines running, but were too afraid or cautious to investigate. Yambo was ready with a camera attached to his collar and silently slipped out of the ship. He understood fully that his mission was to find people hidden inside, but remain unseen and stay in the shadows. He had an earpiece inserted inside his ear and listened to Rex' orders. Rex had taught Yambo to accept the earpiece and he was not afraid of it. Rex would watch the images from Yambo's camera on his screen and once he knew where the men were hiding, he would instruct Yambo to 'come back'. Without his implant, it may not have been possible to make Yambo understand his orders.

Yambo silently entered the mine shaft and stayed close to the stone wall while entering deeper inside the mine. It was only dim light in the tunnel, but Rex could still see how the tunnel looked on his screen. First Yambo found the ships, five of them. They were medium-sized and lined up in a row. Now the tunnel became narrower and Yambo was jogging another half a mile and then came to an abrupt stop. In front of him was a lit-up room in the mine where all of them were. Four cages with three girls in each cage and fourteen men sitting around a table eating. *They had not heard the spaceships arrive!* In a low voice, Rex immediately ordered Yambo to come back and within ten minutes he returned to the ship and was pulled inside. Elsa hugged him and told him what a good boy he was and Yambo reciprocated with an affectionate lick on her cheek. He understood he had finished the job to their satisfaction and he got a treat as a reward.

Rex quickly told the crew the details and ordered ships number six through eleven to park on the mining road as fast as they could. Engines off and stun guns and laser guns loaded. The remaining fleet should stay hovering. All pilots from the eleven ships were instructed to enter the tunnel and stun the gangsters before chaining them up. Yambo would ensure they would not try to escape. If they were met with fire, the pilots were told to use their laser guns and shoot to kill, but only on Rex' command.

The men, Elsa and Yambo half ran to the living area and only slowed down when they saw the lights at a distance. They stayed close to the side of the tunnel to ensure they were out of sight. The gangsters were unaware of their presence and had finished eating and sat around and talked. Rex signed to the men to continue with their stun guns drawn and they inched their way to the room without making any noise. Yambo was at Rex' side waiting for orders.

"Harass!" Rex whispered into Yambo's ear.

The sight of Yambo charging into the room, growling and showing his teeth shocked the men to the point they were unable to react. He was a fearsome sight and ran back and forth ensuring no one had a chance to move. When one of the men tried to reach for his laser gun in the holster, a gesture Yambo had been trained to recognize, he quickly caught his arm and with full force bit down on the man's arm crushing it. The screams from the man echoed inside the chamber and the other men were so terrified they could not move.

A sharp whistle from Rex meaning *"Release!"* told Yambo it was enough and instantly he let go. The man's arm looked as if it had been through a meat grinder and would need amputation. It was destroyed. Rex was by nature sympathetic, but he felt these men did not deserve anyone feeling sorry for them.

"Light stun on the men," Rex told the pilots.

The pilots quickly chained the men up and they noticed the man with the crushed arm was dead. He had died from the shock, perhaps suffered a heart attack. Elsa and Rex removed the girls from the cages and they were surprisingly brave. None of them cried.

"Did the men hurt you or touch you in any way?" Elsa asked. She was using a small translation device.

"No, " one of them replied. "We heard them say virgins bring more money."

"How did they catch you?"

"When we went to the restroom in school, they waited for us there and drugged us. We woke up here inside these cages. None of us know how they transported us from the school to the mine. We heard them say they would ship us off tomorrow, so you saved our lives."

"How old are you, girls?" Rex asked.

"We're ten, twelve and thirteen years old."

"Thank goodness we found you in time. Did you see the face of the man who drugged you in the restroom?"

All the girls shook their head.

One of the criminals had awakened from the stun and Rex walked over to him and asked what planet they came from.

"This planet," he answered. "We live on this planet. That's why no one suspected us."

"Where do you send the girls?"

"There are several planets with low moral beliefs and each girl brings a fortune. I regret what we did." His remorse did not sound authentic to Rex and perhaps the man thought he could strike a bargain.

Elsa led the girls out of the mine and Rex followed with Yambo. Rex contacted the police captain and gave him the details of the mission asking him to send several airmobiles to pick up the girls and the criminals. The pilots were told to return to orbit and wait for Rex and Elsa to join them.

Rex talked briefly with the captain and suggested they interrogate the prisoners to find out where the former girls had been sent. Perhaps they could be found and returned to their parents. The captain assured him they would do that and he also told Rex they would all face severe jail sentences. Rex told the captain he would see him in a little while at the station to pick up his fee, but he wanted to visit the girls' school first.

At the school, Rex asked the principal to order all personnel to come to his office, including the teachers. Rex' gut feeling told him there were more guilty people.

"Please line up in single file," Rex told them politely. "Don't be afraid of the dog. He won't harm you."

He bent down and quietly said to Yambo *'seek'*. Yambo knew if he had a lineup in front of him, his job was to find out if anyone was 'bad'. All the hours Rex had spent on training him were now paying off. Yambo slowly walked the line and looked each person in the eye. When he was done, he returned to one man, a janitor, and growled. The man started shaking and looked to Rex for help. Yambo could smell sweat, adrenaline and certain chemicals released when a person is fearful and he also noticed the person's body language. Rex trusted Yambo's instincts.

"Were you involved with the kidnappings of the young girls?" he asked the man and looked into his eyes.

"No," the janitor replied and took a step back.

"Yambo, *seek*," Rex reminded the dog. This was all for show. Yambo had never made a mistake yet.

Yambo growled at the man showing his large teeth. It was a low base sound that made the hair stand up on the man's arms. He inched closer to the man and crouched down ready to leap. The man's eyes showed horror and he fainted. It was obvious he was guilty.

"Call the police and have this man arrested. He's part of the criminal gang." Rex saw to it the principal called right away.

At the police station, the captain was back and handed over the fee to Rex. It was a generous fee and Rex needed the money to pay salaries and get supplies. He told the captain they should make use of the criminals' space ships and the captain replied they would definitely come in handy. At the station, Rex asked for a lineup of all the police officers and the same thing happened. Yambo picked out two of the police officers and they confessed. The captain was shocked and disappointed. He would never have suspected any of his employees to be involved in crime, but watching Yambo told him the dog was right. They would face trial together with the rest of the gang and the janitor from the school

They left the planet and were soon back home. Rex would let his crew rest a month before accepting another assignment. Once they were home, Yambo was the most docile family dog and Rex and Elsa's kids could play around with him and never have to worry he would nip them. Yambo loved his family.

Rex and Elsa were very proud of Yambo's performance and he would prove over the years to be a first-class trooper.

CHAPTER 32

The tripled lifespan of people who had gone through the Nuvirenn procedure changed people's outlook on life. People stopped saying 'I don't have time'. Time was now plentiful and starting different careers, learning new skills and mastering one's psychology were projects people could work on without rushing. Some parents had two families; raising one family when they were younger and years later starting a new family, often after they turned a hundred years old. Their minds were on the upswing and knowledge acquired from a long life was passed on to the younger generation. Deterioration of the mind had been conquered and almost no one suffered from dementia. Mental capacity and consciousness were steadily increasing with expanding creativity as a result.

On planet Earth2, Ássurt, at one hundred and twenty years old, was the proud father of three children and on Earth, Takara and Tojjo-Lin had two children. Takara was considered 'young' at the age of one hundred and sixteen years old.

Were there people who could not adjust to a longer lifespan? Yes, and some ended their lives, but not many made that choice. Most people saw a longer life as a gift.

The Nuvirenn procedure was now offered to pets and horses, but the cost was high and not all veterinarians were trained to perform the process. People who could afford it opted to have their pets undergo the procedure and afterwards, the animals were stronger and seldom succumbed to diseases. Rex and Elsa were planning to treat Yambo when he turned three years old.

No planet had contributed more to people's happiness than Nuvirenn and their gift to humanity was free.

***

On Earth2, Alma had had a happy life with Janus and her family and her marriage of thirty-six years had been nurturing and loving. Their children were adults now and Alma had more time to think back at her life. Where was her little sister Helga? How she longed to see her and be with her again. Alma made a holographic recording of herself and her life and the next time the Frejjan ship arrived, she drove to the ship using her groundmobile and asked to talk to the captain. She explained she was searching for her lost sister and they had not seen each other for forty-one years. The next time he visited Earth to pick up immigrants, could he ask the authorities if Helga lived on Earth and then transmit the recording to her? Alma had addressed the recording to Helga using her birth name. If she was married, it may be harder to find her, but Alma was hopeful. The captain was touched to hear Alma's story and assured her he would try to find Helga and it was no bother at all. He told her many people from Earth had moved to planet Nuvirenn and there was a possibility her sister also lived there. If that was the case, he would leave the recording at the Nuvirenn office on Earth and they could forward it to Helga. The captain refused payment and assured Alma he was happy to help. The travel time from Earth2 to Earth was a whole year and from Earth to Nuvirenn seven months, so Alma knew it would take several years to get a reply from Helga.

Alma had to wait three years until she heard from Helga and it was a long recording with images of her husband Settie and their five children. The same captain delivered the recording in person and spent a day with Janus and Alma. They showed him Bavonilla and he enjoyed having a day off from his duties. The herd of horses grazing on the land impressed him and he truly appreciated the visit. He was such a pleasant man and Janus and Alma asked him to visit them any time he was back on Earth2.

When they were alone, Janus and Alma watched the recording together and apart from the sad story how Alma's parents died, it was heartwarming to see Helga's life on Nuvirenn and how happy she was with her husband. Both Alma and Helga understood they would never meet again as the distance between them was enormous and even another recording was complicated to arrange, but just knowing they were both alive and happy was enough. Helga said in her recording she felt peace knowing about Alma and she knew Alma would feel the same when she received the response from her. Janus spoke English and could understand everything Helga said. Both Alma and Helga felt the two recordings had brought closure to both of them.

***

It started slowly. People on Earth began to feel dizzy and some people complained they could not think straight. A few went to their doctor and were thoroughly checked with a diagnosis of perfect health. The doctor assured them nothing was wrong. Then a man crashed his airmobile and before he died, he whispered to the medics assisting him "I couldn't remember what to do".

Takara and Tojjo-Lin sat on the porch of their house on Neptune Island and listened to the news over the Internet. Neither of them was affected by illness. Their two children were sound asleep. Marigold was already eight years old and her little brother was two years.

"Takara, did you hear that?" Tojjo-Lin said slowly and scratched his head. "It sounds like a virus in the implant. We're isolated here on the island, but it may reach us soon also. We must protect the kids and remove their implants."

"That's a serious thing to do, Tojjo-Lin," Takara said nervously. "They'll be totally bewildered without the implant and their cognition and intelligence will be seriously affected. They may feel slow-witted and panic."

"Takara, I know my suggestion scares you, but we're both doctors and if my hunch is correct and we're dealing with a virus in the implant, the children will be hurt. They may suffer permanent brain damage. If we remove the implant, they'll be in distress for a short time only until the perpetrators are caught and the virus removed. Will you allow me to remove the implants tomorrow?"

"You're right, just do it," Takara said after she thought about it. "We can't risk the kids." She knew the children were cherished by Tojjo-Lin and he was a loving father.

The next day they explained to the children why they had to remove the implant and Marigold was old enough to understand and agreed right away.

"I'll feel dopey for a while. I can take it," Marigold said and laughed. "Go ahead, Dad."

Marigold's brother understood something was wrong and he would get his implant back after a while. He was not afraid. With his implant in place, he functioned as a four- to five-year-old.

Tojjo-Lin and Takara decided not to remove their own implants yet, but at first sign of illness, they would immediately remove each other's implant.

A month passed and more people succumbed. Many died. By now, everyone understood a virus was the cause and people had their implants removed. The police searched the Akashic Records, but could not find anything. All androids were questioned by their owners and none was found guilty. Finally, one police officer realized the virus must have been launched from Mars. Mars was a high-tech center and the biggest brains in the universe had flocked to Martia and the many tech companies there. The police commissioner contacted Martia and explained the situation and they promised to check their Akashic Records right away. They quickly found the guilty person. It was a young immigrant woman from planet Morekia, only seventeen years old, and gifted with a brilliant mind, but lacking understanding of the consequences of her actions. She had created the virus single-handed and launched it on Earth to see how powerful it was, not giving any thought to the misery and deaths it would cause. The Martian police arrested her and ordered her to immediately neutralize the virus. She did and it was not difficult for her to remove it. Once the police explained the horrendous damage her virus had caused, she finally woke up and broke down in tears. She was deported from Mars and returned to Morekia, where she was sentenced to fifteen years in jail without parole.

Takara's children were glad when they got their implants back and people on Earth decided to trust the future safety of the implants and had them attached again. People who had removed their implants had felt lost without them and many had never experienced life without an implant. They were shocked to find out how dull they felt without the cognitive boost of the microchip.

***

On planet Veehnia, Yambo was now four years old and had been through the Nuvirenn procedure. A light sedation made the procedure easier and he emerged as a smarter dog with lots of energy and increased emotional needs. Elsa showered him with affection and Yambo looked to her as 'mommy'. Rex was 'boss' and to Yambo, every space mission was a big adventure when he and Rex worked together. Yambo would give his life for both Rex and Elsa and his devotion to both of them was indisputable. With a new life expectancy of at least thirty-five years, he would make many trips with Rex and Elsa. So far, Yambo was the only working space dog Rex had ever heard about and eventually his efficiency and courage would bring him fame as a super dog. Elsa cooked all his meals herself and brought along frozen, home-cooked food for him when they were away in space. She enjoyed watching Yambo delight in his dinner. She knew it was tasty and nutritious. While she heated his food on the spaceship, he would wag his tail in anticipation of his goodie. It was a generous portion and he easily worked it off on the treadmill.

While traveling on the spaceship, Yambo favored the gravity chamber and he and Elsa worked out together. The treadmill was great fun and Yambo was weighed down with a pair of saddlebags filled with twenty-five pounds of weights on each side. As the treadmill started, he would signal with a woof to Elsa to increase the tempo until he was running full speed on the treadmill with fifty pounds on his back. His endurance was remarkable and his muscle strength had not been impaired by space travel. There he was, running at top speed on the treadmill while Elsa lifted weights and the sight was something to behold. Rex would often stand in the door opening laughing out loud and admire the scene. When Yambo finally was exhausted, he woofed again and Elsa would slow down the machine until it was at walking speed. They worked together as a team. Yambo always wore velcro boots so he could walk on the floor without floating up. The latest design of Leo's velcro flooring was more efficient and prevented the person from floating around.

***

Rex and his fleet were on a new mission to planet Cerros-2, located in the Pleiades star cluster, not far from planet Peturun. Rex did not often accept work in the Milky Way and preferred missions closer to home in the Andromeda galaxy, where Veehnia was located. The distance was two and a half million light years, but travel time was only two months thanks to the eighteen-hour tunnel, a mega portal, catapulting them an enormous distance to the next galaxy. Elsa and Rex took turns piloting the ship through the monster tunnel and Elsa was grateful when they finally were through it. Yambo was strapped down and always took the vibration of the tunnels in stride having full trust in his master. Elsa always encouraged Yambo to use his 'litterbox' before they entered a tunnel. A month remained of the trip and then they would enter orbit around Cerros-2.

The mission was complicated and emotional. Cerros-2 was the size of Mars, but with a dwindling population. To remedy the situation, they had allowed mass immigration of people from a neighboring planet that was seriously overpopulated. Unfortunately, the immigrants refused to integrate and obey the laws of their new planet. Instead, they had become troublemakers trying to throw out the existing government and take over the planet. The Cerros-2 native population was already a minority on their own planet and could not stand up to the aggressive immigrants. In desperation, the government had hired Rex to help them bring about peace and also act as mediators.

The Cerros-2 people were very advanced mentally and did not believe in wars while the immigrants were much less advanced and solved every conflict with military action. Rex and Elsa were not sure how they would reach the immigrants' minds and awaken them to the idea that there are better ways to resolve hostilities than bloodshed.

The population had recently lived through a frightening time and two thirds of the citizens had died from a disease carried by an insect similar to a tick causing a fatal blood disorder. There was no remedy for the disease. When the doctors finally figured out where the disease came from, the insects were quickly eradicated. At that time, the population had plummeted and the government invited immigrants not knowing the mindset of the new citizens. Many of the immigrants were convinced a show of force was the only way to get ahead and had no respect for the 'wimps' on Cerros-2. The fact that the Cerros-2 people were way above them in mental development and sophistication was not recognized by the immigrants. They were ego driven and blind to it. It was not unusual for a Cerros-2 person to face a hostile immigrant who would knock him out just for fun. Then there were the rapes. Young girls were violated and the men were seldom caught. The former so peaceful planet had become a war zone.

With the fleet in orbit, Rex, Elsa and Yambo descended to the surface and met with the government officials.

"Can you deport them?" Elsa asked the leaders as they were briefed about the situation.

"We wish we could, but they're here to stay. We can't get rid of them. They outnumber us and they believe every problem is solved with the fist. If you can reach them somehow and mediate a lasting peace agreement between us, we would be most grateful. We can't live like this. Many commit suicide as a way out. Their leader is exceptionally cruel and his name is Krekkogrym. We ask that you meet with him so you have a rough idea what we're forced to tolerate on a daily basis."

The following day, Rex made contact with Krekkogrym and asked if they could sit down and talk for a while. He agreed. When Rex and Elsa walked into his house with Yambo heeling but not on a leash, he took a step back, but met Yambo's gaze with pretended boldness. Yambo was never on a leash as he would not ever leave Rex' side. Rex quietly ordered Yambo to sit. When sitting, Yambo was tall enough to see over the tabletop. Anyone knowing something about animals could see Yambo would obey any order from Rex. Krekkogrym felt cold shivers go down his back. He had never seen a dog and this huge monster of a thing was sizing him up. He was a very tall, skinny man with spiked, black hair and elongated head shape. Deep facial groves in spite of being young indicated an irritable personality. His eyes were green and mean.

"Krekkogrym, we're hired to mediate between your people and the people on Cerros-2. We're mercenaries from planet Veehnia in the Andromeda galaxy. We understand you want to oust the government and take over. Is this correct?" Rex asked using a commanding, direct voice.

"I guess the leaders of the planet told you that," Krekkogrym said trying to avoid a direct answer.

"This is not a game, Krekkogrym. Respond, *yes* or *no!*" The tone of Rex' voice alerted Krekkogrym here was a man he could not dupe.

"Yes," he finally said.

"Are you not aware you're here thanks to the kindness of the Cerros-2 people?"

"Yes, but they're weak and we would be better leaders."

"By knocking out innocent people on the street and raping the women, is that what you call *better leaders?*" Rex did not back off and maintained strong eye contact with Krekkogrym.

"Some of our men haven't conducted themselves in the best manner, but most of us would not perform such acts."

"That's not what I hear. Many of the natives die by suicide to escape the current living conditions on this planet. If you were to be the leader, what rights would the Cerros-2 people have compared to your people?"

"They would be left alone, but we would rule." The comment was blurted out by Krekkogrym, a slip of the tongue he regretted as soon as he said it.

"I bet you would," Rex said. "How about trying to integrate into this society and then participate in free elections? If you would win the election, you could *lead* the country, but not *rule*. This planet is not a dictatorship with you sitting on a throne. It's *free*. Do you get that? You will never be the king here no matter how much you fantasize about it. We'll see to that. What's your response?"

"You have no authority here, Rex. Why should I listen to you?"

"Because we're hired by a legitimate government elected by the people. We work right now as representatives of the government. You, on the other hand, has no authority here. When you deal with us, you deal with the government. I can throw you in jail, if you don't obey the laws of this planet and I have the backup of my fleet. I prefer not to settle this with a war, but be aware, we're professional soldiers and will not hesitate to take whatever measures we deem necessary to reach a solution. Am I making myself clear?" Rex spoke with a hard, intimidating voice.

"Yes." Krekkogrym looked beaten and his cocky attitude was gone.

Yambo was watching and Rex' tone of voice and body language told him Krekkogrym was the enemy, but Yambo would only respond to commands from Rex and never act on his own.

"Would you and your people consider returning to your own planet?" Elsa asked.

"We can't. It's overcrowded. They wouldn't allow us to return."

"Are you willing to integrate with the native people and stop all criminal behavior?" Elsa continued asking.

"I don't think I can convince my people to integrate and stop abusing the people. They look down on the Cerros-2 people as weaklings and only respect physical strength, not mental power."

"We're staying until your people obey the laws on this planet. They'll have to find out the hard way that law and order must be respected regardless of their own mindset and fantasies. You people don't own this planet, you're guests here and should behave accordingly. You don't run the show here, the government is in charge. I ask you, Krekkogrym, to start advising your people to change their ways immediately or face the consequences. Will you do that?" Rex' authoritarian voice was frightening and for the first time in his life Krekkogrym had to deal with a man superior to himself in mental strength.

"I'll try," he said quietly.

"We'll meet in two days again in your house at noon and I expect a positive report from you."

Rex and Elsa got up and Rex told Yambo to heel. Krekkogrym watched him with fear in his eyes.

As they walked to the spaceship parked a mile away, they noticed a circle of men and muffled screams from a woman trapped inside the circle. She was being violated by an immigrant man with the spectators cheering him on.

"Yambo, charge! NO kill!" Rex would never have given such a serious command unless he felt this was the time to show these people once and for all there are consequences to one's actions. Rex respected all life, even his enemies' lives, and that is why he ordered Yambo to inflict serious injury without killing the victim. So far, Rex had never ordered Yambo to kill and Yambo understood the difference between 'kill' and 'no kill'. A 'no kill' meant injury. During training, Rex had taught him to kill using a dummy, but the command was intended to be used in life and death situations only.

With a hair-rising growl and teeth exposed, Yambo charged with a giant leap right into the center of the circle and bit down on the man's neck with his powerful bite. His jaw strength was comparable to any large size carnivore. The man screamed and was immobile while Yambo bit down on his neck. Rex stood outside the circle of men and waited. He wanted the lesson to be crystal clear.

A loud whistle meaning *"release, come back"* alerted Yambo to stop and he immediately released and returned to Rex waiting for new orders. One man had fainted and the others were backing off too shocked to even understand what had happened. None of them had ever seen a dog and Yambo's speed and precision when he carried out Rex' command was beyond anything they had seen. The rapist had passed out, but was alive. The blood was slowly running from his neck and Yambo's teeth marks were visible. Elsa ran inside the circle and helped the shocked woman to her feet. She was shaking from fear and unable to talk. Her clothes had been ripped off and she tried to shield herself from view. Elsa quickly took her sweater off and put on the woman and assured her they would call the police to take her to the hospital.

Using the translation device, Rex addressed the men in a strong voice.

"To violate an innocent woman like this will no longer be tolerated on this planet. All of you stay where you are. You will be charged with a crime as participants in rape. Anyone trying to leave will have to deal with this dog." Yambo was told to *"guard"*.

No one moved and the man who had fainted woke up and understood there was no escape. Within minutes a police van arrived and loaded up the men and a second police groundmobile escorted the woman to the hospital. She would need psychiatric help to recover from the shock.

When the police had left, Rex stroked Yambo on the head and told him in a quiet voice he approved of his performance. On his own, Yambo would not hurt anyone.

From his house, Krekkogrym had seen the whole incident and understood Yambo had seriously injured the rapist as he was removed from the scene on a stretcher. He was overwhelmed with fear.

Soon, the whole town knew what had happened and the government officials assured Rex all the men would face rape charges. No mercy would be shown. None of the government leaders disapproved of Rex' decision to use Yambo to establish law and order.

The following day, Krekkogrym appeared on the Internet and gave a speech to his people asking them to do their best to integrate into the society and abandon all criminal behavior. He had been up the whole night thinking about what had happened and soon realized they could not win by bullying the population and it would serve their interests better if they cooperated with the native people. As the leader of his people, Krekkogrym was an intelligent man and knew when the game was over. He also wanted peace in his life and his nerves were frazzled.

Rex and Elsa watched the speech on their ship in orbit and realized they were watching the beginning to a solution. The crew members had been informed what had happened.

The next two weeks, Rex asked his pilots to patrol the whole planet at low elevation, uncloaked, and search for any immigrants involved in criminal behavior. They found nothing and apparently the lesson with Yambo had made a difference. The sight of the fleet spreading out over the planet was reassuring to the native population and threatening to the immigrants. Rex and Elsa knew they had to change the mindset of the immigrants permanently so they would not revert to criminal behavior as soon as they were off the planet. They met with the government officials every day and with Krekkogrym at least a few times a week for briefings.

Rex and Elsa were walking briskly to Krekkogrym's house to hear the latest news and found his house on fire. It was not fully engulfed in flames yet, but the flames were rapidly spreading. They knew Krekkogrym was most likely inside.

"Yambo, rescue, hurry!" Rex kicked in the front door and without hesitation Yambo ran inside full speed and started looking for Krekkogrym. He had been in his house several times and understood he was supposed to save the man's life. He heard Rex shout *"crawl"* and dropped to the floor to continue his search. He found Krekkogrym on the floor in the kitchen alive, but unable to move. He had been shot. Yambo had trouble breathing because of the smoke, but grabbed the man's shirt with his teeth at the neck and as fast as he could he dragged Krekkogrym outside by walking backwards. Yambo could easily manage his weight, but the floor was slippery and he had to use his full strength to drag him out. The flames were now right next to Yambo, but did not touch him yet. At the door opening, Rex and Elsa grabbed Krekkogrym and quickly pulled him out and laid him down away from the house. He was conscious and looked at Yambo with awe. He knew Yambo had saved him from burning alive.

Yambo was sitting and breathing heavily. Rex, Elsa and Yambo traveled along with Krekkogrym to the hospital and one of the doctors quickly gave Yambo oxygen to inhale. It helped and soon he was back to normal. The doctor scanned Yambo's lungs and found no damage. Krekkogrym's bullet was surgically removed and the killer had used an old-fashioned pistol as he probably had no access to a laser gun.

An assistant to Krekkogrym had shot him and then put the house on fire. He could not accept they were asked to integrate into the society and just 'give up'. Krekkogrym told the police officers his name and he was soon arrested and put in jail. The house had burned down and was a total loss.

Rex, Elsa and Yambo went to see Krekkogrym at the hospital and he was doing well and healing fast. He turned to Rex and asked him how he should thank Yambo.

"Shake hands with him. He understands it means you're grateful," Rex explained with a smile.

Krekkogrym was in a wheelchair and in spite of still fearing Yambo, he stretched out his hand to Yambo. Yambo immediately responded by offering his paw and they shook hands. Krekkogrym had tears in his eyes and the formerly so cruel man seemed to have mellowed quite a bit. He held Yambo's paw in his hands a long time and the two of them looked into each other's eyes. For a moment their souls connected. Krekkogrym offered his gratitude and Yambo accepted it. It was a touching moment.

When Krekkogrym was out of the hospital things moved fast. With firm resolution, Krekkogrym and the government agreed to a peace treaty and Krekkogrym assured the government his people would obey and respect all laws of the planet and integrate fully with the native population. If any of his people broke the law, they should face the consequences according to the law.

The government paid Rex his fee and conveyed how relieved they were the situation had ended so favorably. When Rex and Elsa said goodbye to Krekkogrym, he assured them he would not return to his old ways and he looked forward to a new life without warfare. He would post a message on the Internet emphasizing the immigrants and natives should live in peace from now on. He never forgot Yambo and talked about him for the rest of his life.

Rex and his fleet were home again and the mission had taken five months. Yambo had a month off to enjoy his beloved family. His training with Rex continued between missions, but to Yambo, training was fun time.

CHAPTER 33

Planet Xellisun was barely functioning and the society was close to collapse. Most of the money was owned by a small group of people while the citizens had become poverty-stricken and stripped of humanity. Food was scarce, violence was everywhere and chaos made life unbearable for the people still alive.

Not all the rich people were bad and ten affluent families had teamed up and hired Vitzoll and his fleet as well as Rex and his fleet. Vitzoll's eighty-five ships and Rex' twenty ships were on the way to Xellisun to try to restore the planet, have a new government elected and write a new constitution. The planet had to be reborn; new laws and a totally new system that was fair to the people must be created. The ten families had agreed to share the fee for the mercenaries and felt they had nothing to lose. Money was losing its value, but the families owned gold and were willing to pay most of it to the mercenaries to restore the planet. They had earned their money by hard work, not looting the people. To leave the planet and start a new life on another planet was Plan B, but the ten families preferred to restore law and order on Xellisun and hoped the two fleets of mercenaries could do the job.

Planet Xellisun was half way between Earth2 and Bantizza and the travel distance was not far. It had been an advanced planet in the past with a fair government working for the people, but corrupted people had managed to dupe the citizens to vote for them and once they were in office the changes started. The people lost free speech; surveillance was everywhere; privacy was non-existent; money was not backed by gold and slowly lost its value; taxes had skyrocketed. There was limited medical care and the schools were closed. The corrupt government was still in office with the heavily bribed armed forces protecting them. The planet was large, at least the size of Veehnia, and the population was five billion people. To get the job done, the ten families felt two fleets were necessary.

During the flight, the fleet discussed options and they had a few ideas, but no final plan. It would be a challenge to restart a new society from scratch and they had to earn their fee, which was substantial and would most likely reduce the wealth of the ten families considerably. Both Rex and Vitzoll and their crews had seen similar deterioration on several planets. Most of the time, it was possible to restore a planet to normal conditions, but not always. There was never a guarantee their mission would succeed and Rex and Vitzoll knew each assignment was different and required original solutions.

Rasufilus traveled along on Vitzoll and Janus' ship as advisor and his experience was highly valued. Yambo was also onboard Rex and Elsa's ship. When they arrived, all the ships went into orbit. Vitzoll and Rex toured the planet with their ships cloaked. The planet had a small fleet of thirty fighter ships and they had been warned the native pilots were aggressive and trigger-happy. From the air, they saw the planet was a mess with trash everywhere, gangs roaming the streets and mayhem all over the planet. Some shoppers walked in groups to a grocery store as no one dared to venture out alone. They watched as people left their place of work and apparently some companies were still in business as the number of people leaving to go home was substantial. The tax these people paid supported the government and there were several police officers on the streets protecting them.

The following day, Vitzoll contacted the government from orbit and explained they were mercenaries and asked for a meeting. He explained his fleet was in orbit and they would descend to the surface unarmed. The government officials seemed surprised at first, but agreed to a meeting and guaranteed their safety. Vitzoll, Janus and Rasufilus as well as Rex, Elsa and Yambo sat around a large table with armed guards lined up against the wall.

"Remove the guards *at once!*" Rasufilus demanded in a thundering voice. "This is a peaceful meeting, not warfare."

The president was not used to being told what to do and hesitated at first if he should obey orders from Rasufilus, but the stern look on Rasufilus' face told him this was a man of courage who would not back down. He waved to the guards to leave the room. The president was a short, stocky man with crew cut red hair, beady eyes, a thick beard and an elongated head. He looked cruel.

"I'm president Cegros and I'm in charge here on Xellisun," he started. "I know who you are. My first question is who is funding you?"

"We're not at liberty to disclose who hired us," Rex responded calmly. "We have a fleet of a hundred and five fighter ships in orbit and are prepared to use them, if need be, but we would prefer if you agree to cooperate with us. We're hired to bring law and order to this planet and write a new constitution. There will be a presidential election and you can run for office with the same rights as the other citizens on this planet. Your armed forces will have to take their orders from us and we expect you'll advise them to be at our disposal."

The president looked indignant and furious.

"We had elections two years ago and we won," he said loudly and it was obvious he had trouble controlling himself.

"We heard the election was rigged and massive fraud was taking place," Vitzoll stated. "If you're correct and no fraud was involved, then you have nothing to worry about in the next election. If the people reelect you as president, we'll honor their decision. Please ask the leader of your armed forces to join us here in this room, right now."

"I will *not*. I have not agreed to obey you." By now the president was visibly irritated and his red face revealed his anger.

Rex gave a command to Yambo in a low voice and he walked over to the president and made eye contact with him. A low growl alerted the president he was advised to obey or face the dog. There were no dogs on the planet, but the president had seen them on the Internet and knew the danger of a trained dog of Yambo's caliber. Using his communicator, he contacted the leader of the armed forces, a man named Hesco, and he showed up within minutes. His oversized laser gun was in a holster and in full view.

"Go ahead and instruct Hesco that from now on he and his men take orders from us and no one else," Vitzoll declared.

Hesco was shocked and looked at the president to make sure he heard straight. He was also short and stocky like the president with deep wrinkles on his forehead and long, dark hair in a ponytail. It was obvious this man was merciless and without patience.

"Hesco, you and your men will work under the command of these mercenaries from now on," the president said. "Is that clear?"

"Why? What right do they have to give us orders?"

"I'll explain later. Just agree you will follow their orders and then leave the room."

"I will do so," Hesco mumbled. He glanced at Yambo with hate in his eyes and left the room.

The meeting continued until the president had been informed of all the changes that had to take place on the planet with a new government working for the people, a new constitution and a society without crime. The president listened with a steely face and his pursed lips showed his disgust. The crew left and they walked back to the spaceships. They all knew Hesco was trouble. Before they entered the ships, they shared their thoughts.

"Hesco will order his fighters to attack us in orbit," Rasufilus said. "They have only thirty ships, but they may take a chance and attack us during the night. We'll have to establish night watch. I also believe Cegros has no intention to cooperate with us. He faked it. You may have noticed how he said 'I'm in charge here' and a man of that conviction will not give up power. I suggest we shoot down all their ships if they attack us during the night, if they're uncloaked. Otherwise, they'll keep coming back. Hesco will not submit to us and he and Cegros will concoct a scheme using any means they have including full warfare. Be prepared, they may go into hiding to avoid us."

The rest of the crew all agreed with Rasufilus. They knew he had years of experience and his reading of the situation was right on the money.

They returned to orbit and Vitzoll opened the communication channel and informed the rest of the pilots about the details of the meeting and the real possibility they would soon be under attack. He advised them they would have to take turns sleeping while one of them stood guard and to remain cloaked at all times.

"If Hesco's ships are cloaked, take off into space as fast as you can and we assemble outside orbit until the ships are gone," Rasufilus added.

Nighttime arrived and towards the early morning Hesco's ships attacked. They were cloaked, but the crew heard them and took off at full speed. The whole fleet escaped unharmed and the pilots on Hesco's ships realized the fleet had left and returned to the planet.

The fleet entered orbit again and when Rex tried to contact Cegros, there was no answer. Rasufilus was right again. They had gone into hiding.

"We have two spy drones with cloaking capability, one for each fleet," Rasufilus said. "Let's launch them right away and if we're lucky, we'll find where the ships are hidden. We must take out their ships."

For two days the drones scanned the whole planet while the crew waited in orbit. No ships were found. Overnight, they left orbit and hovered cloaked outside orbit in case the fighter ships would return. They did not. Perhaps the pilots realized they would never catch Rex' and Vitzoll's ships.

"The ships are either camouflaged or hidden inside hangars. Let's see if the drones can find any hangars tomorrow," Rasufilus said. "We can't give up on the ships. They'll have to be destroyed."

Another two days went by and one of the drones transmitted an image that might be a hangar. It looked more like a warehouse, but should be investigated. They launched the drones again in the middle of the night hoping they would be able to hover them outside a window and take pictures without anyone seeing the drones. It worked. The pictures were blurry because of the low light, but when Elsa ran them through the computer and enlarged them, the shape of thirty ships were visible. The crew celebrated.

"I suggest we use twenty of our ships and leave before daylight so we arrive at the hangar at first light," Rex proposed. "Twenty ships will blow up the hangar in a few minutes and we can make a fast getaway. They'll never catch us and our ships can take a direct hit without too much damage. They may have guards outside, but there were none on the pictures."

Everyone agreed to the plan. Vitzoll and Rex would lead with nine each of their ships following. This would be the first time Yambo witnessed firing from the ships and Elsa would observe how he dealt with it. The ships left that same night in the dark without lights and fully cloaked. The pilots could not see each other, but knew the location of each ship from their instrument panel. Each ship had a radio transmitter and the beacon was visible on the control panel. It was a long distance to fly and when they arrived at the hangar, the sun had just come up.

"Descend to five hundred feet," Rex informed the pilots. He knew they had to be fast and finish the mission before anyone had time to react.

With the ships lined up in front of the hangar, they all fired on Rex' command and the building literally exploded. Their weapons had tremendous power and the ships inside were all on fire and destroyed. The scene in front of them looked like a hell with exploding ships inside the building and a roaring fire was now consuming the hangar.

"Retreat! Fast!" Rex shouted and all of them were gone within a minute. No one had guarded the building and, apparently, Hesco had trusted the mercenaries would never find the ships as they were hidden inside the hangar.

Yambo had observed the attack on the hangar with intense interest, but without fear. He knew his Master always did what had to be done. The sight of the building on fire and the explosions had shaken him somewhat, but he kept his calm and when Elsa reassured him with a loving hug, he understood what he had witnessed was necessary to get the job done.

Back in orbit, Vitzoll posted a message on the Internet addressed to the president with the simple message "Ready to talk now?" There was no response.

"We have to find the president's hiding place," Rasufilus said. "If we find Hesco, we find Cegros. I suggest we catch one of the soldiers and hope Yambo can make him talk. The drones should be able to spot the barracks where the soldiers live. The easiest is to grab one of the guards, stun him, and interrogate him at a safe distance from the barracks. We can drop him off on the opposite side of the planet and by the time he manages to return to his unit, we have probably finished our mission and his former world is gone."

The plan was accepted and the pilots were told what would happen next. The cloaked drones were launched and within a day a large area with buildings lined up could be seen on the pictures one of the drones transmitted. It was obvious it was a military camp and armed guards confirmed it was.

"Since we plan to use Yambo, Elsa and I will take our ship and land about two miles or so from the camp," Rex started to explain. "We'll leave from orbit in the middle of the night when they sleep. They won't be able to hear the engines from that distance. Elsa stays with the ship. Yambo and I will use the portable engines to reach the barracks. We approach the soldier, stun him and then fly the ship to the opposite side of the planet and land. I knew Yambo will make him talk. We drop him off without his weapons and communicator in the wilderness. It will take him weeks to find a house where he can alert his superiors. I don't foresee any problems."

"It's a good plan," Rasufilus said and Vitzoll nodded in agreement.

Nighttime arrived and Rex and Elsa took off without lights and cloaked. Rex slowed the engines down to minimum and they landed two miles from the camp without making much noise. Rex strapped an engine onto Yambo and attached a sturdy handle to the back of his engine and then put his own engine on. Yambo was thoroughly familiar with the engine and accepted it as part of the job. They took off and Rex held on to Yambo's engine keeping him close. Yambo traveled in an upright position like a person. They landed a short distance from the barracks. Rex wore dark clothing and it was hard to see him in the dark. There were no guards visible and Rex walked carefully around the perimeter of the camp making sure he was not visible. Yambo heeled and was told to be silent. At the back of the camp, they found a guard relieving himself and not paying much attention to his surroundings. In a flash, Rex ran up to him and fired his stun gun set on medium. The soldier had no time to react and just dropped to the ground unable to move or make a sound.

He was heavy and Rex could not run too fast with the soldier on his back. Yambo carried his weapon in his teeth. Rex quickly strapped the engines onto the soldier and himself and tucked the weapon inside the soldier's boot. He ordered Yambo to follow, started the engines and they left. He held on to the soldier using the handle. Yambo ran full speed right next to Rex and had no trouble keeping up. Back at the ship, Elsa helped to drag the soldier inside the ship and they took off. The soldier would probably not be missed until the next day and there was nothing his unit could do anyway. Hesco would most likely figure out what had happened.

Rex flew the ship to a wilderness area of the planet where no people were living and landed. The soldier was awake and in shock. Just the sight of Yambo next to him paralyzed him with fear. Rex ordered him to exit the ship and Yambo made sure he would not try to run.

"On your knees! Where is Cegros hiding?" Rex asked in a hard voice. No response from the soldier.

Rex gave Yambo a command. He approached the soldier, who was on his knees, and grabbed his throat and started to bite lightly. Yambo knew he was not supposed to kill the man, only harass him. The soldier fainted. Rex was in no hurry and the soldier woke up after a few minutes.

"I will talk. Just get your animal away," he cried out. He had never seen a dog and was not sure what Yambo was, but he did understand he was dangerous.

The soldier revealed where Cegros and Hesco were hiding and the size and locations of the armed forces. He also told Rex the planet had six cargo ships and there were no additional fighter ships hidden on the planet.

"We noticed many people still go to work," Elsa said. "The tax rate is high on this planet. Where does the tax money go?"

"Cegros takes it. He pays the armed forces and then keeps the rest of the money for himself."

"Does he spend it?"

"No, he's hoarding it. He's cheap as hell. No one dares to confront him, not even Hesco. He pays Hesco just enough to ensure he obeys and then all the tax money goes into his own account. Cegros is a dangerous man and he has no feelings for the people. He considers them to be his slaves. If they all died, he would take his money and move to another planet. He couldn't care less what happens to this planet or the citizens here."

"Do you support him?" Elsa asked.

"Hell, no. I hate him. You may not believe me, but I wish your fleet killed him. I do feel sorry for the people and would like to have a *real* government in place. The last election was a joke and a total fraud."

"Do the other soldiers also want a new government?" Elsa continued asking him.

"Yes, we all do, but we can't say anything. If we do, they would kill us on the spot. The only one who likes Cegros is Hesco, maybe because he's a true sadist and enjoys cruelty and inflicting pain on others. Neither of them is married and there's no one telling them to stop."

"Couldn't the soldiers just grab Hesco and throw him in jail?"

"He's never alone. His body guards protect him. The same goes for Cegros. It's impossible to get near them."

"You have told us what we need to know. Our plan was to leave you here. If we return you close to your camp, will you cooperate with us? If you do and work for us, we can remove Cegros and Hesco from power and restore this planet to a democracy." Rex sensed this man was honest and could speed up the mission.

"You have my word I will cooperate. All of us soldiers suffer. We have no hope for the future the way it is now. We might as well be dead."

"I'll return your gun and communicator and we'll drop you off close to the camp. Make up a story you were sick or something and passed out. I'll give you the code to our communicators and you'll have to memorize it. Don't enter it into your communicator. They would kill you for treason if they scanned your communicator and found our code in there. I'll write it down for you and on our trip back, you can memorize it. We expect you to notify us of anything you hear, no matter how insignificant it seems to you."

"I promise you I will do it. My name is Voren."

As they flew back, Voren was busy making sure he had the long code memorized and they dropped him off a few miles from the camp and returned his gun and communicator. Rex hoped he had made the right decision.

Back again in orbit with the fleet, Rex and Elsa informed the pilots everything they had learned. The pilots told Rex they had full confidence in his judgment that Voren would cooperate. He did. The same day the first message came in from Voren telling the crew his story had not been questioned and they all believed he had passed out and was sick.

"I suggest we catch Cegros and Hesco as soon as we can," Rasufilus explained over the communication channel to the pilots. "Voren gave us the locations where they hide. Let's start with Hesco. If he's out, Cegros has no backup and is easier to catch. Hesco is hiding in an underground bunker that's heavily guarded. We'll launch the spy drones right away to establish his routine so we can catch him when he leaves the bunker. Cegros is holing up in a cottage outside the city. No one would suspect a president to live in a tiny cottage and Cegros and his five bodyguards are crammed inside that little house. The neighbors may know he's in there, but would never dare say a word."

Rex and Vitzoll launched the two drones from their ships and kept them at a high enough elevation so they would not be heard from the ground. They directed them to hover and just take pictures. It only took a few days to establish Hesco's routine. Every morning he left to confer with the other leaders and he always returned to the bunker in the late afternoon. A groundmobile was used and it appeared to be the same vehicle every day. From the pictures, the crew noticed it was a heavier than usual vehicle and reinforced to withstand a direct hit. The families funding the mission had requested the president and Hesco should not be killed, but must stand trial for their atrocities.

"If we use six of our ships and hover above their groundmobile, they have to stop," Rasufilus said addressing all the pilots. "Any weapon they fire at us can't harm our ships and we can fire a warning shot to show them they have no way out. Once they're out of the vehicle, we stun them and chain them up and Voren can most likely direct us to a warehouse or small building to keep them until this mission is finished. After Hesco is out of the way, we deal with Cegros. Let's wait until we hear from Voren."

The same evening Voren contacted them to ask for instructions. Rex asked him if he knew a safe place to hide Hesco and his bodyguards and Voren suggested an isolated warehouse. It was seldom used and no one lived close to the building. It had a restroom, but no cooking facilities. Rex instructed Voren to contact him the next day at a specific time for further directives.

Rex and Vitzoll hovered cloaked above the route Hesco used and four additional ships were next to them. When Hesco's vehicle was approaching, the ships uncloaked and fired a shot in front of the groundmobile. It was obvious Hesco and his men were shocked to see the six fighter ships right above them and the driver stopped the vehicle. There was nowhere to go.

"*Get out of the vehicle!*" Vitzoll barked, using his loudspeaker.

Nothing happened and no one came out. On Vitzoll's command, Janus fired a laser gun into the engine compartment killing the engine. Still, no one exited the groundmobile.

"Let's give them a scare," Rex said. His communication channel was open so the pilots could hear him. He lowered his ship and slowly landed on top of the vehicle, bearing down on it inch by inch with a crushing sound. The men went berserk inside the groundmobile and the door flew open. They rolled out while screaming in panic. Elsa quickly opened the door and Yambo jumped out of the ship. She yelled "*harass*" and he ran back and forth ensuring none of them reached for a gun. One of the men had passed out and the other five men appeared to be in shock, including Hesco. Rex landed his ship on the ground and gave each man a stun and they were immobile. The other pilots also landed their ships and quickly put chains on the men. All the guns from the groundmobile were confiscated and put inside one of the ships in cargo bay. The groundmobile had been reduced to scrap metal. The pilots found guns inside the men's clothing and removed them. A few vehicles had seen them, but turned around and disappeared believing they would get killed.

In the meantime, Voren came through on the communicator and gave them the directions to the warehouse. He would meet them there. The six men were loaded up in the cargo bay of Rex' ship and they took off. The building was large and on Vitzoll's order, two of the ships slowly rolled inside the warehouse and the four pilots were told to guard the prisoners. It would only be for a few days and the pilots would live on their ships. Each prisoner was chained to a sturdy column and would have to stay there until the president was caught and the armed forces surrendered. They would get two bathroom breaks per day under heavy guard.

Voren arrived in his groundmobile and told Rex he could sense the soldiers were ready to work for the mercenaries, but he did not know if the leaders would submit. He unloaded a small amount of food for the prisoners he had managed to take from one of the barracks and returned to the army camp. So far, no one knew he worked for Rex. Before he left, Rex gave him five gold coins.

"Voren, please accept these coins as a partial payment for your services. Without your help, we may never have found the hiding places of Hesco and Cegros."

"Thank you so much. I wasn't expecting to be paid, but thanks anyway." Voren smiled and gratefully accepted the coins.

The ships returned to orbit and next on the agenda was the president. By now, he may have heard Hesco never arrived to his meeting, but it was not for sure. The pilots knew they had to catch him before he fled and decided to repeat the same maneuver at daybreak the following day.

Six ships hovered above the little cabin where Cegros and his guards were hiding.

"President Cegros, come out of the cabin unarmed with your bodyguards," Vitzoll called out to him.

No answer and no one came out. Janus fired a shot through the window. Still, no one came out. A second shot had no effect either. A third shot blew out the front door and they were able to see inside the cabin. It was empty.

Vitzoll landed his ship and Janus quickly put on a protective vest. With his laser gun in hand, he entered the cabin. It was empty.

"Maybe we should check Hesco's bunker," Elsa suggested.

The ships flew to the bunker and found the entrance. It appeared to be an underground concrete structure with only the door above ground. On Vitzoll's command, Janus fired a shot blasting the door aside. Another shot straight into the bunker was answered by a massive fire response of high caliber weapons. The bunker was occupied. The ships were not hit and hovered a few hundred feet above ground.

"I'll launch the mini drone," Rex announced on the communication channel. It was a cloaked drone no larger than an inch and equipped with a camera and made very little noise. Elsa steered the drone inside the front door and into the bunker. A long staircase led to the living quarters and they saw about twenty armed men waiting and ready to shoot. One of them ran up the staircase and fired out the open door at the ships, but missed.

Elsa brought back the drone and Vitzoll notified the pilots he would shoot a vial with tranquillizer inside the bunker. It would explode on impact and release the tranquillizer throughout the room. Its effect was rapid and would put all of them to sleep within a minute. Vitzoll maneuvered the ship as close to the front entry as he could so Janus could shoot the vial aiming it down the staircase. It was a difficult shot requiring good aim and had to be executed fast to avoid being hit by the men's weapons, but Janus had good eye-hand control and did not miss. The vial flew down the staircase, hit the wall and exploded. Within seconds the room was filled with tranquillizer vapors and by the time the men reacted, it was too late. The gas had already hit all of them and they just dropped to the floor and were unconscious.

All the ships landed and with gas masks on, the pilots ran inside the bunker and quickly dragged the men out and put them in chains. They were fully asleep and would not wake up for two hours. Cegros was not among them. The pilots loaded the men inside the ships in cargo bay and took off to the warehouse. Once there, they were chained to the columns with the other men.

Rasufilus suggested they should contact Voren so he could identify the men.

"I suspect we have caught the top leaders of the armed forces," he said. "There is no danger now if we communicate with Voren. The soldiers won't hurt him and if he's in any danger, he can stay here with the pilots until it's safe for him to return to camp."

Voren was surprised to see the message on his communicator, but jumped into his groundmobile and arrived quickly at the warehouse. He confirmed it was the top brass of the armed forces they had caught.

"Do you have any idea where Cegros is?" Rex asked him.

"He's shrewd. I think he's probably traveling around and only staying in one place overnight and then moving on. If you offer a reward of a few gold coins on the Internet to anyone who has seen him, you'll catch him in a few days. The people have nothing and can't afford to pass up such an offer."

Elsa posted the message right away on the Internet offering three gold coins as a reward if the person could give the location of the president. It was a winner. The same day a person contacted Rex on his communicator giving the exact location where the president was hiding, namely in the house next door to his home.

The crew had stayed at the warehouse hoping to hear from someone about the location of Cegros and when the message came in, they took off right away. It was a short flight and when the ships hovered above the little house, Cegros came out with his bodyguards unarmed. They knew they had no chance to escape and did not resist when they were put in chains. Besides, Yambo made sure there was no talkback.

Elsa ran over to the house next door and found the person who had contacted them. It was an elderly couple who accepted the reward with tears in their eyes. They told Elsa the people had suffered tremendously under Cegros' dictatorship and looked forward to a new life with freedom for all.

The pilots transported Cegros and his men to the warehouse and from there they called the police force to come and arrest Cegros, Hesco and their men. Several groundmobiles arrived and Rasufilus informed the police chief who they were and why they were on the planet. The police chief only needed to look at the prisoners and recognized all of them and understood right away a regime change was taking place. He sighed with relief and assured Rasufilus all the prisoners would be locked up.

Elsa posted a message on the Internet the government had fallen and soon an election would take place. Any citizen was welcome to run for office. People celebrated and went wild when they heard the hated Cegros and his sidekick Hesco were under lock and key. The ten families contacted Vitzoll and they met for the first time face to face. It was a long meeting and they had already written a new constitution and new laws they hoped would be accepted by the new government. Cegros' bank account would be emptied and the stolen tax money returned to the treasury. The new money system would be gold backed and they would assist in any way they could to get the economy on the right track. They assured Vitzoll and the crew everything would change and full democracy would be established. They themselves were businessmen and would not run for office, but they would advise the new government and ensure a new system would be in place as soon as possible.

The families paid the fee to Vitzoll and Rex in gold and told them how grateful they were the mission had ended so well and a new government would soon be in place. The fee was very generous and after Vitzoll and Rex had paid the salaries to the pilots and the expenses related to the mission, it was a nice pile of gold left to be distributed. Both Rex and Vitzoll had the same system; half of the extra money was saved to maintain the ships and the rest of the money was shared evenly by all the pilots. Rex was debt free and had paid off his loan to the Veehnian government.

Before they returned home, Rex contacted Voren and shook hands with him. He paid him ten gold coins, a fortune for Voren. Without his help, Rex knew the mission may not have ended so favorably. Voren also shook hands with Yambo without fear. He held him in high regard and admired him.

CHAPTER 34

Rex and Elsa's son Adrian was now an adult and twenty years old. He wanted nothing to do with his parents' adventurous lifestyle and had a sensitive, caring personality. His sister, Sophie, on the contrary, was a copy of Elsa and every time her parents returned from a mission, she wanted to hear all the details of what they had lived through. Elsa and Sophie discussed every space trip in detail and Sophie soaked it all up. She had asked her parents to teach her how to fly a ship, but they felt she should finish school first and then they could discuss it.

When Adrian announced he wanted to become a member of the clergy, his family was mildly shocked. Where did he get those ideas from? As an android, Rex was logical and very caring, but not religious. Elsa and Sophie were agnostic, totally openminded, but unsure what to believe. They did not attend church and did not read any spiritual material. Not so with Adrian. He had a deep faith he had never revealed to his parents and felt a strong bond with a higher power. Rex and Elsa decided not to interfere in any way and told him they would support any choice he made and help him achieve his goal. Adrian entered a theology school and started studying religion, philosophy, advancement of the soul and sacred writings. It was a three-year program with a heavy course load and the students had to work hard to keep up. Adrian did not regret it. He knew he was in the right place.

Religion was important on Veehnia and there was only one faith. Half the population attended church services regularly. Their faith involved belief in the Creator or, as he was referred to, The Natural God, meaning the Creator had no connection to any religion or government. God is a Spirit and beyond the material universe. Marriage was encouraged for all clergy members and roughly half of the students at Adrian's school were women. When the students graduated, they would be called 'minister'. Some ministers became hermits for a while to achieve a closer bond to the Creator, but most returned to their church after a few years. Adrian was planning to follow this route and immerse himself in prayers and meditation, but only for a while. He wanted to have a wife and family and to serve his parish.

***

Adrian graduated and his parents and sister were proud to have a minister in the family. At first, they thought being a minister was a 'wimpy' profession, but as they learned more of what Adrian was doing, they realized they had been wrong and supported him. Elsa and Sophie asked him to give them lessons in meditation and found they gained mental strength and inner peace, feelings both of them embraced. Meditation became a habit they practiced almost every day.

Adrian had his own parish and once the members of his church knew him, they showed up for service and enjoyed listening to him. He was very personal, supportive and a superb listener as well as nurturing and showing great sensitivity. His plans to become a hermit for a few years never materialized as his church members asked him not to leave. They needed him and when Adrian heard that, he abandoned the idea.

Adrian and his family were invited to Tothellim and Amelia's house. All of them were pilots and often visited each other to discuss their missions in space. Adrian often talked to Tulema, who was by now fourteen years old, and found her interest in his church heartwarming. They would walk into the garden and talk and neither of them wanted to listen to 'space talk'. Tulema was born on a spaceship and had spent the first six months of her life on the ship, but she was a landlubber and preferred firm ground under her feet. A loner by nature, she was a fan of old, old printed books, a true rarity, as all books were in electronic format. She loved reading old printed books; some of them were over two hundred years old and very fragile. Adrian's church had a library of printed books and she was allowed to borrow one book at a time provided that she wore gloves when handling the books.

Tothellim and Amelia noticed their daughter's interest in Adrian and his church and knew she had faith. As parents, they did not interfere and felt she had free will and was capable of making her own decisions. They often visited Adrian's church and listened to his service. Tothellim had developed a strong faith ever since Emrak had visited him in his dream after his death and Amelia shared his faith. Their seventeen-year old twin boys, Aten and Seleus, always came along and enjoyed listening to the sermon. Rex, Elsa and Sophie also attended his church regularly and even though Rex was an agnostic, he found he did enjoy the tranquility of Adrian's church and always left with a feeling of increased peace within. In many ways he was no different than a human and his feelings constantly evolved.

Adrian taught Tulema how to quiet her mind and listen to her inner voice and transcend. When they met, they grew together. Both knew they were soulmates.

***

Yambo was the father of a litter of six puppies, four males and two females. One of the males was given to Tothellim and Amelia to be trained as a space dog and they named him Iljo. Eric, the captain, was in favor of a dog as a crew member. He had seen Yambo and loved him. Vitzoll was offered one also and accepted the offer. He and Janus felt the six months roundtrip travel time to Veehnia was worth it to get Yambo's son and they would keep him in the gravity chamber onboard. During the return trip, they would work on his training.

Vitzoll and Janus landed on Veehnia and it was the first time they saw the planet. They liked it, but felt it was too 'busy' for them and preferred the peacefulness on Earth2. Rex and Elsa invited them to stay a week with them. After hours of studying the male puppies, Rex had selected two puppies, Iljo and Zakki, to give away and Iljo and Zakki looked like Yambo looked as a puppy and had strong personalities. Both were intelligent and very alert. By the time Vitzoll and Janus arrived, Tothellim, Amelia and Rex had finished Iljo's and Zakki's initial training. Vitzoll and Janus were enthusiastic to meet Zakki and participate in his training. There were a few dogs now on Earth2, but they were rare and there was no dog comparable to Yambo on Earth2. Vitzoll would be Zakki's master with Janus acting as a secondary master.

An intense week of training followed and it was time for Vitzoll and Janus to return home with Zakki. They had a good understanding how to train the puppy, command words to use and veterinary requirements. Rex had done a good job preparing them and they thanked Rex and Elsa many times for the gift of Zakki.

Both Iljo and Zakki turned out to be as efficient as their father Yambo and the pride of their owners. They wore implants and went through the Nuvirenn process at age three. Both dogs started working at age one and became first class crew members.

*****

At the young age of seventeen, Tulema married Adrian. Tothellim and Amelia had hesitated and felt she was too young while Rex and Elsa felt Adrian was twenty-six years old and perfectly capable of supporting a wife and care for her. In the end, Tulema and Adrian made the final decision and their devotion for each other was unmistakable. Their parents wished them happiness and Tulema continued her education after she married. She loved being part of the church and often helped Adrian write his sermon. It was a happy union.

*****

The year 2248 had arrived and most planets were doing well. Peace and prosperity on the different planets in the universe were more prevalent than war and chaos and several mercenary forces were available for hire to maintain law and order. Standard of living was good to excellent on most planets and consciousness and awareness were on a steady upswing. The difference between the humanoid populations on the planets was in reality less than met the eye and the similarities were noticeable. The different peoples were tied together with the same basic goals and requirements and the inner need to achieve peace and transcend trivia. Development of the mind was valued, but not at the cost of forgetting that living life, laughing and enjoying the journey was just as important. Reaching the finish line with a smile on one's face is a good indicator the voyage through life is worth the occasional pain we endure. At that time, we are ready to join our Creator, a reward waiting at the end.